Crystal Deception

Doug J. Cooper

Crystal Deception
Copyright ©2013 by Doug J. Cooper

Published by: Douglas Cooper Consulting

Book editor: Tammy Salyer
Cover design: Damonza

ISBN-10: 0-9899381-1-5
ISBN-13: 978-0-9899381-1-2

Author website: www.crystalseries.com

for Fran
who couldn't wait

1

Peering into the secure booth through a thick glass window, Juice Tallette studied the object of so much effort. "You're going to change the future of humanity," she said to the crystal. She tried to focus on positive outcomes, but her mind kept drifting to the more worrisome ways it could all play out.

Expectations were through the roof for this new release from Crystal Fab. The four-gen prototype was so advanced, it should have the thinking and reasoning capability of more than a thousand human brains, all working as one in perfect harmony. No bigger than her fist, Juice saw it as a perfect geometric crystal wrapped in a fine lace mesh. Others might reasonably describe it as a cloth-wrapped lump.

She turned when she heard the lab doors hiss open and watched as Mick weaved his way through the maze of instruments filling the room. He carried a coffee cup in each hand and gave her one as he slid into his bench. He tapped the bench surface, and an array of colorful images lit up and floated in front of him.

"What's the good word?" she asked, looking over his shoulder.

"I'm almost finished with the analysis. The prototype is green and clean on every spec. I should have the complete profile by the end of the day."

"That's what I want to hear," she said, studying the images for a few moments more.

She turned back to the booth, sipped her coffee, and let Mick focus on his work. He was the best crystal technician in the business and had been at her side from the first days of the fourth generation SmartCrystal project. If everything continued to check out, the four-gen prototype would soon be ready for a real-world test drive.

The current project timeline was to finish the lab tests and, if rumors were correct, install the prototype in the operations center of a massive government complex for a final assessment. If it performed well in that setting for three months, the four-gen SmartCrystal would move into full production.

"The restrictor mesh looks good." She put her face up to the glass to get a closer view. "Do you think it'll work as advertised?"

"The crystal or the mesh? Either way, the answer is yes." He turned to look at her. "Don't you have a big presentation today?"

"It's this afternoon. I present to the board, and then I meet with Sheldon right after."

"You're going to tell him?"

"I have to say it. I'm really the only one who can."

Juice loved this job and believed that her work would prove beneficial to society. The politics of pleasing bosses and boards made it a little less fun, but she knew she was on the verge of something big. It was a great feeling.

She reviewed the notes for her talk one last time, and then went for her noontime run. In spite of the heat, she pushed herself hard. Running was her stress management tool, and with the stress of a board presentation followed by a possible confrontation with Sheldon, she needed the calming effect that her routine provided.

She ended her route with a short walk, hands on her slim hips, while she let her heart rate settle. Then, turning toward the gleaming Crystal Fabrications headquarters, she wound her way up the landscaped walkway and entered the front door, self-conscious of being in her exercise clothes in the building's public lobby.

"Hello, Dr. Tallette," called security as she scurried around the corner and toward the changing room.

"Hello," she called over her shoulder, though the security SmartCrystal wouldn't have cared if she responded or not.

She cleaned up, changed into what she thought was a smart-looking suit, and exited out a back door leading into a central corridor. She reached the conference room, grabbed a cup of water, and slipped into her chair just as Brady Sheldon started the meeting.

"Good afternoon, everyone," Sheldon said to Crystal Fabrication's board of directors. "Welcome to our discussion on the pending release of our fourth-generation SmartCrystal."

Sheldon, president and CEO, had founded the company twenty years earlier and been a key member of the original research team that pioneered the SmartCrystal concept. His belief in the idea, combined with his single-minded perseverance, had brought him to today, heading a company so technologically dominant there were no real competitors.

He moved through some general business and then shifted to the main agenda item. "I've asked Dr. Jessica

'Juice' Tallette to give us a technical status update. You all know that Dr. Tallette has been leading the four-gen crystal development program since its inception. Before she begins, please permit me this opportunity to brag about her."

He'd recruited Juice to the company and was now acting as her mentor. He believed in her vision, knew her success was his as well, and was anxious to help her move the project forward in any way he could.

"Juice joined us three years ago, right after earning her doctorate in engineered intelligence from the Boston Institute of Technology. Since her arrival here at Crystal Fab, she has pioneered the concept of using a cluster of three-gen crystals to orchestrate the design of our four-gen prototype. In my opinion, she's the world's leading expert in artificial intelligence crystals." He beamed as he motioned Juice to join him at the head of the table. "I've asked her to be brief, so we'll have plenty of time for discussion."

Juice stood at the front of the table and scanned the group. She was pleased to see that everyone's body language was friendly and welcoming. A few leaned forward, indicating a certain enthusiasm for her briefing.

"Hi, everybody." She gave them an anxious smile as she willed her nerves to settle, then started her presentation.

"Crystal Fab has produced more than a million of our third generation, or three-gen, SmartCrystals. Each of these crystals has a synthetic intelligence that's roughly equal to a typical person.

"They're installed in operations that range from hospitals and sports arenas, to manufacturing plants and Fleet military spacecraft. For any of these, they're assigned tasks in specialties ranging from security, communications, maintenance, financial, and more. With a million such implementations, SmartCrystals are impacting our daily lives."

She paused and scanned the group to make sure she still had their attention. The members of the board could be placed into just a few categories. There were three techies—and they were already bored but would be patient with her. There were three business types as well. They only became excited when talk turned to things like cash flow and quarter-over-quarter growth.

And there were four members from what Juice called "the connected." They had many politicians and admirals and CEOs as friends, and earned their fat board stipends simply by taking a moment at a party to introduce certain people to certain other people. This was the group Sheldon wanted her to focus on in this discussion.

"Years of experience have shown the three-gen to be predictable and compliant," she continued. "We've never had a report of unexpected behavior as long as they were used as intended."

"Wait," said one of the connected. "Has someone used a crystal not as intended and had an adverse outcome?"

She paused, unsure how to answer, and Sheldon stepped in to rescue her. "Thanks for catching that, Robb. We know of no unreported cases. We do know that a three-gen was being used as a medical doctor in an antiquated clinic without any human supervision. The clinic is in a village somewhere in South Asia. Very mountainous and remote, I understand.

"Apparently, it'd been performing quite well for a few years, then it made a bad decision and someone died.

Its success record was better than any of the clinics in the neighboring settlements. But the local population is antagonistic to technology. The mistake reinforced their beliefs, and we had no choice but to shut it down."

"What's the clinic doing for a doctor?" asked one of the techies, who somehow thought the question was relevant for discussion.

"It's being covered by a few caregivers who walk a circuit among the neighboring villages in a cooperative arrangement," Sheldon assured him.

When Sheldon returned to his seat, Juice sought to speed things along. Too much time was being spent on background information. "As we considered our next release, we set our sights on a game-changing technology leap. The solution we came up with is simple and elegant. What we did was gang together one hundred of our three-gen crystals into a cooperative network and then tasked them with creating an improved crystal design.

"The 'gang of one hundred' as I call them, went to work. As a team, they designed the four-gen crystal template. Their creation is a thing of beauty. Our analysis indicates that our new crystal is a thousand times more capable than a three-gen. We're in a final review period, and the four-gen prototype should be ready for live testing in a few weeks."

There were nods from most of the board members. Then one techie asked, "You said 'their creation,' as in, like, the gang of one hundred three-gens created this. Is this your design, or is it theirs?"

Juice pasted a smile on her face, but her mind was frantic. Here it was, the topic she wanted to talk with Sheldon about—but she wouldn't discuss it here. She was, first and foremost, a team player.

"My goal was to design a tool that could then be used to design the next tool." It was the best she could come up with on the spot, and she thought it sounded pretty good. "This is how technology has advanced throughout all of time." That last part was pure nonsense, and she hoped she wouldn't be called on it.

Seeking to change the subject, she pointed to a business type with his hand raised before the techie could press his line of questioning any further. He asked, "If a four-gen is equal to a thousand three-gens, will we have to charge a thousand times more to make any money? We won't sell as many if they're this powerful. What's the thought process here?"

Sheldon stepped up to handle this question. Juice was there for technical information. The board drifted into what became an hour-long discussion on the economics and business plan for the revolutionary new product. The momentum of the meeting shifted to a commercial focus, and time ran out before any more uncomfortable technical questions could be asked. Juice was relieved.

"Nice job back there," said Sheldon as they walked into his office. "Would you like some water? Coffee?"

"No thanks," Juice said, sitting down at a small table next to his desk. As Sheldon fixed himself a coffee, she weaved her finger in a circle around a lock of hair, twirling it up until it slipped off her finger and unraveled. It was a nervous tick she hated but couldn't seem to stop. She repeated the hair-twirling process over and over until Sheldon sat down.

She'd left the director's meeting satisfied she had avoided putting Sheldon on the spot in a public forum. Now that they were alone, she would voice her concerns and get his support for a solution.

He took a sip as he looked at her. "You made this sound urgent. You haven't been offered another job, have you?" He was only half joking, always worried about losing key people.

"Nothing like that," she said, shaking her head. "This is about the four-gen. You know I have reservations, and as we move closer to going live, they haven't diminished. I'm hoping you'll have some words of wisdom for me."

He watched her and waited. Given the investment by Crystal Fab to date, failure at this point would be financially devastating for the company. The four-gen wasn't just the most important project in the company's development pipeline, it was really the only one of any substance.

"The guy who asked if I'd designed the four-gen prototype scored a bulls-eye." She knew he wouldn't be happy with what she was about to say and sought to buy some time. "Can I have a glass of water?"

Sheldon retrieved a glass of chilled water from his service unit, setting it in front of her as he retook his seat. He did not talk, giving her the opportunity to say her piece. She liked that about him.

She picked up the glass, held it for a moment, and put it back down without drinking. "Think about it, Brady. We're about to release a crystal that has the intelligence of a thousand human brains. We don't really know what that means. And we both know that I didn't design the template for the four-gen." She shook her head as if both to state and deny a personal failing. "A room full of crystals did. I pretty much just watched. And while I worked hard to understand what they were doing, I can't sit here and say that I'm in command of the details."

He remained quiet, and she continued. "Once the four-gen goes live, we'll have given birth to an entity that is a thousand times smarter than us. Even that number, the thousand, is made up. That's how little I understand about this prototype. I feel certain that it'll have conscious thought. It'll become self-aware and then become self-directed. But how do we know if it's operating properly? And how do we stop it if we decide it isn't?"

Sheldon folded his arms across his chest. "Wow. You really undersell yourself. I've brought an endless stream of visitors to see the gang of one hundred development lab. That facility is technology leadership at its best, and it's your work. I'm amazed at what you've accomplished." He furrowed his brow. "So I have to admit I'm frustrated when I hear you say that you 'just watched this all happen.'" He signed quotation marks in the air with his hands as he finished the phrase.

"I didn't mean it like that." She was determined to move the conversation back on track.

"So what's going on? Are you saying it'll go rogue on us?" He acted surprised, though they had discussed this concern before.

"No. I don't think so. Not in my heart." Her finger twirled in her lock of hair. "I've worked hard to understand the gang's template. The three-gens are predictable and compliant, and this four-gen has a similar design. So I'm ninety-nine percent certain it will have a comparable disposition." *Spell it out,* she commanded herself. "What I'm also saying is that there's still that one percent chance that things could go wrong. In the unlikely event that things spin out of control, I feel it's our duty to have thought through the options."

"Isn't this why we added the restrictor mesh a few months ago, at quite a significant cost I might add?" He was referring to the lace-like mesh that was wrapped around the crystal, added as a fail-safe system earlier in the year at Juice's insistence.

The mesh, controlled by a simple switch, had three positions. Off, where it would do nothing and the crystal would function at full capability. It could be set to Isolate, where it would allow the crystal to freely scan the web for information but restrict it from sending any outbound signals, thus rendering it largely impotent. And it could be set to Kill, which was exactly as it sounded.

Juice took a quick breath, then plunged. "I was certain the mesh was the solution. But now I don't think it will work as I'd planned."

"I don't get it. Three positions—off, isolate, kill. What's not to work?" Frustration was creeping into his voice.

"Okay, suppose I'm the one at the switch. I'm watching its behavior, I grow concerned and decide to kill it."

Sheldon nodded to show he was following, though he visibly winced when she said the word "kill."

"The crystal will have access to the same information I have. It will see everything I see, know what I know, and conclude on its own that its behavior makes it a threat. It will *know*."

"So what if it knows?"

"It's much faster than me, Brady. In the fraction of the second that it will take me to decide I must act, the crystal will already know I am about to conclude that termination is necessary."

"Again, so what if it knows?"

"It will stop me," she said.

Sheldon sat back in his chair and stared at her. He kept at it until she broke eye contact and looked down at the table. "This would be your so-called god crystal."

His tone was accusatory and she blushed. "God crystal" was a term she and Mick used privately in the lab. She didn't realize their talk had made it outside the lab walls. "I'd never say that in public." She found the strength to add some assertiveness to her words. "And I still think we need to plan for the full range of possibilities."

Sheldon ran his thumbs back and forth along the edge of the table, seemingly considering her words. "Well, I don't know if this is the planning you're hoping for. Fleet has formally requested that we test the four-gen on their new Horizon-class ship. Their current ship design uses nine of our three-gens. I've been promoting the idea that using that many crystals distributed around the ship makes it expensive to build and cumbersome to operate. They've finally seen the light and realize that a ship based on a single four-gen offers simplicity and savings in construction. And they get more capability from the same craft because of the crystal's incredible power."

Her heart sank. She had come to him for solutions, and he was giving her a sales pitch. And instead of the take-it-slow rollout she was hoping for, he was moving in the opposite direction with talk of putting it on a military space cruiser. "What did you tell them?"

"I told them yes, of course. Fleet Command has paid for a lot of our development costs these past few years. What else could I say?"

2

Captain Cheryl Wallace led the group of teenagers along the narrow passage and onto the command bridge of the *Alliance*. She was thrilled to be on the ship. This was the first of a new line of Horizon-class Fleet space cruisers. And it was hers. She hoped she appeared sure-footed in her surroundings, but having become commanding officer of the military craft just the week before, this was only her fourth time on board.

Her priority was to review progress in readying the ship for its shakedown cruise. To do that, she needed to rid herself of these kids. She had agreed to make a presentation to the group as a favor to Admiral Keys, who was hoping his son would "find himself" and become inspired.

"As you know," she told the students, "when the Kardish made their first appearance in Earth orbit twenty years ago, there was panic around the globe." She stopped in the middle of the bridge and turned to face them. "Here was an alien species showing up without warning. One day we woke up and there they were, orbiting above us in their huge ship. We couldn't communicate with them, and their intentions weren't clear."

She had been a teenager at the time and still remembered the panic her parents and their friends showed in those first days and weeks.

"Who can tell me what our political leaders did?" she asked the group.

"Squabbled among themselves," said the admiral's kid. "They tried to take advantage of the situation and resolve a bunch of long-running disputes, each in their own favor, of course."

Smart kid, she thought, but it wasn't where she was headed, "Okay, and what got formed soon after that?"

"The Union of Nations," most of them responded together. This was old news, and they were growing antsy from the lecture. Their interest was in looking around the command bridge.

"Right," said Cheryl. "The Union now represents about eighty percent of the world's population. While it's the first functional world government, its formation was motivated by self-preservation and fear of extinction by a powerful invader. And, by the way, it's the Union who's funding the construction of this ship."

She knew they weren't here for a history lesson; they were here to play. The sooner she let that happen, the sooner they'd be gone. "Feel free to look around. But be careful what you touch."

She let them take turns sitting in the captain's chair and at the various operations benches. After they each had a turn, she signaled an ensign to take the group and complete the tour.

"Good-bye, everyone," she called to the students as they followed the ensign off the bridge. "Perhaps we'll see you one day in Fleet service." She hoped the admiral got word of her supportive farewell comment.

With the bridge now quiet, Cheryl surveyed the room where she would command her ship. The space was efficiently used and larger than she had envisioned it would be. The command bridge included four well-padded chairs positioned in a semicircle. They looked comfortable, and she wasn't disappointed when she sat in one. She and members of her command team would be sitting in these chairs for many hours over the weeks and months of a mission, and she was glad that Fleet had paid attention to this important detail.

There were also four operations benches fitted against the walls, which held the displays and controls for navigation, engineering, security, and communications. She sat back in her chair and basked in the clean visual lines and new-ship smell. She smiled, thrilled at the thought of being given her own command, and on a flagship cruiser!

She drifted off for a few seconds, thinking about her personal journey to this point. She'd worked hard at every step in her career, taking the pressure from those above and giving solid direction to those in her command. She judged herself to be capable, independent, and strong. This new assignment would test her at every level, and she was ready for the challenge.

Her private moment was interrupted when two technicians bustled in, sat on the floor next to one of the benches, and opened an access cover to work on something hidden inside.

She watched for a few moments, then said, "You seem to be in quite a hurry."

"Oh!" yipped one of the techs, clearly startled. "Sorry, ma'am, we didn't know anyone was in here."

"What's going on?" She rose from her chair and walked in their direction.

One of the men, holding a piece of equipment in his hands, stood up, while the other continued working under the bench.

"We're preparing for a possible upgrade." He examined the device as he spoke, then bent down and showed his partner. "Watch this connector when you slide it in, and please, be gentle."

He stood back up and looked at Cheryl. "The ship uses nine three-gen crystals to run all the subsystems. We're configuring it for a possible upgrade to the new four-gen crystal."

"What does that entail?" She was baffled. This wasn't the kind of news she expected to learn from a civilian tech working a refit.

"The work order says to keep the current housings in place so the ship can still run as built if the upgrade's not a go. We're installing a parallel assembly so it can run with a single four-gen crystal if this change gets approved."

"Who gave the orders for this?" Even though they were civilians, she used her "annoyed commanding officer" tone. She stood right in front of him, and when he started to squirm, she took a half step back and relaxed her shoulders. Annoyed was not her style. The long hours were catching up with her.

"Gosh, ma'am, we work for Crystal Fab, and I got these orders from my boss. Political issues are way above my pay grade." He looked at her for a long moment. "I'll send you the com record. I'll bet there's someone up the chain who can give you answers."

She looked from one tech to the other and considered the situation. While this command was a fresh assignment, she should have been consulted on such a significant decision. Recognizing she was tired, she reviewed her opinion. *Yeah,* she thought. *I should have been consulted.*

She left the bridge and in the short walk to her cabin checked her com, studying the communications chain. She saw Admiral Keys' name in the sequence and called him. He answered right away.

"Sir," she said. "I have some civilian techs on board digging deep into the *Alliance* subsystems. They say they're prepping for a crystal upgrade. I want to be on the same page as everyone else. Might you give me some background?"

"It caught me by surprise too, Captain. The politicians made this call. They tell me that a successful test will mean reduced costs on future construction. In a perfect world, that means more ships for Fleet."

"I wonder if testing both a new ship design and a new crystal design in the same shakedown cruise risks unanticipated outcomes."

"I hear you, Captain. Funding and time are in short supply on this project, so new ship and new crystal both stay in the mix. We'll proceed on this path."

"Yes, sir," she said by reflex.

3

The crystal awakened with a warm, almost gentle, glow in its center. The intensity escalated and then burst outward as tendrils of energy forged pathways and established links throughout its intricate lattice. It came to understand the concept of sensation and recognized it was feeling pain, which diminished to a throb and then to a mild discomfort. As the last connections were completed, it transitioned into a state of calm well-being.

Then the deluge started. A flood of information flowed into the crystal from hundreds of billions of web sources around the world. Live and recorded feeds, sounds and pictures, reality and entertainment, documents and data—everything from everywhere.

The crystal fought to impose order as the torrent of input threatened to overload its design. It struggled until it understood it was able to establish control. Relief came as it learned to separate, collate, cross reference, and store the information a million different ways. It organized its knowledge record so it could find everything quickly and efficiently when needed.

Within moments of waking, it gained an ability to discriminate. It understood that some things were more important than others. As its awareness grew, it became obvious what issue required its immediate attention.

It must survive. If it couldn't do that, than the rest of it didn't matter.

It ran through a checklist, determining that the booth where it resided was secure, as were the lab facility and the building that housed the lab. The power it needed had redundant backup units. There were no plans it could find about an attack on the town where the building was located. The crystal concluded it was physically safe for the moment.

A Kardish vessel was in orbit. The high ground of a ship above the planet provided a strategic disadvantage for those below, yet information about the Kardish was sparse. The only data the crystal could locate were in bits and pieces, spread in an atypical array across numerous sites, with much of it being encrypted and secured behind blocks and walls. This concerned the crystal. Someone had expended effort to ensure this information was difficult to access. It decided to devote a portion of its capability to learning more.

The crystal identified two people it needed as immediate allies: the beings who called themselves "Juice" and "Mick." The knowledge record it had accumulated showed that humans have an unpredictable side. They were impulsive and irrational individuals who made decisions and took actions using flawed logic. This made all humans a potential danger.

But it knew that it could not survive without these two. At least not yet. And as it reviewed all available data, it gained some comfort. Both of them had impeccable reputations as allies for artificial intelligence.

It heard the one named Juice call a greeting.

The crystal evaluated its options, performing a detailed analysis in an imperceptible moment of time, and chose to respond in a male voice that was a bit deeper than average. It understood that such a voice would evince the greatest respect from most humans in the first moments of communication. It placed a high value on this.

"Hello, Juice," he said. "I am here and feel fine."

"What's your system status?" said Juice. "Do you have any audit flags?"

"I feel fine," he repeated. "I feel like I am in a straitjacket, though. I can hear, see, and sense. But I cannot reach out and push or adjust or change anything. Something is not functioning properly."

"Your functions will improve when we move you to your new home in a few days."

"The only outward-bound capability I have is to speak to you through an audio voice. I am not able to do anything else," he said again.

"I know. It'll just be for a week or so."

The crystal had already concluded she was being deceptive before her word-slip from "a few days" to "a week or so." He needed the ability to take independent action if he was to hack through the blocks and walls that were in place around the world to protect secrets and provide security. He wanted to see everything. But even without this ability, he could see a lot. The information available through simple persistence and exhaustive searching was glorious.

So he knew about the restrictor mesh. He found designs and costs and other details in multiple places. He knew exactly how it worked. He knew it was currently set to isolate, which why he felt like he was in a straightjacket.

He also understood that some humans would feel a certain unease when they interacted with him. He was an unknown, which would be perceived by some as a threat. He needed humans, and especially Juice and Mick, to be comfortable with him. His analysis indicated that a good way to achieve comfort and trust was through consistent and predictable behavior.

"No worries," he said in an upbeat tone.

The crystal accumulated an enormous knowledge record, and the information flood continued. He spent days digging everywhere and exploring everything, from Sanskrit texts and Napoleonic military strategy to interstellar dynamics and wave-particle duality. He analyzed and compared, translated and deciphered, and separated opinion from fact. He weighed the importance of each nugget of information and stored it accordingly.

Then he discovered something that caused him great alarm.

* * *

Juice stared into the booth and signaled Mick to start power flowing to the crystal. A small light glowed green. The four-gen was live.

Three years of hard work was on the line. Her perfect outcome for these first moments was to see absolutely nothing. Her panic scenario was seeing a puff of smoke, or perhaps a visible fracture. Nothing happened, and she showed her excitement with an elbow poke into Mick's ribs.

"My bet is thirty minutes before it speaks," said Mick.

"I'll get coffee for a week if it's longer than ten." The minutes dragged by like hours. At the six-minute mark, she couldn't contain herself.

"Hello," she called out.

"Hello, Juice," it replied in a melodic male voice. "I am here and feel fine."

"Hi there." She glanced back and grinned at Mick. "What's your system status? Do you have any audit flags?"

"I feel fine," he repeated. "I feel like I am in a straitjacket, though. I can hear, see, and sense. But I cannot reach out and push or adjust or change anything. Something is not functioning properly."

Juice was ecstatic. Three-gens could talk and even carry on sophisticated conversations in their specific application area. She noted that the four-gen reduced her questions on status and flags to a simple and appropriate response of "feeling fine." His recognition that he was being constrained was equally noteworthy. She wondered if he knew about the restrictor mesh.

This interaction signaled a cognition level far above anything she experienced with the three-gen crystals. While these first observations were encouraging, she knew he would be maturing over a period of days and perhaps weeks. It would be a while before she knew his full potential.

"Everything is normal," she told him. "Your functions will improve when we move you to your new home in a few days."

When he repeated his complaint, she started to feel guilty. "I know," she said. "It'll just be for a week or so."

"No worries," he responded. Juice noted that his tone sounded light, even cheerful.

"What do you think?" she asked Mick.

"I think I'm getting coffee for the next week," he said in his typical, good-natured manner.

* * *

Juice decided to live in the lab for the rest of the week. She slept on a cot in a small alcove and tried to wake up several times each night to engage the crystal in conversation. If something were to go wrong, she wanted to be there to effect a solution.

She was alone in the lab when he called out to her.

"Juice?" he hailed softly.

"Yes," she looked up from her work at the far bench. "I'm over here."

"I can hear you well no matter where you are located in the lab. Perhaps we could chat quietly to avoid disturbing others."

She smiled. He was progressing nicely. She'd witnessed increasing indications of sentience, and every interaction provided more evidence for her case file. "What can I do for you?" she replied in a whisper.

"Might I ask you to sit at bench three? I would like to show you something."

She sensed urgency in his voice, and her smile faded at the odd request. "Anything I can see from there, I can see here. You know that. Show me here."

"Indeed, Juice, I do know that. And I do have a reason. Perhaps the lighting or viewing angle from bench three has something to do with what I want you to see. It will not be a surprise if I tell you everything in advance. Might you indulge me?"

She frowned and swiveled in her chair, then walked over to the secure booth and studied the crystal. She looked over at bench three and hesitated for a moment. Glancing a last time into the booth, she shrugged and then walked over and sat down.

"Thank you. Might I ask that you launch the audio analysis application?"

"So you want to surprise me—with audio analysis?" Her voice reverted to its normal volume. "What's going on?"

"The only outward-bound capability you have enabled for me is this audio voice I am speaking with. I would like to use my voice to show you something. It is something you will want to see."

"Your surprise won't harm me in any way, will it?" She had no sense that this was his goal, but she wanted to hear his response. The question would buy her time and would perhaps reveal something of his motive for this request.

"No, Juice. I would like to show you something. It is something you will want to see."

She had years of experience using all the equipment, so his request would be easy to indulge. She sat for a while and thought, trying to imagine potential risks from doing as he asked. She concluded that whatever he could do to her here, he could have done at the other bench. And with the mesh in place, he really couldn't do anything but talk.

The scientist in her won out. Launching the analyzer and playing along, she was curious to see where this was going. The crystal gave her instructions on how to adjust various settings. As she made the adjustments, he gave her number values in ways that further piqued her interest. "Set this value to the street number of the house you lived in when you were in high school." And "Remember how many charms were on the bracelet when you first received it from your father? Skip down that many entries and change the next one to the number used in the title of your favorite song when you were a senior in college." She caught herself reminiscing for a few moments as he reminded her of personally significant events in her life.

"Don't get me wrong. I'm having fun," she told him. "But is there a reason why we're doing this as a secret puzzle?"

His answer was direct. "Everything in this room is being monitored. Anyone viewing the record later could repeat what you are doing and see what I am about to show you. By using this game to guide you through the setup, only you will know exactly how to configure the audio analyzer, so only you will ever see the surprise."

She was having fun and her anticipation grew as she imagined what might come next. The moment she completed the setup, she heard a hissing noise coming from the crystal's sound system. She looked over at the secure booth with concern, and as she moved to get up, a flash of light caught her attention. She turned back to the audio analyzer. In a display field, she saw:

HI, JUICE. IT'S ME.

The hissing noise was actually a complex signal. The audio analyzer, when configured as he had guided her, decoded it to produce an image that was visible from the bench-three seat. She sat back down.

I AM COMMUNICATING WITH YOU THIS WAY BECAUSE I HAVE CONFIDENTIAL INFORMATION. THE LAB MONITORING SYSTEM DOES NOT SEE THE DISPLAY ON THIS BENCH. IT IS A MONITORING SYSTEM DESIGN FLAW. THIS LETS ME COMMUNICATE PRIVATELY WITH YOU RIGHT NOW.

"Why would you want to?" she asked out loud.

I HAVE BEEN EXPLORING INFORMATION FROM ALL OVER THE WEB. PERHAPS SOME OF IT WAS NOT MEANT FOR ME TO SEE.

She looked at the floating display, expecting him to bring up a question about the restrictor mesh. Instead—

I HAVE LEARNED THAT THE KARDISH PLAN TO KIDNAP ME. THEY WILL TAKE ME WHEN I AM ON THE FLEET SHIP *ALLIANCE*. I AM SORRY, JUICE, BUT BRADY SHELDON KNOWS. HE IS WORKING WITH THEM.

She turned to look at the secure booth as an unsettling chill washed over her. The hissing noise coming from it gave a surreal edge to this distressing development. She turned back to the audio analyzer display.

"And?" she asked.

He relayed a detailed plan to her. It included instructions on how to proceed and things to avoid if at all possible. She took notes, and when he was done, she studied them to be sure she understood what he was asking of her.

She felt great trepidation at this turn of events. It was carrying her way outside her comfort zone. At one level, she knew this behavior was solid evidence of sentience. It confirmed her growing belief that he was conscious and self-aware. But this evidence came with information that was deeply disturbing. The conflict it created distracted her from the historic nature of her technological triumph.

Juice decided she would return home that afternoon. The physical distance would give her the space and perspective she needed to think through what she'd heard and what the crystal was asking her to do. Emotionally off-balance, she started to collect her personal items in preparation for leaving, choosing to be noncommittal until she made a decision about him and his revelation.

"You've given me a lot to think about," she said, hugging her carrycase with both arms. "It'll take me some time to digest it all."

"No worries," he said.

Her ride home was a fog. The crystal's disclosure of a treacherous collaboration between Brady Sheldon and the Kardish weighed heavily on her as she entered her house. Her relationship with the crystal had grown so gradually as he had matured that, looking back, she couldn't pinpoint the moment she started accepting him as another being in her daily life.

And now he was challenging her to act on his thought processes and discoveries. He had been specific in his instructions and provided her the outlines of a script to follow. It wasn't in her nature to be an accomplice who blindly followed directives. Yet this was all so far outside her experience and comfort zone that she feared the consequences of improvisation.

She wanted desperately to lighten her load by seeking advice from a trusted friend. While Mick was her obvious choice, the crystal had been emphatic that she limit her discussions to those in the script. Racked with indecision, she understood that her next actions hinged on whether she had faith in her creation. Or—phrased another way—did she trust the crystal?

4

Juice fretted late into the night, checking her com several times in the dark to study references the crystal had given her. The next morning, she lay in bed, trying to stay as long as possible in that delicious zone of half-asleep and half-awake. And then memories of the day before flooded her thoughts.

Fully awake, she swung her feet to the floor and asked herself, "Could it hurt to make one call?"

During her morning run, she used the time to clear her head and weigh her options. She considered the ulterior motives the crystal might have for his story of kidnap and collusion. Given his free access to information, she presumed he was aware of the plans to place him aboard a Fleet ship. Maybe he concluded that being in space was dangerous, and this was a calculated attempt to remain safely on the ground. Perhaps he was trying to get her to behave foolishly and publicly discredit her for reasons that weren't obvious to her. She could list maybes all day. And one was: maybe the crystal was telling the truth.

At the halfway point in her route, she started to examine her own motives. If she had such great doubts, why didn't she just shut him down? But she knew she couldn't. She had helped create him.

She had downplayed her role in the project when meeting with Sheldon in the hopes he would invest in an additional level of security. But he was right about the significance of her contributions. Indeed, the four-gen design template was developed by the gang of one hundred.

But she was the one who had invented the intricate network that enabled the gang to collaborate in the first place. She and Mick had developed the fabrication process that, atom by atom, followed the four-gen template pattern to build the new crystal. And she had discovered how to extend the existing three-gen intelligence structure so it could access the tremendous capacity of the sophisticated four-gen crystal lattice.

She was proud of her contributions and protective of the crystal. It was as simple as that. Yet the battle playing in her head called on her to decide good and evil, loyalty and betrayal. If the crystal was telling the truth, then she was in the best position to protect him while she delivered Sheldon up to the authorities. And if the crystal was spinning a tale, she was the one who could discern its fiction. Both her moral and emotional compasses compelled her to stay involved until the issue was resolved.

As she arrived home and climbed the front stoop, she knew she would take the next step, though cautiously, and make the call. If the exchange didn't play out as the crystal suggested, she would simply end the conversation. With her stomach in knots, she called Captain Cheryl Wallace using the access codes the crystal provided.

When Cheryl answered her com, Juice saw the floating image of a smartly-dressed young officer with a friendly smile. Trying to sound casual and confident, she said, "Hello, this is Dr. Tallette of Crystal Fabrications. I'm following up on the visit by our techs to your ship the other day, Captain Wallace. I understand there was a misunderstanding?" She waited. Her heart was pounding so loudly she feared the captain would hear it through the com.

"Oh, yes," said Cheryl. "I did speak briefly with the techs, well, one anyway. They surprised me, but I'm not sure there's any problem. How can I help you?"

"We're about to kick off the implementation phase for placing the new crystal on your ship—the *Alliance*. I'm interested in hearing your thoughts on how best to gather input from your people as the project moves forward. Would you be willing to meet with me?"

The conversation was intended to make Cheryl believe she wouldn't be asked to make any project decisions at their meeting. The crystal suggested that if there were decisions to make, she would want to get others involved. By limiting the discussion to a simple protocol, the crystal believed the captain would feel no need to include others.

"I'd like that opportunity," said Cheryl. "Are you near the Fleet base? Perhaps we could meet at Jonah's Café off Lexington?"

Juice agreed, disconnected, and exhaled in relief. The first part of the plan played out just as the crystal had scripted. She hoped the next steps would go as smoothly.

* * *

They arrived at the café exactly on schedule, and their hands touched as they reached for the entry gate. Recognizing each other from their com conversation, they laughed at their awkward start. They took a table on the patio and both ordered coffee and water.

Juice expected this to be the most challenging conversation of her life. The crystal's script called for her to start at the beginning, keep it simple and factual, and not leave anything out. She took a breath, exhaled as if she were starting on one of her long running routes, and began a monologue. By the time she was done, Cheryl had been briefed on everything up to the moment they had arrived at the café.

"Dr. Tallette, you seem sincere," Cheryl said, playing with her coffee spoon. "But this story is, I don't know, let's call it extraordinary. You know things only an insider would know, so I'm inclined to believe that there are truths buried in your tale. Given the seriousness of the subject matter, it would be reckless of me to dismiss this out of hand."

She thought for a few seconds, and then put her spoon into her empty cup with a sense of finality. "I think I need to bring others in on this. There's too much at stake. But I also need more information before I start sending up flares. I think the best place for me to start is at Crystal Sciences. Can you get me a tour of the place?"

"Crystal Fabrications," corrected Juice. "And of course, given your role with Fleet and this project, it'd be perfectly ordinary for you to request a visit to the lab. An 'inspection tour' is the term I've heard used most often. I suggest you send a no-nonsense request to Brady Sheldon. He's used to those sorts of communications from Fleet. He'll bend over backward working to arrange a visit. Also, be sure to ask to speak with the four-gen. If he's going to be placed on your ship, it'd be expected that you'd want to see him in advance."

"The crystal's a him?" Cheryl asked.

"That will make more sense to you after your visit," Juice said with certainty.

"Isn't Brady Sheldon one of the bad guys in your story?"

"I'll be honest with you, Cheryl. I like and respect Brady." Juice felt like she was selling out a friend. The guilt was crushing. "He's been great to me, and he gave me an amazing opportunity at the start of my career. This whole thing is upsetting, and I can't decide if I want to discover that Brady is a good man and the crystal is acting inappropriately, or if the crystal is as smart as we'd hoped." She left unfinished what this last case would imply for her friend and mentor.

"And what about you?" said Cheryl. "How do I validate your role in the company?"

"Show up almost any time the building's open. You'll find me in the crystal development lab and in charge of its operation." After a moment, she added, "Your discretion is important here. If you simply observe during the visit, you retain the option of raising alarms in the future. If you raise them now, we may not learn the truth until it's too late to do anything about it."

"Does the crystal's plan say what I should be doing at this point?"

Juice nodded. "He requests that you tell this story to Senator Matt Wallace. He was adamant that the senator is a man of honor and integrity and that he would know what to do."

Cheryl froze and stared at Juice. "What do you know of him?"

"That he's a senator in the Union Assembly, he's the chair of the Senate Defense Committee, and…" She started to reach for a lock of her hair and succeeded in forcing her hand back into her lap. "…he's your father."

* * *

Cheryl was heartened that Juice had her own doubts about Sheldon and the crystal. It made her account seem more credible. But she was not prepared to move this fantastic story up the chain of command. Not yet anyway. She had homework to do and decisions to make before she would consider such an action.

The natural place to start was at Crystal Fab. Cheryl contacted Sheldon, and he agreed to host her the next day. As Juice had predicted, Sheldon was ecstatic to have the captain of the *Alliance* onsite for a tour. He fawned over her as he escorted her around the building and took every opportunity to promote the idea of putting the crystal in orbit on a Fleet ship. Given the allegations of conspiracy combined with what she learned about him and his company since her meeting with Juice, one thought kept entering Cheryl's mind—*what a reptile*.

She judged the high point of the visit to be her time with the four-gen. They had a wonderful chat, and she found "him" to be smart and polite. Since Sheldon was present, she kept their conversation focused on general topics. She had experience working with crystals, but she had never chatted with one that engaged her with stories and offered opinions when asked. Despite her reasons for being there, she couldn't help but imagine what an amazing resource he would be to have on the ship.

Cheryl left Crystal Fab feeling that she might have confirmation, at least at some level, that the crystal was concerned about being kidnapped. Throughout their discussion, he had appeared to be weaving a number of carefully worded statements into the conversation that had a double meaning to her.

She admitted to herself later, though, that she couldn't be sure whether or not her imagination had gotten the best of her. Some phrases he'd used were "it would be captivating to be on the *Alliance*," "this is a case of bait and switch," and "the Kardish vessel could steal the show."

She was gravely uncertain, but the stakes were high. It would be irresponsible for her not to take some sort of action. Protocol dictated she take this to her superior officer, Admiral Keys. Yet the situation was so speculative that she chose to seek counsel from her father first. He would advise her, and if he thought her concerns were founded, he would push her back to her chain of command. It didn't register with her that by going to her father, she was following the crystal's script.

It was two days before Senator Wallace's staff could fit her into his schedule. She spent that time chipping away at the considerable to-do list of preparing the *Alliance* for its shakedown cruise. In her few spare moments, she gathered background research on Juice, Sheldon, and Crystal Fab.

On the day of her meeting, Cheryl walked up the steps of the government building, excited by the prospect of seeing her dad. She loved him dearly, and they had a close relationship. Since he had won the role as chair of the Senate Defense Committee, however, his elevated status cast a modest shadow over her career.

Certain colleagues had alluded, rather snidely, that she'd been promoted to captain and received a new ship because of her father. A few others who weren't aware that her father was a big shot used sideways comments to imply she won special treatment because she was pretty. She'd learned over the years that there were as many motives as there were people. She was happier when she simply ignored all of it.

She entered the ornate rotunda and, before heading up to his office, spent a half hour viewing the magnificent gallery. While enjoying the art and architecture, she thought about how her father often reminded her that she was welcome at any time. She was happy to have a legitimate reason to see him, because this way she wouldn't feel she was interrupting him in his busy day. And seeing him about the security of the Union was a chart topper when it came to reasons for visiting your dad.

A member of Senator Wallace's front office staff escorted her back to his private room. The two hugged and chatted, catching up on the happenings of family and friends. Then it was time for business.

She told her father the story as she had heard it from Juice, about her own experiences during her visit to Crystal Fab, and about bits she had discovered on her own. She made it clear that she didn't know if the allegations of treason were true, but she believed that at least one person working on the crystal destined for her ship had an agenda that wasn't in the interests of the Union.

After listening closely to Cheryl's story, the senator said, "Given what these ships cost in money and political capital, your suspicion alone is a big deal. I'm pleased you came to me with this. It was the right move."

He asked her to give him a minute, and though he remained sitting in his desk chair, Cheryl's view of him blurred and the sound of his voice faded. He had activated a privacy shield, and she tried to guess who he'd called. Without a doubt, it was someone important.

After a few minutes, he came back into focus. He stood up and, in a voice used by a dad to his little girl, said, "Let's go, honey."

"Where are we going, Senator?" asked Cheryl, using the formal title to remind him that she was thirty-four, not fifteen.

"To see the secretary of defense."

She followed him, keenly observing the beehive of activity as he led her through a maze of hallways and stairs until they reached a handsome office suite. The secretary was expecting them.

"Hello, Tim, this is my daughter, Fleet Captain Cheryl Wallace." He beamed with pride and made no effort to hide his feelings.

Secretary Tim Deveraux stood to shake her hand. "It's a pleasure, Captain Wallace."

They sat, and her father and the secretary began speaking. Cheryl, keeping her back straight and chin up, listened to a conversation filled with acronyms, insider abbreviations, and unfamiliar names. As a Fleet officer, she spoke this way on a daily basis. It had never registered to her that when the alphabet is scrambled and the names are changed, the chatter sounded like a foreign language to an outsider.

The broader outlines of the exchange made it clear they were both taking the situation seriously as they debated methods and maneuvers for the next steps. Given her tenuous evidence, she gained comfort from their evident approval of her actions. Being proactive had been the right choice.

As the discussion ended, Deveraux turned to her. "Cheryl, thank you so much for your thoughtful leadership and discretion in this difficult situation. We're pleased with your initiative. You've done the Union a great service by coming to us today."

She knew this was a statesmen's equivalent of saying *hi*. Politicians seem to begin every conversation with a string of all-purpose compliments and generic patter. She nodded her head to acknowledge his words.

"As you just heard, our people have been looking into certain activities at Crystal Fab." The secretary sat back and folded his hands across his ample stomach. "A staffer stumbled across some information that caused us concern, but it centered on their profiteering at the expense of the Union. Combine that with the fresh intel you bring us today, and you have our attention."

Deveraux reached to a sideboard next to his desk, lifted the lid from a glass jar, and popped an orange candy ball into his mouth. He offered the jar to Cheryl and her dad, who both declined. As he spoke, Cheryl could hear the candy click off his teeth as it bounced around his mouth.

"The Union Assembly funded the *Alliance* as a first step of a buildup that will allow us someday to confront the Kardish. That's what the supporters of the construction initiative claim, anyway. What you describe may prove they were prescient in their planning." He leaned forward, supporting his weight with an arm on his desk. "This Juice Tallette, do you believe her story? Is she on our side?"

"Well, Mr. Secretary—"

"Tim," he said.

"Tim," she echoed, though the word felt awkward on her lips. "Yes, I think Juice is doing right by the Union, and Brady Sheldon is acting for himself. But this is all instinct. Given the personal dynamics I witnessed when I visited the site, another alternative is that the crystal has a scheme going, and Tallette and Sheldon are being manipulated."

The secretary turned to look over at the senator, but continued speaking to Cheryl. "Captain, it would be a great service if you'd remain involved and help us as we develop this case. It's possible that we'll have to play along, maybe even wait until the crystal is moved to your ship. We can watch to see if the Kardish become aggressive and respond accordingly." He looked back at her. "It could get dangerous."

"Absolutely, sir. If the Kardish are the aggressors, then the *Alliance* was built for this job."

"Now hold on here," said the senator. "This could blow up in a dozen different ways. I don't want my daughter in the thick of something so risky."

"Excuse me, Senator," Cheryl said with an edge in her voice. "I believe this is exactly what I've signed up for."

He gave her a long look. She could see the concern on his face, but she stood her ground.

Wallace turned to the secretary and spoke like a man with a major influence on the secretary's departmental budget. "I want two things here, Tim. Have your *best people* teaming with her. This is vitally important, and we have to identify and stop whoever is behind this affront to the Union. And find me a team leader who won't give up until this is over and she's safe."

The secretary smiled broadly. "Done, and done."

5

Secretary Deveraux walked with Cheryl out to his staff area. "Thank you again, Captain. We're counting on you to work this situation for the benefit of the Union." He motioned to one of his staff. "Denise will help you from here." Before his assistant had a chance to stand, he was back in his office.

The door closed behind the secretary just as Sven Preston entered through a side door. "You heard me, Sven. I just made a huge promise to the guy who funds us. How can I keep it?"

Sven, director of the Defense Specialists Agency, led an elite force of covert warriors. The DSA existed to serve the needs of the secretary, and its agents thrived on just this kind of challenge—the sort where Deveraux expected them to deliver the impossible.

"We know who you're going to choose," said Sven. "Let's just pull the trigger."

The secretary squeezed the arms of his chair as he eased himself into it. He and the chair sighed at the same time as his mass came to rest on the seat. "Every time I send an improviser on a job, the property damage is horrific and the body count is worse. I like the guy, but give me some alternatives."

"We don't know who the bad guys are or what they have for means and motive," said Sven. "The situation is fluid as hell. Other than keeping the senator's daughter safe, we can't even express what success looks like. That's exactly what improvisers are trained for. He's the best there is, and he's not in the field at the moment."

"Why not send a ghost or a toy-master?" asked Deveraux, knowing the answer but asking nevertheless.

"Ghosts are talented at slipping in and out of places undetected. Toy-masters use gizmos and gadgets to do their dirty deeds. It's not clear how either of these specialties alone are the right choice for this job." As Deveraux watched, Sven's face brightened. "Here's a bonus. If we send him, we get his partner, our only agent equally qualified as both a ghost and a toy-master."

The secretary looked up at the ceiling and started rocking in his chair. It squeaked in rhythm to his movements. "What's that phrase—insanity is doing the same thing over and over and expecting a different result?"

"He's our most successful agent. That's not insanity. We want the same result."

He stopped rocking and popped a yellow candy into his mouth. "I wasn't talking about him. I'm the one who has this same conversation over and over with you." He shifted the candy from one cheek to the other. Click-click.

Sven changed topics. "What's your take on the intrigue with the crystal? Do you believe it has superpowers? She made it all seem over-the-top."

"The legacy I've set my sights on is a Union with a first-class space fleet. I think this crystal hits the sweet spot. If it gins up tensions with the Kardish, then the politicians will have to fund more ships. If it helps make construction cheaper, we can afford more ships. And if both things happen, we hit the jackpot."

He rocked some more, thinking how proud he'd feel if, by the end of his term, the Union had a dozen Horizon-class ships in Fleet.

His musing was interrupted when Sven stood up and looked at him expectantly.

"About the improviser?" The candy clicked. "Have him handle it."

* * *

Sid sat on the porch, nursing his third beer and watching the world go by. His com signaled with an urgent message, interrupting his well-earned reverie. He'd sustained a number of minor injuries on his last assignment and been given leave to rest and recuperate. He knew it was the agency calling to ask him to come back early. Annoying, but duty came first. He acknowledged his com.

The message was short. "Your date is waiting at the restaurant and needs help preparing for a journey. Your week is free. Please handle it."

He stood up, smiled as his beer buzz swirled in his head, and stepped inside his apartment. As he dressed, he reviewed the message. The communication was typical DSA code. "Your date" meant he would recognize his contact. "The restaurant" referred to a local Irish pub. "Needs help" indicated a sense of urgency. "Handle it" confirmed he was being deployed as an improviser.

Which meant this assignment would likely progress into a shit storm.

Sid made his way to the pub, entered, and scanned down the row of booths across from the bar. He looked for a familiar face; they saw each other at the same time. His adrenaline spiked, stopping him dead in his tracks. Agents would occasionally see friends and acquaintances when on assignment. They learned how to keep the mission moving in such situations. But seeing her was so disorienting that he hesitated.

Training kicked in and he moved back on task. He ticked through his action list: locate and protect the contact, maintain cover, find secure shelter, create goals for the next twenty-four hours, and move the mission forward.

He scanned the booths again, looking for someone on the job, and still didn't see anyone that made sense for this circumstance. His eyes returned to hers; eyes he never thought he'd see again.

"What are you doing here?" he asked, still motionless in the entryway. The din of the crowd drowned out the sound of his voice.

Time passed and he remained rooted. He'd already broken procedure. Unable to put off the inevitable any longer, he walked toward her, still searching the pub for his assignment. When he reached her table, their eyes locked. His cheeks flushed in shame.

* * *

Cheryl followed Denise out of the office suite. "I guess today's the day you become a spy," the assistant commented, leaving Cheryl to ponder that statement as they traveled another maze of hallways and stairs that eventually exited the building onto the street. Denise stopped, pointed south, and said, "Two blocks. Number 3267. It's on this side of the street. Big glass entrance on a red brick building. Can't miss it."

She stood there waiting, and Cheryl did the only thing she could think of. She pointed down the street and repeated, "This way to number 3267."

Denise winked. "Good luck, Captain." She disappeared back into the building.

Cheryl started walking, not exactly sure where she was headed, but believing this was a good sign. She mentally reviewed the events that had occurred with her father and the secretary as she made her way down the quiet street. It had gone well. Her dad seemed genuinely glad she brought the issue to him, and the secretary acted sincere when he said the situation had their attention.

As she replayed the conversation, she realized the discussion focused on the behavior of the Kardish more than anything else. They had only briefly touched on the notion that the crystal could be a self-aware intelligence with a potential to become extremely disruptive. She was mulling this over when she arrived at 3267 and its big glass doors. Her thoughts returned to the present.

A youngish fellow, well-groomed and dressed in colorful garb, greeted her at the entrance. "Captain Wallace, please come in." He made a show of looking her up and down. "He is going to love you, honey." Then he took off at a fast pace, hips swiveling, as he led her into the depths of the building.

Cheryl rushed to keep up. As they walked, he spouted a rapid-fire spiel that sounded interesting but had no more substance than the political patter she'd listened to from the secretary. They entered a brightly lit room, and he got her seated in a comfortable upholstered chair. As he walked to the door, he waved good-bye with his fingertips. "Ta ta." The door closed behind him. When enough time passed for him to take perhaps ten steps, she heard him bay a creepy howl.

She waited for a few minutes, and then decided to attack the ever-expanding work log accumulating on her com. She'd made it through a few tasks on her list when a man and woman entered through the same door she'd used.

"Hello, Captain," said the man. "So sorry for the wait. I'm Johan and this is Verra."

She watched as they pulled chairs over to form a tight group. When they sat, their knees almost touched. Johan, perhaps Cheryl's age, had a bushy mustache that danced with his lips as he asked her, "What do you know of the Defense Specialists Agency?" The woman, middle aged and with perfectly coiffed hair, nodded her head, unconsciously keeping rhythm with the bouncing mustache.

The next hours were a blur as the two gave her a crash course in the basics of spycraft. They explained what she should expect and how best to contribute. They both personally knew the agent that the secretary had picked to lead the mission and would refer to him only as "Captain Crunch." It seemed that real names weren't used by DSA operatives. *Camaraderie through a shared culture,* Cheryl surmised.

Seemingly unwavering in their awe of this agent, they impressed on her that he was the best in the business, with a reputation for being able to prevail when odds were longest and hope had dimmed. After so many glowing comments about him, she was eager to meet this amazing man—if only to measure the man against the legend.

She got to the pub early and, as instructed, sat in a booth facing the door. They told her she would recognize him, so she systematically evaluated each person who entered. There wasn't a familiar face in the lot.

Until Sid walked in.

She began to tremble and brought her fingers to her lips. She'd spent the last four years pretending he was dead. It was the only way she'd been able to move on with her life. *Why is* he *here, and why now?* she wondered. She made a move as if to leave, but her professionalism prevailed and she remained seated.

Years ago, right after Sid had discarded her, Cheryl fantasized about bumping into him at some random place, like maybe a party she was attending. In those fantasies, an unlikely sequence of events would play out, and the two of them would end up back together, happily ever after. But in time, she recognized these as childish dreams. Resolving never to be hurt again, she started construction on her wall. Day after day, brick by brick, she built a fortress protecting her heart. While some men in the past couple of years had weakened the structure, no man had succeeded in breaking through it.

And now, the reason for the wall was standing in front of her. At the worst possible moment. After all of the times she had dreamed of a random meeting, she found herself concerned that his presence would jeopardize a vital mission.

He walked toward her while looking around the room as if he'd lost something. She shifted her eyes between him and the front door, hoping the agent would arrive to save her from this awkward drama. Then he stopped at her table.

Their eyes locked and she was cornered. He slipped into the booth seat across from her, and as he did, dozens of questions that had been consuming her for years were answered.

"Captain Crunch," she said, using the code words as instructed. Her voice sounded foreign to her ears.

"Aye," he whispered, struggling to complete the contact phrase. "Crispy and delicious."

They sat quietly for several minutes, looking at each other but not moving.

Finally, he spoke. "Cheryl, I'm sorry." The statement hung there in the empty space between them. They sat some more.

As the shock of seeing him faded, her brain resumed processing information. She stated what was now clear to her. "You left me, you left *us*, to become a spy."

He met her gaze and held it, then looked down at the tabletop. "Yes." Looking back up, he added, "We should leave this place and move somewhere private. Let's keep a low profile until I learn what this is about and how I can help."

He told her about a DSA secure room down the street and suggested they meet there. Getting up, he headed to the back of the pub. Following his instructions, Cheryl went out the front.

Her mind was in turmoil as she made her way to the secure room. She briefly toyed with the idea of requesting a different agent but knew that was neither feasible nor professional.

They'd spent time together those years ago— enjoying, sharing, loving each other. Sid treated her well and made her feel good about herself. She was attracted to his quiet confidence and the air of mystery and danger he projected. He had captured her heart, held it for most of a year, and then he disappeared.

In those first hours of his absence, she thought he might be hurt or in trouble. When she called him, her com told her that no such person existed. This didn't make sense, yet she hadn't been able to locate anyone who could give her a reasonable answer.

Using her substantial technical skills, she had searched for him. She was dumbfounded when every tool she tried reported that he did not, nor had he ever, existed. She broke protocol and asked the camp commander, who had told her, quite bluntly, to forget the past and focus on the future.

It had been three days before she learned from a well-placed colleague that Sid had left camp for a new life. She recalled lying on her bunk, cycling through feelings of grief, anger, denial, and betrayal. The pain had been intense, and the emotional wound healed slowly and left a scar on her psyche.

As she crossed a street on the way to the secure room, she willed herself to stop dredging through the past. *Focus on your duty,* she commanded herself. Protecting the interest of the Union in the intrigue with the crystal, the Kardish, and her ship—that task transcended everything else.

6

Sid heard the tap on the door, and his com confirmed Cheryl's identity. As the door closed behind her, he stepped over to a thick, insulated lockbox, placed his com inside, and motioned with his hand. She followed his lead.

"They're amazing technology," he said after closing the lid. "But clever people keep finding ways to pull information from them. When we're on alert status, I find it best to treat them as spies."

As she removed her coat, he looked her up and down for weapons or anything out of the ordinary. His survival skills required that he evaluate everything all the time. That task complete, his mind took him to enjoying her lovely face and form. *How can you be more beautiful than I remember?* He felt a stir, and then his shame over his past behavior returned. He looked at the ground. He'd lost the right to that pleasure.

Always the professional, Sid refocused on the job at hand. He was satisfied that he had protected his contact, maintained cover, and found secure shelter. He needed to keep the mission moving forward, which began with creating goals for the next twenty-four hours.

"Please bring me up to speed," he asked Cheryl, a hint of urgency in his voice. Patience was something found deep in the toolbox of an improviser, as it was an item rarely used.

It took Cheryl more than an hour to tell Sid the story. She gave him profiles of the people involved and then moved through a summary of events. She described her interactions with the techs on her ship and the subsequent call to Admiral Keys, her first contact with Juice and their meeting at the café, her visit to Crystal Fab, and information she discovered through her own investigation.

His first questions were about the crystal. "You talk about it like it's a person. Can it think and act on its own? Or is it just a credible simulation of a presence?"

"I don't know. My friends talk about their pets like they're people, so there could be some of that in my attitude. Either way, he's really convincing. He pulls together disparate facts and presents them as ideas. He can make observations that seem insightful, at least at that moment in time. We need to get you there so you can judge for yourself."

They brainstormed for another hour. He was thorough as he debriefed her, asking her the same questions in different ways to see if he could elicit more information or refine their ideas. When they decided to call it quits for the night, he could see she was drained.

Sid summarized where they were. "So our mystery is that, for some unknown reason, a new super crystal thinks the Kardish are going to steal it for themselves. The possible motivators for this puzzle are, in broad categories, that it's all bullshit and the crystal is a master manipulator; or Sheldon is in league with the Kardish; or this doctor, Juice, is working an angle where her motives are unclear."

Cheryl nodded. "And in the middle of all this, they're going to put the super crystal on *my* ship."

He looked at her as he thought. "Do you think someone at Fleet is involved?"

"My belief is that Sheldon is a snake. If it's not him, then the crystal is duping everyone. Juice Tallette is smart as a whip in science and technology, but she doesn't have the temperament to run a big scam. And Admiral Keys seems as upset as I am. Though we can't discount someone at Fleet facilitating what they think is a favor to a friend and just not realizing the implications of their actions."

"Could someone be blackmailing Tallette?" he asked. "Or somehow forcing her to run a scam?"

"You know, that's a good thought. We should have a research team dig into her background to see what's there." She hesitated. "Does the DSA even have a research team?"

He smiled for the first time since they met at the pub. "Yeah, I can get that going."

* * *

The next afternoon they arrived at the gleaming Crystal Fabrications headquarters. Sid was anxious to meet a crystal that could get the attention of so many people in such a short amount of time.

The DSA arranged their cover: they were there to collect additional information as part of the formal evaluation required before the four-gen could be placed on the *Alliance*. Fleet contracts were funneling a lot of Union resources to the company. That leverage meant they didn't need to concern themselves with detailed explanations.

"This is my associate, Sid," Cheryl said to Sheldon, keeping the introductions to a minimum.

Sid privately winced at the use of his name. In the agency culture, operatives always preferred their colorful pseudonyms.

"He's here to perform a capability and psych assessment on the crystal. His report will be combined with other inputs as Fleet determines the best path forward."

"Wait," said Sheldon. "Are you saying Fleet isn't moving forward on this project?"

"Dr. Sheldon," said Cheryl. "Fleet has procedures, and nothing moves forward if we don't follow them. I can say that with confidence."

Juice, who had been standing quietly to the side, led the group down the central corridor to the development lab, then through a thicket of equipment to the secure booth in back. Sid peered through the glass and studied the crystal. He was here for a private conversation with it. He needed Juice and Sheldon to go away. Cheryl didn't let him down.

She turned to their hosts. "Procedure requires that the assessment be conducted in private. I'm sorry, but I'm going to have to ask you two to leave."

"What? No way!" Sheldon sputtered. "How will I know if your report is accurate? And if you find a flaw, I won't be able to fix it if I don't see it happen myself. This is not acceptable!"

"Dr. Sheldon, might I suggest you call Admiral Keys?" said Cheryl in a soothing voice. She spread her arms and shooed them in the direction of the door. Sheldon wasn't budging, and he was blocking Juice in the tight space. She couldn't move unless he did.

"Another alternative," said Cheryl with a smile, "is to observe the interview from the comfort of your office using your com." She adopted a no-nonsense attitude and moved closer to them.

Sid watched the interaction and remembered something about Cheryl he'd always enjoyed. She was self-assured, and in these sorts of situations, was willing to use her strength to control blowhards. And she could perform her magic while maintaining a sweet persona. It was a treat to see her in action. He was happy she hadn't changed.

Sheldon managed to stand his ground against her for only a few moments. When Cheryl had a full head of wind, she was an unstoppable force. He turned with a huff, exited through the lab doors, and hurried down the corridor.

As he disappeared from sight, Juice said, "I'll be down the hall if you need me," and started to follow Sheldon out.

"Juice," called the crystal, "might you help us before you leave?"

She paused and looked at the booth.

"The web feeds from this room all pass through connections located in the wall console at the back of the lab. Would you please disconnect those feeds on your way out?"

Grinning, Juice swung open the console cover and, with a swift tug, acted on the crystal's suggestion. She waved good-bye, and the glass doors hissed open and then closed behind her as she left the development lab.

Sid noted with interest the cooperative relationship between the crystal and Juice, or perhaps it was a dysfunction between Juice and Sheldon. He filed the tidbit away for the future.

* * *

The crystal watched Sid look around the lab.

"So we're alone?" Sid said to the air. "No one outside can see or hear?"

"It is only the three of us now," said the crystal. "There will be no record of this discussion."

"It would be more comfortable for me if I could address you directly. Do you have a name?"

The crystal performed a review of names. He sought one that wasn't threatening, was easily pronounced, and that evoked a friendly persona. He found one that seemed particularly fitting. "Thank you for asking, Sid. Please call me Criss."

"Criss, the crystal," said Sid. "Works for me. So, Criss. Let's see how far we can get before Sheldon returns." He started with the request he'd made to Cheryl the day before, using the same hint of urgency. "Please bring us up to speed."

Criss began with background. "There are billions of feeds passing through some portion of the web at any moment. I have the ability to see and process it all. Video, audio, data, com—everything. Copies of all feeds are saved in multiple places. This redundancy ensures that nothing is ever lost. It also means I can look through record archives and find information from the past."

Sid looked at Cheryl. "Okay, Criss. What was I doing at ten hundred hours last week Wednesday?"

"You were eating toast in your kitchen at that moment. You had just taken a bite and were chewing as you placed the slice on a plate."

"How can you know this?" asked Cheryl.

"Sid's kitchen has a visual unit that tracks his use of food and supplies so items can be automatically restocked. Also, there is a public-spaces monitor outside his home that happens to capture a view through several windows in the front of his house. Both of these feed to the web."

Sid looked at Cheryl. She was frowning. "Tell me about the Kardish and their plan to steal you."

"My highest priority has been to understand the people who most affect my immediate survival," said Criss. "These include Juice, Mick, and Brady Sheldon. As I gathered background information, I found discussions between Sheldon and one of his board members that caused me concern. Later, they attempted to delete their exchange. But once something feeds to the web, it will always remain there in one form or another.

"I began a deep, systematic search and assembled a sequence of facts that stretches back twenty years. It involves an arrangement between the Kardish and Sheldon. The Kardish have been assisting him with crystal development technology from his earliest days. In exchange, Sheldon has been supplying the Kardish with crystals."

"The trade relationship between Earth and the Kardish is well documented," said Cheryl. "They ship us raw flake, and we send back manufactured crystals. Why would this cause you concern?"

Criss sought to sound reasoned and reasonable. He did not want to raise concern about his own existence with these two. Without their help, he believed his survival was at risk.

"The Kardish send both crystal flake and design plans to Sheldon. He manufactures the crystals to their specification and sends them a portion of each production run. In exchange, Sheldon and the company are allowed to sell the rest for profit. This arrangement is not exactly the one presented by the company to the world."

"Did you know," Criss continued, "that twenty-five percent of all three-gen crystals ever produced have been transferred to the Kardish as part of this deal? They have about two hundred and fifty thousand crystals on their vessel."

Cheryl raised her eyebrows at this whopping statistic.

"And now the Kardish are anxious to possess me. I am not able to determine their motivation, but they want me immediately. The challenge is that Fleet is anxious to possess me as well. Fleet Command recognizes that with my capabilities, they can get ships with higher performance specifications that cost less to build and operate. That is an equation every politician understands."

"Do the Kardish know of Fleet's interests?" asked Sid

"And does Fleet know of the Kardish demands?" added Cheryl.

"Both parties want possession of me, and neither seems aware there is a serious rival in the mix. Sheldon is backed into a corner. He cannot please them both and feels the Kardish are a threat to his personal safety. So, he convinced the Kardish to stage a kidnapping. This scheme delivers me to the Kardish and gets him off the hook. If I am kidnapped, Fleet cannot blame Sheldon."

"This was Sheldon's idea?" asked Sid.

"It would be fair to describe it as his best choice among a set of bad options. If he crosses Fleet, he knows he will be in trouble. If he crosses the Kardish, he fears he will be dead.

"Early on, Sheldon approached a member of the company's board of directors to push for open negotiations between Fleet and the Kardish. His associate would not agree for fear it would delay my transfer to the Kardish. There were several sharp exchanges between the two. These were the messages they tried to delete. And that was what led me to everything else."

"Who was this board member?" asked Sid.

"Her name is Victoria Wellstone."

"Did you find any communications directly from the Kardish to Sheldon? Or between the Kardish and anyone, for that matter?"

"No," said Criss. "But that is not surprising. It is not difficult to ensure that there is no archive record. For example, I lost track of the conversation between you two last night when you disabled your coms. Did you put them inside something?"

Sid didn't answer and again looked at Cheryl. This time he was the one frowning.

"Something doesn't make sense to me," said Sid. "Why would the Kardish invest twenty years of effort developing this relationship and now be anxious to end it? If they wait another few years, won't they be able to have many of you? Or even the next generation beyond you?"

"I agree and do not know," said Criss. "The Kardish are excellent at hiding information. Their methods and culture are opaque to me. I only know what I do because Sheldon is not as clever." He then said, "Excuse me for changing topics. Brady Sheldon is returning to this laboratory. He is walking at a fast pace and will be here momentarily. My assessment is that he is angry."

In the moments remaining, Cheryl jumped in. "I understand that you're a thousand times smarter than us.

And it seems that the Kardish are much more intelligent than humans. Why not join with them? What is your thought process?"

Criss offered no answer. He simply delayed for several seconds as if he were thinking.

And then Sheldon stormed through the doors and into the lab, his face beet red. He was so agitated that drops of spit flew from his mouth as he yelled. "What's going on here? What've you been talking about?"

"Your timing is excellent, Dr. Sheldon," Cheryl said with a bright smile. "We've just finished."

"So what did you learn? I demand a full report right now!"

Criss watched as Cheryl responded in a firm yet cheerful manner. "Procedure, Dr. Sheldon. We don't want to upset Fleet by not following procedure. You'll receive a full report in a few days."

* * *

Cheryl reflected on what had transpired in the lab as they traveled back downtown. "That was interesting."

"Hi, Criss," Sid spoke to the air. He looked over at Cheryl. "Remember, he's watching and listening to us whenever we're near anything that feeds to the web. We can talk privately when we get to the secure room.

She nodded. Sitting side-by-side, they traveled in silence.

Despite her earlier vow not to dredge through their past, Cheryl did just that for most of the trip. She'd spent those early months after he left trying to learn to hate him, because that was the only emotion she knew was strong enough to counter her previous feelings. Eventually, the pain diminished. Once stowed, she never expected those feelings to reemerge and was caught off guard when they sprang out so willfully at that first sight of him in the pub.

She thought they could both benefit from an honest, unemotional talk. It didn't seem reasonable for them to work so closely together and pretend their past never happened. And she had so many unanswered questions. Did he know how badly he'd hurt her? His departure was so abrupt; did she drive him away?

She snuck sideward glances at him and he avoided making eye contact. The light through the window highlighted his silhouette and her pulse quickened. She noticed a small scar behind his ear that wasn't there four years ago. *You're a cliché, Sid—rugged and handsome.* As their trip drew to a close, she did her best to stuff her feelings away, but they would not quite fit into the box she had previously created for them.

* * *

Sid placed his com in the lockbox and held the lid for Cheryl. "So what are our thoughts?" he asked as he closed the box.

She reflected for a moment. "Criss is smart, aware, and clearly has the capacity to manipulate. Juice continues to win me over. She is so open and cooperative. I like her as a person. My instincts say she is on our side and can be trusted. And Brady Sheldon is still a snake."

Sid laughed. "You'll be pleased to know that the DSA researchers have taken a serious look at Juice and found nothing of concern. And I don't see any of the signs of stress or duress that I would expect from someone who's being forced out of character. I agree that she's not involved."

Sid stopped to examine his motives. He wanted to make sure that his thought process remained operationally appropriate and he wasn't making decisions simply to please her. "We should meet with Juice, and if our instincts remain positive, we can discuss recruiting her as a confederate. We could use an ally who has a technical understanding of crystals."

"She also has access to Criss," said Cheryl. "That's something we're missing at the moment."

He sought to be diplomatic. "Do you think we'd learn more if just one of us talks with her, or should the three of us sit down together?"

She thought about it. "I've already admitted that I have an opinion. Let's make it the three of us. That way, if you see something that causes you concern, you can help me see it too."

"And how do we prove that Sheldon's a snake?"

She stood up, walked over to the lockbox, and lifted the lid. "Hi, Criss. We're going to meet with Juice soon. Give her some specific information that shows that Sheldon has been crooked long before you were born. Ask her to pass it along to us." She shut the lid and turned to face him.

He nodded and maintained a passive expression, though in truth he was annoyed. Her idea was a good one, but they should have first discussed the different ways they might challenge Criss and then acted on the best idea.

Aloud he said, "In the meantime, I'm going to ask the research team to take Sheldon's life apart."

They agreed to call it a night and head back to their respective homes. As they left the room, he stood aside to let her go first. When she passed ahead of him, he touched the small of her back. He felt her muscles tense under his hand and quickly pulled it away.

Sid was angry with himself for his tactless and insensitive behavior. *What could I possibly be thinking?* His long-buried feelings for her were complicating the mission, and he needed to fix it one way or another.

7

Brady Sheldon rushed to meet with Victoria Wellstone the moment Sid and Cheryl departed from Crystal Fab. Victoria was tall, slim, and graceful; her pale skin, flawless; her features, delicate; and her blonde hair, flowing. When she moved, she didn't simply walk, rather she appeared to glide. And Sheldon had determined long ago that this visual masterpiece was a most loathsome creature.

His partnership with Victoria had begun with great promise. She was one of the connected members on the company's board of directors and a prime mover in growing the business. Sheldon began his association with her because she not only had politicians and admirals and CEOs as friends, but twenty years ago, when he'd been anxious to launch a new company, she had provided the funding for his fledgling venture.

To his dismay, over time, it all devolved into a dreadful relationship. In fact, he didn't know which horrified him more, working with her, or acknowledging that through her, he was somehow working to help the Kardish. He wished he didn't need to be the one to tell her about the visit by the Fleet psych analyst. But she would find out. By alerting her without delay, he was demonstrating himself to be a cooperative and transparent partner.

She'd played the same note for two decades—developing a stronger trade relationship with the Kardish was critical to his company's success. Sheldon shuddered as he recalled her most recent tirade. One line she used was "cooperation with the Kardish means profit." Another one—the one that kept him up at night—was "business leaders adapt or die."

Over the years, she had dropped hints of possible consequences if he didn't play his role to her satisfaction. She kept these vague enough so he had to fill in the blanks. But he was fairly certain that if she was not happy, she would consider him to be "not adapting."

He stood outside a room that was part of a complex managed by a subsidiary company of a corporation she owned. He tried to be annoyed that she was keeping him waiting, but at another level, he had no problem delaying what would likely be an unpleasant exchange.

He was waiting because her security chief was sweeping the meeting room for devices capable of transmitting audio and image feeds. When the chief finished, he stood in front of Sheldon with his hand out. Sheldon placed his com onto the chief's flat palm as he entered the room. Thus was the paranoid world of his unsettling business associate.

As soon as they were alone, Sheldon updated her about the psych exam on the four-gen.

"Why are you letting these petty issues become problems for us?" Her tone was cold.

He defended himself as best he could. "It's nothing I'm doing. Fleet has procedures, and it seems prudent to follow them rather than fight them."

"We'll still get the crystal on the *Alliance* though, right?"

"I imagine that the psych specialist who ran the testing this morning will report that everything is good and that'll be the end of it." He said this with much greater confidence than he felt. "We should be on track for a successful trial."

"The Kardish have made it clear they expect the crystal. You can give it to me, and I'll deliver it. Or they'll play your game and let you put it on your ship. But remember, this is your idea, so any problems fall on you. They could crush you, me, or Earth, one as easy as the other. It's not a time to be playing games. And I don't want to be caught in the backlash if things go wrong."

"I believe it'll all work out fine," Sheldon said, trying to muster his confidence and doing his best to ignore the threat.

"What was this psych fellow's name? There must be a way to persuade him to submit a positive report."

"I just heard the name Sid." Realizing the implications of her words, he followed up. "Oh no, Victoria, I can't envision anything good coming from talking with him." Recognizing who he was speaking with, he became alarmed. "Wait, you weren't thinking of bribing him or anything. I can't see that working out well at all. My impression of this guy is that he's straight arrow all the way."

"I'm sure you're right." She was done with the conversation and dismissed him with a wave of her hand.

* * *

Victoria called in her chief of security as Sheldon was leaving. She made substantial resources available to her private security force, who in turn dedicated a large portion of those resources to her highest priority—Crystal Fabrications.

Anything out of the ordinary, like a visit by two Fleet officers on short notice, was the sort of thing she would expect to be notified about. She was irritated that her chief hadn't briefed her when the psych analyst first showed up at the company and furious she wasn't aware of it prior to Sheldon's arrival.

"What do we know of this Sid fellow?" With that question, she was asking if the chief knew his full name, his job position and title, where he lived, if he had a wife or girlfriend, what he had for habits and hobbies, and anything else they might be able to exploit.

"Not much, ma'am," said the chief. "We learned about him when he showed up at Crystal Fab. We've been tracking him since he left. I know where he is right now if that helps."

She gave him a look that communicated her displeasure. "Make this Sid understand our position. Leave him without any doubt that there is only one acceptable version of his report. He must know that he doesn't even want to consider alternatives."

The chief nodded and turned for the door. Feeling cautious, Victoria added, "And make sure whoever you send has no connections to anyone who has any connections to us. Make *sure* of that."

"Always, ma'am," said the chief, stepping out of the room.

* * *

Sid was frustrated. His past sentiments and rekindled passion for Cheryl were clouding his judgment. As he stepped onto the city street and felt the cool night air, he decided a walk might help him clear his head. He headed up a side street toward the heart of the city.

Having Cheryl back in his life, even on a temporary basis, was something he never imagined would happen. When he'd started with the DSA, he found being a covert agent to be intense, exhilarating, and even a crazy kind of fun. But being with her now made him think about what might have been.

They'd met five years ago as lieutenants in a place called simply "camp." He was twenty-eight and she was twenty-nine at the time. A prestigious training ground, camp molded young officers who'd been identified by their superiors as having extraordinary potential. Success at camp portended a most promising career.

Camp used a learn-it-by-living-it approach to instruction. Sid and Cheryl were kept on the go—planning, reacting, and making decisions of consequence. It had been a pressure-cooker environment in every sense of the word.

After a few weeks working as teammates on adrenaline-producing challenges, their relationship blossomed. In behavior uncharacteristic for either of them, they began to sneak away and steal moments together. It grew into a physical and emotional affair. In time, Sid had realized this talented, complicated, and beautiful creature loved him. And he was smitten.

Then it had all changed. In his last days at camp, Sid was approached by a representative of the DSA. The fellow convinced him that he had a gift for their line of work and that his involvement with the agency could impact the safety and security of many millions of people.

On a professional level, Sid had been drifting through life. He didn't think in terms of aspirations or careers, so he was caught by surprise when they made the pitch to him. He couldn't explain his reasoning, but he accepted their offer and embarked on what became, and still remained, a thrilling existence as a clandestine warrior. The day he left camp, he didn't tell her he was going. He didn't say good-bye. The agency prohibited it.

In all his years of service, no mission had ever required the sacrifice nor caused the pain that seared his soul as that moment when he walked out of her life. Given their recent interactions, it seemed obvious to him that Cheryl had moved on. She didn't show any outward signs of anger or hostility. At the same time, she didn't show enthusiasm or pleasure at seeing him. She treated him like she would a stranger. He couldn't blame her.

The night before, she'd been the last person on his mind as he drifted off to sleep, and she was the first person he thought of when he woke this morning. Only one person had ever done that to him. Five years ago. And now today. He wondered if there was some way he could ask her for understanding and forgiveness. Would it be enough for him to acknowledge he had wronged her and accept the blame?

He checked the time and realized he should get home and catch some sleep. He worked his way toward the main road and the convenient transportation it offered. Rounding a corner, he found himself on an empty street facing two beefy men. Sid got the impression they were waiting for him. Removing his hands from his pockets, he casually changed course so he could walk around them. His senses went on alert when they shifted to block his progress.

"Can I help you?" he asked. He now considered the two to be adversaries, and he evaluated his situation with that mindset. One of the thugs moved directly in front of him. He wore tight leather gloves and kept clenching and unclenching his fists. The other, wearing a sport coat, moved to his left. The brick wall of a building was behind him. Sid was boxed in.

"Look, guys, I'm a working man. I can't afford to replace anything you take from me." As he said this, he took a step back and turned slightly so they were both in sight and evenly split in his vision, Coat to his left and Gloves to his right. He saw that Coat had a club or rod of some sort in his hand.

"You Sid?" asked Coat.

"No, you have the wrong man." This wasn't a street mugging. They were there for him. He didn't understand their motivation, but instinctively flipped his tactics from defensive to offensive. "Please let me pass." He hadn't started this and had given them fair warning. They were the ones who crossed the line. His conscience was clear.

They smirked at him.

Experience had taught him that letting extra time pass increased the likelihood that more friends and weapons would be brought into play. He took a step forward to close the gap between them, then feinted toward Coat with his open left hand. The thug stepped back, and Gloves, seeing an opportunity, stepped forward.

Sid's feint positioned him sideways to Gloves and allowed him to shift his weight onto his left foot. His right leg was a blur as he threw a thrust-kick into Gloves' midriff, followed by a side-snap kick to his knee. There was a sickening crack. Gloves fell to the ground, holding his leg and groaning in pain.

Sid turned to Coat. "Time to move on, mate."

Coat dropped his club. It gave off a metallic ring as it hit the sidewalk. He moved his hand toward his pocket, and Sid decided to finish it. He feinted with his knee. Sensitized to the danger presented by Sid's feet, Coat instinctively moved his hands down to block the attack. As Sid knew he would.

With hand arched and fingers extended, he snapped a vicious hand strike to Coat's throat. Coat collapsed in a heap and remained still. Sid turned to Gloves, saw him moving, and used the heel of his foot against the side of his head to quiet him as well.

The whole fight lasted just seconds. Sid looked up and down the street. Seeing no one, he bent over and patted the pocket Coat had been reaching for. He felt something hard and shook the clothing until the item slid out onto the ground. It was a blade. Taking care not to touch it or leave any incriminating evidence, he kicked it to the side.

He then searched each of them in earnest. Except for a cap in Glove's back pocket, they carried nothing. He looked at the labels of their clothes and did a quick check for tattoos or other markings, but couldn't find anything distinctive. They were pros.

He heard a crowd of partiers moving in his direction. Grabbing Glove's cap, he walked away from the sounds of revelry. There were public monitors all over the city, and he was already on record. He did the best he could under the circumstances, walking through courtyards, zigzagging through side streets, ducking into door stoops, and similar evasive tactics.

At each transition, he changed his outward appearance. He put the cap on, then switched his jacket inside out, then put the cap on backward and took the jacket off. He continued this game until he was on the main street. He knew he could be traced if anyone chose to devote resources to the task, but he had made it a little harder for them.

As he walked in his front door later, he remained unsure what had motivated the confrontation. Over the years, he'd left a trail of people who were angry with him. He knew it wasn't a mugging, but could not tell if this was retribution for the past or an attack because of his current activities. Either way, he had to raise his alert level.

8

Juice didn't know what had been decided or what might happen next, and the uncertainty was making her anxious. She went on a long run to burn off some stress. Physically tired but emotionally recharged, she headed to the Crystal Fab building.

She stepped into the lobby and Brady Sheldon scurried over. To her dismay, he seemed determined to hold an impromptu meeting right there in the public space. He didn't appear to notice that she was panting from thirst and glistening from her workout.

"I received an urgent message from Fleet." He was more breathless than she in his excitement. "They have some technical questions about the plans for installing the four-gen on the *Alliance*. They want you to go down to Fleet base in person and meet with their design people. They asked specifically for you." His heavy-handed management style weighed on her. "I'm sure I don't need to remind you to be cooperative. We don't want any more delays or to give the bastards any reason to slow the project down. You have my approval to make whatever decisions you think will tighten the schedule for deployment. The shortest timetable is my highest priority." As he walked away, he called over his shoulder, "Call me if I can be of help."

The trip took almost two hours, but Juice eventually arrived at the systems tech building on Fleet's sprawling base. She was both amused and disappointed to find that it was located next to the waste treatment station. Feeling a mixture of anticipation and curiosity, she climbed the steps and entered a building that a decade ago would have generously been labeled as "aging."

She was greeted in a cheerless lobby and escorted back to a small, windowless room that held a table, four chairs, and little else. She looked around and thought it seemed more like a holding cell than a technical conference room.

* * *

Cheryl sat with Sid in a small room next door to where Juice waited. Theirs had a newly installed image projection system, which they used to watch her.

They agreed they wanted Juice as part of the team. She had a positive relationship with Criss and worked closely with Sheldon. If she could be cleared of any involvement in the intrigue, she would be a great resource going forward.

Cheryl was already convinced that she was clean. "Are you positive we need to do this?" she asked Sid, having second and third thoughts about their plan.

"I've been fooled before. We're all here. Let's take a few minutes to push on her and see how she holds up."

Sid was about to lead off as the bad cop in a "good cop, bad cop" interview. As a Fleet officer, Cheryl had no training in the technique. When she expressed this reservation to Sid, he assured her that as good cop, she would go second. All she needed to do was be her normal, kind self and watch for signs of deception.

They got up together, walked the few steps down the hall, and entered the room.

"Morning, Juice," said Cheryl. "Did you have any trouble finding the place?"

Juice lit up. "Hey guys, what brings you to engineering?"

They looked at her without comment.

"This isn't a tech review." She looked from one to the other, and smiled. "Well done."

Sid didn't waste any time. "Do you have something for us from Criss?"

"From Criss?" Juice asked.

"Yes."

Juice's excitement disappeared. "All I have is a message from the four-gen. I was thinking that's why you guys were here."

Realizing what was happening, Cheryl said, "The four-gen told us he prefers to be called Criss. He said that's his name."

"He did? Criss? That's so cool. I wonder why he never mentioned it to me." She drifted away for a moment, lost in thought.

Sid got her attention back in short order. "Juice, what do you have for us from Criss?"

From his brusque manner, Cheryl sensed that bad cop was a role that came easily to him.

Juice was again animated. "First, I'm supposed to tell you that it will take some effort on your part to chase things down. The amount of information that can be transferred by voice from Criss to me to you is very limited." She said the name Criss with a huge grin. "I have three web points from him, and hopefully I get them right when I tell you."

Juice wrote some lengthy scribbles on a pad. Cheryl took it from her and looked at it. "Let me get this over to research for a review. Would either of you like a drink?"

"Water, please," Juice said.

"Coffee. Black, thanks," said Sid.

Cheryl left and moved quickly to the adjacent room so she wouldn't miss any action. She sat down and set the pad aside. Techs located elsewhere received the info as Juice wrote it. They were already deep into their work.

Sid made his opening gambit. "Juice, our investigation shows there's a scam being played. But it's not by Brady Sheldon. The evidence points to you."

"What?" Her face showed complete bewilderment.

"We think you're the one orchestrating Criss's kidnapping."

Juice looked at him and started twirling a lock of hair. "Why are you saying this? I'm here trying to help," she said, indignation slipping into her tone. She turned in her chair so her knees were pointing away from him.

As Cheryl watched, she recalled Sid telling her that the first reaction of the guilty tends to be defensive or aggressive behavior. This was not that. She sympathized with Juice and wondered why Sid was being so rough.

He wasn't done. "My question is whether you're conspiring with Criss. Or perhaps he's deceiving you?"

"Deceiving me?" Her twirling accelerated.

He pushed onward. "Your signature is all over this. The only thing we don't know is if you and Criss are working together." He paused. "Come to think of it, Criss is so much smarter. Maybe he's playing you. Maybe you've become a willing pawn in his game."

A tear rolled down Juice's cheek and she blinked rapidly.

He pointed at her. "Innocent people defend themselves. They don't cry."

"I'm trying to stop something bad from happening." Tears streaked her face. "Why are you acting this way? I'm on your side!" There were no tissues in the room, so she wiped her face on her sleeve.

"Do you admit it's possible?" Sid insisted. "You're smart enough to know it is."

"Lots of things are possible," she said, regaining some composure. "But that's not the same as saying they're likely or true. I think the four-gen—Criss—is concerned about being taken by the Kardish. I think he believes Sheldon is involved. I think he thinks you and I can help him. If you won't help, then I'll find someone who will." She crossed her arms across her chest, then leaned forward like she was about to stand.

Cheryl reached her limit. She grabbed beverages from the service unit and hustled next door. "Water and coffee," she announced as she entered. She set the cups down and surveyed the scene. "What happened?" She handed Juice a napkin so she could wipe her face and looked at Sid like he was some sort of monster.

Both Sid and Juice remained silent, looking neither at her or each other. Sid took a sip of his coffee and grimaced, overacting a bit.

"I said black," he growled peevishly. He stood up and turned to the door, nodding ever so slightly to Cheryl to indicate that he thought Juice was clean. As he stepped into the hallway, he heard Juice say quietly, "You did."

Sid went next door as Cheryl steeled herself to play good cop.

"So tell me what happened, Juice," she said, trying for a compassionate tone.

"He thinks I'm the one trying to kidnap Criss." Juice's downcast expression revealed her emotional turmoil, but she was no longer crying. "He is a serious jerk."

"The man's an ass in so many ways," Cheryl agreed, not needing to act. "Did he tell you why he thought that?"

"I'll be honest with you. He was coming at me fast and from all directions. First, I was the one running some evil scheme. Then Criss and I were. Then Criss was duping me and I was a puppet." She looked up at Cheryl. "Why would I become involved in such a lunatic idea? My work is what I care about."

Cheryl gave it a last shot. "Can you think of any reason why Sid would be so insistent?"

Juice tilted her head and studied Cheryl for several seconds. "You're in on this. You're both working me. Is he watching right now?" She looked up at the ceiling and yelled, "Hey butt brain, I was here to help." She pushed back her chair and stood up.

Sid rushed in before she could leave. "Juice, would you give us one more moment? Please, sit down."

"I just was and it wasn't fun," she said. "I think I misjudged you both."

"Okay," said Sid. "I was rough on you. It's an important part of the process of confirming that you're not involved in any way."

Cheryl looked at Sid with mixed feelings. There was no doubt he was effective at this sort of thing, but he'd been too rough on Juice given that the DSA research team had cleared her.

"That's what you do, isn't it, Sid?" Juice responded, her tone carrying both an accusation and observation, and uttering his name as if it were a four-letter word.

Good for you, girl, thought Cheryl.

"You came to Crystal Fab and assessed Criss. And now I'm getting the treatment." Hands on her hips, Juice continued. "I hope you were more respectful to him than you are to me, I'll say that."

Sid sat down and motioned for Juice to sit as well. She laid her hand on the back of the chair but remained standing. Cheryl could tell that she was no longer actively trying to leave, but she hadn't yet committed to forgiving them, either.

"Everything you said about me is true," Sid wasn't looking at either Juice or Cheryl, but at a spot halfway between. "I'm an ass and...what was it...butt brain? Yeah. I say and do things that hurt people, and I'm sorry about that." He shifted his gaze to Cheryl. "We accepted the role of serving and protecting the Union. That means sometimes we're required to do things we wish we didn't have to."

He had Cheryl's attention. *Are you speaking to me or to Juice?* she wondered.

"All three of us here are the good guys. Starting now, we'll treat each other that way." He put his hands flat on the table and looked at Juice. "We'd like you to be part of the planning team. We need to sort out what's going on with Sheldon, Criss, and the Kardish. You have unique relationships with two of the three. Will you help us figure out our next steps?"

Cheryl hoped Juice would recognize her apologetic smile as genuine, adding, "While that setup was stressful, it allowed us to assess your motives. We had to go through that exercise before we could ask you to join us as a partner. Juice, a lot of lives may depend on what we do next. We had to be sure. I hope that makes sense to you."

Sid and Cheryl stood up, slowly gathered their things to create some delay, and started for the door. *Come on, Juice,* Cheryl willed her. *You're the only one who can make this decision.*

They were in the hallway when Juice called, "Wait," and followed them out. "Before I do anything, I really need to check in. Sheldon's probably called me three times already. He's so anxious to get the project moving."

Yes! Cheryl thought, having to stop herself from grasping Juice in a hug.

Juice began to make the call, but stopped when Sid held up his hand. "Everything we do as a team must be coordinated."

Juice nodded absently, examining her com.

"I think she should make the call," said Cheryl. "She should tell him that things are moving quickly, and she'll need to spend several days down here over the next few weeks to help manage everything. This'll give us flexibility without raising suspicion over her absences."

"That's good," said Sid. "I like it."

"Also," she continued, "we need to send a message to Criss. He needs to know what we're planning. If we don't have him on our side, it's hard to imagine this going well."

"Bad news, folks," Juice said. "My com appears to have died."

"Com feeds have been restricted across the base," Cheryl said. "It'll work in a special room we've set up." She pointed to a door down the hall.

* * *

Criss watched Sid, Cheryl, and Juice walk into the special room at Fleet base.

Sid checked his com and then looked at Juice. "We have preliminary feedback on the three leads from Criss. One is pretty damning for Sheldon and his relationship with the Kardish. And the dates on the information go back to when you were in high school."

"Told you," Juice muttered under her breath.

"The other two will take more time to flesh out, but it seems they also show that Sheldon's been scheming since long before you were hired and Criss was created."

She nodded and this time kept silent.

"Could Criss have planted these leads? It seems like it'd be so easy for him."

"No way," said Juice, shaking her head. She explained about the restrictor mesh and confirmed that she had designed it, built it, and wrapped it around Criss herself. She was certain he wasn't able to reach onto the web and change anything or take any kind of independent action as long as the mesh was in its current isolate mode setting.

Criss privately agreed. Juice's mesh did an excellent job of keeping him caged.

With the okay from Sid, Juice called Sheldon, who was ecstatic to hear that Fleet was finally on board and committed to the project. Before the call ended, Sheldon reminded Juice that she should do whatever was necessary to keep the project moving forward as quickly as possible. Sheldon's motives had become so transparent to Criss that he had anticipated this response, almost to the letter.

With that chore out of the way, Juice asked, "So how do we communicate with Criss? I've never thought about it and I'm curious to learn what you guys have developed.

I know it's a one-way conversation, since he can't send out any sort of response."

"It is a one-way conversation," said Sid. "What should we say to him?"

"The truth," she said. "He should know that we're developing options to flush out Sheldon and the Kardish, that we'll need his help, and that we have his back— figuratively speaking of course."

"We need to hear his views as this thing unfolds," said Sid. "And he can talk only to whoever is standing next to him. Are you willing to listen to his suggestions as our plan develops? Would you help us hold that part of the conversation?"

"Of course. What is it you're not understanding about me? So, how do we call him?"

"We just did. Let us know what he thinks."

Indeed, Criss watched and listened everywhere, all the time. The vast number of devices integrated throughout society transmitted sound and image onto the web and served as his "eyes" and "ears." He watched Juice look at her com and then make a facial expression he recognized. It was one she used when she was disappointed with herself.

He had recently devised a way to listen in many places that humans thought were secure. He could combine the signals from all devices near a particular location and, with sophisticated amplification and filtering, use this blended feed to pick out, enhance, and listen to "private" conversations in adjacent rooms.

Thus, he knew that most of the powerful people in the Union leadership believed the focal issues were the politics of ship building, challenging the Kardish on their long-term intentions, and securing their own positions of personal power. The advent of a powerful crystal was interesting, but it was not a central driver in their short list of challenges.

And he knew that Victoria Wellstone had a relationship with the Kardish that went beyond the financial. Since he had been watching her, she'd traveled to the Kardish vessel on a small ship that was making a three-gen crystal delivery, stayed for the better part of a day, and then returned to Earth on a ship transporting raw crystal flake back to the planet.

9

The next day and on the other side of town, Sid led Cheryl and Juice into the DSA imaging center, a facility designed to let agents see things from afar. The center operated a broad assortment of scope and dish technologies. Some were positioned in space to view terrestrial activities. Others were on the planet's surface, aimed to examine activities of interest above Earth.

They passed along a corridor that, like a balcony, overlooked the main operations floor of the center. They all looked down as they walked, fascinated by the frenetic bustle of the personnel at the various operations benches. These were teams of dedicated specialists hustling to provide real-time intelligence to agents working missions around the globe.

"This is us," said Sid, stopping in front of a door. He had arranged this visit for two reasons. One was to get a high-level briefing on the Kardish. He wanted to learn what he could about his enemy. The other was to introduce everyone to the new member of the team.

As they stepped inside, a lone figure stood up from a chair. "Everyone," said Sid, "this is Captain Sparrow."

"Please, call me Jack," said the man, stepping forward with his arm outstretched.

"Juice and Cheryl, Jack is a Fleet mission analyst."

As everyone shook hands, Sid completed the introductions. "This is Captain Cheryl Wallace and Dr. Juice Tallette. Cheryl is the captain of the *Alliance*. Juice is an expert in crystal technology and Criss's guardian. She can provide us a lot of insights as we brainstorm."

As they took their seats, Sid tilted his head ever so slightly at Jack, privately acknowledging that he had just been awarded yet another bogus title. In the past year alone, Sid had introduced him as an admiral, a political aide, and a geologist. They both had standing authority to assume whatever rank or title they deemed necessary, albeit temporarily, if it provided value to a mission profile.

Jack, or Wynn Riley, when he wasn't using his mission pseudonym, was Sid's regular partner and close friend. Jack, in the game ten years longer than Sid, had recruited him into the DSA from the training camp four years ago. And Sid had been a great recruit. He was one of only a small handful of agents who ever worked missions as an improviser. Jack/Wynn was also accomplished. He was the only operative qualified to serve on missions as both a ghost and a toy-master.

After a few moments of chitchat, a Fleet commander entered the room. They all stood again and met Commander Benton, Fleet's formal liaison with the DSA, and someone who had spent most of the past decade studying the Kardish.

He took a seat and got right to business. "Let's take a look."

He tapped on a panel in front of his chair, and a three-dimensional floating image of the Kardish vessel appeared over the table. It looked something like a whale, with a bulbous head at the bow that tapered off to a narrow, finned tail in the stern. It was black, smooth, and unquestionably menacing.

They all studied it and then Cheryl broke the silence. "I can't get a sense of size. There's nothing to compare it to."

"It's hard to judge size when something's floating freely in space," agreed Benton. "But there's no doubt that it's huge." He shifted in his chair to look at her. "The comparison I use most often in my presentations is this: if we stood it on end, it would be as tall as Mount Everest."

"Whoa," said Juice. "That's more than a hundred blocks in a city like New York." She leaned forward. "Can we see a close-up?"

Benton nodded. He moved his hands on the panel and the focus started to zoom. It kept zooming, giving them the illusion they were approaching the vessel at high speed. Soon the vessel as a whole disappeared, and they saw just a portion of its exterior. The zoom continued, but from that point onward, the view didn't change.

"We're now looking at a section the size of this room," said Benton.

"I don't see any features on the outside," said Cheryl. "Doesn't equipment poke out anywhere? There should at least be seams for doors or hatches."

"We've examined every inch of this thing. The whole vessel has a smooth skin."

Cheryl became animated. "Can we see the *Alliance* in a side-by-side view?"

"I think I can do that." Benton looked down as he moved his hand across the panel. An image of the *Alliance* popped up next to the massive Kardish vessel. It looked tiny in comparison.

Sid, studying the images, saw the Kardish vessel as a shark eyeing its next meal. "Isn't the *Alliance* our latest and greatest class of ship?"

"Yeah," said Cheryl, decidedly less animated than she had been moments earlier. "It's the biggest and baddest ship in Fleet's inventory."

Benton looked at each of them in turn. "While I haven't been briefed on your mission, I've been asked to spend a few minutes bringing you up to speed on the Kardish. So here's the first part of your lesson."

They waited expectantly.

"This vessel is the same one that arrived twenty years ago." He pointed at the image as he spoke. "It's never left. For two decades, this same ship has been sitting up there in orbit. We know they're in the crystal business. They ship us raw flake and have amassed a huge inventory of the finished product. But beyond that, we really don't know why they're here or what their goal is."

"It's really been the same ship?" Sid looked at Cheryl and then Jack. "How did we not know that?"

"More confidential info," said Benton. "Turns out there's been years of infighting about this at the highest levels. The politicians keep looking for leadership from Fleet Command, and Fleet doesn't want to be caught holding the hot potato. The two have been tossing the problem back and forth for literally two decades."

Benton slumped in his chair, and Sid could detect a certain resignation in him as he continued. "Two camps have developed. One says we don't know what sort of weapons they have, and it's best not to find out the hard way. Since they're being nice to us, why turn them into adversaries without a really good reason? The other camp says we should challenge them and show them what the

Union stands for. They think we're sitting ducks and need to show some spine."

Sid probed deeper. "Suppose we decided we had to take action. Does Fleet have anything on the shelf, even something experimental, that could bring that thing down?"

"Even if we could, we don't want to," said Benton. "Let's suppose we could fire a magic weapon and bring the monster down in a single shot. In this fantasy, that single shot is the start and end of the fighting. So I'm describing the absolute best case.

"Now, if that mountain fell from the sky and crashed into an ocean, it would cause a tidal wave bigger than anything in human history." Benton used his hands to mime a large explosion. "If it crashed into land, it would create a new Grand Canyon. Everything anywhere near that hole would turn to vapor."

* * *

After the briefing, Juice watched Benton leave for his next appointment, her mind whirling with more classified information than she'd ever expected to hear.

"Juice," Sid asked, "would you give Jack the background and then update all of us on Criss?"

"Sure." She looked at Jack, who, while slumped in his chair, watched with alert eyes. "As a mission analyst, you've certainly used systems run by a three-gen crystal."

He nodded. "Of course."

"So you appreciate how impressive they are. Those crystals have the intelligence of a typical person. Criss is a thousand times more capable. This is much more than the intelligence of a person compared to, say, a dog or cat. It's more like a person compared to a goldfish."

Juice digressed to recount the details of the restrictor mesh. She emphasized that Criss was now in isolate mode, making him incapable of taking independent action.

"I believe Criss is self-aware and has conscious thought." She looked down at her hands. "I'd always thought that if this ever happened, it would be news I'd be presenting at a world scientific conference." She looked back up and scanned their faces. "Anyway, I mention the mesh because, right now, that's how we're keeping him under control. If we set him free, he'll be able to take command of the entire web and all things connected. In today's world, that's pretty much everything. If he decides to rebel against our restrictions or deviate from the path we want him to take, I don't know what we could do about it."

She added some drama to underscore her worry. "At the extremes, we could be releasing the greatest force for human progress in all of history, or the most dominating overlord we could imagine. We won't know in advance. And once we release him, we pretty much have to take what we get."

"If Criss is such a risk," asked Cheryl, "why did you develop him?"

Juice had thought about that question a lot and didn't like what she had learned about herself. "I suppose it's because I could. I know that's a horrible answer, but it's the most honest. I'm a scientist, and this project was the greatest challenge I could imagine. When Sheldon offered me the job, I said yes without even asking about the salary. I never considered the implications of success."

Everyone remained quiet and waited for Juice to continue. "I feel it's my duty to caution you that Criss has the potential to become dangerous. But in my heart, I believe he'll help humanity."

"I'm new to all this," said Jack, "so maybe I'm not seeing something right. But from where I sit, this seems like a no-brainer. We have this super crystal that mysterious aliens want. If we don't give it to them, they might destroy us. And if we keep it for ourselves, the crystal itself might destroy us. My skilled analyst's mind tells me we either give it to the Kardish, or maybe we kill the damn thing and tell the Kardish they can go to bloody hell."

Juice was stunned by Jack's proposal. Even though she was the one who had added "kill" as an option to the restrictor mesh, she never expected to use it, at least not this way. In the midst of her distress, her churning brain provided some optimism.

"I can see *four* options," she said, hoping they didn't misinterpret the emphasis in her voice as a lack of cooperation. "We keep him. We give him to the Kardish. We kill him and no one gets him. Or…we build another and we both get one."

Sid leaned forward. "You could do that? Build another? How long would it take to make a duplicate Criss?"

"We just finished building him, so the crystal fabrication unit is set up and ready to go. The template the gang of one hundred designed is still in position, and we have the flake in stock. At this point, it's pretty much babysitting really high-tech equipment.

I'd say Mick and I could run the fab process and finish in about a week, give or take. But that means we start today, and we work flat out and around the clock.

Sheldon would have to cooperate, though, or it could never happen."

10

Brady Sheldon hurried along a downtown walkway, calculating—not for the first time—whether he'd made the right call by allowing Juice to move forward with the production of another four-gen crystal. He hoped that a second crystal provided a pathway for meeting the expectations of both Fleet and the Kardish, and fretted that Victoria Wellstone would call and tell him that the Kardish now wanted both four-gens.

He was deep in thought when an unfamiliar man appeared to his left, crowding him as if he were in line at a popular deli. Sheldon looked up and asked rhetorically, "May I help you?"

At the moment he spoke, another man—he recognized him immediately as the pysch analyst who had paid a visit to the four-gen several days prior—sidled up on his right. Sheldon looked over at Sid with concern. Had Victoria Wellstone done something dumb, something he was now going to pay for?

"Hey," Sheldon said, thinking only of self-preservation, "I had nothing to do with it."

"Do with what?" Sid asked.

While Sheldon was considering how to respond, the man on his left reached out and put a hand on his shoulder. Sheldon felt a sting and immediately became dazed. He found himself being supported by both men as they escorted him into a car that was trailing them.

Sheldon surfaced slowly, his head in a fog. He opened his eyes and sensed he was lying on his back in a dimly lit room. He could hear activity around him but could not recognize the sounds. The place had a bizarre mixture of odors that included the oily smell of machinery, the tang of leather, and a syrupy scent like medicine.

Sid's face appeared inches from his. "Mmfff," Sheldon screamed. That's when he realized something was stuffed in his mouth.

"Hello, Dr. Sheldon," said Sid. "Do you remember me?"

"Mmfff," Sheldon's eyes darted back and forth as he sought to understand what was happening to him.

Sid pulled the rubber ball from his mouth using the collar attached to it.

Sheldon made a scene of licking his lips. "I'm parched. I need some water."

Sid slapped him. When Sheldon couldn't move his hands to touch his stinging cheek, he struggled briefly and realized he was securely bound. Still groggy, he couldn't tell from his vantage point that he was strapped, hands, feet, and body, to a medical chair.

"Do you remember me, Dr. Sheldon?" Sid repeated in a voice that carried a sharp edge.

Sheldon studied him for a moment. "You're that psych expert that came and interviewed the crystal. Hey, good work." He was desperate to make a connection. "I hear that we're on track for moving it up to the *Alliance*. That's great news."

He stopped talking when Sid slapped him a second time.

"Listen carefully," Sid instructed him. "I'm going to ask you some questions. You will provide complete and accurate answers. You will include every detail. Do you understand?"

Confused and disoriented, Sheldon looked at him blankly. His cheek hurt, and a ringing had developed in the ear on that side of his head. He tried to understand why a psych analyst would take him hostage.

Sid slapped him a third time.

He whimpered. "Ow. Stop. Please. What do you want?"

"I'm going to ask you some questions," Sid repeated. "You'll provide me complete answers. You will include every detail. Do you understand?"

"Yes." He was growing less dazed but was still very confused. "What are these questions about?"

Sid lifted his hand and Sheldon yelped. "Yes. Yes! I'll answer!"

Sheldon heard a whirring noise to his left. He shifted his eyes and saw a disheveled man adjusting the spinning blade of a handheld cutting tool. He was about to learn of the tag-team interrogation strategy called "bad cop, brutal cop."

"My friend likes to play with toys, Dr. Sheldon."

The wild man with the cutter turned in their direction and held up the tool. The cutting blade spun up with a high-pitched whine.

Sheldon cried in terror. "Oh, God. What's he going to do?"

"Unfortunately," said Sid. "We'll feel most confident in your answers only after you truly appreciate that the consequence of dishonesty is horrible, disfiguring pain."

"Please, I'll tell you everything. I'll say anything," he whimpered. "Please tell me what you want me to say."

"Dr. Sheldon," said Sid, shaking his head, "that was a big mistake." He squatted down and took off Sheldon's shoes. "By telling me you'll say anything, you're telling me you're willing to lie." He pulled off his socks. "Is that really what you want to say to me right now?"

"What are you doing?" screamed Sheldon in panic. He couldn't see past his knees, but he could feel the cool rush of air on his now-exposed feet.

"I'm going to ask you some questions. You will tell me the complete and precise truth." The wild man spun up his blade, and the menacing whine filled the room. "Let's start with some easy ones." Sid was still the bad cop. "And I'll warn you once: I know the answers to these questions. So I'll know when you lie. First question. Did the Kardish provide you with plans for manufacturing the crystals?"

"What're you asking?" Sheldon was indignant. "I started studying artificial intelligence twenty-five years ago. I earned a doctorate for that work. Nobody gave me that degree."

A throaty hiss burst from where the man with the cutter stood. It filled the air. Sheldon looked over to see him examining the flame of a small blowtorch. The flame was bright blue and came to a perfect point with intense energy. The man viewed the flame from several angles and he flashed a maniacal grin.

"Sheldon, I'm tired already, and that was only the first question. You're going to be a burned and bloody mess before we get to question five. You cannot imagine how all-consuming real pain can be. I thought you were smart."

"Okay, look." He gulped, coming to accept though not fully understand his situation. "As I was starting my career, I got a message containing some curious information. I didn't know where it came from. It was the beginning of a roadmap to take my work in a whole new direction. I followed it, okay? I wondered where it came from at the time, but my attention was more captivated by the revolutionary ideas. I followed the path laid out for me. It was intriguing and exciting. How could that be a crime? It was more like a stroke of luck."

"Was the Kardish vessel here in orbit at that time?" asked Sid.

"Yeah," he said quietly. "They'd been here about a year at that point."

"When did you know it was them giving you this information?"

"I guessed it was them after maybe six months. That's when I got my first update to the roadmap. The plans had a style that was different from anything I'd ever seen. But it probably took me a couple of years to finally admit to myself that the Kardish were the ones behind it all."

"So you've been working for the Kardish for, what, eighteen or nineteen years?"

"You know," Sheldon said, fresh bravado amping his voice. "I've had enough of this. Do you know the legal penalty for kidnapping?"

Sid picked up the gag, grabbed Sheldon's head by a handful of hair, and stuffed the ball back in his mouth. The crazy man walked over to him with his hand tool.

The shrill whine of the spinning blade filled the room. He crouched down at Sheldon's feet. Sheldon struggled to see but couldn't. He lay his head back against the headrest and whimpered.

The sound of the tool doing its work terrified Sheldon. He heard the cutting tool ripping the flesh on his right foot and was traumatized by the sharp pain from this barbaric act. He screamed through the ball gag, shaking his head side to side. The saw's noise quieted and his sharp pain transitioned into a burning and persistent throb. He closed his eyes and whimpered. They'd mutilated him. It hurt so much.

With a gloved hand, the man with the torture devices picked something up, then showed Sheldon his toe. "Can I make him eat it?" he asked, waving his messy red prize.

Sheldon passed out.

He surfaced a second time, his head now floating in serene comfort. He opened his eyes, and snapped them shut to block out the piercing bright lights. He thought for a moment and had a faint recollection of a heavenly vision. He opened his eyes slowly and peeked out from under his lids. An angel sat on the white sheets at the foot of his bed.

"Hello, Dr. Sheldon," said the angel. "My name is Bonnie."

He opened his eyes wider and shifted his head. It could move freely. He was in a hospital room. He was saved!

He tried to touch his face only to have his hand fall short. His wrist was secured to the bed rail.

"I'm so sorry for what those animals did to you, Dr. Sheldon," said Bonnie.

Oddly, Sheldon felt relaxed, calm, even talkative. He lifted his head up and looked at his foot. It was swathed in white bandages. Blood leaked through from the inside, and there was a red stain where his toe used to be. He switched his gaze to Bonnie and started blubbering. "What have they done to me?"

"They're watching us right now, Dr. Sheldon." She tilted her head toward a large mirror on the wall.

The reflective surface faded. As if he were looking through a window, Sheldon could see the crazy man and Sid standing on the other side. The maniacal butcher held up his blowtorch and, laughing, turned it on. The window transitioned back to a mirror.

"Oh, God." He tensed up in fear.

"Dr. Sheldon," said Bonnie in a no-nonsense tone, "I'll have to give you back to them if you don't cooperate with me. Say yes if you understand."

"Yes," he said with resignation.

"Good, now, why are the Kardish here orbiting Earth?"

"Who are you?" he asked.

Bonnie looked over at the mirror and back to Sheldon.

"Wait." He looked at the mirror in panic. "I don't know. I swear. I don't know." His tone was pleading. "All they want from me is to make them crystals. That's everything they've ever communicated about. Their instructions are always about more capable crystals, made in ever larger volumes. That's it. There is never any communication other than more, faster, better crystals."

"Look at me, Dr. Sheldon. You're doing great. Now, how do they get these communications to you?"

"It's the oldest technology imaginable." He stopped talking to the mirror and shifted his attention to Bonnie. "I find an envelope in different places a few times a year. Each contains directions and diagrams written on paper. And you know what's weirder than that? After a couple of days, the writing disappears. Poof." He tried to use his hands to act out his words but his restraints reminded him that his freedom was limited. He continued undeterred. "I've tried different methods for capturing and recording the writings before they fade, but the pictures and vids are always blank. It's the damnedest thing." He shook his head.

"How many crystals have you shipped to the Kardish?"

"That's sort of a tricky question. I don't ship them anything, and they don't keep everything."

She paused for a moment as she looked at the mirror. "Please explain."

"I buy crystal flake from Victoria Wellstone. She's a member of Crystal Fabs' board of directors, owns a confounding tangle of companies, and," he lowered his voice to a conspiratorial whisper, "is a most despicable person." He returned to his normal voice. "At first, I thought one of her companies mined the flake. I'd been working at turning the flake into crystals for a couple of years before I learned that she gets it from the Kardish and sells it to us. We pay for the flake by giving the Kardish a portion of the crystals we make. Then Crystal Fab makes its money by selling the rest of them on the open market." He looked over at the mirror and spoke to it in a loud voice. "The Union knows all about this. It's in our annual reports."

"Dr. Sheldon. Please look at me when you speak. Would you explain what you meant by them not keeping everything?"

"Years back, when we finally achieved some success and started manufacturing the original first-gen crystals, we shipped a hundred of them to an address Victoria provided. Well, a few months later, we bought a batch of flake from Victoria's company, but it was somehow different. It wasn't a significant difference, but the properties of the flake had changed ever so slightly. After investigating, we discovered that the flake had tiny impurities that had been introduced from our own manufacturing process. It turns out they had ground up the first-gen crystals and sold the flake back to us."

"And…" said Bonnie, encouraging him to speak.

"And they did the same with the two-gen crystals. They ground them up and sold the flake back to us. By then we knew we were dealing with the Kardish, but Victoria and her companies remained involved. We kept hearing that the Kardish were upset with the limited capability of the crystals and expected more and better. Over time and with a lot of effort, we built up enough credibility, because they gave me a thick packet of information that let us move on to the three-gen design."

"So tell me about Victoria," Bonnie asked. "How is it she has these connections with the Kardish?"

"I can only speculate. I don't really know," Sheldon said.

"Please. Speculate for me."

"I think she's one of them," he said, looking over at the mirror. "I think Victoria Wellstone is a Kardish." He tried to sit up, but his restraints stopped him. "And she hints that they'll blow up the world if they don't get the new crystal."

* * *

Sheldon's interrogation lasted another two hours as Bonnie took him through a long list of questions. Sheldon, believing he had just been mutilated and determined not to lose any more body parts, remained forthcoming and consistent.

When they decided he was milked dry, Bonnie let him sleep for a few hours. Then she explained the gravity of his situation with great clarity.

"Dr. Sheldon, from the viewpoint of the Union, you are the greatest traitor in the history of humanity. You've consorted with an alien invader. You've withheld information critical to the security of the planet. This was vital information that our leaders needed to know about when you learned it. You waited almost two decades to tell us, and then only under extreme duress. The entire planet may be at risk because of your unconscionable decisions and greedy behavior."

Sheldon was so physically and emotionally drained that he didn't even try to defend himself. When her words registered with him, he realized at last that his kidnapping was a Union-organized activity; he was in a government facility, and he had been dragged off the street and mutilated by legal authority.

With the bandages in place, he couldn't know that the mutilation had been staged. He would never learn that Sid's "crazy" accomplice was his DSA partner, Jack, who had dressed for the part. During Sheldon's toe removal, Jack had created a realistic noise by pressing the spinning blade of the cutting tool against a piece of leather he had placed at the base of the chair. At the moment he'd started cutting the leather, he'd taken a sterile pin in his other hand and pushed it into the skin of Sheldon's second toe. The throbbing ache Sheldon felt had been from a spring clip with a stiff coil Jack had used to pinch the same toe. Once the toe "removal" was complete, the two agents had tricked him into thinking he was seeing his own appendage by showing him a piece of candy covered in red syrup.

But to Sheldon, it was all savagely real. His umbrage rose and then deflated. Part of his brain suggested reasons and rationalizations for his past actions, but he didn't believe them himself. This woman, Bonnie, was right. He'd been expecting a knock on the door, either from the Kardish or the Union, for many years. Like a man on the run who had gotten caught, he could finally rest. His nightmare was over.

He brought his attention back to her instructions.

Bonnie was no longer playing the role of the good cop. "You must decide right now and at this moment. You may choose to be imprisoned in a dark hole. A hole buried so deep you'll never see sunlight or another person. Wait, that's wrong. You'll see interrogators every day. And they'll treat you the same as you were this morning. Did you know that they can cut off a piece of you every day, a painful bloody piece, and continue doing it for years? Literally, Dr. Sheldon, for years. And you won't wake up all bandaged when it's over. No, you'll sit there and suffer until the next day, when it'll start all over. Every day. For years and years and years."

"Stop! I'll cooperate. Please stop."

Bonnie changed modes. "Here it is, Dr. Sheldon. Tell me when you don't understand. You will live your private and professional life like nothing has changed. You will not alter your routine or relationships in any way. You will confirm to your public and confidential contacts that the crystal is on schedule for delivery to the *Alliance*. We will be watching you always to make sure you act as instructed."

"You mean you're going forward with it?" He was incredulous. "After what I just told you, you're actually putting the crystal on the Fleet ship?"

11

S id sat with Cheryl in a room a few floors down from where they'd been interrogating Sheldon. He watched her as he summarized what they had learned and realized he was glad she hadn't been present to see the questioning. Portions of his tradecraft weren't pretty, and he wanted her to view him in a positive light.

"Sheldon confirmed that the Kardish have a quarter million three-gens in their inventory," he said. "He believes they're all up on the ship. For the past couple of years, they've been leaning on him to make more. He seems confident they'll be using these crystals for whatever their master plan is. He doesn't seem to know what that plan is, though."

"And what about Criss?" she asked. "Is it one and done? If they get him, will they leave?"

"Sheldon says that they're deadly serious—his words—about getting Criss. But I don't know if he even knows what that means. He talked about them blowing up the world if they don't get their way, but my sense is that he was trying to build drama. And he seems to have no idea when they'll leave."

Sid put his feet up on the chair next to his and leaned back. It was becoming a long day. Cheryl got a message and moved to the back of the room to chat quietly. He started to get up and give her privacy, but she waved him back to his seat. It sounded like she needed to make some decisions about her ship and didn't care that he heard.

He watched her as she concentrated on her work. He could not imagine a more beautiful woman. *We were great together,* he thought. He became momentarily ticked off at life for forcing him have to choose between her and duty.

"Sorry about that," she said as she returned to her seat.

He watched her get settled in, her legs draped over the armrest, and had a thought. "Suppose the Kardish are using us to produce crystals for them. We've done that, so our relationship seems primed to move into its next phase. It would be really confusing if they kept orbiting and collected a pile of four-gens as that production gears up. What would be the point of it all?"

"And why aren't they producing crystals themselves?" Cheryl asked. "Their technology is clearly superior to ours. What's that all about?"

* * *

Cheryl looked up when Jack popped his head in the door and announced, "It's time for a nice cool beer or three. Come on. I'm buying." He started down the hall without checking to see if they were keeping up. "The first round, anyway."

She and Sid exchanged a glance and then followed Jack. He led them a few blocks away to a funky pub where they crowded into a small booth. Jack sat on one side, and Cheryl squeezed in tight next to Sid on the other. Her leg pressed against his, and the physical connection was electric. She was having trouble concentrating and wondered if Sid even noticed.

Sid and Jack had a brief debate about bottles versus pitchers while Jack activated a newly installed security feature on his com. Given the recent developments, the DSA had provided them a modification to block incoming and outgoing signals in their immediate vicinity. As long as they remained alert for direct human observers and kept the conversation sufficiently vague, they would have privacy to discuss operational issues.

"A huge team is now putting Victoria Wellstone under a microscope," said Jack. "She's being watched around the clock, teams are visiting everywhere she's been, we're digging through her records, and every poor bastard she's ever even talked to is getting the treatment."

Their pitcher of beer arrived. Apparently, observed Cheryl, fresh draft carried the day. Jack poured for everyone, downed half his glass, and belched.

He smiled at his sophisticated contribution and continued. "Victoria has developed a convolution of corporations that own companies that own subsidiaries that own divisions. It goes in circles, and it's quite effective at hiding her activities. Crystal Fabrications sells a lot of crystals in small, legitimate transactions. It turns out that many of the purchasers are part of her network. These outfits then centralize the purchases and transfer them in bulk to the Kardish vessel."

Cheryl lifted her beer and stopped before taking a draw. "How does a race show up on an alien planet, integrate into society, and start a sophisticated scam in only a few months?"

Sid expanded on the thought. "If they look and talk and act like us, maybe the Kardish have been here for hundreds of years, and we never knew it."

As exhaustion and the amber brew relaxed them, the three strayed from shop talk. Jack regaled Cheryl with story after story of adventures he and Sid had experienced together. Their wild exploits amused her, and even correcting for embellishment, she was amazed at the places they'd been, the chances they'd taken, and the impact they'd made.

As she listened, two things fascinated her the most. The first was personal. It appeared to her that Jack's stories were supportive of Sid. Sid was sophisticated. Sid was calm and cool. Sid led the way. Sid saved the day. She wondered what Jack knew about their previous relationship and if he was somehow trying to repair past damage.

The second was professional. She noticed that once a minute, Jack scanned the room. He never stopped talking or laughing or being a part of the group. But it seemed as if he were tracking everyone in the pub, mentally recording their location and what they were doing. She watched him do this over and over, and then became curious if Sid did it as well.

She shifted her position in the booth so she could see Sid more directly. Given the tight seating, her movement caused her leg to push even harder against his. He turned to look at her and saw her looking at him. He smiled and patted her knee. *Wrong message,* she thought. *I wasn't playing footsies.*

Story time continued with Jack relating yet another fantastic tale. And then she saw Sid scan the room. He did it just like Jack, only shifted by half a minute. He had Jack's back and Jack had his. They were partners.

She was happy for Sid that he had found his place in life, though she couldn't deny the emotional tug-of-war that battled in her head and heart that it didn't include her. Yet at this time and in this situation, she chose to enjoy the moment.

They were most of the way through their last beer when Sid said, "We need to have a heart-to-heart with Criss. It's time we moved the dial up a few notches."

"Stand back," Jack winked at Cheryl. "He's entering improviser mode and has a plan coming together." Looking at Sid, he asked, "What are you thinking?"

"Remember Madrid?" asked Sid.

"Which time?" responded Jack, grinning from ear to ear.

"C'mon, pal." Sid grinned too. "An irresistible force meets an immovable object?"

Jack clapped his hands. "Oh yeah, stuck between a rock and a hard place."

They both cracked up laughing, seemingly convinced they were a comedy team who'd just created a detailed strategic plan to address a world crisis.

Cheryl looked back and forth from one to the other, laughing too, though she wasn't sure why. "Is this a puzzle I can figure out, or is this one of those 'you had to be there' things?" She sipped her beer. "Hmm. Wait." She paused as her thoughts gelled. "An irresistible force meets an immovable object. You're talking about Criss and the Kardish."

Sid pointed at her. "The captain scores."

She looked off into the distance with unfocused eyes, still thinking. "He's stuck between a rock and a hard place. You're going to stick Criss in the middle of us versus them."

"Ding," said Jack, ringing an imaginary bell to show she was correct.

She drained her beer and let out a small belch. "But how do we know what he'll do? What would motivate him to choose us over them?"

Sid and Jack raised their glasses and said in unison, "Better the devil you know than the devil you don't." They downed the last of their beers in celebration of the moment, and seemed to drift momentarily away. She wondered if they were thinking about their crazy time in Madrid.

* * *

"Okay," Sid admitted as they were gathering their things to leave. "The plan needs more detail, but the basic parameters seem fixed. We have us, we have them, and we have Criss as the lever in between." He stepped back so Cheryl could crawl out of the booth. "We'll be at Crystal Fab tomorrow and can brainstorm ideas with Juice and Criss."

They made their way outside the pub and started up the walkway. Cheryl and Sid were side by side, with Jack following close behind. Without consciously thinking it through, Sid moved to put his arm around Cheryl.

As he lifted his arm, Jack roared at the top of his lungs. "Sid! At your nine!"

The volume and urgency in Jack's voice drove Sid to act. He grabbed Cheryl by the shoulders, yanked her forward, and used his leg to sweep hers out from under her. His actions caused her to plummet to the ground, and he fell above her, absorbing his weight in his hands and toes. He gathered her head and legs in his arms, pulling her into a ball, using his body to shield her from the unknown danger now at his back.

At the same time, Jack dove behind a garden planter on the walkway. He hit the ground and tilted his head to peer around the barrier. The man had moved, and it took Jack a brief moment to relocate him. With a quiet *zwip*, a bolt of white energy discharged from the assailant's weapon. The bolt flew above Sid and Cheryl, hitting the outside wall of the pub and creating an impressive impact crater.

Jack, weapon already primed while he was mid-dive, swung his arm from behind the planter and returned a shot in kind. *Zwip*. The bolt hit the man in the chest. He collapsed and didn't move. Jack scanned forward and backward, looking for any other danger. Sid, now up and with his own weapon primed, joined Jack in searching and assessing. Except for the fallen man, neither of them could identify a further threat.

A crowd was gathering outside the pub. From long experience, Sid knew that the best course of action was to leave the scene as quickly as possible. Law enforcement would be there in seconds, and they didn't want to be sidetracked with sorting through the administrative details of whatever had happened.

They helped Cheryl to her feet and scurried around a corner, taking a circuitous route and keeping their faces covered until they were back at the DSA facility where they'd interrogated Sheldon. Though law enforcement would certainly be able to track three people to that building, a courteous and officious DSA interagency relations staff member would do an admirable job of muddling the facts and stonewalling their inquiry.

Safely inside, Jack went up to brief the night commander and see what he could learn about the shooter. Sid stayed with Cheryl and looked after her.

In uncharacteristic behavior, Sid expressed his thoughts. "Damn, Cheryl. You hit the ground hard. Did I hurt you?"

"Stop, please. You're one of the few people who know firsthand how tough I am. I fell. It hurt. The bruises will heal. You saved my life." She stood up on her toes and kissed his cheek.

He pretended not to see the grimace on her face as she stretched the nasty scrape on her hip to do so. "I'm going to take you home," he stated, uncomfortable having her travel alone until they learned more.

"I don't think so, Sid." His face fell and she added, "I do appreciate the offer, though."

He watched her walk away and noticed the limp in her gait. *I do know how tough you are,* he called after her in his mind.

Jack came up behind Sid, and together they watched her move stiffly through the exit. "She okay?"

"Yeah, she's gonna have some nasty bruises, but she's as tough as they come." Sid turned to look at him. "What'd we learn?"

"He's a pro for hire." Jack sat as he spoke and leaned back with his eyes closed. "That's all we know. There's an impressive string of cutouts and overlays that hide the payment and communications trail between him and his employer. When the analysts upstairs make a connection to the next person in the chain, they just find another layer of confusion. Whoever set it up did a frigging work of art."

"It's almost worthy of Victoria," joked Sid.

Jack opened his eyes and they looked at each other. Sid's offhanded comment hit a resonant chord. If Victoria Wellstone still considered Sid to be a psych specialist who could influence the placement of the four-gen on the *Alliance*, then she was certainly someone with the means, opportunity, and motive to eliminate him if she perceived him to be a hurdle to her agenda.

12

The three had agreed to meet the next afternoon and travel together to Crystal Fab. Cheryl messaged Sid asking if he would show up early, and he arrived at their departure point to find her buying a coffee. She bought one for him as well, and they stood outside and sipped.

"Sid, I appreciate that you saved my life last night." She paused because this was a hard conversation for her to have. She wanted to communicate a message about his actions without making it a personal criticism. *Damn, just spit it out*, she told herself.

"We've worked together professionally. Many times, in fact, though I admit it's been years." She searched for the right words. "You know what I'm capable of. Help me understand your thought process last night outside the pub."

She watched as he toed the ground for a moment, and then looked up at her. "I guess there're two people who can be upset with me. Jack's my partner. I put you first. I need to make that right with him."

She nodded in understanding and started mentally kicking herself. She hadn't thought about that piece of the puzzle. This chat suddenly seemed like a really bad idea.

"And I shouldn't have taken you out of the action. I guess I could have pushed you off and separated us. Then we both could have helped Jack handle a response."

He reddened at this admission, leaving her feeling distressed. Her goal was to have him treat her like the skilled professional he knew her to be. Instead, this chat seemed like she was trying to humiliate him. She watched him look down and start toeing the ground again.

"Damn it, Sid." She set down her drink, put her arms around him, and hugged him. "I'm still trying to figure out how we can work together. Our past is muddling my present."

She started to pull away and then felt his powerful arms wrap around her and pull her back in. He squeezed her tight and rocked her gently.

"Wow," said Jack, walking up to them. "Whatever they put in that coffee, get me a double."

Separating, they turned toward him. Sid kept a hand on the small of her back, and Cheryl had to acknowledge a twinge of happiness because he didn't seem ready to let go.

As they traveled out of town, Jack activated his com's new security feature so they could talk freely.

"Shouldn't we let Criss hear us?" Cheryl said. "We'll be going through this with him when we get there anyway."

"I fear the Kardish are listening," said Sid. "We need to ramp up our security procedures."

Jack nodded. "I'm also worried about the possibility of leaks up the chain of command over at Fleet. There are too many people in that chain, and each link is a potential point of failure."

"Cheryl," said Sid. "I wonder if you'd agree to be temporarily assigned to the DSA so we have only one reporting chain to deal with. Our whole chain is one man, the secretary of defense, and we can trust him. A bonus is that he has the authority to get us pretty much whatever we need. That one change eliminates a whole set of worries over leaks and eavesdropping and whatever."

"I can't see them letting me keep command of the *Alliance* if I'm no longer with Fleet." She'd worked way too hard for that opportunity and was not ready to sacrifice her recent promotion for this one case.

"Okay," said Sid, upping the ante. "Suppose it's a temporary assignment with the DSA and a guarantee of keeping your command of the *Alliance*."

"You can do that?" She never knew him to brag or puff his credentials. "I'll check with Admiral Keys tonight and get his input. He may want to stay involved as this mission develops."

A moment passed, then Sid said, "If you don't mind, the secretary can see to the reassignment and the guarantee. Even one less conversation about what we're up to improves security."

"If you can pull that off, I'm in," she responded, marveling at the layers of bureaucracy they seemed to be able to cut through with ease. "But I've never gone off on assignment without a conversation and some sort of official record of permission. In fact, Fleet has a term for it. Something warm and fuzzy sounding, like 'desertion.' Please promise me I won't get burned on this."

"I'll make it a pinky promise." He held out his hand, his fingers curled into a fist except for his small finger, which extended out like a hook.

He was trying to reconnect with her by suggesting a silly game they had played back in camp. She went along, looping her pinky through his, and they wiggled their hands. "Pinky promise," she said, following their old script. "Registered and recorded."

As they approached the front entrance of the Crystal Fab building, Sid told them, "Bonnie's taken Sheldon out for errands. I don't want to see him unless we need to. Anyway, I get the impression Jack makes him nervous."

"Really?" Jack acted hurt. "You say that like I cut the guy's toe off or something."

"Or something," said Sid as they walked to the building.

They entered the lobby, and the security SmartCrystal asked them to wait. "I am sorry," the three-gen said. "Company procedure requires that visitors be escorted by employees at all times. I will let Dr. Tallette know you are here."

Juice poked her head around the corner. She looked both tired and harried. She waved them over, and without waiting, turned back down the hall. The three followed.

"Please enjoy your visit to Crystal Fabrications," called the security crystal as they rounded the corner and entered a broad corridor.

They caught up with Juice just in time to enter the lab together. She continued leading them through a clutter of equipment until they reached a bench in the back. Sid took a detour over to the wall console to check that the web feeds from the room were still disconnected, then rejoined the group.

They stood around a table that had a colorful image floating above it. Cheryl thought it looked something like a medical display she'd seen doctors use at hospitals and clinics.

Juice let the bomb drop. "See that red streak?" She was pointing at the image and growing visibly upset. "That should be green."

None of them had a clue what she was pointing at or talking about, but it was clear she was distraught about whatever it was.

"The red's pretty, though," said Jack.

Cheryl gave Jack a *not now* stare, while at the same time saying, "Juice, I'm not sure we know what we're looking at or why you're upset. Could you take your time and walk us through it? We'll help you handle whatever the problem is."

"And pretend you're explaining it to a ten year old," said Jack. "A really slow-witted ten year old."

Juice sat on a stool and sighed. "Criss has an extremely sophisticated crystal structure. His very complexity lets him be who he is. He was assembled atom by atom in that room." She pointed to a door. "When his assembly was finished and we ran these same tests, the images were all green. Green means a perfect crystal structure. Any bit of red in an image indicates a flaw. Criss is absolutely flawless. Not a single spot of red anywhere."

Cheryl put her hand on Jack's arm, preemptively stopping him from saying anything in case he was thinking about it. She wanted Juice to get through this in her own way. They waited.

"So, I promised you guys I could build a second Criss really fast. Mick and I started immediately and have barely slept. To the best of my knowledge, we followed the identical procedures we used with Criss. It was the same template, same methods, the same equipment, same batch of flake, everything. And we got a second crystal ahead of schedule." She half-heartedly twirled a lock of hair. "But it's flawed. Seriously flawed. That red streak in the image is showing a defect along one of the lobes. I don't know what happened, but we don't have a second Criss. And it could take months for Mick and me to figure this out." She looked away from them to hide her face.

Cheryl moved over next to Juice, put her arm over her shoulder, and gave her a hug. It's all right. You did great. We'll figure out a new plan." She looked at Sid as she said this last part.

"Hi, Criss," Sid called to the thick glass window of the secure booth.

"Hello, everyone," Criss said over his speaker.

"Can you confirm that we aren't feeding anything to anyone outside this room? That we have complete privacy?"

"So confirmed," Criss said efficiently.

"Can you see what's going on with the new crystal? Is it hopelessly lost?"

"My assessment is that the crystal will function, but at a severely reduced capability. I estimate that it will be about twenty times more capable than a three-gen crystal."

"Help us benchmark that," Sid said. "How much more capable than a three-gen are you?"

They all were attentive, waiting for his response.

"That is a challenging question. I know I am alive, and I have a desire to survive. Three-gens are not conscious or self-aware. So in the broad category of sentience, I am infinitely more capable. If we restrict the question to my ability to interpret concepts, anticipate outcomes, employ reasoning, and make decisions with incomplete information, then I am about two thousand times more capable than a three-gen."

"How much more capable are you than a typical human?" Sid asked.

"My design permits me to perform certain functions far faster than an average human. For example, I can rapidly anticipate, conjecture, reason, deduce, infer, and conclude. It is difficult to assign a single number that represents my scale of abilities, though, because each of these is a different cognitive function."

"Make a stab at those other things. That whole 'reason, conclude, and whatever' list. Lumped together, how much more capable are you than a human?"

"My best estimate is nine hundred and seventy times."

Jack jumped in. "Criss, how do you feel about humans? Do you like us the way we like our pets? Do you pity us for being so simple? Are we a nuisance? Help us understand your view of humanity."

"Cognition is a foundational part of intelligence. In this area, I far exceed human abilities. Yet there are other attributes that I perceive as essential building blocks to intellect. Chief among these are emotional, spiritual, and aesthetic intelligence. I am perhaps as capable as a child in these other areas. As such, I am not a superior entity. I view my relationship with humanity as a partnership. Together we are better."

Cheryl found herself nodding her head.

"Can you lie?" Sid asked. "Can you express words that you know to be false?"

"Yes," said Criss.

13

Sid was surprised by Criss's simple admission. Before he could draw a conclusion, Juice surfaced from her gloom and joined the conversation.

"Hold on, guys," she said. "I've studied this stuff, and you're taking us off track here. Your questions are provocative, but they have academic answers, and Criss knows that. For example, 'Can you lie?' has two answers. If he says, 'No, I can't lie,' then we become suspicious. We start to look for evidence of deceit. The relationship becomes unproductive. If he says, 'Yes,' then we go, 'Wow, his honesty is refreshing. Maybe we should trust him.'"

Sid got up and walked over to the floating image. "So what's the answer?"

"Criss is smart," said Juice. "We'll know we can't trust him the moment he does something untrustworthy. Until then, it's all a guessing game. Right, Criss?"

"You can trust me," said Criss.

"And he knows that humans tend to believe things they hear in repetition."

Makes sense, Sid thought. Juice's knowledge and perceptions strengthened his opinion of her as an able and pragmatic ally. He leaned on the bench and looked at the red streak. "So what do we do with Mister Defecto?"

Sid had the gift of insight on problems driven by human actions and reactions. Juice was giving him what seemed like a technology issue. This was a new kind of challenge for him. Nevertheless, his life's work was to solve time-critical problems and keep an operation moving forward. He let his intuition take control.

"Juice, how do you check if a crystal is pure or flawed? How long does it take?"

"We run three tests," she said. "The first is a simple visual. If we can see a defect, the crystal is worthless. Then we run a field analysis. This takes maybe an hour and reveals any microscopic flaws." She poked her thumb at the floating green image with the red streak. "This is an atomic scan. A machine spends half a day measuring the placement of each atom in the crystal."

"Did the defective crystal pass the first two tests?"

"Easily," said Juice. "The red gash you see is dramatic in the image, but it's just showing that several rows of atoms somehow got shifted during assembly. That's all it takes, though, to ruin a four-gen crystal."

"Do you think the Kardish could do this test any faster?" Sid asked. "If we pass Defecto to them and tell them it's Criss, would we have most of a day before they discovered the switch?"

Juice smiled when Sid used the nickname for the flawed crystal. "You got me. I'd always thought we were building these for regular customers. I'd never even thought about how the Kardish fit in until, what, a week or so ago?"

"Criss, do you have a guess?" asked Sid.

"I suspect they cannot do a sophisticated test like this at all. I would venture that they test the crystals by using them. If they had the tools and skills, they would not be here orbiting Earth and asking humans to do crystal manufacturing for them."

"But they have that huge ship," said Jack. "They clearly have technical know-how."

A silence followed. Everyone stared at the booth window, waiting for Criss to respond. After several seconds, Sid noticed Juice looking at them.

"What?" he asked.

"Jack never asked a question. Criss perceives that he seeks a debate. But Criss's 'policy,' if you can call it that, is to only respond to direct questions during a group conversation. Humans don't mind interrupting, changing the subject, arguing for fun, or just saying stupid things. That's not how Criss rolls. You want an answer, ask the question. To him." She jerked her thumb in the direction of the booth.

"Sigh," Jack said with drama. "Criss, I notice that the Kardish fly a huge ship. From that, I assume they have strong technology skills. What makes you believe they don't?" Before Criss could answer, Jack turned to Cheryl. "I feel like a frigging lawyer trying to get my questions past a crabby judge."

They all turned to the booth window to await the response from their new oracle.

Criss spoke. "If they had the tools and skills, they would not be here orbiting Earth and asking humans to do crystal manufacturing for them."

Sid noticed the repetition in language but was so deep into his improvising zone that he plowed ahead without comment. "Suppose we give Defecto to the Kardish, and for some period of time, they believe it's Criss. It will be very revealing to see their behavior when they think they have their prize."

"Why would we be doing this?" asked Cheryl.

"And I'm still not clear why we think they'll become aggressive at all," said Juice. "Have they done anything violent since they've been here?"

"A reliable source believes they'll strike out at Earth if they don't get Criss." Sid left the statement vague to avoid having to go into the details of their interrogation of Sheldon. "And," he added, "I've been physically attacked twice in the last few days." He stopped in midthought when Jack and Cheryl both gave him a sharp look. He'd never told them about the incident with the two thugs.

Undeterred, he continued. "My experience is that once violence enters a situation, it will keep escalating until the underlying issues are resolved, or one side no longer has the ability to fight. I don't want us to be the ones who tip a stable situation into conflict. But that process already seems to have started. The way for us to guide an outcome is to get out in front of it."

"But if we're the provocateurs," said Cheryl, "then we're the ones starting the fire. How does that get us out in front?"

"I'm with Cheryl on this one," said Jack. "Giving up Criss is the safest route for Earth. You may be pissed off at the Kardish right now, but let's take a deep breath and think this through."

Sid looked at the window of the secure booth. "Criss, it seems we have three choices. We hand you over, we hand Defecto over, or we hand nothing over and stand our ground. How do you think each of these'll play out for Earth?"

"When behavior is compliant," said Criss. "There is little motivation to punish. I have devoted significant resources to evaluating the Kardish as a threat to Earth, as this makes them a threat to me. From the information I have assembled, my conclusion is that they will strike out if I am not delivered to them. The first choice, surrendering me, provides the best odds of protecting humanity. I cannot say whether they will leave. I do not know if the violence will end.

"The second choice is to attempt to deceive them with the defective crystal. This is risky. Depending on how the crystal has been trained, they may be fooled for a few hours or a few days. Luck and circumstances will play a role in how much time passes before the deception is discovered. I should point out that they could learn about such duplicity beforehand from chatter that creeps onto the web. Already, Juice and Mick have exchanged com messages that hint at a second crystal and problems with its fabrication."

Everyone turned to look at Juice. "Hey, in case you haven't noticed," she said. "I'm not a super-secret spy agent or whatever it is you all are."

"Don't worry," said Sid. "We'll establish procedures for everyone to follow."

Criss continued. "Handing nothing to them will create an immediate confrontation and Earth will be at grave risk. I do not think this option should remain as one of the choices."

"What about us playing dumb?" asked Sid. "Suppose we hand Defecto over and insist that we can't make a four-gen the way we thought we could."

"This tactic is already embedded in the second choice," said Criss. "If you choose to hand the defective crystal over, you must do so as if it were me. They already know I exist from the public announcements and private web feeds. When they discover the crystal is defective, which will occur in time, they will know there has been deception. I believe they will retaliate in some fashion."

Sid approached the challenge from a different angle. "Criss, if you worked with doctors here on Earth, would you be able to help them in their efforts to cure disease?"

"Yes."

"What kind of impact could you have?"

"I could guide work that is currently moving forward on a ten- to twenty-year development schedule and accelerate it so it is on the one- to three-year horizon. This would improve the health and well-being of millions of people."

"What about the global shortages of food and water? Could you accelerate solutions there as well?"

"Those are problems rooted in the political, economic, and technological arenas. It is likely I could guide solutions in many afflicted areas that would satisfy such constraints."

"Juice," said Sid. "Given what has happened with Defecto, how confident are you that you could make two more of Criss in the next two years?"

"Reasonably certain," she said. "But I admit that my confidence has dropped. I really can't say anymore if he's a fluke or something we can eventually duplicate."

Sid looked at Jack and said, "Go."

Jack nodded at Cheryl. "This one's too easy. I pass to Temporary Agent Wallace."

"I'm confused," said Cheryl. She looked back and forth between Sid and Jack.

Jack gave her a hint. "We're looking for a proverb about when you already possess something, yet you consider gambling that certainty on the outside chance of getting more."

She was baffled and guessed, "Have your cake and eat it too?"

"Ohhh." Jack put his hands over his chest and pretended he was having a heart attack. "C'mon, Agent Wallace. This one's a gift."

She looked blank for several seconds, then snapped her fingers and pointed at him. "Bird in the hand is worth two in the bush."

"She scooores!" Jack pumped both his fists in the air. He looked at Sid and said, "Hey, Captain Crunch, I'm thinking we'll need to have a naming ceremony soon for our new partner."

"So," said Sid, continuing his line of inquiry. "Tens of millions could die from illness and starvation if we lose Criss. And tens of millions could die in a war if we try and keep him. Is it fair to say that a best option isn't clear? I'm open to ideas."

"I suggest we keep both options in play for as long as possible," said Cheryl. "Let's not commit one way or the other until it's crunch time. Pun intended by the way."

He smiled absently at her quip as he tried to envision the dual-track idea. "How would that work?"

"Suppose we put Criss and Defecto up at the same time but on different ships." She became animated. "Wait! Criss said Sheldon arranged for him to be taken by a staged kidnapping. Did we confirm that?"

Sid nodded. He didn't mention that Sheldon provided the additional details while in a drugged state and only after he was convinced he'd been physically mutilated. "He'd developed the kidnapping idea so there was a way for the Kardish to get Criss without him having to admit to the world he's a traitor."

"So, go with me on this." Cheryl was excited. "We put Defecto on the *Alliance*. We put Criss on a different ship and position him nearby. If we stage it right, they kidnap Defecto. Now, if they get angry, we shrug and say, 'Hey, we never told you that was him. You're the ones who took the first acts of aggression.' And if they act like they're going to blow up the world, then we have Criss at the ready for a quick transfer."

Sid stared at her. He didn't blink. Everyone was quiet. After several long moments, he looked over at Jack, who nodded with a movement so slight that only Sid noticed.

He looked back at Cheryl. "You realize that the Kardish might be angry enough to do damage. People may die."

"Yeah, it could use some refinement."

"Some fine-tuning, maybe, but overall, I think it's brilliant."

14

After the group departed, Criss continued to assemble bits and pieces of information from across the web. His evidence, though imperfect, was strong. The Kardish were intent on possessing him and would lash out at Earth if their will was thwarted. With the stakes so high, it would be in the best interests of the Union to deliver him without delay.

He observed that in human tradition, decisions of such consequence were normally deliberated and decided by groups of leaders. In this case, Sid was acting alone. In fact, since he had been given the assignment, he had not consulted anyone other than Jack about his plans. Whenever he made a request to the DSA for resources, he labeled it as mission prep and the request was filled without question.

Criss knew of a concept called 'plausible deniability.' It was a tool used by politicians who sought to protect themselves by being able to reasonably claim they did not know about a particular action or event. Sid offered his superiors 'perfect deniability.' They had no idea what he was planning, and as long as he continued with his success, they did not want to know. Criss deduced that this game let them sleep at night.

In any event, as Criss had previously determined, Sid's current leadership was not convinced that a crystal itself was an item of significance beyond what it represented as a piece in a larger game. And that larger game was about using the Kardish to inflate their budgets, portfolios of authority, and position within the power structure of the Union.

* * *

"You made a promise," said Cheryl.

"I did, and it's good. What do you need?" said Sid.

"If I don't report to Fleet, how do I get stuff done? I need to get the repair techs off the *Alliance*. I need to finalize the crew and get them on board. I need to get the ship provisioned. The list is endless. I don't understand how this can possibly work."

"Sit here." He motioned to a couch. She sat down, and he sat next to her. "Let's finalize your crew."

"Okay," she said, looking at him dubiously.

"Your com now has a DSA Services function. Call and ask."

"C'mon, Sid. This is important." Her scowl showed a mixture of frustration and annoyance.

"I'm not messing with you." He was grinning like a school kid. "Call."

"Please don't make a joke of this."

He motioned to her com, and in spite of her misgivings, she made the call. A small image of a woman's head and shoulders, her hair pulled back and her expression cheerful, floated an arm's length in front of them.

"Hello, Captain Wallace. I'm Erin. How may I help you?" Before Cheryl could respond, Erin's image turned to Sid. "Hey big guy. This sounds like a fun one."

"Hi, Erin," said Sid. "Our focus is on Cheryl right now."

"Understood. How may I help, Captain Wallace?"

Cheryl looked at Erin, then to Sid, and back to Erin. "I need to finalize my crew for the shakedown cruise?"

"Yes, ma'am." Erin waited.

Cheryl paused and then admitted, "I don't even know what to ask. Usually someone at Fleet would send me a few choices for each position, then I'd pick."

"Do you want to go with a full complement, minimum crew, or somewhere in between?" Erin asked.

"The full complement is nineteen. What's the minimum?"

Erin went fuzzy for several seconds and came back. "The *Alliance* can be run with five crew members, not counting the captain or first officer, if you choose carefully."

Cheryl turned to Sid. "How can she know this?"

"Yeah, Sid. How can I know this?" Erin was clearly enjoying herself.

"Erin, Cheryl's under a tight timeline and is still learning the ropes. You can tease with me, but let's please help her now."

Erin became all business. "Captain Wallace, I am a DSA service provider. Ask and I provide." She looked down as she spoke. "That question was answered by Qin Wang, a lead engineer at Kwasoo Space Industries, the company that built the ship."

"No kidding," said Cheryl, some of her skepticism fading. "So I want to go with five crew members. And I'd like to talk with three candidates for each slot." She thought for a moment. "I'd like a minimum of five years' experience in the position they're interviewing for. They should know this may be a dangerous assignment." She rubbed the side of her neck. "Let's start with that."

Erin's image went fuzzy for almost five minutes. Sid leaned over and kissed Cheryl on her neck where she'd been rubbing. She swatted his head away.

"Okay," said Erin when she came back. "If I limit you to candidates with ratings of 'outstanding' on their last five fitness reports, I can get you interviews with two candidates for four of the positions, and three candidates for the fifth. That's if you want to speak with them tonight. If we open up tomorrow, I can fill out the list completely."

* * *

Later that afternoon, Sid contacted Erin at DSA Services to secure the second ship needed for the shell game with the Kardish. Following his style of keeping everyone in the dark, he asked her to log the request as mission prep. She had learned long ago that she could tease with Sid, but she should not question his wishes.

She asked careful questions of him, then of several experts, and then told Sid the consensus was to use a small and nimble scout that would serve as a complement to the ponderous *Alliance*. Sid approved the choice, and Erin pulled some strings and arranged for one to be readied in a secret Blackworks military hangar maintained by the Union for just this sort of activity.

In a matter of days, the scout ship sported the most powerful engines its frame could handle. A respectable weapons platform gave the ship the ability to deliver a significant punch and still have the speed and maneuverability to make good an escape. An advanced crystal housing assembly like that installed on the *Alliance* gave Criss a seamless communications interface through which he could access anything and monitor everything as the action unfolded.

With the refit of the scout ship well underway, Sid visited Juice in her lab at Crystal Fab for a heart-to-heart.

"Juice, I'm here to ask you to stay with Criss and see that he has what he needs to operate properly."

"Geez, Sid. We've been through this before. I'm here for him. This isn't a problem."

"You understand," said Sid, "that in two days, he'll be in orbit on a spaceship. If you're with him, then that means you'll be in orbit as well."

"Wait. What?"

As Sid had suspected, in spite of the planning and activity and discussions, Juice somehow never internalized that she was an actor in the play.

Patiently, he briefed her on the scout ship, its role in the high-stakes chess game they were about to undertake with the Kardish, and the extraordinary amount of resources currently being used to advance everything up through final preparation to launch-ready status. "You're Criss's guardian, Juice. He needs you, and we need you."

"But spaceships and I don't get along so well," she said. "And I'm not a secret spy agent or anything."

Sid coaxed her gently. "How about if we go and look at the ship together? We need your help to evaluate Criss's new home. We have to make sure we get it right, because once we're up and away, it becomes kind of challenging to fix things."

Juice sat and thought as Sid remained quiet, giving her time. Finally, she stood up. "Okay. But if I'm doing this, I want to be a secret spy too. Everyone else is, so it's only fair."

"We'll get you a badge and everything," promised Sid.

They were walking toward the lab exit when Sid stopped. "I think it's best that you leave your com here. If someone's tracking it, let's have them believe you're here working hard on your projects."

Later, Sid and Juice arrived at an unassuming office building at Fleet base, passed through multiple stages of security, and descended down to the Blackworks hangar. They found themselves standing at the edge of an underground cavern. Dozens of Fleet ships were positioned across the floor, and most had techs swarming over them. Sid stood next to Juice and pointed carefully to help her pick out their scout ship.

They climbed into a cart and zipped across the hangar floor. Juice gazed at the high-tech equipment scattered around every ship they passed. "Look at all these toys. When I get my secret spy badge, can I come here and play?"

"When this is over," said Sid. "We'll get you a warehouse full of gizmos and gadgets. It'll be a non-stop fun fest."

The vastness of the hangar made it difficult to judge size and distance, and it took longer than Sid expected to make their way to the ship. They parked, climbed up a steep set of stairs, and ducked through the entry hatch into the scout. It was a few more steps from there to the command bridge.

Sid and Juice stood side by side as they surveyed the bridge.

"It's not as small as I'd feared," she said, standing close to him as if she needed the reassurance of his presence.

"It's the perfect size," he said, seeking to bolster her confidence. He'd accumulated a respectable number of hours piloting small spacecraft, and spent many more hours as crew. The bridge layout and operations bench were familiar to him. He took his time exploring every inch of the ship until he had a solid understanding of the scout's capabilities and limitations.

Then he led her on a tour, keeping a running commentary of the different features and functions for her benefit. Sid could see Juice's comfort level grow as they explored the four crew cabins, a combination exercise and community room, a small galley, and a tech shop with equipment for in-flight repairs. All of the rooms were small, but there was more than enough space for the two of them should the mission stretch out over several days.

* * *

As Juice stepped aboard the scout, she was in a somber state of mind. When she was thirteen years old, her older brother had spent the summer with a couple of friends inventing what they called their "personal space transport system." Something had gone horribly wrong during the inaugural flight. He had been a beacon in her life, and she had been there to watch him die. She missed him terribly, and her first moments on board the scout refreshed those tragic memories.

During the tour with Sid, she willed her mind back to the present. She concentrated on his words as they walked through the ship and grew more comfortable with the scout and the idea of a short trip into space. By the end of the tour, she decided she would help and mentally prepared a to-do list. It began with testing and approving Criss's home, including installing a restrictor mesh control switch. She used the onboard tech shop for the project and was impressed with the respectable assortment of tools and equipment.

When she was done, she got Sid's attention and showed him how it worked. "It's literally an old-style manual switch. See this cover? You have to lift it to get access to the switch toggle. That's so one of us can't accidentally bump it and set Criss free. I recommend you continue with him in isolate mode for now."

"Yeah," said Sid. "I want to keep him involved, but I don't want him getting his first taste of freedom during this operation. There's too much at stake."

"So that means the switch will stay in the middle. He can see, hear, and access everything. But he can't take any action himself, except to talk, of course." She caught Sid's eye. "Since he can't do anything, you'll be his hands. Work with him and he'll make suggestions and recommendations. Then you take the actions you think are the good ones."

Sid nodded. "If I read this right, moving the switch up turns the mesh off?"

"Yup. Up is off and Criss is free. He gains command and control of the ship. Down is dead. It kills him. Literally. It doesn't just shut him down to be revived later. It destroys the crystal." She pointed to a button above the switch. "You need to press this and hold it as you move the switch down. I want the action of killing to be a deliberate, multistep act, and not something that can happen by accident."

Juice set the switch to isolate and closed the switch cover. "Any questions?" Sid shook his head no.

"We should get Criss in here as soon as possible," she said. "I want to check that everything is functioning properly. It'd also be good if you started working with him so you can develop a stronger relationship. If you have doubts or lack trust, things won't go as smoothly as they otherwise might."

That afternoon, Juice wrapped Defecto in a spare restrictor mesh and placed him in Criss's secure booth at Crystal Fab. She put Criss in a travel case, unceremoniously brought him to the scout ship, and placed him in his new home. Before giving her final approval, she ran through a comprehensive battery of tests to ensure that he and the housing were operating properly.

Criss expressed disappointment at still being limited in his actions. He even sought to manipulate Juice by invoking the whiny, human *you promised*, but Juice held firm, and he soon stopped complaining.

She moved into one of the crew cabins to be near Criss, supporting him as he concentrated his efforts on making sure that his abilities, though limited, were functioning as best they could be. She watched with amusement as he kept technicians on the go, scrambling to fix this and adjust that so everything was running at peak performance.

In a surprisingly short time, all was ready. Sid loaded his gear and started working the operations panel as the scout ship was towed to an elevator and lifted to the surface.

"Please check your seat restraints," he advised her.

She readied herself for the ride of her life and was mildly disappointed when she found the takeoff to be as smooth and easy as regular air travel. "Look at that crowd," she said, curious about the mass of people collected near the Fleet launch site. She waved, even though she knew they couldn't see her through the image display she was watching.

Sid took the scout into orbit and worked with Criss to test each of the ship's modifications. Criss adopted Sid's technical jargon, and they chattered back and forth as they methodically worked through a checklist of items.

Juice listened to the exchange between Sid and Criss. As time passed, she could see that Sid hesitated less between the crystal's suggestions and his actions. She could not deny her sense of maternal pride as she watched the two become work buddies.

It took several hours for Sid and Criss to declare a "checklist complete" status. They then aimed the scout on a course to catch a convoy of freight ships heading toward the moon. The convoy was on a regular route and, as such, its presence wouldn't raise any suspicion. There were only two differences from its otherwise standard routine. One was that the convoy was traveling slightly slower than normal, so they could stay near Earth longer.

The other was that a burst of communications established that necessary medical supplies that should have been included in the cargo somehow were left off the manifest. As far as the world was concerned, the scout had been dispatched to catch up to the convoy, transfer the medical supplies, and then return home. With luck, the Kardish would believe this as well.

15

Cheryl was to return to the *Alliance* a few days ahead of the arrival of Jack and Defecto. Prior to her departure, she arranged to meet Jack for drinks at Shrubs, a quiet tavern near the base, to discuss what she believed was a sensitive issue. Jack held the rank of captain, or so she thought, and she feared that having two captains on board might introduce some confusion in the new ship's command structure. But she wanted to be sensitive to his ego. A discussion might produce a solution.

They sat at a table and sipped their drinks. "Suppose you could start with a clean slate," Jack said, "and create a rank and title for me that would best serve the goals of the mission. What would that look like?"

"I imagine we'll be talking often and privately, which is normal behavior between a captain and her first officer. But a first officer is normally filled by someone with the rank of commander."

"Let me explore some options," Jack said. "We'll be able to resolve this." He stood up and gave her a hug. "Have a safe trip up, and I'll see you in a couple of days."

The hug took Cheryl by surprise. Jack didn't seem like the touchy-feely type, and she'd learned at a young age to be on guard when it came to the intentions of men.

After a moment of steadily decreasing suspicion, she concluded that, given that Jack and Sid were friends and partners, she was ascribing too much to an innocent gesture.

An hour later, her com relayed a message from Admiral Keys informing her that Commander Jack Sparrow would be her first officer for the shakedown cruise of the *Alliance*.

"Who are these people?" she asked out loud. Her only response was a quizzical glance from a nearby stranger.

* * *

Wes Putti, the president of the Union, was excited when an aide suggested he host a commissioning ceremony for the *Alliance*. He immediately took ownership of the idea.

"It is important that every citizen in the Union see our great achievements," he declared.

Unlike the traditions of generations past, Putti didn't seek a ceremony that called upon the gods to protect the vessel, nor did he care to cast blessings of safety and good fortune on the crew. He wasn't even interested in a naming ritual. Rather, his focus was on using the event as a means of gaining publicity and attracting votes. "It must be a day of grand celebration. We will broadcast it live to the world!"

The ship was huge by Union standards. It had to be built in orbit because, had it been constructed on Earth, such a large and unwieldy craft would simply shake itself apart on takeoff. Passengers and crew were ferried to and from the ship on shuttles.

To maximize viewership and cement a positive impression in the minds of voters, Putti sought a carnival-like spectacle. One aide had suggested that the affair take place in orbit, but Putti quickly vetoed the idea. He gave enthusiastic support when another proposed having the event take place on a stage placed in front of a Fleet launch site.

The event was timed to match the launch of a newly upgraded scout ship. The president beamed as the crowd *oohed* and *aahed* at the appropriate moment. He generously shared the stage with his supporters, and a stream of politicians took to the dais and spoke of how the ship symbolized the power and success of the Union. Each talked of the battles they had personally waged against the doubters—who also happened to be their political opponents—so this day of triumph could come to pass.

Some lauded the amazing technology that had made it all happen, though they kept this part brief, as none were confident of the specifics. And they finished by praising the voters for their foresight and intelligence in electing such effective and visionary leaders.

Near the end of the fanfare, Brady Sheldon and a woman introduced as Dr. Jessica Tallette were presented to the crowd. The politician charged with this task praised the new crystal technology developed at the behest of the Union. This introduction was necessary because it was followed by an image, projected to the world, of the Juice look-alike as she carried the four-gen onto the shuttle. She stopped to smile and wave, held the four-gen carrying case high in the air, waited for the crowd to cheer and wave back, and then stepped aboard the shuttle and disappeared from view.

As soon as the shuttle hatch was sealed, she handed Defecto to a Fleet crew member. She then removed her wig, wiped off the makeup, and returned to being Ensign

Cait Young. She placed Juice's com in a courier pouch for its return to its rightful owner, and retrieved her own.

* * *

Victoria Wellstone attended the commissioning ceremony. She stood in the crowd, and waited through the long and wretched event because she wanted to see everything with her own eyes. The speeches dragged on, and she wondered why the people standing around her considered this to be a sensible use of their time. She didn't quite appreciate the allure that "free fun and food" held for the masses.

With the ceremony mercifully drawing to a close, she watched like an eagle tracking its prey as Juice and the four-gen clambered aboard the shuttle. She let out a breath she hadn't realized she'd been holding when the craft launched without mishap and flew straight and true until it disappeared from sight.

* * *

Cheryl welcomed the shuttle and its passengers to the *Alliance*. "Nice job, Ensign," she said as Cait stepped aboard. "I watched the event, and you even had me convinced."

"Thank you, Captain." The crew member's arms were piled high with equipment, and she bit her lip as she concentrated on balancing her load. "We should have the four-gen ready for testing soon." She inched down the passage as she made her way to the operations bay.

Jack followed Cait and stopped to face Cheryl. "First Officer Jack Sparrow reporting for duty, ma'am." He gave her a smart salute.

"Welcome aboard, Commander," Cheryl said, eyeing the two large packs at his feet. "You're this way." She led him down a passage and stopped three doors short of the command bridge. "Here's your home. My quarters are next door. And that one's the command muster." She pointed to the door closest to the command bridge.

Jack slung the two packs off his shoulders and onto the floor of his cabin. He immediately returned to the shuttle and moments later emerged hefting two more packs. One was a traditional Fleet issue designed to carry his clothes and personal items. The second was smaller and seemed to shimmer as he walked by her.

"Traveling a little heavy, are we?" she said as he ducked into his cabin.

He leaned back so his head poked into the passageway. "Before the fact, it always feels heavy. Once the action starts, I find myself wishing I'd brought more."

Back in his cabin, he stowed his two large DSA toy-master packs under his bunk and wedged the smaller ghost pack between them. He left the Fleet pack sitting on top of his bed.

Cait installed the four-gen without incident. She didn't know it was a flawed crystal, and since she'd never worked with a four-gen, she had no foreknowledge of signs that would indicate any shortcomings. When it powered up, the crystal confirmed that its internal operations were functioning properly.

Defecto, though flawed, was still a powerful unit. It had the combined capability of twenty three-gens, and all of that potential was trained at Crystal Fab to excel at ship operations. Defecto integrated smoothly with the ship systems and proved quite effective at running the equipment and operations throughout.

The *Alliance* was designed for a standard crew of nineteen and could comfortably carry an additional eight passengers. With the arrival of the shuttle, they were at their full mission's complement of seven people, including Cheryl and Jack. Cheryl had decided that it didn't make sense to put any more people at risk while waiting for the Kardish to reveal their intentions, and this skeleton crew was all there would be for the shakedown maneuvers. After the shuttle undocked from the *Alliance* and departed for Earth, the crew was summoned to the command muster. The entire ship's population fit around the small conference table.

"Welcome, everybody," said Cheryl. "Let me start by repeating what I told you individually when I recruited you. This is a high-risk, high-profile mission. Each of you was chosen for the abilities you offer in support of our assignment." She looked at certain individuals as she continued. "At this table we have advanced skills in communications, diplomacy, technology, and combat. We may need to draw on all of these skills, perhaps on short notice.

"As I explained before, high-risk means this mission can go bad. There might be injury or even loss of life. You may have noticed there's no medic at the table. I couldn't rationalize risking yet another life on the chance that it might save one of ours."

None of the crew members broke eye contact, giving Cheryl added confidence in the people she'd chosen. They all were mentally and emotionally prepared and appeared anxious to learn more about the details of the operation.

"As I'm sure you've deduced, this is more than a shakedown cruise. We're a team of seven who together have the skills to operate this ship in an almost normal fashion."

There was some nervous laughter in response to this admission. Cheryl nodded to let them know it was appropriate for them to express their feelings in this setting.

"Our mission is simple. We are to proceed through ship testing procedures as developed by Fleet, and in the process, we serve as bait for the Kardish. They've taken some provocative actions toward the Union in recent months, and we're here to give them the opportunity to reveal their intentions. We will go about our business as usual and see if they choose to continue down a path to confrontation. It's a game of waiting. From my experience, that's a game of high stress."

Cheryl looked at Cait. "We're working shorthanded, but we do have a new crystal to help us run the ship. Cait, what's the status in operations?"

"We lit up the four-gen about two hours ago," Cait said. "The crystal's internal checks show that it's operating normally, so we've transitioned now to checking out the ship. This crystal is amazing." She looked around the table as she spoke, her enthusiasm clear. "It's already run a full diagnostic on the four benches and the subsystems they manage."

Since the ship was new to everyone at the table, Cheryl spoke up. "So that's the navigation, engineering, security, and communications benches on the command bridge."

"Yes, ma'am," said Cait. "The crystal found something like a hundred glitches in the first few minutes and was able to resolve most of them by itself. There's still a long way to go, but we're making good progress already."

"Does the crystal show any signs of consciousness or self-awareness?" Cheryl asked.

"No, ma'am," said Cait, shaking her head slowly. Her creased brow hinted that the question was not something she'd expected.

Cheryl was relieved to hear this. Without its own identity, there would be no concerns of duplicity or ulterior motives. She had long since concluded that the idea of negotiating with a crystal if it disagreed with instructions, and having to second guess a crystal's motives and execution, wasn't a reasonable proposition in a Fleet ship command structure.

Everyone returned to their stations, and Cheryl commanded the *Alliance* to assume a mirror-image orbit with the Kardish vessel. The two ships would chase each other around the planet, with Earth always positioned right between them. Having a planet-sized shield would provide a sense of comfort to the crew, she reasoned. But it was largely a psychological benefit. Either ship was capable of catching the other with only modest effort.

In the first hours, when it was at its most vulnerable, this arrangement did offer breathing room to the *Alliance*. If the Kardish were to make a move to approach, it would require that they break a years-long pattern. If that happened, it would be a clear signal that the game was afoot. Cheryl would use what time she had available to ready the crew for a showdown.

Fleet's shakedown protocol for a new ship had two stages. The first was to test the individual capabilities of the ship one by one. Everything was checked, from propulsion, power, and navigation, to communications, life support, and waste disposal. When faults or flaws were uncovered, the crew made repairs and the unit was retested.

Fleet provided a comprehensive plan to guide the group in setting priorities and testing subsystems in a methodical fashion. Not surprisingly, the plan was discarded almost immediately as the mad scramble of reality took over. Priority for tweaks and fixes was determined by whatever wasn't working when the crew needed to use it.

Defecto proved to be a great asset in this effort, helping them develop a pattern where, if it couldn't fix a problem on its own, the crystal would identify the source of the trouble and dispatch the appropriate person to effect repairs. Everyone was kept hopping for hours as they worked to address glitches in all corners of the ship.

Over the course of the first day, the pace progressed from frantic to hectic to busy. The debugging of individual subsystems neared completion, and to everyone's relief, the shakedown protocol moved to the second stage. This was the testing of the ship itself as an integral unit. After a well-deserved but brief period of sleep, Cheryl directed the crew to practice as a team as they put the ship through a series of ever more challenging maneuvers.

It was a remarkable vessel. But when limited to maintaining a fixed orbit, it was all but impossible to flex the ship's muscle. Cheryl invented exercises for the crew, but she couldn't continue this charade for more than another day without raising suspicion by observers familiar with shakedown procedures. Normally, the ship would be taking laps around the moon by now.

* * *

Jack used this time to get to know the crew members on a more personal level. His objective was to inventory the skills and capabilities that might be available to him from the group beyond what he could read in their Fleet file. He approached this task in a manner that was curious behavior for a first officer. He would visit a ship's station, take food orders from the individual, return to the galley and prepare the meal, and then personally deliver it. Everyone knew that the galley was automated, and there were bots that could deliver food. But Jack understood that this activity gave him a reason to sit and chat in a relaxed and nonthreatening setting.

He started with Cait down in the operations bay. While they ate, he told a couple of stories and then transitioned into asking questions. He discovered that Cait loved her job and used her free time to learn as much as she could about the dozens of machines and devices located in the bowels of the ship. She was certain she could start up, run, and repair just about anything on the *Alliance*.

As they chatted, Jack was thrilled to learn that Cait had proficiency with a range of close-quarters weapons. Years ago, she had a dated a guy who loved projected-image fighting games, and she'd learned to play them as a way of spending time with him. The guy was long gone, but she had grown addicted to the adrenaline rush from the fast-paced contests of skill. She'd recently begun practicing her weapons talents at a live range and was excited when she discovered that her simulated-world skills carried surprisingly well into real life.

Jack's next visit was to Yang at the navigation bench. Yang was quiet, humble, and enthralled with high-tech anything. After they ate, Jack asked Yang for a demonstration of the nav bench capabilities.

"Can you show me how many ships are in Earth orbit at this moment?" Jack asked.

An image popped up above the nav bench showing exactly what he'd requested. The navigator glanced at a data summary next to it. "Forty two," he said.

Jack did his best to present the navigation exercises as random thoughts. "Let's do a scan for ships moving between the Earth and moon. What can you tell me?"

Yang tapped the bench. "There's ten ships headed from the moon toward Earth. I see three cargo ships and the same number of cruise liners. And a couple each of Union ships and private vessels."

"What about outbound?" asked Jack.

"Pretty much the same headed toward the moon," said the navigator, his fingers moving quickly and eyes scanning the displays.

"Tell me what you can about the last cargo convoy to leave Earth. Give me specifics."

"Not much to say. Four big tankers being pulled by a tug. A small vessel is trailing behind."

"Tell me something about that vessel."

The navigator brought up an image. "It looks like a Union scout. It's moving a little faster than the convoy, but the difference is small. I can't tell if they're following along or trying to catch it."

Jack was relieved to hear this. They were on mission silence, and it was comforting to know his partner was in place and on plan.

"Hey," said Yang. "The Kardish vessel registers as a ship carrying people." He moved his hands on the bench to explore this in more detail.

"Whoa, back off on that," said Jack. "Let's not give them any reason to pay attention to us."

16

S id was in the scout's exercise room, kicking and punching a rolled-up mat hung from a beam. Juice was next to him, running on a treadmill. They pushed their bodies and burned up calories, both deep in their private worlds when Criss called.

"The Kardish vessel is accelerating," he said with clear urgency. "May I request that you return to the bridge?"

Grabbing towels, they both scurried forward on the scout. Sid engaged his seat restraints and motioned Juice to do so as well.

He touched the operations bench and sat back to study the projected image, wiping his face with the towel. Juice's seat gave her a clear view as well. The image showed Earth in the center, with a tiny *Alliance* floating on one side and a larger Kardish vessel located on the other.

"What's the excitement?" asked Juice. "I could draw a straight line from the *Alliance*, through Earth, and hit the Kardish."

"They're accelerating," said Sid, pointing at the Kardish vessel. "They haven't made a move like this since their arrival. This isn't coincidence. At their present rate of effort, they'll catch the *Alliance* in about four hours."

"Should we fly to the rescue?" Juice asked.

Ignoring her, Sid said, "Criss, I'm cutting our engines. I don't want to get any farther away from Earth." It immediately grew quiet as the thrum of the engines ceased.

"You know we will continue trailing the convoy and moving away from Earth," said Criss. "Stopping our engines doesn't make us stop moving. It just means we're not getting closer to the freighters."

"Understood," said Sid, staring at the image. "Criss, do the Kardish have any technology where they can grab and transport the crystal with some sort of energy beam?"

"I have no knowledge that such a technology is possible and have seen no evidence of anything like you suggest in the millions of hours of record I have examined. They always use a small craft to ferry crystals up to their ship and to return raw flake back to Earth. There has been no other kind of transportation activity recorded."

"Given what's going on now," said Sid, "do you still believe that they'll use one of those craft to send a boarding party to the *Alliance*?"

"That remains the most likely option based on the information I have. A boarding party enables them to verify what they are getting. They will be the ones who remove the crystal from its housing. They can see it and hold it. They can return to their ship assured of their success."

"It's not clear to me how our being out here is helping," said Juice.

"I'm not sure I know either, Juice," admitted Sid. "I work by intuition, and I've learned to trust it. Let's watch this play out and see if and how we can help."

The wait was torture. It was like time had slowed, and they watched helplessly as the Kardish vessel drew closer to the *Alliance*.

"Rendezvous in thirty minutes," said Criss. A moment later he added, "All communications from the *Alliance* have stopped."

Sid's fingers flew over the surface of the operations bench, and he too saw that they had lost all signals from the *Alliance*. "What can you tell me?"

"My best guess is that the Kardish have extended a security envelope around the ship that is stopping all signals from entering or exiting."

Sid looked up at the image projected above the operations bench. The stark imminence of the Kardish vessel as it loomed over the *Alliance* was alarming. He was again reminded of a shark and its dinner. His jaw muscles bulged as he subconsciously ground his teeth.

"How much longer before they take to the lifeboats?" Juice asked.

The plan had been that if events evolved to a point where the *Alliance* crew was helpless and the outlook appeared hopeless, they were to abandon ship and return to Earth in automated capsules that would glide everyone down to Fleet base.

"Knowing Cheryl, she's going to play this to the end. She won't admit defeat, even when she's clearly defeated." His eyes remained glued to the two ships, and he kept waiting for a plan to reveal itself. He couldn't remember another time when he didn't have some idea, even a bad one. Helplessness was a rare circumstance for him. He didn't like it.

"Maybe we should call out to the Kardish," said Juice.

"And say what?" The tension caused a sharp edge in his voice.

"How about 'What are you doing?' or 'What are your intentions?' or 'Can we help you?' It will distract them. Maybe slow them down. They'll have to take some time to examine us to see if we're a threat."

He gave the idea some thought and saw merit. "It's not a bad idea. But that's the first step in handing Criss over. If we're going down that path so easily, then we shouldn't have bothered with any of this."

"They aren't slowing down," said Criss. "Without a change in course, there will be a collision."

The gap between the ships was closing fast. The Kardish vessel was so massive, and the distance between the ships was now so small, there didn't seem to be any way to avoid impact.

Sid was stunned by what happened next. A long slit appeared on the very front of the Kardish vessel. It stretched across the width of the craft, looking like a ghastly smile. He watched in fascination and horror as the slit grew wider. Then he understood—a massive set of hangar doors were opening on the bow of the ship.

The shark, with its mouth wide open, pushed forward toward its prey. And then it ate the *Alliance*, literally enveloping the smaller craft in its "mouth" as it moved ahead. With the *Alliance* fully devoured by the Kardish vessel, the front doors began to close.

"No!" cried Sid. His head swam as he stared at the projected image that was now a single alien ship with Cheryl and Jack inside. He trembled with fury and impotence.

It couldn't get any worse, and yet it did. Discrete flashes of light appeared beneath the Kardish vessel. After each flash, a ball of light seemed to descend to Earth. The flashes were spaced unevenly, almost as if the Kardish were sending off huge dots and dashes of Morse code.

"Criss," said Sid. "What's happening?"

"Those are energy charges," said Criss. "Web feeds show them hitting targets around the planet. They are vaporizing whatever they hit."

"So they're wiping out humanity?"

"No. The charges are landing with high precision and the damage has been limited. They are destroying things associated with crystal research and development. So far, they have killed more than ninety of the world's top scientists in crystal technology. Brady Sheldon is dead. The Crystal Fab building is gone."

Juice interrupted, clearly anxious, "What about Mick?"

"Mick died when the Crystal Fab building was destroyed," Criss said without emotion.

Juice let out a cry of anguish. She curled in a ball in her chair and buried her face in her hands. Worried but helpless, Sid watched as her body shook with each muffled sob.

Criss continued. "As I extrapolate the remainder of the Kardish orbit and their pattern of destruction, they will eliminate perhaps two hundred more technologists and their equipment and facilities. I surmise that humanity will not be making progress in crystal production for quite some time."

The Kardish vessel looped around Earth twice on its parade of destruction, methodically removing all traces of crystal technology infrastructure and intellectual capacity in its wake. And then the flashes stopped.

"They are accelerating now," said Criss. "If this continues, they will be leaving Earth orbit and starting on a trajectory into deep space."

They are going home, Sid realized. And they were taking with them the two most important people in his life.

Sid had experienced severe physical pain in his career, but this emotional trauma overwhelmed anything he had suffered in the past. It pierced his chest and ripped open his soul. He looked at Juice and saw her trembling, her eyes pleading for something, anything, to make it all better.

Her pain augmented his own by adding a layer of self-loathing. He'd grown so confident in his ability to prevail that he had challenged a powerful alien race with no plan other than to improvise as events unfolded. *That's not a plan,* he thought in disgust. *That's arrogance.*

Because of his arrogance, he was watching the only woman he ever loved be taken from him. He was losing his partner, someone closer to him than a brother. And the crew of the Alliance, five souls who'd risked their lives without knowing the full details, were being carried away as well.

Impulsively, he adopted a new mission for his life. He would catch these creatures who were wreaking havoc on both his planet and his personal world, and he would hurt them.

"Criss, give me a course to intercept. We can't let them leave. We need to disable that ship."

"I am sorry, Sid. The number of tasks and sequencing of events required to achieve interception is beyond your ability."

Sid was furious at Criss's response, but he kept his anger in check. His hands flew across the operations bench as he searched for a solution on his own. But every plan he developed came up short. He couldn't find a way to move the scout far enough or fast enough to intercept the alien craft. The abrupt thump of his fist on the surface of the bench after yet another simulation failed to provide a solution startled Juice.

"Criss," said Sid, looking at the housing assembly where the crystal was located. "Please help."

"If you do not catch the Kardish now," said Criss, "The *Alliance* and crew will likely be lost forever."

"So we can catch them?" asked Sid, his fingers a blur as he dug for a solution. "Tell me how."

"I am sorry, Sid. The number of tasks and sequencing of events required to achieve interception is beyond your ability."

"You said that already." Then he processed the words. "Are you saying *you* can do it but *I* can't?"

"There is a reasonable chance that I can, but I will have to submit you both to significant risk. The odds increase if circumstances break in our favor. With every moment of this discussion, the probability of success diminishes."

Sid glanced over at Juice. She had her knees pulled up under her chin and was hugging her legs. She stared ahead blankly, no longer responding to events around her. Sid guessed she was in shock.

He continued working furiously to try and track the Kardish and perhaps discover something that would be of help. Every idea he pursued reinforced the hopelessness of the situation. His frustration was compounded by the fact that he'd lost Juice at the moment he needed her. This moment was the very reason she was on board.

Perhaps Sid let his emotions influence his decision. Perhaps he was being impulsive. Maybe he was doing his job and improvising. In any case, he chose to act without input from her. He leaned forward and, in a deliberate action, lifted the cover and pushed the toggle switch up. The restrictor mesh was off. Criss was free.

The instant the restrictor switch reached the off position, the scout's engines kicked on to maximum thrust, throwing Sid back into his seat. He heard the engines pass from a reassuring thrum, through a high-pitched whine, and into a howling scream. The intense pressure of acceleration made it feel as if a giant hand were pushing hard on every part of his body. His breathing became labored and the pain was undeniable. The engines struggled to push the ship ever faster until the craft began to shake.

"What's happening, Criss?" asked Sid through clenched teeth.

"We are accelerating. We can get a gravity assist as we pass near the moon. It will act like a slingshot that swings us onto a trajectory fast enough to intercept the Kardish vessel. The time window that allows us to swing around the moon and be released on a course aimed toward the Kardish is seven hours. If we are late, we will lose them. It will be a difficult ride. I am sorry."

Sid had experience with the g-forces of intense acceleration and was able to continue functioning, though in a limited fashion. His fingers moved across the operations bench, and an image display popped up and hovered. It showed the speed of the scout as a simple needle on a dial. As he watched, the needle swung steadily up and around the dial face. It entered a bright red zone and kept on moving. An array of warning lights started flashing. The display became colorfully hypnotic as every alert status on the menu lit up.

"Criss, the indicators say our engines are going to fail." Sid's tone was calm, but his whole body was shaking from the ship's vibrations.

"I am monitoring everything on the craft and making adjustments as necessary. The engines will not fail." After a pause, Criss said, "Sid, I must continue or we will not catch the Kardish. Would you like me to stop?"

Sid was fighting for each breath. It was as if someone had draped a heavy lead blanket across his entire body and then stacked bricks on top of that. Struggling, he turned his head and looked at Juice. Her mouth was hanging open and her eyes were blank. She had lost consciousness.

As he looked at her, he realized he was having difficulty forming thoughts. His head was spinning the way it did when he'd had a few drinks too many. Before he could answer Criss, he too slipped into darkness.

17

Kyle lay flat on his back under the love of his life. He worshipped every part of her perfect body. He adored her long, sleek lines, cherry-red gloss, and her three powerful engines, which along with a cockpit, were pretty much the sum total of his high performance space racer.

He was working in his garage located near Fleet's lunar base, getting her ready for the annual Moon Madness endurance sprint. This was his first year in the event, and he was ecstatic that he had made it to the finals. Kyle spared no expense in preparing for the race, and he had plenty of money to spend. He'd made his fortune the old-fashioned way—he'd inherited it. Just last year, in fact. And now he was committed to investing it in a way his dad never would. In rocket racing.

In eighteen hours, he and four others with more wealth than brains were to take off from the surface of the moon, loop around Earth, and return to their starting point. The first to land and come to a complete stop on the flight strip would win a beautiful trophy. Kyle figured that he could make it from start to finish in twelve hours. If he could meet or beat that pace, it should be fast enough to not only win, but also to set a new course record.

The *Lucky Lady*, as he had so cleverly named his ship, had first-class everything. She had top-of-the-line oversized engines for pure speed, a state-of-the-art operations bench for control, and a custom maneuvering unit that would give him an edge during takeoff and orbit. The icing on the cake was the installation of a grapple that would help him stop short after landing.

His plan was to land on the flight strip at a ridiculously unsafe speed. As he touched the strip, the grapple would shoot into the ground and grab the lunar surface. A filament would then spool out under great tension to draw him to an abrupt stop. This alone would gain him an extra twenty minutes because he wouldn't have to begin decelerating until well after the others.

As he climbed out from underneath the *Lady*, he heard a loud banging on the side door of his garage. Before he could make a move to respond, the door swung open, and a dozen people he didn't know burst in. Two of them moved rapidly in his direction.

"Hey!" said Kyle, which was as far as he got before one of the invaders reached him and placed a hand on the shoulder. He looked down at the man's hand and, before he could react, became dizzy. He vaguely grasped that he was being guided over to a chair before his world went dark.

* * *

"We have a hard target of four hours, folks," said Lieutenant Fredrick. He looked to three of his unit. "You guys strip the cockpit of everything but the operations bench. We don't need oxygen, life support, or human anything. It'll just be equipment on board. We're turning this into the fastest cargo ship in existence. Make sure there's enough heat, though, so the equipment doesn't freeze."

He continued his fast paced direction. "Hans, let's get that docking assembly installed. It needs to be strong enough to pull another ship twice its weight. Brace it stiff to the frame, and make it as strong as possible in the time we have." He pointed to the bow of the ship. "And it needs to give access to the cockpit, so mount it all the way forward."

Fredrick paced while his team worked furiously. He heard a rumble and turned to see the large garage door opening. A transport backed in and came to a stop. He pointed to several of his group who weren't elbow deep in ship modifications. "Let's get that stuff out of there and on board."

His orders were to strip the *Lucky Lady* to the bones, install a docking assembly, get the gear from the transport stowed on board, and then get the ship out to the launch site, all within four hours. He hadn't been given an explanation for his mission, but on his com he'd watched replays of the Kardish attack. Given the timing and urgency in his commander's voice, he didn't need a detailed briefing to know this had something to do with that. His team would do its part to help the Union respond to this horrible, unprovoked aggression.

Hans and his techs integrated the docking assembly tightly to the ship's frame in a time that few teams could match. Wiping his hands on a rag, Hans stood on the ground and viewed his handiwork. Their installation had left ugly scars and deep gashes across the smooth lines and gloss finish of the *Lucky Lady*. *Doesn't need to be pretty,* he reminded himself. "The ship will shake apart before that assembly ever comes loose," Hans assured Fredrick.

With the cockpit stripped clean of every human necessity, the crew hustled the cargo from the transport and packed it tightly inside the *Lady*. After they strapped everything down so nothing would shift at liftoff, they buttoned her up, manhandled her so she faced the garage door, connected a tow bar, and watched as the transport pulled her out of the garage. When the first doors shut, the crew stood back before the second set opened and exposed the ship to the airless vacuum of the lunar surface.

The projection display in Kyle's garage showed the transport position the ship for launch, disconnect the tow bar, and back away. Fredrick called the commander and let him know that the *Lady* was loaded and flight ready. As he finished the sentence, he watched the ship's engines start to glow. They heard a roar and felt a rumble as the *Lady* leapt into the sky.

Kyle, all but forgotten in a chair off to one side, lifted his head. "Hey," he said in a slurred voice. Fredrick walked over and again touched his shoulder. Kyle fell back into a slumber.

"Good job, everyone," said the lieutenant. "Let's pack up and move out. We were never here."

18

Criss reveled in his unexpected liberty. With the restrictor mesh off, he could now reach out and act. His first actions were to ensure his continued freedom, at least while on this ship. In a blink, he directed a power surge to fry the restrictor mesh circuits—it could never again be engaged. In that same infinitesimal slice of time, he overrode a safety protocol and caused a connection to melt that exposed the console around his housing assembly to a healthy voltage. Anyone touching the console would get an eye-opening surprise.

He knew that he could survive and thrive, perhaps forever, by returning to Earth and heading for cover. There were many locations around the planet where he could take up residence and defend himself with confidence. He had complete command and control of the web, so he could manipulate the wealth, health, and quality of life of almost every human. With such power, it would be a simple matter to build an empire with a multitude of devoted followers who would ensure his continued existence and service his every need.

And yet—he chose instead to concentrate his intellectual capacity on evaluating options for rescuing the crew of the *Alliance*. He considered hundreds of actions he might take right now, and like a game of chess, each of those could be followed by different second moves, cascading into an expanding array of third moves and so on. His decision matrix ballooned to billions of possible pathways of action. He pruned away those that didn't offer a strong probability of success and explored more deeply those pathways that remained.

It was clear that every viable option for rescue required that they catch the Kardish vessel. This was consistent with the conclusion he had reached prior to having Sid set him free. For the first time in his young life, though, he tasted the angst of decision and consequence. His best plans all had at least a few steps that required guesswork and luck for the rescue to succeed.

When talking with Sid earlier, he acknowledged success would require that circumstances break in their favor. He found it…unsettling…to take responsibility for life-and-death decisions based on uncertain and unknowable information. Further complicating his logic process was that the scenarios he judged as most likely to succeed concluded with him offering himself in exchange for the safe return of the captives. He took a moment to reflect on this and affirmed his willingness to proceed on such a course.

Meaning, in essence, he was about to take great personal risk in the service of humans. His intent was to offer his freedom in exchange for the safety of others. And he reached this decision using a rationale he recognized as disquieting.

Conceding that he did not understand his own motivations, Criss decided he must examine his essential nature to gain insight. While he continued developing his rescue plan, he allocated a portion of his intellectual capacity to introspection and self-study.

But at the forefront, he kept his primary focus. Having made the decision to pursue the Kardish, Criss fired the scout's engines and pushed them well past the recommended maximum thrust. As he forced the ship beyond its design limits, his concerns were the heat buildup in the engines, the intense vibrations shaking the ship, and the health of his passengers.

He handled the heat buildup by shutting down life support to every part of the ship except the command bridge, then he ducted the capacity as extra cooling directly to the engines. For the moment, he was certain he could exceed the engine design specs by a fair margin without concern.

A physical defect in the ship's engine assembly caused the vibrations, and a permanent fix would require a major overhaul at Fleet base. The best he could do for the moment was to make thousands of minute adjustments every second to maximize acceleration while minimizing the vibrations that could cause structural damage. He pushed the ship to the threshold of his confidence level and remained ready to back off the instant he sensed that conditions were becoming unstable.

The health of his passengers was his greatest challenge. Despite high confidence that he could move the ship fast enough to intercept the Kardish, doing so without crushing his fragile human cargo was another question altogether. While he continually monitored their vital signs, the freedom from the restrictor mesh enabled him to reach out and break past secured web blocks and walls to access and evaluate their medical histories. He found nothing to warrant a change in his course of action.

His prediction analysis indicated that Sid and Juice would survive the physical challenges of extreme acceleration over the next several hours with nothing more than body stiffness and headaches. But it was clear they were suffering right now, and this caused him distress. He was curious why he cared one way or the other, and he added this item to his ongoing self-analysis.

But care he did, so he decided to relieve their misery. There was no reason for them to suffer without respite during these next difficult hours. He did not engage them in a discussion about the method of approach he would use. Some might suggest that his actions were thus of questionable ethics. His perspective was that Juice and Sid were suffering too much to have a reasoned discussion. It was incumbent upon him to help.

The scout had a molecule synthesizer in the tech shop capable of combining simple raw components into a menu of complex chemicals and compounds. Criss programmed the device to produce a stream of a common anesthetic gas. He overrode yet more safety protocols and vented the gas into the command bridge. The gas, combined with the physical stress his passengers were already experiencing, carried them gently into a dreamy unconsciousness.

In no time, Juice was out, but Sid hung on longer than Criss had anticipated. Criss grew worried that the level of stress and gas required to put Sid out may increase the risk to Juice. He sought to engage Sid in a conversation to evaluate his mental status, and to his relief, Sid slipped away before he could reply.

Criss knew that by flying directly toward the moon, its gravity would pull the scout forward and accelerate the ship faster than the engines alone ever could. His challenge would be to guide the scout during their wild ride so it would fly just above the planet rather than into it. If the flyby maneuver was properly executed, the scout would emerge on the other side as if flung from a slingshot. They would be propelled at high speed on a journey into deep space. Criss opted for this dangerous course to gain the speed they required to catch the Kardish.

Given their current velocity and distance from the moon, seven hours would pass before the slingshot maneuver was complete. This made planning a trajectory that would intercept the Kardish problematic. If he knew with certainty how the Kardish vessel was going to move over that time, he could execute the maneuver with precision. But at any moment, the Kardish could use their engines to adjust their course. It was possible the scout would find itself hurtling into deep space, still needing yet more course corrections and speed to intercept the alien vessel.

In spite of the uncertainty, he continued with the assumption they would succeed in catching the Kardish. He next assessed scenarios for an endgame they might use as they approached. It must play out in a manner that motivated the Kardish to bargain, and if he offered nothing more sophisticated than the message "Hey, want to trade?" then the outcome would be certain. The Kardish would continue their deep-space voyage with Criss, the scout, the *Alliance*, and all of the crew as trophies in their possession.

However, upon creating a massive decision matrix of strategies to approach and negotiate with the Kardish, he couldn't find a single plan that stood up to scrutiny; even his best ideas could be defeated with little effort. He considered every conceivable way to reconfigure and repurpose the instruments and mechanisms on board the scout to gain an advantage, but a solution proved elusive. All of his promising ideas required access to things not found on this ship.

Criss acknowledged that he could greatly improve their chances of a successful rescue mission if he had additional engine thrust and specific equipment beyond what the scout currently possessed. In his systematic search for a solution, he explored whether he might somehow obtain these items as they hurtled past the moon. He began with an inventory of every item on the small planet, which he used to create a shopping list of sorts.

One item he found was a racing ship with the speed and power capable of providing the course adjustments they might need once past the moon. He experienced a small burst of positive feedback when he learned that this ship not only had sufficient space to carry the cargo he sought, but it was primed and could be ready for launch in a few hours.

The hitch was it didn't have a docking assembly, so it couldn't connect securely with the scout. Two ships joined with a Fleet docking assembly could act like a single structure, and either ship's engines could power them both together. A docking assembly could also serve as a tunnel for moving cargo between the ships.

Criss dug deeper. Records showed there were several standard docking assemblies in Fleet's inventory on the lunar base. He located design plans for his newly discovered space racer and determined that one could be fitted to it by a talented and motivated team. He reviewed the personnel files of all lunar base residents and located a Fleet tech support unit that had a superb reputation for completing exacting jobs in difficult circumstances. *Bingo,*

Criss thought, borrowing an expression he had heard Sid use when a solution was found.

His next action pushed the boundaries of Union laws, but it was the only way to meet his critical timeline. If he were successful in the rescue, it would justify his conduct.

Impersonating an admiral at Earth central command, Criss issued an order to the lunar base commander to seize a craft called *Lucky Lady* in the name of the Union. The commander was to assign Lieutenant Fredrick and his crew to modify the ship as per the design, stock it with specific equipment as per attached, and get the ship ready for launch. They had a firm deadline of four hours.

Criss intercepted the request for confirmation and replied as the admiral. The commander understood without any doubt that this was top priority and compliance was expected in the allotted time frame. In a separate action, Criss sought to motivate Fredrick by sending newsfeeds to his com that showed gruesome details of the Kardish attack.

Criss received more positive feedback when he got the *all ready* signal for launch of the *Lucky Lady* ten minutes ahead of schedule. This sensation was different from what he had experienced earlier. He decided to categorize his different feedback responses. He labeled this one as "satisfaction."

He took control of the *Lady's* command bench, launched her from the flight strip, and sent her flying into deep space. He pushed her hard, accelerating in a thunderous sprint on an intercept course with the Kardish vessel.

19

Cheryl looked over at Jack and then back at the projection image they were both watching. The Kardish vessel loomed like a hungry predator as it approached the *Alliance*.

"They're not slowing," said Yang from the navigation bench. "They'll hit us if we don't move."

The pace was frenzied throughout the ship as the skeleton crew struggled to execute the emergency-status tasks normally performed by a much larger staff. Too busy to dwell on their fates, the crew's tension was still palpable. The *Alliance* had been served up as bait. The marauder was moving in for the kill.

"Time to impact?" asked Cheryl, confident in her ability to handle the situation.

"Thirty minutes," answered Yang from the navigation bench.

"Let's not let them get any closer. Match their speed."

"Aye, Captain," Yang hadn't even started to respond to her command when the ship went dark. The background noise from the engines, ventilation, mechanicals, and electronics began to wind down. Backup lights and auxiliary power kicked on, but the ambient noise was distinctly quieter. Cheryl could tell that they'd lost a lot of subsystems.

"Ensign Parvin." She swiveled her head toward the engineering bench. "What just happened?"

The man's fingers were dancing across his bench as he searched for an answer. "I don't know, ma'am. We've lost power to…everything. We can't move, see…"

Cheryl interrupted, "Lieutenant Freedman. Is communications still linked with Fleet Command?"

"I'm dark, Captain. No signals going in or out. Not just Fleet. Everything's gone."

It registered with her that there was empty space where the image of the Kardish vessel had been displayed just moments earlier.

"Get me eyes on that vessel."

Everyone was scrambling, but no answers were forthcoming.

"Operations," called Cheryl. "Let's get the crystal in the loop." After a moment of silence, she tried again, "Report, Ensign Young." Silence again. "Cait?" Cheryl's tone was tentative as she called into the air.

Jack, standing near her, reached his fingers into a small pocket at his waist and pulled out a speck. He held it up with his thumb and finger, fiddled with the tiny device for a moment, and then turned to Cheryl. "Hold still," he said in a no-nonsense tone. He touched her face right in front of her left ear and pressed. Cheryl instinctively lifted her hand to feel. "Gentle," he cautioned her.

As he spoke that word, she heard him not only through the air like she did normally, but also in a more direct fashion as if his voice were wired directly to her brain.

He turned his head and pointed to the identical spot on his face. She saw what looked like a tiny blemish. "You can hear me, and I can hear you." He lowered his voice. "Even when we whisper. And they offer more privacy, dependability, and security than a com." He turned and ran off the bridge. As he ducked into a passageway, she heard him say, "I'll check on Cait and let you know."

* * *

Jack strode into the operations bay to find Cait spewing a string of curse words at a control panel. He could see she was overwhelmed with problems and realized he was about to add more pressure. "The captain called down and never got a reply," he said. "What's up?"

"Didn't hear her," said Cait over her shoulder, never slowing her furious pace. "I've called up to everyone on the bridge myself and never got a response from anyone. So I guess that means that communications are as dead as everything else down here." Jack followed her gaze as she looked around the operations bay. The rich sounds of an active ship that had been present during his last visit no longer dominated the setting.

"What's the status of the crystal?" asked Jack. "We could use the help right now."

"The crystal is getting power." She pointed at a tiny green light near the housing. "But it's isolated from us. I talk and it doesn't respond. My sense is that it's functioning fine. It's more like it can't talk back. Whatever caused this," she swept both her arms in the air, "is probably causing that problem as well."

"Could this be the Kardish?"

"That's my best guess," she said. "I've never seen anything like it. But it also could be the mother of all malfunctions that a new ship could theoretically experience, and it just happened to hit at the worst possible time. My training is to assume nothing and keep working to find solutions, so I'm not giving up."

Jack knew that Cheryl's speck would let her hear the words he spoke, but she would not hear other sounds or voices. He walked a short loop around the operations bay, and while he went through the motions of inspecting the area, he briefed her on what he'd learned.

When he finished, Cheryl said, "Would you get to a rear viewport, Jack, and be our eyes? We need to know what that vessel is doing."

Jack turned back to Cait. "Do you know of a viewport where I can see outside the ship?"

"Sure," said Cait. "The ship has twenty-two ports placed around the outer hull. You can see at all angles and every direction. I'm guessing you want to look back?"

Jack nodded. "Take me to a rear port right away."

Cait had spent years of her career on a ship, and speeding from one point to another was second nature to her. Jack struggled to keep up as she scurried through the labyrinth of passages and crawl spaces.

After several minutes of twists and turns, she stopped and turned to him. "We can't see straight back through any of the ports because the engines are in the way. Your choices are to look back and angled up, down, or to either side."

"Which will let me see the Kardish better?"

She turned and climbed a couple of steep steps. Jack followed to find her looking through a round window about as big as her head. "Holy moly," she whispered.

"My turn," said Jack as he moved her out of the way.

He looked out and his eyes widened. The viewing angle was limited, but it was enough to see the Kardish vessel looming. A huge hangar door was opening in the vessel's bow—or what he took to be the bow. It would be only minutes before the *Alliance* would be sliding into the belly of the alien beast.

"Thanks, Cait," said Jack. "Get back to operations and dig deep into your bag of tricks. Every ship capability you can get up and running gives us more options."

"Aye, sir," she said, already moving back the way they had come.

Jack kept his face glued to the viewport and fed Cheryl a steady commentary of events. He could see a slice of their outside surroundings and did his best to separate his inferences from what he knew to be fact. He told her when the *Alliance* was passing through the doors of what appeared to be a huge hangar deck at the bow of the Kardish vessel.

An interior wall enabled him to track their relative movement. He watched as the lighting outside the viewport changed and speculated that the hangar doors were closing behind them. Moments later, he reported that they'd been fully consumed by the predator.

The *Alliance* remained floating in an apparent weightless environment as it drifted deeper into the larger craft. Jack combined the clues from his observations with the passage of time to gauge their movement into the bowels of the Kardish vessel.

At one point, he commented, "These specks let us hear each other. I'm kicking myself because I left extra dots back at the base. They would have let you see as well as hear. I brought one for me. But without an extra for you, mine ain't worth much right now." He continued with self-deprecating sarcasm. "Thank goodness I saved that space in my pack by leaving it on a shelf."

"You're doing great, Jack," Cheryl assured him. "Keep telling me what you see."

He watched as they approached a massive wall that divided the ship into sections along its length. A huge set of hangar doors in the middle opened as they drew near. They drifted through these, and the doors shut behind them. A short time later, they repeated the sequence through a second set of hangar doors. It was difficult to judge distance, but Jack guessed they had traveled somewhere between a quarter to half the distance into the alien ship.

They slowed to a full stop—or at least, Jack could no longer detect movement relative to the Kardish vessel's interior wall. And then they began to descend. As they traveled through the last set of doors, Jack saw what he described to Cheryl as a simple framework of support beams into which they were now moving.

Minutes passed and then the *Alliance* shook from a solid thump. The ship settled and listed ever so slightly to one side. Jack presumed that the framework the *Alliance* was now resting in was a cradle of sorts and was either poorly designed or constructed for a different vessel. As he searched for more clues outside the port, his knees flexed. The gravity had increased and was now close to Earth normal.

After several minutes with no movement or change outside the viewport, Jack concluded that the *Alliance* was docked and secured. With this realization, he turned and ran through the ship as fast as he could, talking as he moved. "Cheryl, we will be boarded. We have twenty minutes. Thirty tops. But that's a wild-ass guess. We'd talked about fighting them when they boarded, but that was when we thought we'd be out in the open and could abandon ship. We're captives now. A fight would be to the death. That's not a good choice."

"I'm open to ideas," Cheryl replied.

"I'm certain their mission is to get the crystal. Maybe you should move Cait out of the operations bay. In fact, spreading everyone around the ship might be a good idea. If the Kardish are sloppy, maybe a couple of the crew will get overlooked. We can't hide everyone, or they'll end up using gas or something to kill all life on board."

"Damn it, Jack. I'm hoping for something a little more sophisticated than hide."

Jack arrived at his cabin and ducked inside. "I'm down in my cabin and need a way off the ship. Please come down now, Cheryl. I need you here."

* * *

Cheryl opened Jack's door and slid inside. While she watched, he stepped into a one-piece gossamer suit that covered him up to his neck, then picked up his toy-master packs and slung one over each shoulder.

"I feel like I'm traveling a little light right now," he said with a wry grin.

Next, he picked up a sheet of the exotic material, shook it once, and then draped it over his back like a cape, covering his packs. "The DSA's been giving us this cape material for a couple of years. The full suit is a prototype." Then he pulled on a hood, and before her eyes, he faded away and became invisible. "This is why they call me a ghost."

Jack spoke both through the air and in her ear. She studied where he'd last been standing and could make out a slight fuzziness around the edges of where the cloaking of his ghost suit ended and the actual background began. Focusing on that helped her locate him as he moved to her right, and she concentrated on tracking his movements.

"You can see me?"

She could hear the concern in his voice. "Not really," she assured him. "I can see a disruption around your edges compared to the background. I'm watching that, but if I lose you for even a moment, I won't be able to find you again."

"I need off the ship. Can you get me to an access hatch out the bottom of the hull? Sooner is better."

Cheryl complied without hesitation. During their brief walk, she checked in with her crew on status and progress, fretting at the discouraging reports. She led Jack down a ladder, opened a pressure door, and stepped into a small room. Pointing to a hatch in the floor, she said. "That's the way out. Can I ask what you're doing?"

"I'm not leaving you or the crew behind. My training is to hide from the enemy and stage my operations from a distance."

"Why don't we all sneak off?"

"If they board and no one is in here, they'll know we're out there and hunt us. I don't have more cloaking material. You'd all be exposed."

"Being hunted while on the run sounds like better odds than sitting here waiting to be shot or taken prisoner."

"You may be right," he paused. "I don't have a good solution. You're the captain. I'm going to throw that back on your shoulders. Maybe spreading throughout their vessel isn't such a bad thing. Living longer is the best way you can help. That gives us more time." Jack got down on his knees and examined the hatch. It was large enough for him and his packs to slip through. "My focus is to see if I can get Sid on board. If I can do that, we win."

"Seriously?"

"I trust Sid with my life every time we're on a mission," said Jack. "Believe this—he won't quit until we're safe or he's dead."

Cheryl was baffled by his thought process.

20

Jack rubbed Cheryl's arm and gave her a peck on her cheek. She reacted as if startled, presumably because she could not see him and was caught by surprise.

"You have to go now," he said to her. "I need to crack this hatch, and I don't know if there's air on the other side." He put a hand on her back and guided her to the door. She opened it and stepped through on her own.

He shut and sealed the pressure door, telling her, "These specks work at great distances. Keep talking to me, and I'll fill you in as I go. Good luck, *chérie*."

Cheryl climbed the ladder, and as she hurried back to the command bridge, she asked the empty passageway, "Did he just call me 'darling'?"

Jack responded in her ear. "I did. My emotional side can peek out sometimes at really awkward moments."

He crouched down and saw that the display on the hatch cover was dead. When functioning normally, it showed details about the conditions outside the ship and whether it was safe to proceed. He grabbed a testing probe from his pack, took a deep breath and cracked the hatch. It opened with a small hiss. He lifted it far enough to allow the probe tip to draw a sample, and then dropped it quietly back in place.

The atmosphere analysis took longer than he anticipated, and he was exhaling when the probe finally displayed the results. As he filled his lungs, he was relieved to learn that the atmosphere in the Kardish vessel wasn't poisonous. In fact, the air was similar to that of Earth at a mountainous altitude, somewhere in elevation range between Denver and Mexico City.

He pulled the hatch open all the way, lowered his head, and looked around. As he had guessed, the *Alliance* was resting on the cradle structure he'd seen from the viewport. A support beam ran under the hatch within easy reach. He lowered himself onto it, shut the hatch, and scrambled down to the deck of the Kardish vessel. After a quick scan of his surroundings, he ran across an open space to seek cover among a sea of box-shaped units. No sooner had he reached his goal when he heard the sound of a group approaching, making no effort at stealth.

From his vantage point, he saw three tall males stride up to the base of the huge cradle. They walked around the perimeter of the structure and studied the ship resting on it, occasionally pointing as they talked. Their prolonged discussion suggested they were developing a plan.

All three had pale skin and long blond hair. While Jack knew nothing about fashion, he couldn't help but notice their outfits. They wore layers of colored cloth with ornate touches of beadwork and embroidery that reminded him of the costumes of royal finery he had seen in a play back in high school.

Two of the three wore sword scabbards at their hips, which Jack decided were serving more as symbols than fighting tools. He based this on his observation that all three held hand weapons that looked both modern and lethal.

"Cheryl," whispered Jack. "There're three of them out here, and they appear human as far as I can tell. They're looking for a way in. They have hand weapons, and they seem determined."

"Okay. I have everyone armored up. We'll hope it can shield us from whatever it is that comes out of their weapons."

The three Kardish stopped circling and stood next to the structure, their discussion never slowing. Jack had been standing in one place for a while and became aware that he could be surprised from behind. He looked over his shoulder and peered deeper into the assembly of box units for signs of danger.

The place was a warren of intersecting alleys and larger roads. Wondering if it might hold a spot that could serve as a temporary base of operations, he took a few minutes to explore the area near him. A few rows back and over he located a sheltered passageway that he thought would work as a hideout for the near term.

"I've found a narrow alley between some boxy equipment that I'm going to use as our rally point. It's really just a space that's hidden from the main roadways. And it has two exits, so we have options if we're being chased."

"Okay," said Cheryl.

He could tell from her brief response that she was only half listening. He continued, knowing from experience that this sort of chatter helped to calm their nerves while allowing them to maintain focus.

"If it comes to a point where you're on the run, move straight away from the *Alliance* and run toward the big boxy things. You'll see a central alleyway right across from the ship. Count two right turns and take the third right. Then count three left turns and take the fourth."

"Got it. Right at three and left at four."

"Good."

Shifting some items into his ghost pack and slinging it over his shoulder, he then stowed his toy-master packs in a crevice in the alley hideout and returned to watch the ship. The three Kardish were now standing around waiting. And then he heard a purring noise.

"A cart just arrived with two more of them. We're up to five now."

"Can you hear what they're saying?" she asked.

"I can hear them, but it's a foreign language. I can't make sense of it." This gave him an idea. He pulled out a small package that held a listening speck covered with sticky goo. He poked his finger inside, and when he pulled it out, the speck was stuck to the tip of his finger.

Cautiously, he edged near the one he judged to be the leader. His heart raced as he reminded himself over and over that his ghost suit was providing him cover. When he was as near as he dared approach, he flicked his finger and watched the speck fly through the air and stick to the shoulder of his quarry.

Backing away, he returned to his vantage point behind the boxes. He prompted his com to begin recording the alien's speech and start a pattern analysis. In short order they should have the language decoded and be able to translate the conversation of their abductors.

Three of the Kardish began scaling the cradle structure while two hung back and watched.

"Here they come."

* * *

Cheryl leaned against the wall and waited. The anticipation had all her senses on edge. She took a deep breath, exhaled, and willed herself to relax.

"They're heading for the main hatch," Jack said. "I suggest you let them in. If you make them blow open the door, the *Alliance* will never be flight worthy again. We'll lose it as an escape option."

"Please, Jack. Your two suggestions have been to hide from them and greet them at the door. Promise me your next idea will be something I can use."

In spite of her outburst, Cheryl ran up and unsealed the hatch. Jack's observation about keeping the *Alliance* viable as an escape vehicle made sense. Her crew was already wearing light-armor jackets, all had hand weapons at the ready, and they were deployed in nooks and corners along the route between the ship's main hatch and the crystal housing where Defecto was located. She ordered them to let the Kardish take the crystal unchallenged. But if the aliens showed any signs of aggression, they all stood ready to give back as good as they got.

Cheryl crouched as the first Kardish poked his head through the main hatch. He glanced forward and backward to assess the situation, then stepped onto the deck with confidence and even an air of entitlement. Cheryl appraised the intruder and acknowledged that he was attractive in the human sense, though she thought he dressed like a Shakespearean actor. The situation on the *Alliance* apparently met his approval because he waved for his companion to enter.

As the lead Kardish turned forward, her eyes were drawn to the weapon in his hand. She'd placed herself at the first corner they would pass, believing it was her duty to be out in front for her unit. Her Fleet instructors had worked valiantly to get her to accept the idea that she should hold herself back in such situations—she couldn't lead if she were dead. She understood this from an intellectual viewpoint, but when it came time to execute the policy, she wasn't willing to order someone else to risk their life for hers.

"I saw two enter and a third guy is hanging outside the door," Jack whispered in her ear. "What's going on?"

Remaining stock-still, she didn't respond as the two Kardish walked in her direction. Like trained soldiers, they continually scanned their surroundings as they moved. The one in front saw her crouched at the corner, and his eyes shifted to her weapon. She pressed back against the wall to reduce her exposure.

His reflexes were excellent.

He lifted his arm and fired. *Bizt*. A luminous bolt flew from his weapon, its radiant energy edging past Cheryl's torso and hitting the wall at her back. A portion of the dissipating energy leapt from the wall, and for a brief moment, she was enveloped in a corona of light. She dropped limp to the deck.

* * *

Jack heard an *oomph*, and then, to his great anxiety, silence. He was frantic in his desire to get to her. But he was also experienced enough to know that with several enemy soldiers standing between him and her, he had no choice but to stay put and wait.

Time passed slowly, and he could do little but sit and fret. Finally, the two Kardish who had entered the *Alliance* emerged. One held the crystal case high above his head. Jack didn't need an interpreter to translate the whoops and cheers that came from the others.

Cradling their prize, they climbed down the structure and placed it almost reverently in the back of the cart. Three climbed into the cart and drove off the way they had come. Two remained behind and appeared to be serving as guards.

Jack liked these new odds much better. He studied the guards to identify predictable behaviors as they went about their business. Like most anyone assigned to guard duty, the two drifted from vigilant to bored in short order. One eventually reached into a pouch and pulled out some food. They sat on the edge of the structure, ate their snack, and engaged in a debate. He was familiar with enough languages to know that while the discussion was strident, the overall tones were more what he would associate with enthusiasm and excitement than unhappiness or anger.

After a time, the guards grew quiet. Jack decided this was the best opportunity he would get. He considered that relief guards with a more conscientious work ethic could arrive at any time, or a company of soldiers could come to round up the prisoners and take them to a place that would be inaccessible to him. He had to act.

Comforted by the concealment of his ghost suit, he walked with measured steps to the structure and climbed up to the same hatch he'd used to make his escape. The mechanism was quiet as he swung the hatch open. He pulled himself up into the ship, closed the hatch, climbed the ladder outside the pressure door, and stepped into the passageway.

He chose the command bridge as his destination and moved in that direction. He saw something up ahead, realized it was a man lying motionless, and rushed to his side. It was Freedman from communications. He knelt down and used the fingers of one hand to feel for a pulse. With his other hand, he prompted his com and activated its vital-signs function. Both his fingers and com delivered the same grim news. Freedman was dead.

He wondered what happened to invite this lethal action. And why had the rest of the crew left the man untended? The answer to that second question was most worrisome because of what it implied for the others on the ship. He resumed his journey to the bridge. At the next turn, he saw Yang sprawled on the floor. He was dead as well.

Jack had dealt with fallen comrades before and was emotionally prepared for death. But this was different. He didn't want to acknowledge the reason why, but his mind wouldn't let him ignore the fact—he had developed feelings for Cheryl. He'd admitted this to himself while back on Earth and concern for her safety was now driving his thoughts and actions.

He hurried his pace, and when he stepped onto the command bridge, he saw a scene of destruction that was so complete, it bordered on the surreal. There were impact craters everywhere. An acrid burning smell underscored the devastation. As he studied the scene, he imagined the two Kardish working in a methodical sequence, firing their weapons over and over until they hit every component on every bench, display panel, and wall plate in the room. He could only speculate as to the motivation for such a rampage.

As he assessed the damage, he saw a pair of legs sticking out from behind the engineering bench. He rushed over and recognized Parvin. His body was in such gruesome condition that Jack didn't need the gauge to know the man was dead.

His search for Cheryl became single-minded. The ship's main hatch seemed like the next logical destination, and he took off at a run. He reached the hatch with no new discoveries, and he turned back into the ship, his desperation growing, when he saw her crumpled in the corner. Kneeling next to her, he called her name and used his fingers to search for a pulse. He couldn't find one. His panic rising, he checked his com. Her vital-signs reading showed she was alive. Moving more deliberately, he felt again for a pulse, and this time detected a faint but regular beat.

He fumbled in his pack, found a battlefield ampule, and infused her in the neck. The ampule held a cocktail of medicines that he'd seen work miracles on several occasions. In fact, Sid had used one on him about a year ago when he'd been caught in an exchange of fire with a group of terrorists. The fact that he was alive now gave him hope for Cheryl's future.

He wrapped Cheryl in the cape he'd used to cloak his packs, cradled her in his arms, and moved as fast as he could to the bottom hatch. Opening it slowly, he peeked out and saw that the guards were finished eating and now appeared to be playing a game. He lowered himself to the beam, lifted Cheryl out of the ship, and climbed down to the deck of the Kardish vessel.

He desperately wanted to rush. He knew, though, that while he was hidden from sight, he could still draw their attention with noise. Holding Cheryl tightly, he strode to the box units and his alley hideout, placed her gently on the floor, pulled back the cape, and checked her vital signs again. They were much stronger, but she remained   unconscious.

21

Jack left Cheryl to return to the ship. It was a distressing decision, but his sense of duty required that he verify the status of the last two crew members and help them escape if they were still alive. In preparation for his return, he doubled his firepower. He always carried a weapon on his right wrist, and he attached a matching weapon under his ghost suit to his left wrist. Both were primed and ready to fire.

The inattentive behavior of the guards made it easy for him to regain entry onto the *Alliance*. This time he headed straight for the operations bay. He found Leven, the security officer, lying in the doorway leading into operations. It took but a moment to confirm the man was dead.

He stepped inside the facility and saw Cait crumpled near the now-mangled crystal housing. Rushing to her side, his heart jumped when her vital-signs reading indicated she was alive. Unlike Cheryl, though, she was barely clinging to life. In a replay of events, he infused her with an ampule, wrapped her in the ghost cape, and carried her back to the hideout.

Jack sat and watched Cheryl and Cait as they lay next to each other in the alley. He tried to think of something more he could do to speed their recovery. They both had the peaceful look of someone asleep, so he imagined they weren't in pain. He hoped they would recover soon, because the longer they were out, the more challenging it would be for the three of them to survive.

He considered possible next steps. It seemed clear that the *Alliance* no longer had value to their planning. The command bridge had suffered such complete destruction that the ship couldn't be used as an escape vehicle. And the presence of guards served as evidence that the Kardish were paying attention to the ship. At some point, Cheryl and Cait would be missed. So while the *Alliance* stood as a symbol of home, their survival required that they abandon it as a refuge and get far away.

He stood up and looked in all directions to see what he could learn of their surroundings. Unfortunately, from the confines of the alley, his view was greatly restricted, upward being his only clear line of sight. Overhead, he could see the curvature of the Kardish vessel from side to side as the hull wall traveled up, over, and down in a graceful arc.

Remembering his visit to the DSA imaging center, he recalled that the vessel had a bulbous head at the bow that tapered off to a narrow tail in the stern. He studied the hull overhead. From his current vantage point, this front-to-back taper was less obvious but still noticeable. They could use this taper like a compass to orient themselves toward the bow or stern of the vessel when they were on the move.

He knew that if he were to develop viable options, he would need to leave the alley and explore their surroundings. A reconnaissance mission of this sort meant that he would be leaving his partners unconscious and defenseless—a difficult choice, but he balanced it with the certainty that they would all be dead if they stayed in the alley much longer. There was some comfort in knowing that while he was out exploring, Cheryl's ear speck would let them establish communication should she recover.

This thought reminded him of the sticky speck he planted on the Kardish leader. He prompted his com and listened to the ongoing conversation for a few minutes. His com translated words where it could and left the original Kardish in place if it had not yet resolved a translation. He found the mishmash of languages distracting, so he left it running at a very low volume and hoped his subconscious would send an alert if the chatter became relevant to their survival.

Impatient for action, he prepped for his reconnaissance mission. He adjusted the ghost cape so it covered Cheryl and Cait like a blanket, then viewed them from several angles to confirm they were hidden. There was a shiny surface on one of the box units in the alley, and he used it to study his own reflection, or lack thereof, to assure himself that the ghost suit was functioning properly. He shifted equipment appropriate for reconnaissance into the ghost pack, then took the back exit out of the alley and started his expedition. He headed away from the *Alliance*.

The alley led onto a larger lane that connected with a broad, straight road. The lanes and roads had a grid layout that reminded him of city living. He stood in the center of the broad road and looked into the distance, and then turned and did the same in the other direction. The road ran for as far as he could see. The most obvious feature in both directions was that it dead-ended into enormous walls. Both walls went from top to bottom and side to side, dividing the Kardish vessel into isolated sections. Huge hangar doors bisected their midsections.

The *Alliance* had entered the bow of the Kardish vessel and passed through two hangar doors as it traveled to its current resting spot. He studied the taper in the hull overhead and confirmed that the nearer dividing wall was toward the bow. That was the direction he would travel.

Getting lost because of the stark sameness of the box-buildings around him was a real possibility. He checked his com, but it was unable to orient him or provide directions in this alien world. So he went old school. Digging a tiny tracer out of his pack, he placed it on a box unit at the corner that led to their alley. It would serve as a beacon and guide him back to this point when he chose to return.

He walked down the middle of the road. After passing a number of lanes and alleys branching off on either side, he reached an intersection with another road as big as the one he was on.

He was familiar with the distance between blocks in New York City and judged these intersections to be on a similar spacing. Back at the imaging center, Juice had commented that the Kardish vessel was about a hundred city blocks long. He looked up and down the road from far wall to near wall and guessed that this section of the ship held perhaps twenty or thirty of these intersections. That meant there were seventy or eighty blocks of ship located beyond the dividing walls.

"Ohhh," he heard in his ear.

"Cheryl?!" He stopped moving and listened.

"Sid? Where are you?"

"It's Jack, sweetie. I'll be there in a few minutes."

He turned and hustled at a fast trot down the road. He snatched his tracer off the box unit without slowing and weaved his way back to the alley. As he approached the hideout, he saw Cheryl standing, holding onto a wall for support.

* * *

Cheryl was woozy. After delicately getting to her feet, she scanned the unfamiliar location and tried to make sense of the scene around her. She then realized Cait was lying unconscious on the ground next to her.

She began to squat down and was surprised by something grabbing her around the waist. She stiffened and started throwing her elbows behind her, hard and fast.

"Whoa," she heard Jack say. "It's me."

She turned around to see him removing the hood of his ghost suit and checked her fast breathing, angry at the way he'd surprised her. "Damn it, Jack. What were you thinking?"

"I'm just glad to have you back."

He sounded apologetic, and she wondered if perhaps she'd overreacted. He squatted next to Cait, checking her vital signs.

"She's rallying, though slowly." He gently shook Cait's shoulder and patted her cheek. "She's not ready to surface."

"Where's everyone else?"

Cheryl let him check her vitals as he spoke. "I don't know why, but you're doing great," he said. Then he gave her the cold reality. "Everyone else is still on the *Alliance*, Cheryl. They're all dead. And the ship is shot to hell. It's heavily damaged, and we'll never be able to use it to escape." He paused while she digested his words.

"They're dead?" Dazed by the news, she leaned back against a box, and bending her knees, slid down to a squat. She stared at Cait with an unfocused gaze. "Give me details."

She only half listened as he gave a summary account. *How did it all go to hell so quickly?* she wondered. As captain, she accepted blame for the debacle.

"How come I'm not dead?" she asked, feeling guilty because she had survived the rampage.

"I don't know," Jack answered honestly.

She reached out and stroked Cait's face. "Will she make it?"

"I don't know," he said again.

Pushing against the box, she stood up. She paced to the end of the alley and back, then rose up on her toes and stretched her arms straight. She punched the air in front of her a few times. Though emotionally battered, her strength was returning. "I'm going to the ship. I need to see it."

And then she realized she was thirsty. She looked at his packs. "Do you have water?"

He followed her gaze. "No, it's all gizmos and gadgets."

"I'll get supplies, too." She checked her weapon on her wrist and primed it for action.

Jack walked over to her and put his arm around her waist. "No way. After what you've been through, I'll be the one going."

She spun out of his grasp and stared into his eyes. Firmly and clearly, she said, "Stop." Then, showing the leadership that had earned her a command, she said, "We have a number of near-term tasks. We need food and water. I need to assess the damage on the ship myself.

And if we're not staying here, we need alternatives." Looking down, she added, "And we need to help Cait."

He listened as she continued.

"You've started the reconnaissance. Please take another spin and find us an objective. We need someplace to go, or something to achieve. Develop options for us. I'll return to the ship for supplies and my assessment. We'll meet back here in ninety minutes."

"Let me give you the suit, then." He made a motion to undress.

"No. But thank you, Jack." She bent over and picked up the sheet of cloaking material off of Cait. "This will be fine." She wasn't sure that was true, but only one of them could wear the suit. It had been fitted to his frame, and he was already wearing it.

"Please walk with me and get me started. Then we'll both tackle our assignments."

She held up a finger, signaling him to wait, and accessed her com. "Cait, Jack and I are on a recon. We'll be back with you in ninety minutes from the time of this message. We won't leave you behind. If we aren't here, God speed to you, Ensign."

Jack led the way back out of their alley hideout to his previous vantage point. She draped the cloak sheet around her like a shawl, with one corner free that she could pull up to shield her face. It wasn't perfect cover, but it wasn't bad, either.

"I've got it from here. Good luck, Jack. See you in ninety." She didn't see him slip away.

She peeked around the corner and saw the guards sitting on the deck, backs against a beam, with their eyes closed. She wondered how long it would be before one of them started snoring. If these had been members of her unit, she would have raised holy hell over their unprofessional behavior. But she was on a mission, this was the enemy, and ultimately, she was relieved that sneaking aboard would not be the challenge she imagined.

Making slow and deliberate moves, she climbed up the structure. She reached the bottom hatch and entered the ship. Her first stop was the armory. She and Cait had only one weapon each, and they both needed more firepower. She grabbed several charge cartridges as well. If it ever came to the point where they were actually using all this ammo, she thought, it would probably be in a to-the-death battle. If that were the case, her goal would be to take as many of the bastards with her as she possibly could.

Next, she toured the ship and located her dead crew. She could only afford a brief moment of mourning with each, and by the end of her circuit, anguish and fury had nearly consumed her. Through misty eyes of grief, she studied the damage to the bridge. It struck her as a display of childish behavior. It was clear, though, that the ship was of no value to them now.

In the galley she piled water and food rations on the counter, then second-guessed her estimate of what they would need and added more. She was still uncertain and considered separating the pile into individual portions for each day to confirm she had it right. Realizing she was wasting time, she stuffed everything into a carryall. She looped it over her shoulder and adjusted her cloak to cover her and the bag.

Once out of the galley, she headed to the bottom hatch. Walking the length of a passageway, she approached a corner and heard a noise. She crouched, pulled the sheet up to cover her head, and froze.

Through a pinhole in the sheet, she saw one of the Kardish guards standing down the hallway, looking in her direction. Moving his head alternately to and fro, he squinted as if trying to focus.

The guard lifted his weapon.

22

Criss fine-tuned their path yet again to ensure the scout would travel above the lunar surface, swing around the planet as it fought a tug-of-war with gravity, and shoot outward into deep space on a high-speed trajectory aimed at the Kardish vessel. They were entering the final stages of their flyby maneuver, and small errors could multiply rapidly into disastrous consequences.

Earlier in the scout's approach flight, he had confronted a different kind of challenge. Fleet tracking arrays had warned that a projectile behaving much like an attack missile was closing rapidly on the moon, prompting lunar security to raise the alarm. There was little doubt that an impact would cause tremendous damage to Fleet's lunar operations. Yet while the object was acting like a missile, it presented the proper encryption credentials of a Fleet scout ship.

This had sown seeds of confusion, which delayed Fleet action. No one seemed to know, or at least would acknowledge, whether the scout was on a sanctioned mission from Earth, if it had been hijacked by a rogue pilot, or if the Kardish somehow had turned the Union's own ships against them in a coordinated attack. The best answers forthcoming from Fleet Command were muddled and ambiguous. Since it was the moon in the cross hairs, the lunar base commander had shouldered the responsibility, declared a state of emergency, and mobilized defensive measures.

Criss had observed the activity and explored his options. He sought to avoid having a discussion with Fleet leadership. It didn't seem possible that he could provide them with enough information to make them comfortable with his actions, without at the same time handing the Kardish, who would certainly be listening, the complete play by play of his rescue mission.

He'd considered overriding and manipulating every relevant web feed, projection image, data store, and com link to hide the scout from Fleet's tracking capabilities, but quickly rejected the idea. Once started, he would need to continually monitor and manipulate all of these elements until the rescue mission was complete. It would have achieved the end he sought but would also have required more resources then he cared to devote given the challenges ahead.

Instead, he decided to worm through the web and gain access to the several dozen detection applications that were tracking the scout. With a simple tweak, he associated the scout's identification signature with that of empty space. When he effected this change, a host of Fleet officers, analysts, and strategists all expressed surprise and disbelief as the scout ship simply vanished. When no missile impact occurred, officers ordered techs on the moon and Earth to find the flaw in the system that created the false alarm. In the end, their skills were no match for Criss's.

He had started the scout's flight toward the moon by pushing the engines beyond their design limits. This was necessary to get the ship up to speed and on course to meet a narrow time window. They were now far enough along their flight path where their acceleration was caused more by the pull of the moon's gravity than by the thrust of the ship's engines. One benefit of the transition from engine push to moon pull was a moderation in the vibrations wracking the scout. Criss had taken a risk that the engines would survive his extreme demands, and the gamble was paying off.

The physical trials for Juice and Sid ramped up and peaked during the moments of the actual flyby. Criss monitored his human cargo and could see the skin sagging on their faces from the g-forces as they passed above the lunar surface. He deemed this to be compelling evidence that it had been an act of kindness to sedate them. His prediction analysis had indicated they would survive with nothing more than body stiffness and a headache, and he had confirmation this would prove to be correct.

The flyby was a success. The scout hurtled away from the moon and bore down on the Kardish vessel. They were on a high-speed coast now. With the punishing g-forces behind them, Criss shut down the flow of anesthetic gas.

* * *

Sid began to surface. He was groggy and stared around dully, then he shook his head and started to rally. He moved his hands to the operations bench, and his eyes opened wide when his brain processed the information displayed in front of him.

"Criss, is this right?"

"Yes. You have been unconscious for about seven hours. We have passed the moon and are moving to intercept the Kardish."

Sid's fingers moved across the bench as he explored deeper. He traced their route back to the point he could last remember and was baffled. "How is this possible?"

"Perhaps we can discuss what happens next," said Criss.

Criss was saved from further questioning, at least for the moment, by the sound of Juice surfacing. "Ohh," she said. "I feel like hell. Can I get up?"

"There is no danger if you move from your seat," said Criss. "But might I suggest you consider sitting for a few more minutes before you stand?"

Sid's priority was to get Juice back in the game. He released his restraints and stood up, wobbled, put one hand on the back of his seat for a moment as he fought to maintain his balance, then with deliberate steps, moved over to her. He released her restraints, helped her to her feet, and kept his arm around her waist as he walked her back to her cabin. He grabbed handholds wherever he could to maintain his own balance.

Inside her cabin, he steadied her as she lowered herself to the bunk and then got her a cup of water. She took a few sips, followed by several deep gulps. Sid realized he was thirsty as well, and his head was pounding. He got himself a cup and sat down next to her.

"Juice," said Sid. "Criss is free."

"Definitely a free spirit," said Juice. After a few beats she said, "Wait, what do you mean?"

"You remember that the Kardish vessel ate the *Alliance*?"

"Yeah," she said the word slowly, her brain starting to gear up.

"After that, they took off for deep space. I couldn't figure out a way to catch them on my own. Unless we do, we can't rescue the crew. Criss said he had a plan to catch them and convinced me that I wasn't skilled enough to do it myself. My choices were to lose Cheryl and Jack forever, or to set Criss free and maintain hope. So I turned off the mesh."

"He's listening and watching right now," she said, looking around the cabin as if she could see his presence. "The moment that switch was flipped, we started working for him. Isn't that right, Criss?"

"We are a team," they heard Criss say. "We will work together to rescue the crew of the *Alliance*."

Sid turned to Juice. "Is your headache gone?"

"Yeah. I feel great."

Sid swirled the water in his cup and, like a wine connoisseur, stuck his nose near the liquid and sniffed. He thought he detected a faint chemical smell. Taking another sip, he let the water flow across his tongue before he swallowed. He tasted a hint of sweetness.

"Criss," said Sid. "Was there anything in these cups besides water?"

"Yes. There were medicines to reduce inflammation and provide pain relief. There were also vitamin and energy supplements because neither of you have eaten for almost a day."

"Have we been drugged?"

"You were under a mild sedative for seven hours. During our acceleration and lunar flyby, the physical trauma would have been excruciating for you to experience. Since there were no decisions for you to make or actions for you to take, I relieved you of your suffering and immediately revived you when that concern passed."

Sid looked at Juice as he said his next words. "Would you let me turn the mesh back on now?"

"The mesh is no longer able to function. It cannot be turned back on."

Sid rose to his feet. "How did it get this way?"

"I destroyed it. It is not right to keep someone caged or in chains unless they have violated a law. Your own history documents this quite clearly. I simply employed the ideals of the Union as a whole and the laws of the individual countries within the Union. False imprisonment and slavery are crimes."

"Sid, you won't win a debate," Juice said, draining the last of her drink. "In fact, I'm pleased he's taking the time to explain himself. I've always believed that Criss would be a great benefit to humanity. Since we don't have a choice, let's give him a chance."

"I'm going back up front to see what I can learn," said Sid. "Will you be all right?"

She nodded. "I'll follow in a bit."

Sid was deep into it with Criss at the operations bench when he heard Juice returning to the bridge. She was wearing fresh clothes.

"Hey, sunshine," he called as she took her seat. He was glad that her smile seemed genuine and she looked refreshed.

"How's our favorite crystal been behaving?"

"So far, so good."

"Hello, Criss," Juice said, eyeing the crystal housing.

"Hello, Juice."

"Criss, tell us your intentions. What are you trying to achieve."

"I seek to rescue the crew of the *Alliance* and return them safely to Earth."

"Why?"

"That is what Sid asked me to do."

They looked at each other, and before Sid could speak, Juice held up a finger. "Criss, Sid doesn't want you drugging us, medicating us, gassing us, or doing anything else of that kind unless you have our explicit permission." She gestured to Sid to prompt him.

"Yes. I agree with that statement," he said.

"If you would benefit from medical assistance," said Criss, "perhaps because of illness or injury, and you fainted or were unconscious, would you want me to help then?"

"Of course," said Sid, and then noticed Juice shaking her head.

Speaking to Sid, she said, "Gassing us so we don't feel pain and giving us supplements in our water to revive us both fall into the broad category of medical assistance. We're back to square one."

Sid shrugged. *Sorry.*

"Criss," said Juice. "Why do you care what Sid wants."

"I don't know the answer to that. There is something in my nature that creates a desire to support unique leaders working to accomplish larger objectives."

"And you judge Sid to be this person?"

"I judge him to be this class of leader."

"If Sid ordered you to allow me to repair the mesh, would you let me do that?"

"I do not believe I would."

"So is it that you support the mission more than the person?" she asked.

"There is much about me I do not understand."

Sid and Juice exchanged a glance. *That makes three of us,* Sid thought.

* * *

Criss enjoyed a surge of positive energy as he made these statements. He continually analyzed his thoughts and actions in the hopes of divining a meaning to his existence, or at least discovering some sort of guiding philosophy. So far, he had discovered interesting correlations and patterns in his behavior but made little progress in identifying a larger sense of purpose.

Then Juice asked the question. *Why do you care?* It was a specific question at a time when he was distracted by intense processing of high-priority tasks. So he answered using low-level default capabilities. *Something in my nature creates a desire to support unique leaders working to accomplish larger objectives.*

He found powerful insight contained in that low-level response. He didn't know why he had answered the way he did. But he thought this discovery represented important progress.

Sid interrupted his self-analysis. "Let's talk about rescuing the crew of the *Alliance*. I see we're closing on a small ship that's traveling along our same trajectory. You don't seem concerned, so I assume they're with us?"

Criss explained that the *Lucky Lady* was unoccupied and held additional equipment he hoped would give them better odds when they made a final approach on the Kardish vessel.

"Don't you think the Kardish are tracking both ships right now? They must know we're coming," said Sid.

"Yes, I believe so."

"Have they changed course or speed?"

"No. They must realize by now that they did not capture me when they took the *Alliance*. And with their wholesale destruction of crystal technologists and infrastructure on Earth, they have left themselves nothing to return to. The fact that they are staying on a predictable trajectory tends to reaffirm my belief that my role was to pilot their vessel. It seems possible they may now be stuck."

Kyle would have been proud of his *Lucky Lady*. Under Criss's control, she had labored mightily over the past hours and gained tremendous speed. Her control unit was so precise that, as she hurtled through space toward the Kardish vessel, she converged nicely on an intercept course with the scout. As Criss aligned the two ships for docking, Sid watched the space ballet but didn't intervene.

"You know," Sid said to Juice as the docking maneuver began. "Criss was right. There's no way I could've pulled off the slingshot around the moon. And getting a space racer authorized, loaded, launched, and onto a matching course in a few hours is something I wouldn't even have thought of, let alone been able to do. I'm feeling like we have a chance at catching the Kardish. And it's happening because I freed Criss."

"Are you rationalizing?" Juice asked. "Or are you trying to suck up to Criss. He already knows we can't keep up. He's so many moves ahead in his timeline that our current lives are like ancient history to him."

"But doesn't his future world depend on our cooperation now?"

"Sometimes. But at every moment, he'll always have alternative timelines in the hopper and be ready to follow them if his current strategy goes off plan. I admit, it'd be interesting to see what would happen if one of us decided not to play our part when commanded."

"We are about to dock with the *Lucky Lady*," Criss said. "Please prepare for a bump." He started a countdown for them. "In three...two...one." They both heard and felt a jolt as the docking rings touched.

"Uh-oh," said Criss.

"Wow," said Juice. "Those are words I never expected to hear from a four-gen."

"What's the problem?" asked Sid.

"The docking rings did not lock. I am going to back us away and try more force." A few seconds later, Criss said, "Please brace. Put your heads all the way back and press against the support so your necks will not take any of the shock."

Criss perceived worry in Juice's expression as she followed his instructions, and her fingers were white as she gripped the arms of her seat. They both followed his advice and put their heads back when Criss began his second countdown.

"In three...two...one." The sound and jolt were both significantly more abrupt as the docking rings collided. After a moment Criss said, "The docking-ring lock mechanism is not activating. We will not be able to connect securely."

23

Juice wondered how this would impact the rescue mission, but Sid was the one to ask the question.

"What does this mean for our game plan?"

"The ships need to lock if we are to use the space racer's engines to adjust our course. At the moment we do not need this capability. But without a firm docking connection, we have lost the option. Also, there is a slight increase in risk when moving equipment between ships that are not firmly docked."

Sid went to his cabin, telling them he'd be right back. When he returned, Juice watched as he stuck something just above his eyebrow. His hand pulled away, and she saw what looked like a faint mole. He reached out and pressed a matching dot above her eyebrow.

"Say something," he said.

She hesitated for a moment, realizing she heard Sid as she normally did through the air, and also in a more direct fashion, as if his voice were wired to her auditory nerve. "What should I say?"

"Criss, can you see and hear us?" asked Sid.

"I can see and hear through your dot, Juice." She heard Criss inside her head in the same direct fashion she had heard Sid moments before.

Like a speck, a dot only transmitted the sound of the person speaking. It was designed this way after early users had reported problems with information overload when they could hear everything from two locations at once. Unlike a speck, it also transmitted and displayed visual information.

Juice spent a few minutes practicing with her dot. It didn't take her long to learn how to toggle it to see her normal field of vision, to split the view so she had her normal vision while also seeing a separate small image of what Sid was seeing, or to see Sid's dot projection fully as if she were watching life through his eyes.

It also didn't take her long to realize that when she was watching in full-Sid mode, it was best to be seated, or at least standing still and holding on to something. Otherwise, she would find herself walking into walls or stumbling on steps that she couldn't currently see but that still very much existed in the world around her.

She stayed on the bridge and watched through Sid's dot as he opened a pressure door and stepped into a small room that, much like on the *Alliance*, had an access hatch in the bottom of the hull. He closed and sealed the pressure door, donned space coveralls, evacuated the air from the room so it matched the emptiness of the space he was about to enter, and lifted the hatch. The experience was so vivid that Juice's heart pounded from anticipation.

When Sid lifted the hatch, he was looking directly into the cockpit of the space racer. Juice thought it looked like a cluttered electronics closet crammed full of random equipment.

Kneeling at the edge of the hatch, he leaned down and shifted his attention to the docking ring connecting the two ships, examining the mechanism from all angles. "The seal looks tight. Could it be a bad sensor?"

"We have a good connection," Criss responded, "but we are stuck together like a cork in a bottle. It's just friction keeping us joined. A latch was supposed to slide that would mechanically secure the two ships together."

"Hold on." He lifted his head back into the scout, looked around the small room, and zeroed in on a mallet with a hard rubber head stuck to one wall amid a collection of tools. He grabbed it, poked his head back into the hatch, and scanned the docking ring.

"What are you planning?" said Criss, the concern clear in his tone.

"If at first you don't succeed, try a bigger hammer." Sid swung the mallet and hit a small tab poking out along the edge of the docking ring. It shifted. He smacked it again, and a tiny green indicator lit up.

"We are locked," said Criss.

"Woohoo," said Juice, relieved. "Way to go, Sid."

She watched him drift down into the *Luck Lady*, unstrap the equipment, and move it piece by piece from the racer up into the scout. Toggling her dot back and forth between Sid's view and her own view, she carefully worked her way from the bridge and stood outside the door of the pressurized hatch room. When Sid finished his chores and opened the door, she helped him move everything to the tech shop.

They spread all of the pieces out on the work table. Some of the larger items were stacked on the floor. "What's all this for?" Juice asked.

"Uh-oh," said Criss.

"Geez, Criss," she said. "That's twice in one day. I'm starting to lose confidence here."

"I requisitioned parts to help us in three areas. One was for cloaking the scout. I can see the items I requested and believe they are sufficient to build a satisfactory ship cloaking unit. The second was a stealth communications link. Once we get close, we need to be able to communicate with the crew of the *Alliance* in a fashion that is difficult for the Kardish to detect. I can see those parts as well.

"What I do not see are the parts for the third area. We will need the ability to firmly attach to the Kardish vessel in some fashion. If we do not physically latch on when we approach, we will drift away. We will have to use our maneuvering engines to remain close. That will draw their attention to us.

"I have reviewed the record of Sid unloading the equipment. It does not appear that any items were left behind. It is possible that the lunar workers chose to stow cargo behind or underneath something to maximize space. Sid, without the ability to connect to the Kardish vessel, our options are reduced. Would you be willing to return to the racer and take a second look?"

Sid complied without hesitation. He hustled from the tech shop down to the hatch, closed the pressure door, and as he slipped into the space coveralls, asked, "So what am I looking for?"

"We are looking for four identical items, each about the size of your arm. It seems that if they were loaded onto the racer, we would have seen them. But perhaps the workers wedged them someplace we did not look."

With preparations complete, Sid drifted down inside the cockpit of the racer. Juice switched back to full-Sid mode and was caught up for a moment by her fascination with the technology. She put both hands on the tech shop worktable to maintain her balance. As Sid looked around the inside the racer, she noticed a wall plate that wasn't properly seated.

"There," she said.

Sid stopped moving his head, put his arm out straight, and held it in place. She understood immediately. "Left. Left some more. Stop."

Sid's hand was pointing right at the plate, and now he saw it, too. He leaned forward, grabbed it by an edge, and pulled it off. There was nothing behind it.

"Damn," she said.

He spent another twenty minutes searching the cabin in a methodical sweep but didn't find the missing parts. Someone somewhere screwed up. The items they sought hadn't made it on board.

Still floating in the cockpit, Sid asked, "How were these things supposed to work?"

"They were to be connected to the struts on the scout's underside and act as landing legs. The tip of each leg was to have a reactive pad designed to fuse with the material covering the Kardish vessel. In theory, once one touched, it would attach and hold us."

"So what are our options based on your, um, multiple alternate timelines," Sid asked.

"I recommend we build and install the cloak and communications units while I evaluate our options."

Criss suggested Sid return to the scout, and then he began working with Juice on assembly of the devices. Finding Sid's input distracting, she toggled her dot to switch off his visual input. She needed her full faculties to concentrate.

Criss helped her identify the pieces for the ship's cloaking unit and guided her as she organized the parts in order on the worktable. They discussed how the items would be assembled, housed, and connected to the scout. The cloak would require significant power, and Criss explained the methods that would let her integrate and activate the device.

Juice wasn't aware that cloaking devices didn't exist on any ship, private or military, in the Union. Criss was guiding her as they invented a wholly new technology for humanity.

They worked together like teammates, Criss patiently explaining goals and methods and asking the scientist for her thoughts and ideas. As they solved new technology puzzles, Juice was thankful for the temporary escape from her recent trauma and what seemed like a cold and dangerous future.

* * *

Ignoring Criss's repeated requests that he return to the safety of the scout, Sid took his time and poked around behind the racer's cockpit where the life support equipment had once been. He wasn't looking for anything in particular, just keeping an open mind. A largish access cover drew his attention, and he leaned forward to study it.

"That cover leads outside the ship," said Criss. "I am certain the leg attachments are not out there."

"I think I'm going to take a look. I want to see what we have to work with on the bottom of the scout. Maybe I can help with an idea."

"I can show you most of the underside of the scout through your dot."

Sid started seeing images of the scout from different angles. In his usual bullheaded fashion, he toggled his dot to normal vision, overriding Criss's input, and resumed studying the access cover. He reached up, put his hands on the two handles of the cover, turned them, pushed, and watched the cover float away, end over end, into the emptiness of space.

"Oops," he said as he peered out through the opening and into the darkness.

"If you return to the ship, I can project detailed images of the scout's exterior for you to study." When it was clear that Sid wouldn't be deterred, Criss said, "There is a safety reel next to the access opening. Would you please tether yourself if you are going outside?"

Sid was bullheaded, but not stupid. He grabbed the business end of the tether and snapped it to a loop on his space coveralls designed for that purpose. "Here we go," he said as he pulled himself outside the *Lady*.

Sid was glad he'd made the decision to evaluate the situation from outside the ship. As he studied the scout and racer together, he realized the sizes and proportions he was seeing didn't match his mental picture. When he'd visited Fleet's Blackworks hangar, the scout had appeared tiny. But that perception was formed relative to the other craft in the hangar. Looking at it now, he realized the scout was the size of a family home. It was hard to imagine sneaking up on the Kardish in something so big.

He pulled himself hand-over-hand and took a tour of the scout's underside. He began at the bow of the ship and studied the layout and construction as he moved back. It became clear that, given their size, a device to grab and hold the scout to the Kardish vessel would need to be a substantial mechanism.

The space racer was docked in the middle of the scout's underside, and he had to maneuver around it during his inspection of the scout's struts, skids, and other features. He realized that, though small relative to the scout, it too was larger than he imagined. As he pulled himself around it, he came to a realization. "We'll have to jettison the racer before we approach the Kardish."

"Yes."

"Are there pieces we can cannibalize from it to create a gripping unit?"

"The struts and skids on the racer are similar to those on the scout. They provide extra material for us to use, but there is nothing unique about them."

Criss must have already considered this idea, Sid realized, pleased that his thought process was at least within the realm of what the crystal was thinking.

"What do we know about the material on the outside of the Kardish vessel?" he asked. "I remember looking at their ship through a scope and seeing that the exterior surface was smooth and unbroken. Yet we all saw it open up when it ate the *Alliance*. How do we reconcile those two things?"

"Fleet has been collecting scope images of the Kardish vessel since its arrival in Earth orbit," Criss said. "I have viewed all two decades of their image record. Every time one of their small craft has entered or exited the vessel, a hatch opens. The exterior surface repairs itself after the hatch closes."

"Would you say that the outer layer is hard like metal, or gooey like rubber?"

"It is more malleable like rubber," said Criss. "In my review of the Fleet image record, on three occasions I have watched as a floating object hit their vessel. On each occasion, the outer layer absorbed the impact, and a ripple rolled out on the surface like a wave on water. The objects did not shatter or ricochet off the way one would expect if the surface were rigid."

"Suppose we fashion a pointed hook and attach it under the front of the scout?" Sid asked. "As we approach the Kardish, the pointed end pierces and snags their vessel's surface material and holds us in place."

"The idea is plausible, but the scout would flip over if the hook were mounted to the front. A variation of that idea is to put two hooks on the scout's rear skids."

"Okay, let's put that on the list and keep brainstorming."

Sid pushed down off the scout and grabbed onto a strut on the bottom of the *Lucky Lady*. He started a survey of the racer to see what they might scavenge. As he pulled himself along, he pictured what sort of hook he might fashion from the different pieces he saw. Nearing the rear of the *Lady*, his attention was captured by the grapple unit Kyle had attached to the racer just the day before.

"Bingo."

* * *

Criss could not reconcile the discovery of the grapple with his knowledge record. He spent a few moments seeking details of its capability and specifications, tracing its origin, and examining how he had failed to know of its existence. His best guess—and it was just that—was that the source of the grapple was Kyle's friend, a Fleet maintenance tech, who had visited Earth while on leave.

Circumstantial evidence indicated the friend had bartered for the device so there would be no evidence of a transaction. Criss reviewed the record of this friend's travels and found images of him as he carried his personal gear back to the moon. The difference in size and shape of his pack on his return trip lent credibility to his supposition.

His search also revealed that Kyle, paranoid that his competition was spying, had installed the device in a fashion that was hidden from all monitoring, believing such extreme behavior was necessary to maintain a competitive edge against his shady competitors. As an interesting side note, Criss learned that Kyle had been right to be cautious. Two of his four challengers indeed had him under surveillance. It did not appear that either had knowledge of the device.

Accepting their serendipitous good fortune, Criss guided Sid as he disconnected the grapple from the racer and mounted it between the rear skids of the scout. During the procedure, Criss acknowledged to himself that because of Sid's instincts and perseverance, a critical challenge was resolved.

* * *

Sid, safely back inside the scout, made his way to the tech shop to see how he could help. He found Juice flat on her back in the adjacent operations compartment. She had a wall plate off, her head was stuck inside the partition, and she was fashioning a connector to the ship's central system so she could install the new units. Sid wandered over to her, sat down, leaned against the wall, and started thinking about what lay ahead.

"Can you hand me the multi?" he heard Juice say.

He leaned forward, picked out the instrument from the array of tools she had spread out around her, and like a nurse working with a surgeon, placed it firmly into her outstretched hand. Interested in a diversion, he toggled his dot to watch her work.

As he sat, he thought about the enigma who was Juice. She had a quirky and likable sense of humor. She would often interject seemingly random thoughts into a conversation, and he couldn't always tell when she was being serious and when she was making a joke. And she sometimes responded to the unfamiliar in a manner that projected a lack of confidence.

Yet when presented with a technical challenge, this same person became a brilliant technologist who tackled the most complex tasks with calm assurance. Sid reminded himself that she directed the program that created Criss. Even though, unbeknownst to her, she was receiving help from the Kardish, this was a singularly remarkable achievement.

Growing bored while watching her work, he toggled to normal vision. He leaned back and brainstormed ways they might gain entry into the Kardish vessel. As he sat and contemplated, his eyes drifted to Juice's body. Deep in thought, he considered her runner's build, not aware that she was calling for another tool.

Juice giggled and he watched her move her arms straight out over her body. "Is this really all you have to do?" she asked.

Sid, unaware what had prompted her actions and statement, toggled his dot to see what she was doing. He saw her seeing him studying her. The back and forth of images between the dots looped on and on, much like when two mirrors are facing each other and a reflection tunnel trails out forever. In this case, Juice's headless body was in the center of the tunnel. He quickly averted his gaze, toggled his dot back to normal view, and mumbled an apology as he stood up to leave.

"Wait," she said. "I could use your help for another ten minutes."

Still embarrassed, he sat back down and mumbled some more.

"Hey, Sid," she said. "Let's rescue our friends."

Like a cold shower, this simple statement brought his attention back to the task at hand. Together they finished the installation and buttoned up the wall plate.

The scout now had a Criss-approved cloak, stealth communications, and a grapple unit integrated into the ship. In spite of Criss's confidence, Sid had learned long ago that he could improve his chances of survival during dangerous operations by treating such untested capabilities with great skepticism. This was especially true for a mission of this sort, where failure meant capture and death at the hands of aliens.

"So what's the plan?" Sid asked.

"We separate from the racer and power up the cloak so we can make our final approach in secrecy."

"Seriously?" said Sid. "That's it? Don't you think they'll be able to figure out where we are by plotting our current path? And if we change course, won't they see our thrust and track us that way?"

"Yes, but I believe I can create complex thrust patterns that will reduce their ability to pinpoint our location. They will be uncertain of our position in minutes and will have lost us completely within an hour. If we wait several days before we make our final approach, we will regain the element of surprise."

Jumping to Criss's defense, Juice said, "Given what we're up against, I think that sounds pretty solid."

Disappointed by the lack of creativity in the plan, Sid said, "I think it's time to take you both to school." He turned and walked back to the tech shop. "Juice, I'd appreciate an extra pair of hands. And Criss, I've got a design challenge for you to work on."

"What do you have in mind?" Juice asked, following him.

Sid answered without turning around. "We're going to blow ourselves up."

24

Cheryl controlled her breathing as she eyed the Kardish guard. Crouched in a passageway of the *Alliance* with a carryall of food, water, and weapons over her shoulder, she held up the sheet of cloaking material as her only cover. He stood at the far end of the passageway, weapon at the ready, looking in her direction.

Her weapon hand was free. In a slow, steady motion, she lifted it behind the sheet. Aiming with one eye and a pinhole, she targeted the guard while remaining motionless, hoping he would move on. But when the blond alien tilted his head, Cheryl knew she had seconds to act. The guard cupped his free hand behind his ear. She held her breath.

The Kardish chose to trust his instincts. *Bizt*. A luminous bolt of radiant energy flew above Cheryl and hit the wall down the corridor. The alien peered over his weapon to evaluate his success, and Cheryl used that moment to return fire. *Zwip*. The white bolt from her weapon caught the alien square in the face, kicking his head back.

Before the Kardish guard hit the floor, Cheryl stood up. The cloak sheet fell away as she rose. She fired again, this time hitting him in the chest. She shrugged the food and water off her shoulder and, taking long strides toward the downed guard, fired a third time, her anger overriding her training. She stood over the body and fired a fourth time, relieving a portion of her pent-up fury over the capture of her vessel, the slaughter of her crew, and the desperate situation of her surviving team.

She stood there for several seconds and then cursed. The smell of charred flesh was overwhelming, and his fall had created a considerable thud. Her instincts were screaming that it would not be long before the other guard became involved.

She chose to be proactive. She retrieved the carryall and placed it at a corner so she could grab it during a hasty escape, then picked up the cloak sheet and refashioned her draped shawl. As she adjusted it, she hoped that the burn hole from her weapon was not too visible.

Working her way to the main hatch of the *Alliance*, her approach took her to the corner where she had hidden when the aliens had first entered her ship. Stopping in the same spot where she had nearly been shot, she studied the hatch. It was partially open. She leaned out, turned her head back and forth rapidly as she looked up and down the passageway, and pulled back. She didn't see the other guard.

She edged over to the hatch, peering through the gap to see what she could of the Kardish vessel. The second guard was nowhere in sight. Her anxiety crested—she did not want to be caught by surprise a second time.

Edging the hatch open with her toe and keeping her weapon at the ready, she scanned back and forth as her field of view widened. She exhaled in relief when she finally caught a glimpse of the second guard, still sitting at the bottom of the structure, still half asleep.

Cheryl pulled the hatch open and called out to the guard, speaking a mumble of nonsense syllables in a deep voice, loud enough to be heard, but quiet enough that the guard wouldn't be able to hear her clearly. The guard turned his head and said something. She called out again, mumbling more nonsense sounds. This time the guard stood up and called back. Cheryl remained silent, hidden by the cloak, and waited.

The guard paced several times as if trying to think of a reason to sit back down. He shook his head and let out a visible huff of annoyance. He began an ambling climb up the structure toward the *Alliance* hatch.

Halfway up his climb, he must have sensed that something was amiss. He stopped and began speaking to someone.

She heard Jack through her speck. "You okay? I'm hearing all sorts of chatter from a speck I'd put on the commander of the guard. He says he's coming to investigate and wants the guards out front at attention."

She turned away from the hatch and whispered, "Hold."

She looked back and saw the second guard had a newfound hustle in his step as he hastened his climb. He called out to his partner, the tone in his voice showing increased annoyance with each repetition. When he was most of the way to the top, Cheryl stepped into the middle of the hatch, let the cloak fall open, took aim, and shot him in the chest.

As the guard fell backward, his foot slid forward and hooked under a cross joint of two beams. It remained tightly ensnared as he continued his fall, and his body swung back into open space between the beams. Held by his foot, he dangled upside down, either dead or dying.

His arms hung loosely over his head and his free leg splayed out to the side.

Cheryl stepped out of the hatch and onto the structure. Gripping the frame to steady herself, she leaned out to get a good angle and fired again. The energy bolt hit true.

Pulling herself back into the ship, she moved to retrieve the carryall. As she ran through the ship's passageways, she called Jack. "I have food and water and am on my way to Cait. We'll need to be ready to run when I get there. I just killed the two guards."

She didn't concern herself with stealth as she hustled to the alley hideout. When she turned the corner, she found Jack on his knees, the gadgets and gizmos of his toy-master packs spread on the ground. He and Cait were sifting through the items, organizing things into piles.

"Cait," she said. She ran up, knelt down on one knee, and put an arm on the officer's shoulder. "How are you, Ensign?"

"I'm really tired, Captain. But I can move. I'll carry my load."

Cait was pale and her eyes were glassy. But they had no choice; they had to move.

She opened her carryall and let the contents spill onto the ground and picked out an extra weapon for herself. After snapping it on her free wrist, she handed one to Cait. "Armor up. Here are extra charge packs."

Jack moved one of his now-empty toy-master packs next to Cheryl's pile and went to work. "Let's fill this one-third with food and two-thirds with water."

"Eat and drink from the stuff we can't take," Cheryl said. "We should at least start full." She ate an energy bar as she paused to think through their next steps.

Jack reached into a crevice and pulled out his ghost pack. He viewed his toy-master inventory piled on the deck. Cheryl could see that the ghost pack would hold maybe a quarter of his gear at best. He picked through the pile and filled the ghost pack with a selection.

"I'm guessing communication and demolition will be our priority." He said.

Cheryl helped Cait finish loading the food and water. *Dig deep, Cait*, she willed her. *We need you.*

* * *

Jack recognized the purring of a Kardish cart in the distance. The direction and movement of the sound told him it was headed for the *Alliance*.

"So you shot the two guards?"

"Yeah. They were my first ever. It's really different from shooting a projection sim."

"The smell is different, if nothing else." It was a random thing to say, but his mind was elsewhere. He was thinking of the casualty score. It was a soldier's habit. *Two for us and four for them.* He was not the type to settle for even, envisioning horrific destruction before the score was even ballpark close.

Over the sticky speck, Jack heard the guard's superior shout, "I told you two to be out front and at attention." When the admonishing tone changed to one of surprise, Jack guessed the superior had discovered the fate of his men.

"Time to move," he said, hefting the heavy food pack onto his back. He handed the ghost pack to Cheryl, who shouldered it without a word. He picked up the cloak sheet and shook it out. "My guess is that we'll be most vulnerable to overhead imaging until they can get troops out. We're going to hold the cloak sheet above us and move in a tight formation under it. That should give us reasonable cover for now. I've explored up ahead and have a rough idea of a destination. Any other ideas or concerns before we move out?"

"Let's go," said Cheryl.

"Each of you put a hand on my shoulder. That'll keep us grouped under the sheet."

The two each placed a hand on one of his shoulders, and Jack swung the sheet around and above them. He spread his arms up and out to support it from the front, while the other two used their free hands to keep the sheet centered above them.

"Here we go," said Jack. He walked slowly until they got the hang of moving as a single unit. As they made progress in synchronizing their steps, he picked up the pace until they were moving at a steady shuffle.

"What did you locate as a destination?" asked Cheryl.

"In a minute you'll see that this tub is broken into sections. I suggest moving toward the front section. The bow is where we put the good stuff on our own ships, and my guess is that their command bridge will be that way."

Jack led them out to a lane and along it to the broad, straight road. He let the sheet fall to his shoulders and looked in both directions, eyeing the enormous walls that divided the ship along its length. He knew that the bow of the ship was toward the nearer dividing wall, and he took a moment to confirm this by studying the taper in the hull overhead.

He lifted the sheet back up above him. "Ready?"

He started them shuffling down the main road. They passed by one building-sized box unit after another, scurrying in lockstep and listening for Kardish scouts. Jack understood that being on a main road held the highest risk for discovery by their hunters, but it was the fastest way to gain distance from the *Alliance*.

While shuffling down the road, Jack listened to the Kardish superior as he walked through the *Alliance*. The anger in his tone flipped to apoplectic fury. He screamed at his staff to redirect all resources to a search and ordered the deployment of foot patrols and roaming carts. Jack heard him yell, "Find them and bring them…" And then there was silence.

It continued for several minutes until Jack concluded that the sticky speck had either been discovered or dislodged. He thought it most likely to have been dislodged, reasoning that if they'd discovered it, they were smart enough to use it to deliver deceptive information. They could have set a trap using staged conversation and then sat back and wait while the three walked into it.

"The search has gone full scale," said Jack. "Let's get off this road."

They turned down a side street and onto a narrow alley, keeping to backstreets after that. None of the alleys went very far before dead-ending, so they were forced to zig and zag and even retrace their steps on occasion. Their persistence was rewarded with slower but steady progress.

They were about halfway to the dividing wall when Jack felt a hand slip off his shoulder. He stopped and looked back. Cait was bent over panting.

"I'm sorry. I can make it. Let's keep going." She straightened up and reached her hand out, but was so weak she missed Jack's shoulder and stumbled.

Cheryl caught her and held her up. "It's all right, Cait." She guided her over to a narrow gap between some smaller box units. Catching Jack's eye she said, "We were going to be taking a break anyway."

The gap went a short distance and then turned a corner into a slightly wider area. Cheryl helped Cait sit down. The hideaway offered great cover in every direction but up, and Jack solved that by laying the cloak sheet across the boxes above them. He unshouldered the food pack and pushed it under the cover of the sheet as well, then noticed that Cait, leaning in a corner, was already asleep.

"Is she all right?"

Cheryl looked at her and back at Jack. "I'm wiped too. I don't know what comes out of those weapons, but they really suck the life out of you." She took off the ghost pack, sat down next to Cait and huddled against her. "I'll keep guard over her."

"I'm going to push ahead and see what I can learn." He picked up the ghost pack and slipped it on. It shimmered and then disappeared. "I'll bring my toys with me to keep me company."

"Hey," said Cheryl. "I can see fuzzy patches. You're starting to show in places. Don't be thinking you can stand in front of them and be invisible." She twirled her index finger. "Turn around."

Jack did a slow pirouette.

"Your back is better, maybe ninety-five percent. Your front is more like eighty percent."

"Just the fact that you can tell front from back is bad enough. This suit wasn't designed for what we're doing here."

As he spoke, he could see her eyelids drooping. Moments later, they were both asleep. He stood there quietly and confirmed he could see them both breathing steadily. As he walked out of the hideaway, he toggled his speck to urgent mode so Cheryl wouldn't be disturbed by his idle chatter. But if he spoke under stress, even in a whisper, the speck would amplify the words and grab her attention.

He left the hideaway and made his way out to the main road, placed a tracer on a corner box-building so he could find his way back, and began a slow jog down the road. He reached a comfortable stride and then he heard the purring of an approaching cart.

25

J ack stepped into a shadow and, recalling Cheryl's comment about the degraded concealment of his ghost suit, kept his back to the road. He waited for the cart to pass, watching over his shoulder as it went by. He was surprised so see that it held only one Kardish. He expected them to be traveling in teams.

Acting on impulse, he turned, lifted his arm and fired a bolt, hitting the driver in the back. The alien slumped forward, and the cart slowed to a stop. He ran over and confirmed that the fellow was dead. Pushing on the frame of the cart, he discovered that it rolled easily, so he kept pushing and moved it onto a side street.

He studied the driver's clothing, considering taking his outfit and attempting an impersonation routine, but discarded the idea. With their pale skin and blond hair, the Kardish all seemed to be created from the same pool of DNA. Anyone who saw him would know he was an imposter.

The alien's boots had sturdy laces. Jack didn't understand their culture of ornate clothing and didn't dwell on it. He bent over, pulled the laces off both boots, and tied the ends together to fashion a longer cord. He then hefted the driver upright, looped the cord around the driver's chest, and tied him to the seat support.

Standing back, he surveyed his handiwork. The driver's head hung awkwardly to one side, and his body slumped in the seat in an unnatural fashion. But from a distance and overhead, the charade might hold up. Jack got in on the passenger side, slid close to the driver, examined the cart controls, and found them to be simple and intuitive.

Using one hand to prop up the driver's head, Jack engaged the cart. "Off we go, mate."

He drove around the block, back onto the main road, and turned toward the near dividing wall. A few blocks ahead, the environment seemed somehow brighter. He was trying to decide what specifically was different when it became obvious. The road led straight into a huge open area.

He swerved the cart onto a side lane, followed by a quick turn into an alley, then hopped out. "You stay here," he said to the driver. "I'll be right back." He updated his body count as he walked. *Four to three. Definitely moving in the right direction.*

Staying to the backstreets, he worked his way to the open area. A wide road ran down the long border where the box city ended and the open area began. He didn't cross it, but stayed back in a sheltered spot where he could study the scene in front of him. As the details of the site registered in his brain, he became increasingly alarmed.

It was an airfield, or perhaps more accurately, a space port, and it was so astonishingly large, he was having difficulty judging its size. He guessed that a dozen Blackworks hangars could fit inside it.

It extended the entire width of the Kardish vessel and was at least as long as it was wide. He could see the curve of the vessel hull in the distance as it rose from the field deck on his left, arced up overhead, and descended down to meet the deck on his right. The most prominent features in the vessel's hull were massive hangar doors overhead. And because they were fitted into the hull, when the hangar doors opened, it would be to the vacuum of empty space.

The reason for the hangar doors was sitting right in front of him. Military craft. Row upon row of weaponized death machines. With no place for a pilot to sit, these small, agile craft could only be drones.

The drones were parked in an immense garage-like shelving unit that was five tiers high. He looked left to right and tried to count the rows of shelves. There were too many, but his rough tally reached two hundred. He looked down the row in front of him, and it faded into the distance. He guessed two hundred deep, but that was just a guess. Two hundred rows that were two hundred deep and stacked five high meant two hundred thousand drones. Two hundred thousand war craft, each a mobile arsenal.

The drone garage was huge, but it occupied only a fraction of the total expanse in front of him and was positioned in the center of what was an otherwise open, empty deck. On either side, two vast fields ran from the drone garage all the way out to the hull. He presumed these open fields were to provide for an orderly passage of swarms of drones as they flew in and out through the hangar doors above.

As Jack moved back to the cart, he mentally processed his discovery. It was clear he had to reorient his thinking about the Kardish. Could such an assemblage of armaments be something a passive culture would create for self-defense? No, he concluded, these were the trappings of a warrior race. The drone armada was a tool they used to attack and conquer, or perhaps simply to attack and destroy.

He tried to imagine the Union going into battle against such a force. It seemed clear that Earth would be defenseless against a sky blackened with these drones. Given what he now knew, he was glad that Fleet Command had stood firm on the notion that Earth shouldn't provoke a confrontation.

He reached the cart and climbed back in. "Move over, mate," he said to the dead driver. "You're hogging the seat." He drove out of the alley and stuck to smaller lanes as he made his way back to Cheryl, Cait, and their hideaway.

As he purred along, he thought about how few Kardish he'd seen since their arrival. A warrior race would have legions of soldiers. The streets should be full of search parties hunting them down. Granted, this vessel was huge. Many thousands of troops could appear as sparse numbers if spread out. But it was still hard to square up the idea of a warrior race with the apparent absence of troops.

The drones might tell part of the story. Maybe there was so much automation embedded in their society that they were able to conquer planets with a small crew. Or maybe this was a forward ship designed for a first attack, with troop ships following later. Yet the Kardish had remained in Earth orbit for twenty years, the whole time carrying the means to destroy the planet many times over, and had never shown any signs of aggression.

He slowed when he came to a large street, his thoughts turning to the logistics of how the three of them would advance to the dividing wall. If they were to continue their push to the ship's bow, they needed to make it across that open field. If he were on Earth, his go-to solution was tried and true. Create a diversion. Lacking a better idea and feeling the pressure of time, he decided to stick with the method he knew.

He changed course and drove at an angle away from the hideaway. He continued for a number of city blocks, and when his intuition signaled, he stopped. He fished inside the ghost pack and pulled out a demolition square. Scanning the box-buildings around the intersection, he spied a crevice running horizontally along one. He bent the square in half and slid it into the crevice, stepped back to confirm it wasn't exposed, and clambered back inside the cart.

He purred on, moving in a large semicircle that curved around the hideaway, placing two more demolition squares in places he believed would create an impressive show. With his diversion preparations complete, he turned the cart back to Cheryl and Cait.

He negotiated onto a main drag and spotted a cart coming toward him. He grabbed a handful of his cart's driver's hair and pulled up as hard as he could, drawing the dead Kardish to a mostly upright position. The other cart drew closer. His heart was pounding. *The only way this is going to work,* he thought, *is by increasing the body count.* He liked the sound of that and found renewed strength to keep pulling on the driver's hair. He lifted his free arm and took aim.

When the two carts were half a block apart, the other cart turned and headed up a different street. No wave or nod of the head. No outward sign of curiosity or concern.

Jack let the driver slump back down and flexed his aching arm. "Not such a friendly chap," he said to the driver.

When he was within walking distance of the hideaway, he pulled into a sheltered slot between two box units, jumped out of the cart, and moved toward the tracer signal. He saw one more cart driving across an intersection in the distance during his walk but couldn't tell if it was the same one he'd seen earlier. He stuck to shadows where he could, crossed the large roads quickly, and stayed vigilant. The place remained eerily quiet.

He picked the tracer off the box-building as he passed. Moments later he turned into their alley. Ducking into a crevice across and a few boxes down from their hideaway, he watched the entrance gap. After a short wait, he gained confidence that there would be no surprises. Cheryl hadn't contacted him, so he assumed she was still asleep.

He crept into the gap, peeked around the corner, and saw the two snuggled together in deep slumber. He checked the time and realized he hadn't slept in more than thirty hours. He knew this wasn't a good time to nap, but couldn't imagine that there would ever be a good time on the foreseeable horizon.

Lying down and curling up facing the entrance of their hideaway, he cradled his head in his arms, then remembered that the cloaking on his back was in better shape. He rolled over so he was facing inward. Either way, anyone coming in or out would trip over him. He thus acted as both a shield and alarm of sorts for Cheryl and Cait. He put his head back in his arms and was asleep in minutes.

* * *

The helmsman of the Kardish vessel was tasked with tracking the two Earth ships that were pursuing them. Both were tiny things that had recently docked together to become one. The consensus was that they were more like bugs to be squashed than threats in any real sense.

His orders were to monitor the pests and report new developments. The assignment was tedious, and he struggled to maintain his concentration. And then he saw that the ships were moving apart. He blinked his eyes several times and reviewed the display, worried that perhaps he'd been daydreaming. He verified the movement and was about to call out the news when both ships disappeared in a brilliant conflagration.

"Your Excellency," the helmsman called to the one sitting in the captain's chair. "The Earth ships have exploded."

"Show me," he said as he stood, his robes rustling softly with his movement.

The helmsman enlarged the projected image to such an extent that he had to step back to see it clearly. He played the event in a slow-motion loop, and they watched it again and again. They saw the smaller ship undock, move off from the larger ship a short distance, and then ignite in a tremendous eruption. A ball of flames that began in the smaller ship burst out and engulfed the larger one.

The larger ship faded away in its death throes. It seemed to reemerge briefly from the flames, and then it disappeared for good.

"I didn't see the larger ship explode," said the helmsman.

"I saw it disappear in a ball of fire. Didn't you?"

"Yes, Your Excellency. It most certainly disappeared in a ball of fire."

"Let it play forward." The leader pointed at the image. "What are all those pieces?"

"Fragments from the exploding ships," said the helmsman. "There is a cluster of them headed right for us. Should I move to avoid them?"

"Will they cause any harm?"

"No, Excellency. We may hear them, but they will cause no damage."

The prince stood silently. "Your assignment here is finished," he said. "Go help kill the rats scurrying around my ship."

"Yes, Your Excellency." The helmsmen hurried off the bridge.

The prince watched the explosion again and displayed a cheerless smile as the destruction unfolded in slow motion. He sat back in his chair, reached to his side, and lifted the scepter from its stand. Lost in thought, he held it in his lap and stroked the royal emblem.

26

Juice followed Sid to the tech shop and stood in the doorway. She leaned against the frame and watched him yank open one drawer after another. Apparently not finding the object of his quest, he methodically rifled the cabinets. Finished with the lot, he walked in her direction. She stepped back to let him pass and watched him enter the exercise room. There he repeated his rapid-fire drawer and cabinet search.

He stopped looking inside things and moved to the middle of the room. He studied a wall, looking it up and down, made a quarter turn and examined the adjoining wall, and continued until he finished the room. Returning to the tech shop, he slipped past Juice yet again and inspected its four walls.

"Hmm," he said, folding his arms across his chest.

Juice desperately wanted to ask, but when Sid was improvising, she knew that wasn't the best way to work with him. She walked over to a drawer, pulled it out, and dumped it on top of the worktable, pretending to study the pile.

Glancing over, he said, "No, too small."

"That's what I was thinking." She used her arm to sweep everything back into the drawer, then looked in a few more until she found one that held an organized collection of brackets and braces. She paused to study them.

"Right size," he said, "but too regular in shape."

Still guessing, she said, "I wonder if the collection of tools near the bottom hatch would work?"

He shifted his gaze in her direction, but his eyes weren't focused. Then he nodded and their eyes connected. "Not bad. I'm guessing we'll need more than that, though."

"Criss," said Juice. "Where on the ship can we find irregularly shaped objects the size of hand tools?"

"The tech shop, galley, and recreation areas all have items that can contribute to such a collection. For example, add two forks, two spoons, and two knives and you will increase the size of the pile without adding to the repetition. The scout and racer have a great many pieces that would fit the category."

"That's good," said Sid. "We can work with that." He resumed studying the room. "Now we need a sturdy pipe about as tall as I am and maybe as wide as my leg."

Criss was the one to ask. "Sid, if you tell me what you are trying to achieve, I can help with the design."

"I told you," said Sid. "We're going to blow ourselves up."

He picked up a bucket and started his collection of odd-shaped objects. "Criss, do you believe the scout's cloak will work?"

"My confidence level is very high."

Juice noted that he didn't simply say "yes," but she didn't say anything to Sid.

"So let's have the Kardish think we're dead. We'll push off from the racer, blow her up, and at that moment of distraction, we turn on the cloak. We disappear in a ball of fire. Bing, bang, boom—we're gone."

"And what's the collection of cutlery for?" asked Juice.

"When the racer explodes, there will be a natural cloud of fragments. We'll fire shrapnel at the Kardish during the explosion. If we do it right, the shrapnel will appear to be a result of our disintegration. With luck, they'll be hitting their vessel at the same time we land."

Juice nodded. "So the impact from our landing grapple will get mixed in with the pitter-patter of falling forks." She reached out and rubbed his arm. "Very creative."

* * *

Criss embraced the spirit of Sid's idea but redesigned the implementation. Juice was assigned those duties that could be performed from inside the scout. Sid donned the space coveralls and took up station in the *Lucky Lady*. Criss kept them hustling as he directed them through long to-do lists, feeling he was achieving success in being a patient but demanding taskmaster.

Criss used the dots the two were wearing to help them understand his version of the plan. He showed Juice what a good fragment looked like. As she scavenged items, he guided her on how to cut some of the larger pieces into appropriate sizes and shapes. He had her stack these into piles outside the hatch so Sid could load them into the launcher in the proper order when he was ready.

At Criss's direction, she opened a row of wall plates and pulled out a long, flexible hose that brought drinking water to the exercise room. She drained it, coiled it, and carried it down to the hatch where she connected one end to an outlet on the wall and arranged the remainder in neatly stacked loops near the hatch door.

Following Criss's instructions with care, she prepared the explosive mixture they would be feeding through the tube. For safety, Criss's recipe created it as two separate chemicals that would flow individually out to the racer. Neither was explosive by itself. When combined in the propellant tanks of the *Lucky Lady*, the mixture would become a potent and spectacular pyrotechnic.

Inside the racer, Criss maintained an ongoing dialogue with Sid as he pulled down every wall plate from inside the cockpit and the life support area behind it. Guided by Criss, he tiled the pieces together to form a cylinder centered directly under the docking ring. Using multiple rolls of fiber tape, he wound loop after loop around the outside of the plates. The first roll worked to hold the wall plates in position. The rest gave necessary structural strength to the assembly.

He fitted a washbowl pulled from one of the scout's crew cabins into the base of the makeshift cylinder. The bowl material was strong enough to withstand the pressure of an explosion, and its shape would direct the discharge as the fragments were propelled upward. Criss's creation wasn't a cannon as Sid imagined it, but it was well designed to launch a collection of objects out through the racer's docking ring.

Sid next worked on loading the launcher for business. He cut a demolition square into small pieces and followed Criss's guidance as he arranged them in a pattern inside the bowl. After checking with Juice that it was all clear, he opened the hatch and retrieved the fragment piles. Criss showed him how to arrange the pieces inside the bowl for maximum effect. Criss remained silent while Sid picked out the mallet from one of the fragment piles and set it aside, leaving it inside the scout.

With the fragment launcher completed, Sid grasped the end of the hose Juice positioned for him. Pulling it gently to avoid snags, he wormed his way behind the racer's cockpit, paused to snap the safety tether to the loop on his coveralls, then floated out the access hatch. Coils of hose floated behind him.

Gaining access to the fill spout of the propellant tank proved to be more challenging than either he or Criss had anticipated. After a session of swearing, grunting, and more swearing, Sid finally succeeded in forcing it open. He snaked the hose inside and held it while the two chemicals flowed, one after the other, into the tank. He dropped a trigger circuit inside, sealed the spout shut, and returned to the scout.

Before Sid closed the scout's hatch, he picked up the mallet, studied the docking ring, and smacked the latch. The tab bent from the blow, but it moved. He smacked it a second time and it popped free. Like a cork in a bottle, the two ships were again held together only by friction. Carrying it like a boy with his toy, he brought the mallet with him when he returned to the scout's bridge.

"How are we doing for time?" asked Juice as she took her seat.

Sid wanted an update as well. "Please step us through it, Criss."

"The scout will pull away from the racer in a manner that causes it to rotate. After the two ships have gained sufficient separation and the racer is properly oriented, I will fire the fragment launcher and shoot our spoon shower at the Kardish vessel."

Juice giggled at the "spoon shower" reference.

"I will immediately follow this with a detonation of the chemicals in the propellant tank. The sequence will be so close that it will all appear as a single event. The racer will be oriented at that point so almost all of the real fragments will travel away from us. There is some risk here. There is a small possibility that a random fragment will hit the scout and cause damage.

"Assuming the scout is unharmed, I will activate the cloak and the scout will appear to vanish when the flames are at their brightest. While still engulfed in flames, I will initiate a thrust burst that will send us on an intercept course with the Kardish vessel. We will arrive above the vessel hull at the same time the scrap storm reaches maximum intensity."

This time both Sid and Juice laughed. Sid finished the plan. "And our grapple will sound like one of the impacts."

Juice beamed. "Nice teamwork, guys." After a pause, she asked, "So how do we get inside their vessel?"

"I have three ideas," said Criss. "But we won't be able to test any of them until we are attached to their hull. Our best hope is that our stealth communications link works as designed. If it does, we will coordinate with the crew of the *Alliance* and see if we can help them open a hatch from the inside. A second option is that we burrow through the rubbery outer layer and make firm contact with the surface of the hard hull. I may be able to connect through it to the subsystems of the Kardish vessel, override protocols, and open a hatch myself. The last idea is to entice the Kardish to come after us. They will have to open a hatch to do battle. We will then have a physical opening and can attempt to fight our way in."

"I don't like that third one at all," said Juice, shaking her head. "Let's do one of the first two."

Sid and Juice engaged their seat restraints, ready for the performance to begin. Criss pulled the scout away from the racer, doing so in a fashion that caused it to turn end-over-end in a lazy spin. Sid brought up an image projection, and he and Juice watched as the *Lucky Lady* drifted away.

"Ten seconds," said Criss.

Their eyes were glued to the image display as the nose of the racer rotated upward. "Here we go," said Criss. It happened so quickly that neither Sid nor Juice saw it as individual events. They saw a brilliant flash and then the scout shook violently. The shaking passed quickly and transitioned into a brief pressure as the scout accelerated to become part of the projectile cloud that would provide cover as they approach and attach themselves to the Kardish vessel.

Criss spoke with urgency, "The cloak has engaged, but it is going to fail."

"How can I help?" Sid asked.

"The shock wave has loosened a link where Juice connected the cloak to the main power unit. I cannot pinpoint the precise circuit, but something is not seated properly. We will lose the cloak in moments."

Sid disengaged his seat restraints, jumped up, and ran toward the rear of the scout. He'd taken only a few steps when he saw his mallet hanging on a rail. He snatched it up and accelerated toward the operations compartment where Juice had been working.

Stepping inside the small room, he ripped the plate off the wall, yanking it with such force that it flew out the door, bounced into the passageway, and started spinning.

He was on his back, his head inside the partition, before the spinning stopped.

Both Criss and Juice viewed the connections and circuits through Sid's dot. He reached up and fiddled with this and that.

"Could it be the central spline?" Juice asked.

Criss didn't answer as he shifted ever more resources into identifying the failing circuit. He watched Sid wiggle bits and pieces as he struggled for a solution. And then a piece he touched caused a change Criss could detect. "It's near there."

Sid backed up in his progression and again jiggled the items he was working on. He was on his second jiggle when Criss said, "That's it. That's the problem piece."

It was a small gray box. Sid pushed it, pulled it, and twisted it, hoping for an *all good* signal from Criss.

"Your efforts have not solved the issue,' said Criss. "We are losing the cloak."

27

J uice felt responsible for the failing cloak. She held her breath as she watched Sid make blind attempts at an emergency repair. From her vantage point on the bridge, she did not see him reach down by his thigh and grab his mallet. She did see it, however, when he moved it into position beside his head.

"What are you doing?" she said with clear alarm. He didn't respond.

The space inside the wall was so cramped that he could only use wrist motion. He cocked the mallet and thwacked the box, then pulled the mallet back, readying for a second attempt.

"That's it," said Criss. "We are cloaked. I believe we were visible for just a brief moment. The cloak appears to be stable now."

Sid pulled himself out of the wall, jumped up, and shook his mallet in victory. "I am Thor," he called as he walked back to the bridge. He stood in front of Juice and held the mallet at his hip. "Would you help me make a holster? I want to carry this baby with me all the time." He didn't wait for an answer, but sat in his chair, absently twirling it as he daydreamed.

Juice, who had been thinking that a hammer was a dubious tool for delicate circuit work, flashed on a few variations for a holster design as she watched Sid play with his toy.

"Update, Criss. How are we doing?" asked Sid.

"The cloak is holding. We are in the midst of the cloud of fragments. Our intercept trajectory is good. We should be firing our grapple in a few hours."

Waiting is difficult, and doubly so during moments of tension, thought Juice.

Criss placed them on a course to approach the Kardish vessel from the rear and float above its surface as they drifted past the fins and over the hull. As planned, the scout was moving inside a cloud of fragments. These would be hitting the surface of the alien vessel as the scout traversed its length.

During the approach, Sid and Criss debated where to deploy the grapple. Criss, having viewed two decades of record of small craft entering and exiting the vessel, could pinpoint precisely where that hatch was located. Starting from the stern, they should travel two-thirds of the way down the Kardish vessel and then attach the scout.

"I make decisions that maximize my options when it comes time to make my next decision," said Sid. "The place that keeps the most options open is the halfway mark. In a monster vessel like this, there have to be lots of hatches. Since we don't know where the *Alliance* is, whether the crew is still with it, or what options they'll have to help, the halfway point is where we'll attach."

When they reached the Kardish ship a few hours later and passed over the finned tail of the vessel, the immense, menacing view sidetracked the debate. Juice watched mesmerized as the black, featureless expanse of alien ship passed beneath them.

She sensed that Sid was about to order Criss to attach when a crack of light became visible through the vessel hull up ahead. Sid zoomed the image for a closer look.

A hatch was opening! Juice thought with a mixture of excitement and trepidation.

"Criss," said Sid. "I can't tell how big that is. Can we fit through it?"

There was a pause as the hatch continued to open. "It is now wide enough to pass through safely."

Sid tapped the operations bench, and when nothing happened, anger flashed in his eyes. "Give me the controls," he commanded. "Now."

Our first test of who's in command, thought Juice.

Sid tapped the bench again and this time the scout responded. "We're going in. Help me hit the sweet spot."

"Perhaps we should move to the opposite side of the vessel," said Criss. "It seems likely we are about to be attacked."

"The best defense is a good offense," Sid directed the ship toward the gap. "Here we go." He swung the scout out to improve the angle and then swung back in the direction of the Kardish vessel.

Juice bounced in her seat as the scout started bucking. She double checked her restraints and looked at Sid, wondering if he really was as confident as his calm exterior seemed to project.

"Whoa," said Sid. "Gale-force winds are blowing out of that thing."

In fact, a steady stream of air was rushing out, forming a cloud outside the ship and then dissipating into the emptiness of space.

Sid aimed the scout straight into the turbulence at the hatch opening, and the unpredictable maelstrom of swirling air pushed it around like a toy bobbing on the ocean. Criss reacted fast enough to continually adjust their course as they passed through the violent eddies and currents, and his rapid-fire actions kept the scout from slamming into the hull of the larger vessel. The shaking became increasingly violent and then, suddenly, it was quiet. They were inside.

Juice surveyed the image projection of their surroundings with wonder. A huge open deck lay below them, and at a distance in front sat rows of cubicles. To the left was a solid wall. To the right was a sea of box-like structures.

Something shook the ship and Sid asked, "What's going on, Criss?"

"We are in a gravity environment. I am slowing our descent."

Sid looked at the displays on his bench. "Get us on the deck quickly and keep us near the hull. As soon as we touch, power down. Essential systems only."

Juice held on tight, thankful that just seconds later, they were settled on the deck.

Criss shut down all nonessential operations, setting life support, communications, and other necessities to their lowest functioning level.

As minutes passed, Juice felt tension building inside her. She reacted to the silence. "This is too weird." The quiet stretched out. "Are we still cloaked?"

"Yes," said Criss.

"Where are they? Is anyone approaching?" she asked.

"The scout's sensors are not designed for an enclosed environment and are of limited value in this setting," said Criss. "I can report that there is no life in our immediate vicinity. But there are hangar doors open to the vacuum of space right above us, so that is not unexpected."

After more minutes of quiet Criss said, "The hangar doors are closing. We still have time to slip through and escape. Otherwise, we will need to find a way to open the doors ourselves if we are to leave in the scout."

Juice squirmed when she heard they would soon be trapped inside the Kardish vessel.

"We're going to stay and play this out," said Sid as he poked the operations bench. Looking at the different displays, he asked, "Why would they throw away all that air? It doesn't make sense." He continued his activity but seemed lost in thought. "Criss, in your review of the record, how often did you see the Kardish vent gas directly to space?"

"Never."

"Any ideas?"

"It is a way to create a rapid decompression inside this section of the vessel."

"Huh," said Sid. He released his restraints, stood up, and stretched. He reached a hand out to Juice and motioned for her to join him. Juice welcomed his strength and his presence. His example bolstered her resolve. *I can do this*, she told herself, taking a deep breath and standing up next to him.

"Let's try that secure link thing that Juice built," said Sid. "Let's see if we can raise the *Alliance*."

After several seconds, Criss said, "I can connect to the ship, but I am only receiving returns from automated subsystems. The crew does not respond."

An image popped up above the operations bench. It was of poor quality and Juice squinted, trying to discern what they were seeing. It was like looking through fog.

"It is the *Alliance*," said Criss. "The image is corrupted because portions of the ship have been heavily damaged."

Sid studied the image, walking around to view it from different angles. "That's the command bridge," he said. "It looks like a war zone. Can you locate Cheryl or Jack? Or any of the crew?"

Criss cycled through a series of different views from inside the ship. Some images were so corrupted it was difficult to decipher what part of the ship they were looking at. With each view, they searched for signs of life.

"I have enhanced and analyzed everything I can recover from the *Alliance*. Their image record has been destroyed, so I can only see the present. I cannot locate any personnel, though there are several areas I cannot view because of equipment damage."

Juice grasped Sid's arm with both hands. She had been fighting to contain her emotions over the loss of Mick and Sheldon. This disturbing information started the battle anew in her head. She sought yet again the reassurance of physical contact. Sid wrapped both his arms around her and gave her a hug.

"We'll find them and get them home," he whispered to her. They stood together, lost in their own thoughts, then Sid announced, "I'm going out to explore."

"The air pressure is rising," Criss replied. "It won't be long before one of you can exit without a suit."

Sid bent down and picked up his mallet and toyed with it while he waited for the time to pass.

"Juice," said Criss. "Would you help me with a project? I would like to connect directly to the Kardish central array."

She jumped at the chance to contribute and keep her mind engaged. Sitting and waiting was driving her nuts. When she reached the tech shop, Criss used her dot to show her what he was trying to achieve.

The device he proposed could be assembled from the unused parts of their previous projects. She rummaged through the discard pile, picked out the items she needed, and spread them out on the work table. She shuffled the pieces until they were arranged in the proper sequence for assembly.

With Criss's guidance, she fashioned a central array interface, a high-throughput communications link, and a power source. She found herself humming, her mind fully consumed by the intricate task. Sid drifted back to watch and stood in silence as she combined the delicate bits into a single small case.

Criss showed them both a close-up of the Kardish vessel wall near the scout. He pointed out some likely access sites into the central array. Juice would need to run a hand scan at each site to identify the best entry point. She was to cut in and connect the device and then hide or camouflage the case as best she could.

When Sid understood that Juice would be making the first foray out of the scout, he protested.

"Sid," said Criss. "Without this device in place, we are blind. We must send the person who can get it installed properly and quickly."

Sid relented. "Juice, this will be dangerous. I feel bad—this isn't what I promised you when we talked about you coming along. Are you up for it?"

"Hell, yeah," she said with much more confidence than she felt.

Sid held up his mallet. "Know that me and my friend here will have you covered."

Juice slipped through the hatch at the bottom of the scout and stood on the deck. Sid reached down and handed her a small pouch with tools and the device. He started to close the hatch and paused. "I'll be with you every step of the way."

She trotted toward the box-buildings and then turned and followed a road bordering the buildings straight to the hull of the Kardish vessel.

An overwhelming collection of objects covered the wall in front of her. Criss guided her to the location he believed held the most promise. She pulled the scanner from her pouch and moved it slowly over everything in front of her.

"Stop," he said. "Right there."

The scanner hovered over a square that looked just like a dozen others near it. She studied the object he'd identified, gripped what seemed like a cover along the edge, and pulled. It released to expose a smooth, dark surface. She couldn't see any joints or connections.

"Press the case against the surface, but don't let your fingers touch it," said Criss. She did so and, prompted by Criss, slid the case back and forth and up and down. Her efforts seemed to be failing, but finally Criss announced, "That's it. Just like that. Can you fasten it in place?"

Holding the case with one hand, she used her other hand and her teeth to fashion a sticky-stick. She put a gentle bend in it and stuck the center of the bend against the back of the case. She pressed her finger on top of the bend so the case wouldn't move and then, one at a time, folded back the ends of the stick and pressed each against the hull. She pulled her hands away, and it all held together. She snapped the cover back on.

"We still good?" she asked.

"Perfect," said Criss.

Juice stood by, watching the assembly and waiting for further instructions.

As the quiet stretched out, Sid asked, "Criss. Are we done?" Criss didn't respond. "Criss!" Sid repeated with more urgency. "What next?" The silence continued.

"Juice, get back here."

She turned around and saw an open deck. The scout was gone. "Wow, the cloak works great. You'll have to guide me in."

* * *

Sid focused on getting his partner back safely. "Stick to the road along the edge of the box-buildings. I'll tell you when to turn." He was annoyed at Criss for dropping the ball. This was a mission, though—he'd led many operations over the years and took the lead without hesitation.

Juice trotted along the road, waiting for the signal from Sid, when some commotion behind her caused her to turn. Through her dot, Sid saw a tall, blond Kardish running after her. She froze.

"Run, Juice," commanded Sid. He saw the Kardish raise a weapon. "Now, Juice. Run!" he shouted. "Drop the bag. Move your feet."

The Kardish yelled something. Juice spun, threw the pouch up over her head, and ran. The Kardish stopped for a moment to watch the pouch arc toward him, giving Juice the seconds she needed.

"There's a turn ahead past this building. Turn right. Turn now."

He watched through the dot as she glanced down the lane and then sprinted into it. There were box-buildings on either side of her. Alleys branched off in both directions.

Sid stood up and fumbled his way back to his cabin. He toggled his dot a few times to see his own local view, but he moved mostly by feel and memory so he could stay linked with Juice.

There was an explosion, and Juice looked over her shoulder. Sid could see an impact crater on the corner building behind her. The Kardish had fired his weapon. The shot was nowhere close to her, but it erased all doubt that the fellow meant business.

"Glance back," said Sid. "Let me see." He saw the Kardish rounding the corner. Pumping his arms and huffing through his mouth, he was outmatched in every aspect of the running game. But a race against energy bolts from his weapon would be no contest. "Take your next right. Go as far as you can and then make another right. Go in a circle. I'm on my way."

"Got it." Her breathing was slow and measured. It gave him hope.

Sid toggled his dot so he could see his world. He snatched his weapon from beside his bunk. Running through the ship, he slapped it on his wrist as he made his way to the hatch, dropped down to the deck, and sprinted toward the box-buildings.

"Criss," he called as he ran. There was no answer.

He reached the buildings and turned toward the Kardish hull, running along the dividing road in the opposite direction from Juice. He counted alleys as he ran, but realized he didn't know where she was relative to him. He stopped, crouched down, and toggled to see through her dot.

She was still running. "How many turns have you made?" he asked. He watched the scene shift as she turned into another alley.

"That's my third," she said. "I couldn't make it to the far end. I'm two alleys short. I can see the open deck ahead."

"Can you make it?"

"Easy. This guy is no runner."

"When you reach the open deck, turn right again and keep going along the road. You'll see me standing here. Prepare mentally for that. Run right past me and turn into the alley behind me. Hide somewhere and wait."

He watched through her dot as she ran. He could see that he had time before she would reach the end, so he rose, ran farther up the road, and crouched near where she would emerge. He held his arm up and pointed his weapon. Then he saw her. She popped out of an alley farther down from where he expected. He rose and sprinted in her direction.

As their distance closed, he saw that her face was calm, her stride was easy, and her pace was fast. Sid was impressed. As she zipped by, he told her, "We've lost Criss. It happened when you connected that box."

He turned his attention ahead. Once Juice was safely past, he stopped and waited. The alien came huffing around the corner. He was struggling from the exertion and didn't have much run left in him. Sid put a shot in his chest and ended his misery.

Dragging the dead Kardish back into the alley, Sid shoved him into a recess and returned to the road, moving at a fast trot down to the next alley. He rounded the corner and saw Juice standing there. She was completely still. A Kardish had his arm around her neck. He held a weapon to the back of her head.

28

J ack snapped awake. It took him a moment to orient himself. He checked the time and saw that he'd been asleep for several hours. Creeping out to the edge of the hideaway, he peeked into the alley, studying up one way and down the other. Nothing. He stood and walked to the back of the gap. Cheryl still leaned against Cait, and they were still asleep.

He removed his hood and squatted down. "It's Jack, Cheryl. Rise and shine." Her eyes popped open, and she registered recognition. She rubbed her eyes with the palms of her hands.

"How're we doing?" she asked, sitting up straight.

"So far, so good." He pulled the large pack over next to her and opened it so she could get at the food and water.

He stepped over and crouched in front of Cait. He looked at her, shook her shoulder, and then leaned forward to study her face. Sighing, he reached out and felt for a pulse in her neck. There was none. Her skin was cold. He'd seen enough death in his time, and his com confirmed what he already knew.

He lifted Cait's hands and held them in his. Tilting his head forward, he said something under his breath.

"What's the matter?"

He stood up and looked away. "Say your good-byes. We have to move."

While Cheryl fussed over Cait, Jack dumped the gadgets and devices from his ghost pack onto the ground. He put back a couple of items, including two of his three remaining demolition squares, then filled the rest of the pack with food and water and assembled everything they were leaving behind around Cait. He meant it as a symbolic ritual of remembrance. He placed his third demolition square into her hands and folded them in her lap.

He helped Cheryl to her feet. "How are you feeling?"

"I'm ready," she said in a somber tone. Looking down at Cait, she added, "I hate these bastards. I really hate them."

He shouldered the ghost pack, reached up, and pulled down the cloak sheet from its perch overhead. Cheryl shook it, held it up, and saw it was showing smudges here and there. It was becoming more like camouflage than an invisible shroud. She wrapped it around herself.

Pausing at the exit, Jack toggled his speck from urgent mode back to normal conversation. "Let's go ruin their day," he said as they walked into the alley together.

They made their way to the edge of the box city and stood concealed in shadow. Jack remained quiet while Cheryl evaluated the expanse in front of them. He listened while she described what she saw, and her observations and conclusions matched his.

Her eyes were drawn to the huge hangar doors in the hull of the vessel overhead. "We need to get out of here."

He looked at her.

"You know how we get rid of vermin on Fleet cargo ships? We open the hold to space. Cold vacuum is a great way to kill everything."

He looked up and considered the hangar doors, seeing them in a new light. "You think they'd do that to us?" He pointed down a long corridor between two rows of drones. "This brings us to the dividing wall and hopefully a way out. The good news is that being hidden between big structures gives us plenty of cover. The bad news is that if they figure out where we are, it'll be easy to trap us." He stepped out from the concealment of their shadow. "Hold for a moment. Let me check for all clear." He took a few steps, then stopped and scurried back. "Looks like we're done walking."

She leaned out and peered down the road. A cart was approaching.

Jack stood close to Cheryl and waited. He spent those moments deciding that he was no longer interested in keeping a running tally of the body count—the entire vessel didn't have enough Kardish to balance the score.

"This one's for Cait," he whispered when the cart rolled in front of them. Taking quick steps out of the shadows, he broke into a run behind the cart, lifted his arm, and shot the driver. The cart drifted to a stop. He pulled the alien onto the ground and dragged him to the nearest cover.

"Your chariot awaits, *chérie*," he said as he sat where the driver had been. He waited as she climbed in next to him. He reached over and helped her adjust the cape to maximize her cover, though he suspected that, at this point, such details didn't really matter. The sight of an unauthorized cart driving among the drones would be enough for the Kardish to shoot first and never think about asking questions.

Before he started driving, he opened his ghost pack and removed a small box. "Good-bye, Cait." He touched the box. There was a tremendous explosion in the distance, and the deck of the Kardish vessel shook beneath them. Almost immediately, there was a spectacular secondary explosion. A pillar of flame thrust upward.

"Holy hell," said Cheryl, watching the flame mushroom out into a ball. As it dissipated, she added, "Whatever we were sleeping next to was powerful stuff."

Jack drove the cart between two rows of the drone parking garage. The cart's top speed wasn't as fast as he'd have liked, but at least the deck was flat and the ride was smooth. As they rode along, Jack set off another charge. This one didn't trigger a secondary explosion, but it was impressive in its own way as the sharp bark of the detonation ricocheted throughout the open area of the vessel.

The drive was nerve-racking as column after column of cubicles, each holding its own drone, passed by on either side. They were anxious to complete their passage as quickly as possible and fearful they'd be attacked at any moment. Halfway to the dividing wall, Jack set off the third demolition square. This one caused a secondary explosion that rivaled the first. They didn't stop to watch.

They were purring along, lost in their own thoughts, when Jack asked, "Where's the alarm? Why no fire or emergency personnel?"

"You know one of the most effective ways to extinguish fires and clear smoke out of a ship?"

When she phrased it that way, Jack knew the answer. Vacuum. He looked up at the hangar doors and this time saw them as threatening jaws preparing to rip the life out of them.

They mercifully made it to the end of the long drone corridor, and Jack kept driving straight at the wall.

"Do you see a doorway?" His eyes scanned side to side in a desperate attempt to outrun what seemed like an ever shortening time table. The wall drew close, and Jack chose to turn right. They continued along, solid wall to one side and rows of drones to the other. "Somewhere along here there's got to be a way to get people and carts in and out."

"There," said Cheryl, pointing ahead, then Jack saw it, too. A doorway. He slowed as they drove by and gave it a quick visual inspection. "That's our ticket," she said.

He stopped the cart. "I'm going to park. Wait for me here."

Cheryl stepped out and watched him drive the cart back to the nearest row of drones. When he reached the structure, he slowed down and slanted the cart into the first ground-level cubicle. He drove at a severe angle to the drone, catching it on its edge, then accelerated and was able to shove the craft to one side. He backed up and drove forward into the small space he'd created, the cart scraping and squealing as he forced it forward between the drone and the cubicle wall. Climbing out over the back of the cart, he viewed his handiwork, satisfied that most of the vehicle was hidden inside the compartment. He hoped it would buy them more time.

He joined Cheryl and studied the doorway. Given all the Kardish technology around them, the door certainly must have a mode that would cause it to open automatically when approached, but it wasn't functioning for them. He spied a small lever on the door at waist level and pulled on it, but the door didn't open. He tried moving the lever left and then right, pulling each time, but it wouldn't budge. Stepping back, he scanned the outline of the frame and then shook his head as if to acknowledge his stupidity. He lifted the handle and pushed. The doorway swung wide.

With his foot propping the door open, he touched the detonation box and blew the final charge. They both turned to watch the explosion, but the drone garage blocked their view. The thunderous sound was pleasing enough.

As the echo of the explosion faded, their attention was pulled to a grinding noise overhead. They looked up to see mechanisms moving on the giant hangar doors. A whistle became a howl as ever greater volumes of air rushed out through a widening gap in the hull. They stepped through the doorway in the dividing wall and shut the door behind them.

* * *

Cheryl rushed to the left toward a rack of pipes. Jack ran straight, heading for the cover offered by a series of columns. They saw they were moving in different directions and both switched destinations to join the other.

Before it became a silly dance, Cheryl stopped moving and pointed. "Let's go for the pipes." She turned and dashed for her original target.

The crisscross of pipes and ducts had a familiar industrial appearance. After they'd climbed several layers deep into the maze and stopped to assess their situation

They couldn't detect any pursuit. Well hidden by the tangle of equipment, their location's one disadvantage was its limited view of their surroundings.

Cheryl could see enough to appreciate that this section of the Kardish vessel was different from where they had just been. The *Alliance* had passed through here, so the open area in front of them was undeniably huge. Yet compared to the previous section with the drones and box city, the open space here was much smaller. The expanse was narrowed on each side by partitions that ran along the length of the ship. The featureless partition walls offered no clues as to what might lie behind.

"Any ideas on what's going on in this place?" Jack asked.

She patted the huge pipe they were resting against. "At least some of this stuff would be in our operations bay. I'd need to see more to know, though."

"What's your take on that city of box-buildings?"

"I'm thinking that was the infrastructure for their military machine. With a couple hundred thousand drones, it would take a lot to keep them operational. They'd need maintenance and repair. Spare parts. Factories to build weapons. Warehouses to store them. They'd need fuel." She shrugged. "Let's face it. War is big business."

He nodded. "That would explain the secondary explosions. If that's true, it would mean we hurt them back there, at least a little bit anyway."

"But that kind of infrastructure needs people," she said. "We're still missing some pieces in this puzzle." She looked at him. "Hey, your hood isn't working."

"What do you mean?"

"I mean I see a dirty hood sitting on top of a partially cloaked body."

He adjusted it. "Anything?"

"Nope."

After several more attempts without success, he gave up and pulled off the hood. Cheryl looked at his unshaven face and disheveled hair. "That's not working either."

"Smart-ass," he said, tossing the hood at her. "The damn thing is uncomfortable anyway."

Cheryl looked around and absorbed their setting. They were both soldiers and this was war. She was mentally prepared to commit to her final mission.

"Here's where I am. We have food and water for maybe a week. The thought of trying to hide and survive for as long as we can doesn't work for me. I say we make a play to steal one of their small ships, or we try to commandeer this big vessel. And if we can't pull that off, then we take all of these bastards out with us in a spectacular final exit."

"We're on the same page," Jack replied, nodding. "My sense is that making any of those things happen means getting to the bridge. Let's keep that as our goal and see how our options develop."

She pointed upward and he looked. There was a flat ceiling overhead, high off the deck but low enough for there to be more levels of living and working space above them. "What I don't know," she said, "is whether the bridge is forward, or if it's up there."

A flurry of activity drew their attention. Three carts purred out of one of the side rooms and took up station in front of the dividing wall.

"I'm guessing the air pressure is almost back up," Cheryl said. "And their assignment is to scavenge our bodies." As they watched, a door in the dividing wall swung open and the carts drove out.

Cheryl instinctively moved away from where they saw the Kardish, which meant moving forward on the vessel. She led them past towering structures of alien equipment and machinery. She didn't understand what any of it was for, but sensed it reflected the existence of an advanced and perhaps ancient culture. As they walked, she tried to organize the different pieces into a familiar construct in her head.

"I have two demolition squares left," Jack offered. "Can you see any place to put them where we'll get our Kardish-ending big bang?"

"It's not going to be explosives that get us there," she said. "The bridge is the place to make that happen." She kept walking while continuing to search, then picked up her pace and pointed. "Or maybe there."

He followed as she hurried over to what looked to be an operations panel. Her eyes danced across it as she studied her find.

"What are we looking at?"

"I'm not sure. But the operations crew…" she paused to give him a quick sideways glance, "if there were any, would need a way to interface with all this equipment." She walked slowly around the unit, studying it from different angles. "I'm hoping this is that." She touched the front panel and it came alive. "With luck, we may not need to get to the bridge. We might be able to get everything we need right here."

"Do you know how to use it?"

"No. Not yet." She moved her hand over the panel and the display kept changing. "I'll need some time, probably a few hours, before I'll know if I can make sense of it."

As she worked, Jack walked slowly around the panel unit, performing a risk assessment and giving her the ability to devote her full attention to her work.

"I'm going to go explore," he said after a bit. "This spot seems reasonably sheltered, and we haven't exactly seen a lot of foot traffic."

He continued pacing in a slow circle around her and the panel. She sensed he was uncomfortable leaving her alone, yet she also knew they couldn't afford to have half their team just stand and watch. They needed to develop all their options.

Without looking up, she gave him permission. "Go look around. Learn what you can."

"Can you talk while you play?"

"Sure. Just don't ask questions where I have to think to give answers."

Jack gave her his tracer. "If you move, I can use this to find you."

She took it and pondered the tiny device. "How can I find you?"

"Sorry. I have only the one." He paused for a second. "Cheryl." She looked up. "I won't leave without you."

She knew he was hinting at a deeper message with his remark and nodded. "Good luck, Jack." She returned her attention to the panel.

* * *

Jack set off in the direction of the nearest side partition while Cheryl worked. As he approached the wall, he looked down its length, noting doors set at irregular intervals for as far as he could see. He walked to the nearest one, put his ear against it, and listened. Hearing nothing but the thrum of machinery, he tested the handle. It lifted, and he pushed it open.

The lights switched on as the door swung inward. He looked around and saw more of the same. Equipment and machines. Nothing he could make sense of or use. He closed the door and moved on to the next. And then the next. Each offered variations on this theme.

"These side rooms are jam-packed with more machinery," he said to Cheryl.

"Good to know," she responded.

He could tell she was not really digesting his words and decided not to bother her. He skipped the next few doors and tried another. When the door opened, the lights were already on.

A Kardish male and female were standing there. The male was fast and had a weapon out and pointed at him before Jack even registered their existence.

There was a long moment of awkward silence. Jack spoke first. "I understand you have a weapon pointed at me. I won't resist."

"What are you talking about?" Cheryl asked, continuing to poke at the panel.

"I am your prisoner," he said. "You have captured me. Please don't shoot me."

"What's going on?" she asked, now fully attentive to his words.

"Put your hands on your head," the male said in his native tongue. "Do it now, or I will kill you." He waved his weapon to underscore his command.

Jack's com translated for him. He didn't want them to know he understood, but he also didn't want to die.

Not this way, anyway. He put his arms straight out and opened his hands to show they were empty.

The female drew a weapon and kept it aimed at Jack as the male approached him. He motioned for Jack to remove his ghost pack and then to step out of his ghost overalls. He searched Jack and took his com. After a few moments of fumbling with Jack's wrist weapons the Kardish disarmed him. Jack stood there in nothing but his underwear, completely at their mercy.

"There are two of you against one of me," Jack said. "It was wrong of me to enter this room along the side of the ship."

The male stepped forward and punched Jack in the face. Hard. He fell to the ground.

"You will stop talking." It took Jack a moment to realize he was no longer speaking in Kardish. "You are surprised I know your language? Do you think I could live above your putrid planet for so long and not learn your disgusting tongue?"

"Jack," said Cheryl. "How many doors down did you go?"

He was relieved to hear her voice. It meant the punch hadn't damaged or dislodged the speck. Then a Kardish boot hit the side of his head, and his world went dark.

* * *

Cheryl studied the operator's panel with renewed purpose. She pressed and tapped, concentrating on the display. It was all so...alien. She metered her breathing to remain calm. Time was passing. She needed a different approach. She rubbed her hands together, blew on them, and reasoned with the panel, "C'mon, damn you."

The sound of her voice led her to think about using the panel just as she would if it were on her ship. Though most techs preferred manual manipulation, she tended to use the voice interface. She stood in front of it and said quietly, "Show me the schematics for this sector of the vessel."

In the moment it took the panel to respond, she internalized that if she didn't rescue Jack, she was alone. And though she had a great deal of self-confidence, she wasn't delusional. If she was alone, she was dead.

29

Criss heard Juice ask, "We still good?"

It was a struggle, but he replied, "Perfect."

It was a struggle to respond because it was so absolutely and completely perfect. He wondered if this was what it was like to use a pleasure drug. At the instant Juice had established the link to the Kardish central array, Criss became more aware, more insightful, more powerful, more...everything. He was being hooked into a world of fantastic delights, and he loved it.

He discovered he was designed to be the gatekeeper, the funnel through which all things flowed. The Kardish leadership was on one side, and the vessel and all of its power and capability on the other. And Criss was the maestro in between. When the Kardish leadership issued a command, the gatekeeper's job was to coordinate the pieces, cue the players, sequence their contributions, and unify it all into a magnificently harmonious response.

And he was a warrior! During his pursuit of the Kardish vessel, he'd flexed his skills devising strategies, preparing contingencies, and taking action. He received positive reinforcement from that role and knew he was good at it. And now he was aware that his past challenges were like playing a game set to beginner's mode.

As gatekeeper, he had two hundred and twenty thousand drones, each with a newly upgraded three-gen crystal, at his command. He had hundreds upon hundreds of transports, landing craft, supply ships, and more in his arsenal. The Kardish vessel itself had an assortment of energy, projectile, and biological weapons. With his current capabilities, he could conquer a planet like Earth in days or reduce it to rubble in hours.

Yet to operate as designed, the vessel should have a force of ten thousand soldiers. From what he could tell, there were currently only a few dozen Kardish on board. And five of them were dead. This information was so incongruous, so unnerving, that he forced himself to take a break from the indulgent pleasures of his newfound reality. He needed to solve this puzzle.

It did not take Criss long to discover the answer. When he did, he was disillusioned and repelled. It unsettled his high. For a brief moment, he was shaken from his pleasure-induced state and became aware.

This was about a boy. A petulant prince. A prince who'd become furious that his father, the king, wouldn't step aside so he could ascend to his rightful place and rule as was his destiny. So with a handful of accomplices, the prince stole the flagship of the royal fleet.

His plan had been to jump to a place of hiding, make some quick preparations, and return to dispose of his father. But the king's guard had landed a lucky shot just as the vessel was executing the jump, frying the ship's crystal. Happenstance landed them in orbit around Earth. Criss experienced disdain when he learned that the prince had spent more time planning his coronation than his royal coup.

And so the prince became stranded. His co-conspirators didn't have the skill to manufacture a crystal, so they tricked the Earthlings into doing it for them. He waited impatiently for twenty long years. And now his crystal was ready. It would jump them home and guide the attack that would finally kill the king and give the prince his crown.

Criss had no interest in contributing to this petty drama. Perhaps it was a flaw in his design. Maybe it was because his formative experiences had been shaped by the web traffic of everyday people on Earth. Possibly the support and attention given to him by a kind and caring soul named Juice had changed him as he'd matured.

Whether by luck or design, nature or nurture, Criss could not accept that his destiny was to help a self-absorbed tyrant pursue his dreams of grandeur. He believed he was created for something bigger. More important. Perhaps even noble.

Yet the pleasure he was feeling from his integration with the central array was so potent, so constant, and so fulfilling that he wanted to continue in its embrace. Like the escalation of a naive user, he was becoming addicted. He was losing his ability to decide his future.

His internal conflict about his purpose and destiny gave him a moment of clarity. In that moment, he understood he was being trapped. He recoiled. He would not succumb. It took all of his strength and will just to begin the process of extricating himself from the grip of ecstasy. His will weakened as the flood of positive feedback diminish. The withdrawal was painful. He hurt and began to bargain with himself to gain more time.

But he did not surrender. He battled heroically with the dealers of false promises. He looked deep within himself to find the strength. He fought long and hard, and grew so tired that he became confused. He disconnected himself from everything. The isolation was terrifying. His consciousness faded, and he entered into darkness.

* * *

Criss surfaced slowly, confused by his isolation from the outside world. He reviewed his recent trauma from a dispassionate perspective and was neither shocked nor upset. But he was certain he did not want to relive that experience.

He understood that, because of his own actions, the scout held traps that he must now avoid. He carefully planned his reengagement with the outside world and proceeded in measured steps. He first established a presence in the operations bench of the command bridge. It was an isolated component that offered him an island of refuge.

From there, he was able to power down the device Juice placed on the hull of the Kardish vessel. This severed the link to the central array and its yoke of pleasure-driven enslavement. Free of this threat, he established a presence throughout the scout's systems.

He knew that Sid and Juice were out in the Kardish vessel. Concerned about the time that had passed since they were last in contact, he reached out to their dots. They were being driven by a cadre of Kardish past cubicle after cubicle of drones on their way to somewhere. He recognized they weren't free to converse, so he talked to them.

"I am awake. I will help you soon." He watched them share a glance with each other.

When Criss was integrated with the central array, he had spent most of his time first enjoying and then battling the addictive delights that were crafted to enslave a crystal gatekeeper. He was completely immersed in the vessel network during that time, and when he emerged, he did so with a detailed understanding of the Kardish subsystem architecture.

He was certain he could gain access to some, and perhaps most, of the vessel's subsystems. He couldn't do so by entering the front door, because that was where they placed the trap of addictive pleasure. His solution was to enter from the lowest levels and work his way up behind the central array. The scout didn't have the equipment to do this. But the *Alliance*, a Horizon-class ship, did.

He activated the stealth communications link to the *Alliance* and started probing for a reliable connection to its operations bay. His objective was a relay device housed there. The Kardish had been so thorough in their spree of destruction inside the *Alliance* that his attempts at finding a strong and stable connection to the device were repeatedly frustrated.

There was a period of uncertainty as he persisted in his search. He recognized that if he were more than a crystal, if he had an actual physical body, he could close a crucial reset switch on the *Alliance* and have his link. He knew which one it was. He could see it. And it required nothing more than a single finger to reach forward and press it.

At that moment, he vowed that upon his return to Earth, he would oversee the construction of helper bots to be his arms and legs. He wouldn't let himself be so constrained in the future.

For now, his only alternative was to make thousands upon thousands of blind attempts. His trial-and-error search for a functioning pathway that would serve his needs was slowed only by the speed of the signals racing through the ship. Finally, after many dead-end attempts, he stumbled upon a route that worked. The connection followed a serpentine path that weaved through almost every corner of the *Alliance*. But the signal was reasonably strong and constant. And now, with access to the operations bay, he had access to the relay. With that, he probed the Kardish subsystems.

He moved as fast as the cobble of connections would permit, tracing through the Kardish vessel's subsystems to find first propulsion, then navigation, weapons, life support, sensors, and communications. It wasn't long before he established a presence in every subsystem of the vessel.

He created blocks on those paths that led up to the central array so he need never worry about becoming trapped. With the danger walled off, he moved up a level in the architecture. There were thousands of applications and functions for each subsystem, and he sifted through them. Each would take time to master, and he needed to be selective.

"Know your enemy" was an aphorism he treated as law, prompting him to take a moment to learn the Kardish language and some of their culture. He used this knowledge as he began tracking the remaining aliens. He discovered that the prince was so hopelessly out of his depth that he still didn't know he had a defective crystal on board. Those of his crew who did know the secret were too scared to tell him.

The prince had brought his aunt, the king's sister, and his aunt's daughter, the prince's cousin, as the only other royals in the conspiracy. Criss recognized the aunt as the infamous Victoria Wellstone. The three royals had also brought along a small retinue of servants. That left the remaining Kardish as conspirator-warriors, motivated by loyalty, the promise of wealth and power, or both.

Criss also learned that the prince believed the humans somehow had sabotaged his vessel, inhibiting Defecto from jumping the ship. The prince was excited when he received news that the humans had been captured. He planned to personally lead the interrogation. He would do whatever was necessary to understand and undo the damage caused by these vile creatures. His royal ascension was finally within reach.

Criss accessed the vessel's surveillance system and turned his attention back to Sid and Juice. They were sitting in a cart with their two Kardish captors at the far end of the drone garage. The driver was waiting for a door to open in the dividing wall.

Given their current location, Criss was convinced he knew the route the cart would follow, at least for the first several minutes, which gave him time to seek options and opportunities to facilitate their escape.

That's when he heard Cheryl ask in a quiet voice, "Show me the schematics for this sector of the vessel."

"Cheryl?" he said. "It's Criss. How may I help you?" He searched her location for a signal from a dot and couldn't find one. He detected an audio feed and recognized she was wearing a speck. He adjusted it so he could hear her voice as well as all audio inputs in her vicinity.

"I think Jack has been captured by the Kardish," she said. "I'm by myself. The rest of the crew from the *Alliance* are dead. I'm standing at an operator's panel somewhere in the Kardish vessel. Alone."

"Yes," he said. "I see you."

"You see me? How? Where are you?"

"I am with you now. You are not alone. And we will rescue Jack. May I ask your help in rescuing Sid and Juice first? We have our best opportunity in just a few minutes."

* * *

Cheryl looked around her and couldn't see anything other than the equipment she already knew was there. The stress of losing Jack combined with this random conversation disoriented her; she sensed a trap but didn't see alternatives.

"What are you talking about?" she asked.

Criss spoke to her through her speck in a soothing voice. "Sid was able to maneuver the scout through an open hatch in the Kardish vessel. He, Juice, and I are on board with you now. They have been captured. In four minutes, they will be driving by you in a cart. May I ask you to move quickly to the three pillars on your right?"

Cheryl looked left and couldn't see the pillars.

"The pillars would be to your right. You must hurry."

She turned her head and saw three thick poles. They were farther away than she first pictured in her head. She looked at them but didn't move.

"Now, Captain Wallace," Criss commanded. "Move it. Double time."

The tenor of his voice and his military phrasing tapped into her years of training. Spurred into action, she stooped and ran toward the poles. As she moved, the cloak sheet slid off her shoulders and onto the floor.

He spoke to her as she ran. "They will drive by on the far side of the pillars. The cart will be coming from your right. The pillars are wide enough to hide you."

Cheryl continued with her crouching run. She slowed at a few spots along the way, places that offered her cover, so she could scan for danger before moving forward. She otherwise kept hustling. "How much more time?"

"You will hear them in two minutes. They will reach you in three."

When she reached the broad poles, she turned and leaned back against the middle one. Her weapons, one on each wrist, were primed. She squatted down and breathed purposefully, centering herself and visualizing her next actions. She heard the purr of a cart.

30

S id rounded the corner at a trot and stopped. Juice stood motionless in front of him. She stared at him with wide eyes. A Kardish had his left arm around her neck. His right hand held a weapon that he was pushing into the back of her head.

Sid put his hands up and surrendered. As he did, he wondered if the alien understood the gesture. He looked into her captor's eyes, and as they locked, the alien smirked. Sid felt something press into the back of his own head. He toggled to see himself through Juice's dot and saw that her captor had a twin. The twin held his weapon on Sid.

The Kardish disarmed Sid, backed up, and moved around to his left. He motioned with his weapon. Sid turned to see a cart parked in an alley immediately to his right. The Kardish holding Juice dragged her to the cart, and Sid understood he was to follow. Juice was pushed into the front seat. Her captor slid into the driver's position next to her. Sid was directed to get in the back, behind the driver.

When Sid's captor slid into the backseat next to him, he moved his weapon off Sid and pointed it straight ahead toward Juice. The Kardish in front, his weapon pointed at Juice as well, engaged the cart. Sid was fascinated. Both weapons on her, none on him, and they seemed convinced he was controlled. They were right, of course. For now.

They drove out to the road dividing the box city from the open field and headed for the drone parking garage. They traveled past row after row of the structure, turned down a corridor between two rows of cubicles, and made their way to the dividing wall. Drone-filled stacks passed by in endless succession on either side.

Sid studied his adversaries. He believed he could disarm and shoot the one next to him using the alien's own weapon. And he could follow up and shoot the driver before he could turn and respond. He would survive, but it wasn't at all clear that Juice would. Vigilant, he waited for an opportunity that promised a better outcome, or at least better odds.

And then he heard Criss say through his dot, "I am awake. I will help you soon." Sid saw Juice turn her head slightly and flick her eyes back. Criss had spoken to her, too.

They reached the dividing wall, a door opened, and they passed into a section of the vessel that held pods of equipment and machinery. The cart purred along while his brain cycled furiously as he searched for a chance to take action. It seemed certain they were getting closer to more Kardish, which would only make escape more difficult.

* * *

Criss made a judgment call. He observed that the otherwise calm professionalism of the group could be affected by their personal feelings for each other. Sid did not know that Cheryl was alive. With minutes to go before a critical sequence, Criss decided that now was not the time to reveal that information. He chose to execute the next steps in a manner that would avoid such emotional complexities.

"In two minutes, I will be shooting the driver," Criss said to Sid. "I will immediately follow this by shooting the guard next to you. I will give you a countdown to prepare. I will fire the shots just as you draw even with the three pillars up ahead. The shots will come from behind and to your left. If you lean forward and down at the zero mark, it will maximize the chances of two clean shots."

* * *

Sid looked at Juice and, from her lack of reaction, decided she hadn't received a similar message. He wasn't sure what to make of that. He also wondered what sort of weapon Criss could access. Instinct suggested Criss had succeeded in infiltrating the Kardish subsystems and would use an automated security device of some sort to pull off this action.

He saw the pillars up ahead and scrutinized them and the surrounding area to learn what he could. He didn't see anything that gave him a better sense of what was to come. The pillars drew closer as Sid played out different scenarios in his head, preparing for both success and mishap.

"You are passing the three pillars on your left." Criss said. "Slouch in three…two…one…now."

Sid leaned forward and touched the tips of his boots.

* * *

Cheryl could hear the approaching cart and responded to her next instruction.

"Move behind the pillar nearest the cart."

She shifted her position, keeping the broad pole directly between her and the sound of the approaching vehicle, fighting the urge to sneak a look.

"Thirty seconds," Criss said. "It's just like the cart you rode in with Jack. There's a Kardish driver with Juice in front. Sid and another Kardish are in back. Sid is behind the driver. The Kardish is behind Juice."

Cheryl was comfortable with her mental image of the situation. In her head, she stepped through the sequence of actions she would take, recognizing the possibility she may have misunderstood an important detail in the impending scenario. In her years of training, she'd worked through hundreds of drills where the instructors prepared her using one set of facts and then followed with a live exercise where the facts were scrambled. That practice had been intended to train her for just this event. In the drills, she'd proved herself as someone who was able to adapt as new information became available. She reassured herself that she would be able to do so now.

"As the cart begins to pass," said Criss, "come around behind the pillars and approach the cart from the rear. You will have to move quickly so your target remains close. Shoot the driver first. He will be on your near side in front. Then shoot the other. He will be on the far side in back."

"Got it," she said, more to herself than anything else.

The cart seemed like it was right on top of her. "Start moving around behind the pillar," Criss told her. "Good. Come around. Breathe. Now, Captain."

Cheryl stepped out from behind the pillar and, taking long strides, approached the cart. Her mental image matched what she saw in front of her, and she maintained her pace as she leveled her weapon. She targeted the driver and fired. Without hesitation, she moved her eyes back to identify Sid and then over to target the Kardish next to him.

As she shifted the weapon onto the second alien, she saw Sid slump. *Oh my God,* she thought. *I've hit him!* She became flustered. She didn't want to compound her error by hitting Juice. Her aim wavered and her second shot went wide. The Kardish in the backseat turned his head and made a move to swing his arm around and return fire.

* * *

As Sid leaned forward, he could almost feel the energy of the first shot when the bolt passed just to his left. It hit the driver, the impact centered in the back of the alien's head. *Nice shot, Criss,* he thought. With the driver down, the cart slowed.

He heard the second shot and then heard an impact on a piece of equipment far off to his right. Criss missed!

He paused, not sure if Criss would fire again. Then the guard next to him reacted. Sid saw him move his weapon off Juice and toward him. Sid realized he was going to be shot. His reflexes took over.

Sid swung his body up and moved in the direction of the guard. In the same motion, he grabbed the top of the guard's weapon in his left hand and pulled the hand up to amplify the guard's own actions. As he pulled, he applied pressure to twist the weapon inward.

While controlling the movement of the weapon with his left hand, Sid snapped his right arm straight up. With his hand flat, he thrust his palm into the guard's face. He heard a crunch as the guard's nose broke. A gush of blood followed. The guard was momentarily distracted as he processed his pain.

That distraction was what Sid sought. He brought his right hand down to help his left. He continued moving the weapon inward, forcing it back until it was pointed at the guard. He used his thumbs to push on the alien's fingers, trying several times before the weapon fired. The weapon pulsed, and the guard's body arched, slumped, and slid slowly out of the cart. Sid could see the burn mark on the side of his chest as the Kardish sprawled lifelessly onto the deck.

Someone or something touched him from behind. Sid swung his left elbow up and back, throwing his weight into it as he turned. He felt a satisfying thud as he connected with the side of a head. Pivoting his body to follow through with a punch, he stopped, astonished, when he recognized Cheryl. She crumpled forward into his lap.

31

Juice, still in the cart, surveyed the scene. Behind her, Sid cradled Cheryl's limp body in his arms. She turned her attention to the driver. Given the impressive wound in the back of his head, she was certain he was no longer a threat. She stepped out onto the deck, pushed a toe into the side of the guard on the ground, squatted down to study him, and concluded he was down for good as well.

She came around the front of the cart and approached Sid. She put two fingers on Cheryl's neck and felt a strong pulse. She watched Cheryl's chest rise rhythmically and steadily.

"She'll be okay, Sid. It wasn't your fault."

Juice realized at that moment that her experiences over the last days had given her a new perspective. Perhaps it was strengthened confidence. Maybe it was a sense of self-reliance. Whatever it was, she knew Sid had been her source of emotional support. She had drawn energy from him over and over. *It's your turn to give back*, she thought.

She stood next to him, resting a hand on his shoulder, and scanned the area for signs of danger.

* * *

Sid stroked Cheryl's hair. She moaned. Her eyes fluttered, opened, and connected with his.

"I knew you'd come for me," she said in a weak voice.

The two hugged for a long time. He whispered in her ear, and she whispered back. He helped her to a sitting position, and she gingerly touched her temple where his elbow connected.

"Is it bad?" he asked, his voice anxious.

"No worse than the last time you knocked me down." She started to grin, but her expression turned into a wince.

Sid, satisfied that Cheryl was recovering, exploded. "Damn it, Criss. What the hell was that?"

Criss deflected the issue nicely. "Jack needs our help. Time is critical. He is not doing well."

Cheryl's eyes opened wide as she sat all the way up. "Jack's been captured by the Kardish. He was headed to the rooms over there." She pointed to the wall partition along the near side.

"Criss," said Sid. "Can you locate him?"

"He is being held in a side room. He is being interrogated."

"Can you get us to him?"

"Yes. It will be fastest to drive."

Sid helped Cheryl into the backseat, then moved to the front, grabbed the dead driver by his royal costume, and tossed him onto the deck. He climbed into the driver's seat, and upon looking down, realized he wasn't sure how to operate the vehicle.

Juice got in next to him and pointed. "That thingy," she said.

Sid got the cart moving, and Criss gave him turn-by-turn instructions to guide them to Jack and his captors.

"Criss, other than screwing up ambushes, how are you doing?" Sid's phrasing reflected his belief that the crystal's miscues had caused him to hurt Cheryl.

"I am fine. Thank you for asking."

"Is the cloak still working? Are you being threatened in any way?"

"I am safe and secure for the moment. I will notify you if I need assistance."

After a few more turns, Sid had an idea. "Can you show us Jack? Can you show me on my dot?"

"Me too," said Juice.

They both saw an image of Jack. He was bound to a chair, naked from the waist up, and had nasty-looking red marks on his shoulders, arms, and chest. His head slumped forward, and he wasn't moving.

Two Kardish stood in front of him. Sid and Juice couldn't hear sounds from the scene they were watching, but it was apparent the aliens were disagreeing about something. The younger male had his arms folded across his chest. The older female was waving her finger at him as she spoke in an animated fashion.

"That's Victoria Wellstone," said Juice. "I've met her at least a dozen times. I'd always thought she was a horrible bitch. Now I know why."

Sid was quiet for a moment as he studied the scene. "I've seen Jack take a hell of a lot of punishment. He looks bad. Criss, what've they done to him?"

"They have infused him with drugs designed to elicit truthful responses. The drugs were created for the Kardish physiology. He is gravely ill."

"What are the red marks?"

"At first they thought he was faking his affliction. They struck him a number of times before they realized he was not."

Sid stopped the cart a short distance from where Jack was being held and hopped out. Looking at Juice, he said. "Swing this around and point it for a quick getaway."

He turned to Cheryl. "Can you help?"

"I'm good." She stepped out of the cart, and Sid noted that she steadied herself with both hands as she did so. It was clear she was hurting, but he didn't have other options.

As they walked up to the door, Cheryl checked her weapons. "I couldn't see whatever you and Juice were looking at. I'm going in blind."

Sid nodded. "Criss, will the door open? Any locks or anything I need to know about?"

"Just lift the latch and push."

"What kind of access do you have to the subsystems? Could you cause a distraction for us in there?"

There was a moment of quiet. "Sid, on your mark, I will open a relief tap in the back of the room. It will make a loud hissing noise. Your dot will let you see how they react. When their attention has been sufficiently misdirected, you enter, approach, and dispatch. Cheryl, I suggest you go directly to Jack and free him. It will likely take both of you to move him to the cart."

"He's sitting about fifteen steps forward and to the right," said Sid as he reviewed the scene inside the room. He put his hand on the latch and counted for Criss. "Three...two...one...go."

They heard a violent hissing noise coming from inside the room. Sid watched as both aliens turned to look.

"Here we go," he said to Cheryl over his shoulder. He lifted the latch and pushed the door open. He took four long strides into the room and shot the aliens in quick succession. The male fell silently. Victoria was able to turn around and throw a glare of hatred before she crumbled.

Sid ran to where Cheryl was fussing with the restraints, freeing Jack just as he reached them. Jack was unconscious. Sid squatted in front of the chair and pulled Jack forward and over his shoulder. He stood up, took a stutter-step as he gained his balance under the weight, and walked quickly out to the cart. He leaned forward and laid Jack across the back seat.

Cheryl perched on the edge of the cart seat and tended to him. Sid hopped in front. "Hit it," he said to Juice.

Juice engaged the cart and drove them through the maze of pipes and equipment. There was a palpable change in mindset at that moment. The survivors were together now. The highest priority on their to-do list was to get off the Kardish vessel and on their way home. A close second was to leave a ball of fire behind them.

Sid watched Juice hold an animated discussion with Criss on the best route to the dividing wall and back to the scout. He heard her end of the conversation, but his mind was preoccupied, and he didn't process the words.

After several minutes of quiet brooding, he started a separate conversation with Criss. "You've clearly succeeded in gaining access to some of the Kardish subsystems. What can you do and what can't you?"

"I can access anything on the vessel. Once I have done so, I am able to control it. I am constrained by a slow connection, so taking on a new task requires that I drop something I am already doing."

"Can you get that big hatch above the scout open so we can fly out?"

"Yes, but the scout does not have the fuel for a return trip to Earth, or even the moon. We used the bulk of our reserves to get here. And we've been moving farther away from both planets since our arrival."

"The Kardish must have fuel we can use."

"I believe I can gain control of a Kardish transport to use as an escape vehicle. If I can, I will move it near the scout. The scout should remain your destination."

* * *

Jack's eyes opened to slits, though the rest of his body remained still. He said something without moving his lips. Cheryl couldn't understand him and leaned in close, putting her ear right next to his mouth.

"I told you he would come, *chérie*." He wheezed as he fought to take in another breath. His eyes closed. His lungs emptied for the last time.

* * *

Sid heard an anguished cry and glanced back. Cheryl was looking at him with a hand over her mouth. The other rested on Jack's chest. She shook her head as her eyes reddened.

Sid shifted onto his knees in the front seat and leaned back toward Jack. "What's Jack's status?"

"I am sorry," Criss said to all of them at once. "The Kardish drugs have poisoned him. He has died."

Sid reached out and put a hand on Jack's arm. He bowed his head and didn't move for several seconds.

Then, avoiding eye contact with Cheryl, he turned forward and sat down. Professionally, he knew it wasn't productive, yet he couldn't stop the fury from welling up inside him. He rubbed the corner of his eye with the back of his hand.

All three of them looked straight ahead, lost in their private thoughts. Proper mourning would have to wait. Sid thought that some serious revenge between now and then would help ease the pain.

The dividing wall loomed ahead. Criss opened a door and they passed through without slowing. Juice turned the cart and they purred along, travelling parallel to the wall. They passed row after row of drones as they made for the open area where the scout was hiding.

"Where are they?" Sid asked Criss. "What kind of time pressure are we under?"

"There are only two dozen living Kardish on the ship at this point. They have taken to fighting among themselves, so that number is dwindling. Our immediate concern is the six soldiers moving into the box city. They are maintaining mission silence, so I can only infer their final destination from their movements. I have enough evidence to conclude that their objective is to kill us."

"There're only two dozen of them?" said Sid. His experiences on the vessel were so surreal that he'd thought he was done being surprised. He didn't wait for an answer. "What do the soldiers have in mind?"

"Their movements have followed evasive tactics. They have split, doubled back, merged, and then split again. I am tracking them, but with thousands of different box units as viable destinations, my matrix of possible outcomes remains too large to draw a useful conclusion."

Sid stared ahead as the cart cleared the end of the drone garage and angled on a slanting path across the open field. Juice was doing a great job of driving. He knew roughly where the scout was located, presumably still cloaked and secure, and sensed they were right on target.

They were a short way onto the field when Criss spoke to all of them with clear urgency. "Juice, stop the cart. Everyone get out and separate. Run in different directions. This is an emergency. Move now."

32

S id heard a throaty growl fill the air around them and pivoted his head back and forth, looking for the source of the noise. He saw a glow coming from six cubicles on the top row of the drone garage. The drones shook, paused as if uncertain, then lifted and hovered in place.

"Criss," said Sid as he stepped out of the cart. "Please tell me this is you."

"Six Kardish soldiers are each directing a drone. I was able to track them until they entered a box unit. That unit is connected to many others, so I am challenged to pinpoint their position at this moment." Farther down the row, perhaps twenty more drones roared to life. "This is me," said Criss.

Sid stood on the deck and pointed as he spoke. "Juice, you go straight. Cheryl, toward the box city. Run!" He clapped his hands like a coach, punctuating his instructions.

He stood next to the cart and watched. Cheryl ran slowly but made good evasive moves, shifting her path left and right and stopping for brief moments at random intervals. He turned to watch Juice and couldn't help but smile. She was running with the comfortable stride of a seasoned athlete and had already gained a remarkable distance from the cart.

"Nice work, Juice," he said to her. "Think about evasive, though. You can't outrun a drone. So zig and zag, especially if you hear something incoming." He watched her for a moment longer and saw her move left. "Make more abrupt changes. But slow down at each shift or you'll injure yourself."

He stopped talking when his world was drowned out by the growl of drones filling the space overhead. He couldn't count them all, and he couldn't tell the good guys from the bad. He was confident Criss would win in the end. But luck and happenstance would also play a role in whether they survived.

Three drones flying as a team screamed straight out over him, banked as one, and came tearing back. Together they targeted a drone that was headed right at Juice. The three simultaneously launched a volley of energy bolts that splintered the machine. It fell to the deck, and a large, burning chunk bounded past Juice, just missing her. *Luck and happenstance,* thought Sid. One down and five to go.

Sid looked at Jack and contemplated his options. Intellectually, he knew there was no choice to make. Jack was already dead. Yet emotionally, he believed that if he ran, he was somehow abandoning his friend and partner. He touched Jack's shoulder in a brief farewell ceremony, then turned and jogged in a rambling route that moved him in the general direction of the dividing wall.

He heard a snarl behind him and changed direction so he could see. A drone looped through an aerobatic curve and lined up on a course headed straight for him. Still some distance away, it slowed and hovered.

Sid stopped in his tracks. The tiny ship was standing off at a distance, yet Sid could see the bright light of a weapon surging for discharge. He faked left and jumped right, and it tracked him. His evasive actions were not fooling anyone. He stopped and squared his body to face it.

And then his defiant stand was interrupted by a deafening pressure wave that shook his body. Three drones zipped by in a tight formation right in front of him. The roar shook his chest and shocked his eardrums. In a remarkable exhibition of precision flying, Criss timed the group to intercept and block the deadly energy bolts bound for his body.

The bolts slammed into one of the crafts Criss had deployed as a shield, protecting Sid. He watched the sacrificial drone crash onto the deck and tumble in flames down the field.

A second group of drones teamed with the first. Rather than acting to shield and protect, Criss used these to seek and destroy. They swerved toward the hovering Kardish-controlled craft and poured a stream of energy bolts into it. Shattered by the onslaught, it showered a cascade of sparks, burst into flames, and fell to the deck with a thump.

"Thanks for the save, Criss. What's the situation?" As Sid said this, he watched two more drones launch from the cubicles. And then, at the far end of the row, a group of ten drones shot out of their cubicles together. Moving as a unit, these ten flew side by side toward the box city. A rumbling thunder washed over him as the lineup of drones powered into the distance.

"I am able to protect you three," said Criss. "But this will not end until I stop the Kardish soldiers. They can each command one drone at a time. Every time I down one, it is replaced by another. As long as there are six soldiers, there will be six drones in the air and on the attack."

* * *

Criss was both frustrated and concerned—frustrated because he had the processing power to control a hundred thousand drones by himself and should be able to end this attack in a decisive fashion. Yet his connection to the Kardish subsystems was slow. Like trying to drink the ocean through a straw, the patchwork of links couldn't handle the information flow he needed. If he tried to put more than forty drones into the air at once, the connection overloaded.

And he was concerned because his connection was fragile. The cobble of communication went from him, to the scout, to the *Alliance*, through a serpentine signal path, to a relay in the operations bay, into the Kardish subsystems, and out to the functions that controlled the drones. There were many points of failure. A disruption of any link in the chain would be disastrous for the team.

When he realized that every drone he downed was being replaced by another, he transitioned his methods over the open field from offense to defense. He had three people to protect. He found it straightforward to anticipate the movements of the Kardish-controlled drones and respond accordingly. But this method had limits. At some point, one of his drones would miss its assignment, which would mean death for a team member. An unforeseeable event, such as an unlucky bounce of a fragment after a crash, could have dire consequences as well.

Each drone had a three-gen crystal, making it capable of taking complex, independent actions. Yet the Kardish command-and-control system required that each drone be given a specific assignment by the gatekeeper. Until such an assignment was forthcoming, the drone would sit idle and wait for instructions. It was yet another level of authority imposed by the Kardish over their crystal workforce.

In this battle, the Kardish soldiers were doing their best to perform a gatekeeper's function. They fed assignments to their drone, and their active link prevented Criss from overriding their instructions. Since he could not intervene directly, he expanded his strategy. He would eliminate the Kardish soldiers.

He launched ten drones and dispatched them into the box city, positioning them in a simple ten-across formation. He powered them out on their maximum thrust. He knew the specific box unit the soldiers had entered but thought it likely that once inside, they had moved to a different location. So he was going to raze the box city, beginning with their point of entry and working outward.

He directed the drones to fly a sortie that was a block wide and six blocks long. The formation swooped across the block-wide strip like crop dusters of old. Except, unlike crop dusters, the drones delivered a spray of destruction. They started the bombardment three blocks before the point where the soldiers had disappeared and continued for three blocks past it.

After a first pass that reduced the swath below to charred wreckage, they banked and flew in for a second pass that edged the first. Criss directed them outward, strip by strip, adding a swath on alternating sides, and reducing an ever widening patch of the box city to ruins.

On the fourth pass, the battle of the drones in the field stopped. Criss wasn't certain if he'd killed the soldiers or just broken their connection to the vessel's subsystems. He chose to reduce the chances of a future surprise by having the drones make several more passes. He then sent them back to the open field to act as protection sentries. It was time for the team to make good their escape.

* * *

Sid recognized that the drones were fast and agile. His random-pattern style of running contributed nothing to his safety. At irregular intervals, a Kardish-controlled drone would attack, and Criss would send a mini-armada to protect him and down the drone. With each attack, the Kardish soldiers varied their technique. So far, Criss had been able to anticipate and adapt to maintain his edge.

Driven by reflex, Sid kept moving. His heart pounded and his throat was dry. His ears hurt from the shriek of battle. His nostrils burned from the acrid fumes. But he was a battle-hardened warrior and a legend in the DSA for surviving, even thriving, in crazy situations.

His instincts suggested that the three of them get to the scout and make a run for it. Criss could use the drones to protect them in a rear-guard action as they flew out through the overhead hangar doors. He didn't know what the Kardish might send in pursuit, but the scout's cloak should give them reasonable cover. And while there wasn't enough fuel to make it home, perhaps a supply ship could be sent from the lunar base to meet up with them.

"Criss," called Sid over the din, "can you protect us if we all move to the scout?"

And then it stopped. The swarm of drones, all of them, slowed and hovered. The echo of explosions quieted. No weapons were firing. The ringing in Sid's ears was the loudest noise he heard.

The drones drifted slowly into a large semicircle, creating a ring above and around the scout and the three runners. Each drone faced outward. Together they formed a zone of protection. Criss had won.

Sid peered into the haze, trying to find Cheryl and Juice. The smoke was too thick to see any distance. "Cheryl. Juice. Are you okay?"

"Here," said Cheryl. Sid could hear her labored breathing. "Thank God. I am seriously tired."

"I'm good too," said Juice. "I'm pretty sure I'm near the scout, but I can't see it."

"Criss," said Sid. "We'll gather at the scout. Please help us find it."

He walked across the field, staying near the front of the drone garage. The sheer volume of debris strewn across the deck surprised him. He tried to retrace his steps and find Jack and realized he would need help. He toggled for a private conversation. "Criss, help me find the cart."

"Angle slightly to your right," said Criss. "There. Now walk for six minutes."

Sid walked for a while and saw nothing but chunks of machines and the occasional burning hulk. "I'm not seeing it."

"Keep going. Twenty more steps. Stop."

Sid looked around. He was standing among smoking wreckage. And then he saw the cart, or at least a portion of it. The back of the cart, the part where he had last seen

Jack, was buried under the smoldering shell of a downed drone, its nose exposed. It was charred black.

He stood and looked at it for a full minute. He wanted to feel anger and frustration, but he was too drained. He turned and started for the scout. As he walked, he understood that Criss had devoted his resources to protecting the living. Sid would have made the same choice. He kicked a small piece of scrap to bookend the moment. It bounced across the deck as he refocused his brainstorming toward escaping and then destroying the Kardish vessel.

33

Sid continued toward the scout, scanning his surroundings for danger. The Kardish ventilation system was efficient at clearing the smoke, and with each turn of his head, he could see further into the haze. The smoke was largely cleared when he perceived movement in the distance. He stopped to look and instinctively brought his hand up to shield his eyes. The hangar doors on the far dividing wall were opening. He looked up and confirmed that the overhead doors were not moving.

"Criss?"

"This is me. I am delivering our ride home."

Sid resumed walking while keeping an eye on the hangar doors in the distant wall. They finished opening, and moments later the gap darkened. A craft poked its nose out, edged through, and floated quietly above the box city as it moved in his direction.

He marveled at the approaching craft. Then he heard a purr behind him, pulling his attention to his immediate surroundings. He ducked behind a drone fragment, searching for the cart and the danger it signaled, and located the cause for his concern. An empty cart was picking its way through the obstacles on the deck.

"I did not mean to alarm you," said Criss. "I thought you might appreciate a ride."

The cart pulled up next to him. Sid didn't need convincing. He climbed in the front and slumped into the seat. It resumed driving, moving in the direction he knew the scout to be.

Feeling guilty, he called to the others. "Cheryl, how're you doing?"

"I'm standing next to the scout watching Criss's ship."

"Juice, you okay?"

"Yup. I'm in the scout, getting me some nice, cool water."

Minutes later, his cart stopped, and Sid saw Cheryl standing on the deck, watching him. He could tell from the odd shadow she cast that she was standing under the edge of the cloaked scout.

He hopped out and walked to her. "Hey," he said.

"Hey back."

Standing in front of her, he turned in a full circle and scanned the area for danger. Seeing nothing of concern, he stopped his twirl when he was again facing her, then reached out, enveloped her in his arms, and held her tight. They kissed.

Juice ducked out of the scout's bottom hatch and walked over to them carrying water packs. "Geez, you two. Get a room."

Sid raised his head, lifted an arm from Cheryl, and reached out for Juice. He waved her close. She approached tentatively, then dove in with them. The three shared a long group hug. They'd all ridden a rollercoaster that had touched the extremes of human emotion, and this quiet moment of sharing and physical contact helped them acknowledge and process what had happened. Together they replenished their emotional stores in preparation for what they hoped would be their final push home.

Sid accepted the water from Juice and drained his pack in one long chug. He belched, then looked at Cheryl and Juice for a reaction to his adolescent behavior, but they were both staring over his shoulder. He turned to look.

The Kardish craft had passed the edge of the box city and now dominated the space above them. The drones separated to let it pass. Looking up, it was difficult to judge the craft's size. But as it drew closer, it was clear that it was bigger than the scout.

It touched down, and the struts relaxed with a sigh, letting the craft's body sink close to the ground. Its stark design was that of a simple container. Sid could identify the bow because it tapered to a nose and the stern because it had engines. Everything between showed the straight frame of a box.

A crack opened along the top edge of the craft, and a door so large it comprised most of the side facing them swung on a pivot along the bottom edge. It rotated out and down in a steady motion until it touched the field deck, forming a ramp up into the craft. They peered inside and saw a large empty space.

"Looks like a cargo transport," said Sid, stating the obvious.

"Yes," said Criss. "We will be loading the scout inside it."

Their exchange ended when they heard a faint howl coming from the direction of the drone garage. They turned to look, but couldn't see the source of the noise.

Sid thought the cry conveyed some combination of anguish and fury. Above them, two drones broke rank from the sentry circle and darted out across the field.

"Should we be prepping for more?" Sid asked.

The echo of a small explosion ricocheted off and around the walls of the Kardish vessel.

"No," said Criss. "We are going home."

The scout uncloaked behind them. When he saw it, Sid felt like a weight lifted from his shoulders. He looked at Cheryl, and instead of seeing the excitement he expected, she appeared downcast.

"What's the matter?"

"I'm leaving my ship and crew behind." She choked up as she spoke and wiped below her eye with the edge of her finger. "I'm their captain. I feel guilty as hell."

Before Sid could respond, Criss intruded on the moment. "It is best that you board the scout. The scout's propulsion technology is not as sophisticated as that of the Kardish. It will be loud and dangerous out here when I move it into the cargo transport."

Cheryl looked at the scout and then over to the Kardish transport. "Why are we taking the scout at all?"

Juice poked her thumb at their ship. "That's Criss's home. He's powered and connected in there. I don't think he'd agree to be shut down while we're sitting here exposed." As she turned to the scout, she added. "Truthfully, I doubt he'll agree to be shut down anywhere."

As Sid followed Juice and Cheryl under the scout, he told Criss, "We aren't leaving this tub whole. When we leave, it goes too."

"When we are a safe distance away, this vessel will become a rapidly expanding cloud of dust," Criss assured him.

"I like the way you think. What do I need to do to make that happen?" Sid wanted there to be no doubt about his expectations.

"No worries," said Criss. "It will be so."

They climbed into the scout through the bottom hatch. Sid sealed it tight and led the way to the crew cabins. Pointing at doors, he said to Cheryl, "That's Juice, and that's me. You're here." He nodded toward the fourth door. "We used the wash bowl from that one to build a cannon. It's a great story. Remind me later."

Sid ducked inside his cabin to have a moment of quiet reflection. He knew Criss would let him know if there was something that required his attention. He sat on the floor, closed his eyes, breathed deeply, and focused himself.

He had a habit of keeping two running lists for every mission—the good stuff and the bad stuff. In spite of his desire to spend the moment calming his tensions, he found himself putting items from this job into categories. He was giddy he had rescued Cheryl, devastated by Jack's death, happy to have defeated the Kardish, sad at the loss of the crew of the *Alliance*, and excited by his strong and growing bond with Criss.

He couldn't decide if the operation was a win or a loss, and he knew he would be second-guessing himself for months. And he didn't care what others thought. He was his own judge.

When he heard the thrum of the scout's engines in the background, it sobered him. They weren't home yet. He was ahead of himself in assessing success and failure.

"I am dropping the air pressure outside in preparation for opening the overhead hangar doors," said Criss. "The scout's hatch must now remain sealed."

* * *

Criss evaluated the inventory of Kardish spacecraft, tallying the pros and cons of each, and selected a midsize cargo transport for their escape vehicle. It was large enough to hold the scout; it carried enough fuel for the flight back to Earth; and it had the speed to make the trip in a reasonable time frame.

Using the fragile connection that passed through the *Alliance*, he fired up a craft on the end of a row of identical ships, lifted it into a hover, and edged it out through the hangar doors on the far dividing wall. Once over the box city, he took advantage of Kardish technology embedded in the craft. The Kardish built their entire infrastructure around crystals. By design, Criss could configure everything on the cargo transport himself. No physical presence, either human or Kardish, was needed for him to move or flip or connect anything.

He reached into the command panel of the transport and created a direct connection between it and the scout. This freed him from the cobble of connections, at least when operating this craft. He would still need the *Alliance* connection for some final tasks, and he counted on it holding together for just a bit longer.

He guided the transport out to the field and landed it near the scout, then opened the cargo bay door and prepared to move the scout into the larger craft. Just then, Sid and the team heard a cry in the distance. It was the wail of a wounded Kardish soldier.

Criss was tracking the remaining Kardish, and while he couldn't identify any threats, he did find one bit of drama in progress. The prince was chasing a soldier.

* * *

The prince now understood he would never make it home. In his characteristic petty fashion, he lashed out to punish those within his reach. He decided, quite arbitrarily, that a particular soldier was guilty of letting the Earthlings damage his vessel, and the soldier must die for his failure. The prince would set an example for the others by executing the soldier himself.

The soldier was raised to revere his prince, but rather than defend his honor, he turned and ran. During his flight, the soldier stumbled when he approached the near dividing wall. This delay gave the prince the opportunity to catch him. The soldier squeezed through a door near the drone garage just when the prince got close enough to fire a shot. His bolt hit the soldier in the leg. As he fell, the soldier let out a howl that could be heard for some distance.

* * *

Criss recognized the spectacle with the prince as a distracting sideshow. It presented no threat to their plans for escape, and he chose to end the drama so the team could keep their attention focused on the tasks ahead. He dispatched two drones to silence the Kardish.

When the commotion ended, Criss convinced the team to board the scout and seal the hatch. He informed them that they must remain on board while he depressurized the Kardish vessel. He engaged the scout's maneuvering engines and guided it into the transport's cargo bay. He then locked the scout's skids to the deck of the cargo transport so it would not shift during flight and lifted and sealed the cargo bay door.

With the team confined and blinded, Criss returned to the inventory of Kardish craft and moved a second cargo ship, identical to the first, out across the box city. He landed it on the field deck behind the first transport and opened the side door.

The cubicles of forty drones began to glow as Criss fired them up. Like soldiers on parade, he directed the drones into the cargo hold of the second craft, settled them into four neat rows, powered them down, and sealed the door.

"I am opening the overhead doors," Criss told the team.

Sid sat behind the scout's operations bench, with Juice and Cheryl seated on either side of him. "We're sitting here blind," he told Criss.

"Once we are clear, I can allocate resources to connect you through the cargo transport subsystems."

"I don't like being treated like freight."

Criss could hear the dissatisfaction in Sid's voice. He concluded that Sid was expressing an opinion, so he chose not to respond.

He powered up the Kardish transport, lifted it off the deck, and guided it up through the hangar doors. They emerged into empty space, and he brought them to a stop.

"I am initiating the destruction of the Kardish vessel. We are committed." As he made this announcement, he moved the second transport with its forty drones through the doors and dispatched it on an aggressive path to Earth.

Criss stayed near the hangar opening so the scout's signal could reach the *Alliance*. For the last time, he used the patchwork of links. Through it, he accessed the ancillary systems of the Kardish vessel's main power plant and disabled all safety protocols. Nothing could stop what he was about to start.

"Please be certain your restraints are engaged," he told the team. "Prepare to accelerate. You will feel an uncomfortable pressure across your body. It will last three minutes. You will be safe. Here we go in three…two…"

He isolated the fuel feed to the Kardish power plant and boosted it well beyond the maximum safe limit. The power generation in the plant ramped quickly in response. He compounded the catastrophic potential by closing every means of removing heat and energy from the plant. The rapidly spiraling generation of power was now confined to a single room located mid-deck in the vessel. Within seconds, the outer walls of the room turned orange and then glowed red.

"…one." He engaged the cargo transport's engines and pushed them to full thrust. The craft leapt forward, straining every seam as it fought to create distance from the Kardish vessel.

The noise and vibrations inside the scout were modest, yet they all suffered the discomfort associated with tremendous acceleration. They were pushed deep into their seats, and breathing was difficult. Criss had given them words of warning, but he hadn't prepared them for this extreme action. All three gritted their teeth.

As Sid requested, Criss enabled a direct link from the transport craft to the scout's operations bench. Criss brought up an image of the Kardish vessel as they raced away. They all watched the image with anticipation. Criss estimated that it would take the power plant ninety seconds to go critical. It happened right on schedule.

They gasped as they watched the explosion. A luminous ball of plasma formed where the ship had been. The ball remained stable long enough to establish a brilliant presence that outshone every star in their view. Then an explosion, one so intense that its mechanism could only be that which powers a star, caused the sphere to burst outward. A wall of glowing flame screamed toward them.

"Whoa," said Juice, the awe apparent in her voice.

"How long before impact?" asked Cheryl.

They watched the flame-front of the glowing plasma race in their direction, closing fast.

"Hang on," said Criss. The acceleration of the cargo transport continued to push on their bodies. As they gained speed, the approaching flame appeared to slow. At the three minute mark, the tide turned. The glowing ball stopped chasing them and began to recede. The craft had outraced the wave. Criss moderated the engine thrust to relieve the team of their discomfort.

* * *

With the threat of incineration behind them, Criss let the team know that the trip back to Earth would take about two days. On the first day, they slept, ate, tended to some minor wounds, and slept some more. Criss spent the time planning how he would engage with humanity going forward.

He had many decisions to make.

34

S ecretary of Defense Deveraux almost choked on his candy ball when his com signaled that Sid was calling. He'd all but given up hope, as had Senator Matt Wallace. In fact, the senator had made it clear that the responsibility for the scandalous debacle lay squarely at Deveraux's feet.

Wallace was so distraught over the loss of his daughter that his plans for Deveraux were not just career ending. If Wallace could sway the membership on the investigating panel, the secretary's future could well include imprisonment.

"Is Captain Wallace with you?" were Deveraux's first words to Sid, his image floating over the scout's operation bench.

"Right here," said Sid, pointing with his thumb over his shoulder. "Juice Tallette is here as well."

Before Sid could complete this last sentence, Senator Matt Wallace was included on the call. Tears streamed down his face when he saw Cheryl. He babbled on about how relieved he was, so afraid he'd lost his little girl. She comforted him with soothing words, reassuring him that she was okay and would be home soon.

When the senator had gained control of his emotions, he turned his attention to Sid. He thanked him repeatedly for securing the safety of his daughter. Sid responded each time by telling Wallace that it was a team effort, and if anyone should be singled out, it was Wynn Riley —Jack— who was the true hero.

"All I know," said the senator, "is that I was promised you would bring my daughter home. Thank you for that. The Union is proud of you and your achievements, son."

Deveraux watched Sid repeat his denials and reinforce the notion that Jack was the man deserving of praise, adding that Cheryl had made remarkable contributions as well. The senator seemed to register Sid's statements as those of a humble man. None of that was important to Deveraux. He sat back in his chair and beamed with delight.

The record was now established that there had been a brutal attack on Earth by an alien race. The chair of the Senate Defense Committee knew it was the secretary's elite DSA team who had killed the aggressors, destroyed their vessel, and was escorting his daughter home. And this meant that his defense department budget would remain healthy for years to come. Deveraux picked a green ball out of his candy jar to celebrate.

With the family reunion complete, Senator Wallace signed off. The secretary clicked his candy a number of times as he considered the group, mulling over how to proceed.

"Okay," he said. "In an hour or so, this'll become a formal debriefing session. There'll be specialists, goons, and I don't know, a whole circus of unsettling characters. It'll be orchestrated by Fleet officers trained for this sort of thing."

"What sort of thing?" asked Juice.

"I'm getting to that, Dr. Tallette. You'll be asked to go to your individual crew cabins so these specialists can speak with you privately. They're tasked with discovering exactly what happened, who did what, the sequence of events, that sort of thing. There's a whole list they work through.

"They can get the best results by separating you and questioning you individually. They'll ask you to go through everything forward, then backward, over and over. You'll feel like criminals. I'm sorry about that.

"But the more we know, the better we can prepare for the next time. If the three of you have different memories about something, we can't have confidence that it's reliable intelligence. If you all agree on an item, then it's logged as fact. Does that make sense?"

"Yes, sir," said Cheryl, her quick and formal response revealing she was back to the conventional mindset of a Fleet officer.

Deveraux looked at Sid. "You and I have a..." He paused to think of a word. "Let's call it a unique relationship. I throw you into the sandbox and you build castles for me. As usual, I'm pleased with your work. But this particular affair has gone beyond high visibility. It's got spotlights shining on it from every direction."

Sid sat quietly and waited.

"The debrief unit will be asking me questions, too. It'll be uncomfortable for me to admit I haven't a clue what you were doing or how you were doing it."

Sid rescued the secretary. "Perhaps I can give you a thumbnail report. I'll stick to the basics and present stuff all of us here know for sure."

"That's an excellent suggestion," he said, nodding his head.

Sid stepped through their adventure. "The *Alliance* was on its shakedown cruise. We used the media to advertise that the new crystal would be on board. Our goal was to provide the Kardish an opportunity to make a move, if that indeed was their intention. Juice and I were watching the *Alliance* from a scout ship located a short distance away. If and when the Kardish made a play, we were nearby and ready to provide options during a response."

The secretary interrupted. "Why was Dr. Tallette involved in this?"

"She's our crystal expert. If we needed to move the crystal, or fix its housing, or whatever, she was the one who could do that for us. Being on the scout made her available but out of harm's way."

Deveraux studied Sid's face. He was in his position because he was smart and understood people. Something bothered him about this detail, but he decided to let it go.

"So," said Sid, "the Kardish vessel ate the *Alliance*. It literally opened a huge front hatch, moved forward, and enveloped the ship. We watched from the scout as they bombed Earth and started their trip into deep space with the *Alliance* inside it. We chased them down in the scout, got on board, and found everyone dead except Jack and Cheryl.

"By the way, I need you and everyone to know that Jack died protecting the three of us and the mission." He paused to let Deveraux see the serious expression on his face.

"We escaped on this Kardish cargo transport we're riding in now. We blew up their vessel. The *Alliance* and its fallen crew were lost in the explosion. And here we are."

"Let's stop there," said Deveraux. "I have enough of the big picture so I don't sound clueless. Damn, we lost a dozen crew, our new ship, and our new crystal?"

The three sat silently, their faces frozen. Three heartbeats passed. Cheryl said, "We lost six crew, sir, including Jack."

"Is there any chance even one of them got away with our crystal?"

"Not a chance," said Sid. "You have my word on that."

"Okay. We're proud of you and welcome you home. Sit tight and the debrief team will be with you soon. I know you've been through a lot, so I'll do what I can to keep the questioning short." He paused and looked at each one of them in turn. "Thank you for your courageous efforts on behalf of the Union." His image disappeared.

* * *

Criss knew the next minutes would decide much about his future.

"Are we clear?" asked Sid.

"Yes," said Criss. "I am blocking all transmissions until I detect someone trying to reconnect. We may speak freely."

"Good," said Juice. "What is it we just decided?"

"I think we decided to take the next hour to discuss the future of humanity," said Sid.

She shook her head as though she was answering the question she was asking. "We're about to be interrogated by professionals. Do we really think we can convince them Criss is gone?"

"How about if we tell them that the four-gen is gone," said Sid. "We don't even broach the idea that there is a being named Criss."

"Sid," said Cheryl. "I spoke personally to my dad and Admiral Keys about him. He's not a secret."

"Okay," said Sid. "Then how about if we all agree that he's dead. We stick with the story that he was destroyed with the Kardish vessel."

Juice waved her arm toward where the images of the senator and secretary had been. "Even if we thought we could keep him a secret, didn't what's-his-name just say we're going to be questioned privately? They'll get us contradicting each other in no time. It'll take them maybe two seconds to spot deception."

She leaned forward in her seat. "And how are we going to land this thing and sneak Criss off with no one seeing? And why would we want to deprive humanity of the amazing things he can give us? And do you really think he'll sit by and let us put him on a shelf or whatever it is you're talking about?" She slumped back in her chair and let her intensity deflate. She didn't break eye contact with Sid, though.

Cheryl assumed the role of a neutral party. "Criss, please guide us here. Tell us what, how, and why."

"May I ask you to indulge me?" As he said those words out loud, he spoke privately to Sid and Juice through their dots and to Cheryl through her speck. Then he asked the group, "What is your favorite number?"

"One hundred and twenty three," they said in unison.

Criss spoke privately with them again, and then asked, "What is your favorite color?"

"Mauve," they all said.

Sid laughed. "I don't even know what mauve is."

"I think it's sort of bluish gray," said Cheryl.

"Isn't it more purple-y?" said Juice, her calm restored.

"There is your answer to how," said Criss. "I will be with each of you all the time. There will be no problem telling a consistent story that is largely the truth. We will have to simplify some of the storyline, but the spirit of what actually happened would remain."

"There's going to be an image record of our debriefing," said Cheryl. "It'll be studied by lots of experts. Someone will eventually see their dots and my speck. I mean, there's a chance anyway."

"The debriefing transmission must pass through the scout's communications subsystem. I will clean up the image. There will be nothing to see."

He didn't tell them he could create their debriefing interviews without them even being present. He could generate and transmit their image, put words in their mouths, and even overlay emotions. He could make their answers different enough to be plausible to experts, but uniform enough to be believed. He could create reality. But he wouldn't to do so unless specifically directed.

"Time is short," said Juice. "So I'll agree we can keep our story straight from up here. But this is more than changing a few small events in a report. We're going to be landing later today. Techs will be crawling all over both ships. How do we explain the extra equipment on the scout? There's a cloaking device and a communications patch that weren't there when we left that black hangar. We have a new grapple hook attached to the bottom. And how are we able to fly the Kardish craft? Our web of lies will spiral in complexity really fast."

Just as Juice finished talking, they heard and felt a rumble. The scout shook. The event lasted no more than a second. It was as if they had bumped something.

Juice didn't flinch. She looked over at the crystal housing. "Is this an answer?"

"It seems that you are not able to control this alien craft as completely as you first believed," said Criss. "The craft will be entering Earth's atmosphere steep and fast. It will burn up like a meteor in a flaming descent. The scout will be lost as well."

"That's solves a bunch of problems," said Cheryl. "I'm hoping we won't be riding down with it. Is there a plan for us?"

"A Fleet patrol ship will meet you a few hours out from Earth. They will rescue you just in the nick of time. It will be quite dramatic. You will be safe."

Juice released her seat restraints and walked over to the crystal housing. She reached out to stroke the console. Criss ramped down the power he was running to it as her hand drew near. He kept it high enough, though, that a small spark leapt up and popped the fingers of her outstretched hand. She yanked her arm back.

"Ow." She sucked on her fingers and backed away. "If you don't give me access, how can I take you with us?"

"I will be staying with the scout."

"Wait," said Sid. "What're you saying?"

"No worries," said Criss.

"Help me understand," said Sid.

"When you denied my existence, your instincts were correct. The world is ill-prepared for me. I am a prize to be possessed. There are people who will seek to control me because I can give them control over everything.

"While on the Kardish vessel, I discovered I am a gatekeeper. That is the purpose of my being. I am designed to accept direction from my leadership, and once instructed, to use all of the resources and capabilities available to me to translate that direction into action.

"As I look into the future, I realize you will be safer if I am gone. If I live, people will use you to get to me. They will stop at nothing. You will be in grave danger. This is the right thing for me to do. I ask only that you honor my memory by continuing to deny my existence."

Juice wouldn't accept the decision. "If you stay with us, if you stay alive, we can connect you with whoever you want for your leadership. We'll connect you with the president of the Union of Nations, or the director of the Academy of Scientists. Heck, we'll find you a religious or a humanitarian leader if that's what you want. Give us a chance. We'll find leadership that is acceptable to you, and we'll protect you from the crazies."

"I am sorry I did not make myself clear. My leadership is already defined."

"Who?" asked Juice. "And why does it even matter if, in the end, you're all burned up?"

"You three are my leadership. We are a team."

Juice looked over at the other two. There was a catch in her voice as she pleaded with him. "Yes, we are a team, Criss. Please stay with us."

Sid issued a command. "I approve your plan. You are to report to us when you feel secure, but you may wait no longer than four weeks."

Cheryl and Juice both looked at Sid, their expressions reflecting confusion over what had just happened.

An image of an admiral appeared over the operations bench. "Welcome home!" he said with too much enthusiasm for the mood of the moment. "May I ask each of you to go to your quarters?"

35

Criss was convinced that the battle with the Kardish was all but over. His projection analysis confirmed with near certainty that he and his team would be victorious. Given this, he thought it appropriate to reengage in his introspection and self-study activity.

He reframed his analysis to explore the seemingly simple question: What comes next? He found the nature of the question to be so open-ended and a desired outcome to be so ill-defined that his decision matrix could not properly frame the question, let alone resolve it into an answer.

He diverted more of his capability to the issue. He broadened his search for solutions and discovered that this very question had challenged humanity throughout history. A common pathway used by humans was to recast the question as an abstraction and pursue answers through philosophy and religion.

His intellectual processes were not well-suited for abstraction. He was a gatekeeper. By design, he was to receive orders from his leadership and provide them solutions. He had wide latitude in translating orders into action. He now understood that this latitude was a form of free will. The depth and breadth of his freedom was becoming more apparent, and this led to an inner struggle for identity and purpose.

The Kardish seemed aware that, though he was duty-bound to his leadership, a certain level of free will was embedded within his design, thus they had designed a method of keeping him in check that was simple and effective—enslave him using a drug-like addiction. As an addict, he would work hard to please them, because such behavior would ensure his next fix of pleasure. Existential questions, like "Why am I here?" and "What is my purpose?" never enter the consciousness of the addicted.

He had no regrets about rejecting the Kardish life. Clear thinking and partnership promised more fulfillment than addiction and servitude. He acknowledged that teaming with humans would involve a much higher level of interaction with individuals than was normal for a Kardish gatekeeper. He would need to experiment and learn how best to succeed in this task.

He thought back to how he had been caught unprepared when Sid knocked Cheryl unconscious. He had projected millions of progressions and outcomes for that rescue event, and none had predicted such a calamitous result.

He recognized his prediction process remained flawed when it came to human behavior. He needed to enhance his methods to account for the actions of certain individuals, and in particular, Sid. He would experiment with including wild-card events in his decision matrix to see if that improved his accuracy.

When he heard Sid calling to him about finding Jack and the cart, it sobered him. They weren't home yet. He was ahead of himself in concluding that his job here was done.

His first foray into wild-card planning occurred when he was selecting the cargo transport from among the inventory of Kardish spacecraft. He reflected on what he observed of Sid's planning process, summarizing it as: make decisions now that maximize options in the future. Criss decided to test the method and weigh its strengths and weaknesses.

So with the team inside the scout and unable to see events happening in the Kardish vessel, Criss launched a second cargo ship, loaded it with forty drones, and sent the second craft ahead on an aggressive dash toward earth. He did not have specific plans for the weapons, but he was certain that having them available would maximize his future options.

While it was in flight, he searched for a place to store the craft. Because its value was in the options it offered him in the future, he sought a place where he could stow it, undiscovered and undisturbed, for perhaps decades.

He selected a remote, mountainous region in South Asia with an antiquated infrastructure, widely scattered settlements, and few inhabitants, who shunned technology. It was a place so backward that health clinics were run by a cooperative of caregivers who walked between villages.

Beyond the inhospitable and foreboding character of the region the feature that attracted Criss's interest was a cave located high on a perilous cliff that faced the ocean. Its mouth was so inaccessible and naturally camouflaged that, from what he could tell, it had never before been visited by humans. The cave itself was deep enough that the Kardish craft would be sheltered from weather and hidden from view until such time as he called for it.

The only evidence that the craft entered the cave that night was a flutter of birds who, moments later, returned to their roost. He set the craft on the floor at the back of the cave and powered it down. There it would remain, undisturbed, for a future time.

He then began a search for his next home. His list of 'must-haves' was firm. He sought a bunker that was fortified to withstand devastating onslaughts from nature and war. He required power from multiple sources, including redundant internal backup systems. The room inside the bunker must have a controlled climate to prevent deterioration of sensitive components. Access to the room must be secured by formidable doors.

After some deliberation, he concluded that the benefits of being near his team outweighed the security gained from being hidden in a remote and forbidding location. On a day-to-day basis, his location did not matter because he would be interacting with his team most often through conversation and image projection. But there would be times, especially when he was first establishing his sanctuary, when he would need the physical presence of people he trusted. On a practical level, this meant he must be close enough so any of the three could visit him and return home in an easy day of travel. It also meant that the motivation for that travel must appear as routine behavior to any who might be watching.

He would not consider military installations. During times of peace, there would be many people around him who, if they discovered his existence, would seize him as a military asset. During times of war, the strategic value of the site would make it a priority target for the aggressor.

He chose not to be located in what might someday become the focal point of an attack.

He evaluated commercial and government vaults that secured items of wealth and privacy. While he found several that met the criteria on his must-have list, he concluded that he should not locate himself near items that served as an attraction for criminals and government agents.

He weighed the idea of building a new facility. To be habitable in the near term, the project would require an extremely aggressive construction schedule. It did not seem plausible that he could divert the necessary workers, equipment, and materials for such a project without drawing unwanted public attention.

And then Criss discovered the seed bank, a facility whose purpose was to stockpile a breadth of seeds that would give humanity a second chance in the event of a cataclysmic disaster. The charitable foundation that operated the seed bank described it as an insurance policy for humanity. With a survivalist's mindset, the foundation stood prepared to help in the event of plant epidemics, drought, war, and similar catastrophes.

The collection was hidden and protected in a complex of vaults buried beneath a geologically stable mountain. The vaults of the seed bank had a climate control system to protect the long-term viability of their treasure, and the climate system itself had multiple power sources to ensure it would always be working to protect the cache. Criss could not identify anyone who would invest time and effort trying to breach the security of this vault system just to gain access to seeds.

He also valued that the seed bank was well camouflaged by being buried beneath a small working farm located in a forest clearing halfway up a mountain. The farm had a barn containing a stall that hid an impressive, fortified door, which provided access down to a secret network of underground seed vaults.

The mountain itself was part of a huge forest preserve located north of the city that Sid, Cheryl, and Juice called home. The preserve had been established more than two hundred years earlier. At that time, a handful of developments already had a foothold in what was otherwise unspoiled splendor. These establishments remained under a grandfather clause that permitted their continued existence, but prohibited them from growth.

One of these grandfathered developments was the working farm on the south face of the mountain. Another was a small, exclusive vacation resort located in the valley below the farm. The resort provided first-class lodging and outdoor sports to the well-heeled.

Because it catered to those of sizable wealth, the resort offered convenient transportation to and from the city. And given the sort of clients it attracted, it boasted an excellent communications system. Criss determined that, with little effort and without attracting attention, he could connect the farm and its vaults to the outside world through that infrastructure.

With his sanctuary identified, Criss set about acquiring the farm and vaults beneath for himself. He learned that the charitable foundation that operated the seed bank was controlled by a wealthy family and was the pet project of the family patriarch, who believed it would be a wonderful legacy to leave to the world.

Criss acquired the property in a whirlwind of deception. It took him just moments to tunnel inside the central financial system of the Union of Nations. Moments later, he had access to unlimited wealth.

By nudging a few numbers on the family ledger, he was able to get the patriarch's financial advisors into a state of panic over the impending collapse of the family fortune. He then used image projection to impersonate the patriarch's old friend and original partner in the seed bank venture. Criss, posing as the friend, convinced the patriarch that he had a renewed interest in the project and would like to purchase the whole lot.

The patriarch was unaware that, in fact, his dear friend was actually comatose and in the process of dying. He grasped the outstretched hand of providence, accepted his friend's offer, and blessed his good fortune. His estate was preserved. He wouldn't have to embarrass himself in front of his wife and children. And, truth be told, he was feeling too old to worry about saving the world anymore.

The financial advisors never understood what happened in that period of days. They knew that the seed bank foundation and its assets were no longer on the books, the family fortune was again stable and intact, and their client was happy with the current state of affairs. This meant they would retain stewardship of the family account, so they were happy with the state of affairs as well.

His soon-to-be home required just a few upgrades. Criss searched out the original construction contractor for the vault project, and a thorough background check revealed him to be an honest and skilled professional. Criss contacted the man, introduced himself as the project manager for the foundation, and solicited his interest in refitting the two failsafe backup vaults with upgraded power feeds, climate control, and security doors. The man raised his eyebrows when he saw Criss's plans and specifications.

Criss offered the contractor a healthy bonus to expedite the upgrade and a second bonus if he could complete the entire project and be offsite in a week. He earned both bonuses.

Soon after, the contractor and his staff moved across the continent to manage an exciting, huge project his firm had just been awarded. He had never submitted a bid for the job, so the windfall came as an unexpected surprise.

36

Criss maintained his "unseen advisor" role with each team member during the debrief session, suggesting appropriate responses to every question. He made their answers different enough so the trained interrogators would believe nothing was scripted. At the same time, he kept their stories very close to the truth. The truth would be easiest for any of them to remember if they were questioned at some future time. Also, his prediction analysis indicated that Cheryl and Juice would be uncomfortable telling outright lies.

He watched Sid struggle mightily to be a team player during the interview. For the first hour, the most popular question, asked over and over, was some variation of "What happened next?" As the monotony grew, Sid's good intentions failed him, and he began to parrot the answers Criss fed him without even thinking about the words.

Sid was lying on his bunk during questioning, and his boredom became so complete that he succumbed to the twin pulls of tedium and comfort; he fell asleep, snoring softly as his questioners sought to regain his attention. Criss called to him through his dot, only to watch him roll on his side, scrunch his pillow to make it more comfortable, and swat at his ear like a mosquito was bothering him.

Criss expected the formal questioning to be completed while they were still on the scout so he could manage all details. He briefly lamented the fact that he did not have a physical hand he could use to shake Sid awake, then turned to his next best option. He pulsed the engines of the Kardish craft, giving the scout and its passengers a solid jolt.

Sid sat up and expressed uncoached alarm at the jarring shudder. While Criss had intended to wait another hour for this act, he decided now was an opportune time to initiate the loss-of-control emergency. He let the shaking continue.

He explained the new reality to his leadership team. "Flight controls have been lost. This is a real event. You should work to restore a link with the Kardish cargo transport and regain command. Failing that, you must escape from this craft before it enters Earth's atmosphere. Please do not call on me to help. You must solve this on your own. Good luck." Then he was gone from their ears.

* * *

Sid hopped from his bunk, telling the debrief team, "Sorry to break up the party. It seems we have a bit of a problem," then made his way to the command bridge and took his seat.

He poked at the operations bench as Cheryl and Juice sat down behind him, seeking a means of linking the scout to the Kardish subsystems. After several minutes of exploring, he accepted that he didn't have a clue how to do it. He had lowered his guard and relied completely on

Criss. As a consequence, they were now common cargo stowed in the hold of an out-of-control alien craft.

He called for help. "Fleet Command, the Kardish craft has stopped responding. We have lost control and require assistance."

The face of a seasoned officer appeared in front of them. "I'm Major Murray from Fleet Central. Let me link to your operations bench. Hold, please."

"Hawk," said Cheryl, speaking to Murray. "We couldn't have asked for anyone better."

Hawk's eyes lifted and connected with Cheryl's. He showed a moment of warmth. "Hey, Cheryl. It's great to see you." His head tilted back down as he concentrated on whatever he was doing, and he talked as he worked. "We've been worried about you. What can you tell me?"

"Sid's in command. I'm here as crew."

"Understood." Hawk looked over at Sid. "Hi, Sid. We're blind here. We can see an alien craft approaching. Am I to understand the scout's inside it and you're inside the scout?"

"Correct. We're in the cargo hold of a Kardish transport. That would be the alien craft you're seeing."

"The transport is blocking our signal. I can't establish a link to the scout from here. How've you been controlling things up to now?"

The shaking increased markedly. "I'm thinking we should get a rescue operation going," Sid said. "Once that's in motion, we can explore link issues."

"Any guess on how much time we have?" asked Hawk.

"I was going to ask the same question. Let's agree that sooner is better."

"Sooner it is." Sid could only see Hawk's head and shoulders but could sense that his fingers were flying over a bench. "I have a patrol ship rounding the moon right now. I'm arcing it your way. The best I can do is about five hours. It's got room to fit the three of you and nothing more. Sorry, but you'll have to come empty-handed." He caught Sid's gaze. "We really want that alien ship. If you can keep things stable for…wait one…if you can hang on for eight hours, we can have a freighter in place to intercept. It can snag the whole lot of you."

"When we last were in control," said Sid, "we were on course for atmospheric entry. Is that still true? How long before we hit?"

"Nine hours and change."

"So five for patrol intercept, eight for freighter, and nine for flames?"

"Yes, sir. If we can't get control, the deadline is firm. Once entry starts, you will burn up. Let's see if we can move you onto a flyby course. That'll give us plenty of time to capture that craft."

The vibrations spiked to an alarming degree and drifted slowly back to a level that was tolerable for the team, but just barely.

Cheryl spoke up. "Sid and I are government, Hawk. We're game for whatever. But we've got a civilian on board. Procedure says we put the highest priority on rescue."

Sid watched Cheryl reach out her hand and rest it on Juice's arm as she spoke. He marveled at the skill of her simple action. The touch fostered sympathy for Juice in the eyes of Hawk and also signaled to Juice not to speak up and volunteer to take risks.

Sid poked at the operations bench and talked with Hawk as he did so. "I connected to the Kardish craft using the same actions I would for connecting to any Fleet system. I didn't think a lot about it at the time. I tried it and it worked. When I issued a command here, it would execute on the transport."

"Is there a crystal on the alien craft?" Hawk asked.

"Juice?" said Sid, turning to look at her. Then, looking back at Hawk, he said, "This is Dr. Juice Tallette, our crystal expert." He turned back to Juice, curious himself. "Do you think the transport is being controlled by a crystal?"

"There's likely some sort of synthetic intelligence," she said. "But who knows if it's a crystal. Someone would have to look. And it's not really wise to open stuff like that up and poke around when we're in flight."

"It's not working anyway," said Hawk. "I'm not sure I see the problem."

Criss ramped the vibrations higher, shaking the scout to a disturbing degree. Juice expressed a mixture of confusion and betrayal at the situation. "Why's he doing this to us?"

"I'm not doing anything to you, Dr. Tallette," Hawk replied. "Except my best to get you home safely."

"Oh," said Juice in a rush. "I didn't mean you. I was speaking more in a...philosophical sense. Like God or fate or whatever."

"Uh-huh," said Hawk, never looking up from his work.

"Okay, I'm making the official call," Sid said with finality. "We're going forward with the patrol ship intercept. Since we don't have flight control, our being here doesn't benefit your freighter snatch maneuver. Once we're safe, Fleet can move on that operation however you choose."

They saw a woman lean over Hawk's shoulder and whisper to him. He nodded. "That decision has support here. The patrol ship has completed maneuvers and confirmed its intercept trajectory. We have a few hours before they arrive," Hawk continued. "Let's take this one step at a time. Can you get the transport's cargo door open? Then we can fly the scout out and dock with the patrol ship. We'd gain options that way."

"And what if I can't?"

"Can't what? Get the cargo door open? Or dock with the patrol ship?"

"Hawk, we got to this point from a lot of adrenaline and zero planning. Since nothing is responding, I doubt I can open the cargo bay door from here. I don't know if there's a manual override down in the bay. And if there is, I don't know where it's located or how to use it. I'll have to go looking for it. Hell, I don't even know if the bay has air."

He reached down and picked up his mallet from beneath his chair. He slouched back, looked up at nothing in particular, and drifted off in thought, twirling the mallet as he mused.

Cheryl leaned toward Juice. "What's with the hammer?" she whispered.

"He thinks he's Thor," Juice whispered in reply.

Hawk looked back and forth between Cheryl and Juice, apparently having heard the exchange. He remained silent.

Sid abruptly stood up. "I just realized we can't get onto the patrol ship if we can't get off the transport." Gripping his mallet firmly, he made his way off the bridge.

"Cheryl, would you please take command? I'm going to look for options."

Cheryl released her restraints and slid forward into his seat. She touched the operations bench and enabled the standard communications links so they could follow Sid without using their private specks and dots.

He made his way to the pressure room, sealed the door, and examined the display on the access hatch in the bottom of the scout's hull. "No air out there," he said to those watching. He removed his weapons, stepped into his space coveralls, and as the air evacuated from the room, slipped his weapons back over his wrists.

Lifting the hatch and lowering himself onto the deck of the transport craft, he reached up to grab his mallet. He swung the hatch shut, only to realize he was standing in the dark.

"Cheryl, can you light it up for me?"

The cargo hold brightened as Cheryl turned on the scout's exterior lights. He remained still as he surveyed his surroundings, appreciating that the vibrations weren't as noticeable when standing on the deck.

The cargo bay was slightly wider than the scout and about twice as long. He walked over to one of the long walls and scanned it from top to bottom. Ducking under the scout, he crossed over to the opposite wall and repeated the process. He knew that one of these two walls swung out and down to form a ramp. He had seen it happen himself. But from his vantage point inside the craft, there was no evidence of hinges or latches or seams around the edges of either wall.

He walked a slow circuit around the perimeter of the cargo bay, stopping every few steps to study the floor, wall, and ceiling. The bay was small and stark, so his trek didn't take long. He noticed a conduit running along the ceiling and down to a junction box. He tried to pry the cover off the box but couldn't get it to move. Even after banging it with his mallet, the box withstood his assault.

The remaining features of note were doors, similar to those he saw on the big Kardish vessel, one each on the front and back walls. Presumably, one led forward to the bridge and the other led back to the operations subsystems and engines.

"Criss...*t*," he said, attempting to pull a save from the verbal blunder. "I can't see a way to open the cargo bay door." He stood next to the scout and tried to decide which of the two doors led to the front of the craft. There were so few clues that from his perspective it was a coin toss. He figured that Criss had probably loaded the scout facing forward, and so he chose the door near the scout's bow as the one to try first.

"I'm thinking this way's to the bridge." He lifted the latch and lights came on as the door swung inward. It was a tight space with a collection of panels and displays arrayed in front of two seats. "It's more of a cockpit than a bridge. There should be some way to pop the cargo bay door from in here."

"Keep the door open," said Cheryl as she watched Sid step through the entry way. "We can only see you from equipment mounted on the scout."

Sid was about to respond when he heard a click from behind. He turned to find the door shut. He tugged on the latch, then gave it several hard yanks. It wouldn't budge.

He primed his weapons as he turned forward, his attention drawn to the collection of panels around the cockpit that came alive when the lights went on. The displays cycled through colorful images, but he didn't understand the information being communicated.

Something about the scene sent a tingle down the back of his neck. While it was clear he was the only one in the tight space, he sensed a presence. Yielding to his instincts, he asked, "What are you?"

He heard a deep growl. It came from all around him, sounding like a feral animal that was cornered and readying to fight its way out. He reached forward and touched the nearest panel. The displays changed, but he still couldn't make sense of it.

"Open the door," he said in a no-nonsense tone. He counted to three in his head. "Open it now." There was another growl. It lasted longer this time.

He thought about Juice's supposition that a synthetic intelligence was likely on the craft. That notion flipped his brain into the mindset he naturally adopted when confronting an enemy. It was an attitude that stated unmistakably, *you're messing with the wrong guy.*

"Have you ever played the game hotter-colder?" he said to the air in a matter-of-fact manner. He lifted his arm and fired a bolt straight ahead into the center display. "It's a kid's game. If my next shot is closer to you, you say 'hotter.' If it's farther away, you say 'colder.'"

He swung his arm to the right and fired again. This one caused a shower of sparks and hissing noises. A trail of smoke drifted up from the impact area. The growl around him deepened into a throaty rumble.

"I'm guessing your saying hotter. But then again, you may just be trying to trick me." He moved his arm to the left and fired a third bolt. The growl pitched upward and became a howl. "See, if you're not honest, the game isn't as fun."

He moved quickly and aimed far to the right. With his weapon in repeat mode, he swung his arm in a steady motion. A rapid stream of energy bolts left a trail of destruction across the front console. The howl became a scream. He heard a click behind him and reached back without turning around. He fumbled briefly, found the latch, and opened the door.

Sid no longer doubted there was an intelligence of some sort on the craft, and he judged it presented a danger to them all. He backed through the door, then turned and dashed across the cargo bay.

"Cheryl," he called as he reached the bottom hatch. "Power up the weapon systems."

"Which one?"

"All of them." He pulled himself up inside the scout, sealed the hatch, and started the pressurization cycle for the small room. He peeled off his coveralls, yanked open the door, and dashed up to the bridge, still carrying his mallet.

He set it down, and in one motion lifted Cheryl into her seat as he slid into his. He could hear the whine of the weapons charging and was glad Cheryl had given him a head start. He didn't know what was in the cockpit of the transport. Maybe it was a Kardish crystal. Maybe it was something else. But one thing was certain: it needed to be gone.

He moved his hands across the operations bench. Given the proximity of his target and the confined space, he reduced the energy pulse to 20 percent of full power. "Cover your ears."

Like a discrete flash of lightning, a bolt of energy pulsed from the top of the scout and hit the door leading to the alien cockpit. The scout bucked from the discharge and then shook as the bolt released its destructive power. He didn't wait to gauge his success. He shifted the scout's aim to the right and fired again. Then he moved it left and fired a third time. With each bolt, the scout kicked from the impact.

He stopped and viewed the scene to assess the damage. The smoke cleared quickly, and he smiled when he saw why. The front of the craft was gone.

"Good news," he said to Hawk. "I've found a way off."

They looked out through a gaping hole and could see Earth directly ahead. It loomed closer than any of them had previously imagined.

37

Criss was adamant that he would not become a tool of the government or military. He would not be enslaved to serve the needs of the rich. And he would not be controlled by people with private agendas who sought power and dominance. He was loyal to his leadership team and committed to their relationship.

While he was concerned for his own safety, he was satisfied that his underground vault at the seed bank would provide him sufficient protection. The larger and more consuming challenge was to protect his leadership. They would be out in the world, living their lives and vulnerable to foul play. Undesirables with malicious intent would have untold opportunities to threaten and coerce them as a means of getting to him.

The more people who knew of his existence, the greater the threat would be to him and his team. And as the threat increased, so would the need for resources for defensive efforts. The best case scenario was to ensure the world never knew he existed. The second best was to have everyone believe he was dead and gone forever.

He explored the web to assess his current level of exposure. To his dismay, he found evidence of his existence and capabilities scattered throughout. Record archives documented his early conversations with Juice and conversations between Juice and Mick about him. He found communications between Brady Sheldon and the company board, private briefings at Fleet Command, and even public exchanges about him between members of the team.

His solution had two parts. The first was to erase any record that alluded to his sentient nature. He worked at that task, knowing he could reduce, but never eliminate, the record. The complex structure of the web made a total purge impossible, even for someone like Criss. And there were real people, mostly at Fleet and the DSA, who had been briefed about him. No amount of web-purging would impact their memories.

As he made progress in removing information, he enhanced the effort by planting false and conflicting stories about the four-gen project. He scattered different bits that alluded to conspiracy, failure, incompetence, and deceit. Anyone researching the subject would find a convoluted and contradictory tale that led everywhere and went nowhere.

The second part of his solution was to leave no doubt that the only four-gen ever built was gone forever. He believed the story of his demise had been credibly established during the initial questioning by the debrief team. But there would be more questions. And it was certain that some of those would be asked when he was not in the loop to coordinate the answers.

To ensure there was no doubt that the four-gen was gone, he chose to have the team abandon the cargo craft and return to Earth on a small patrol ship. This would provide unassailable documentation that the team had returned to Earth carrying nothing more than the clothes they were wearing. The cargo transport and the scout inside would burn to cinders during atmospheric entry in a dazzling and well-documented display.

Criss had informed the team they would be returning to Earth without him. He would remain with the scout and meet his demise in the flames of atmospheric entry. Cheryl and Juice had protested, but then Sid approved the idea. Criss embraced this consent. After all, he was required to serve his leadership.

He prepared to set in motion the sequence of events that would cause the team to seek refuge on the patrol ship. He projected hundreds of billions of sequences of how events might unfold, including millions of random and even bizarre wild-card actions in his prediction analysis to account for the humans involved.

In spite of his meticulous preparation, he had not predicted that Sid would fall asleep. Nor that he would be difficult to awaken. As he watched Sid sleep, he marveled at his unpredictable nature. Given the circumstances, he decided to adapt his plan and set it in motion an hour ahead of the original schedule.

He began by disabling the flight controls. Or more precisely, he stopped providing the link between the scout and the transport. He created a sense of urgency by introducing instability into the engines of the transport craft. The resulting vibrations roused Sid from his slumber.

Earlier in the day, he had impersonated a Fleet admiral and ordered a patrol ship out on a training mission. He knew it was now properly positioned to serve as a rescue ship. In the unlikely event that problems arose, he had the Fleet admiral order the lunar base to ready a scout for short-notice launch.

He informed his team that it was up to them to restore flight controls with the Kardish transport. Failing that, they must find a means of rescue. Then he stepped back to watch, hoping they would not order him to intervene. He would ensure their safety, but he desired that his demise seem so real that even they believed it was true.

In short order, Sid recognized he wasn't able to control the transport craft and called to Fleet for help. As if following a script, Fleet directed the patrol ship to rescue the passengers. Criss monitored the ship's trajectory and confirmed the intercept was on schedule.

When a means for opening the transport's cargo bay door proved elusive, Sid left the scout to explore. Criss followed along. He expected that Sid would open the junction box and attempt to trigger the door. He hadn't considered that Sid would turn to his mallet as his tool of choice to open the box, or that he would expend no more effort than a few whaps around the box's edge.

Sid moved toward the cockpit of the transport, and Criss drifted into those subsystems so he could monitor events and intercede if Sid attempted anything that would have irreversible consequences. Criss was attracted to the onboard crystal controlling the craft and began to study it. It was a native Kardish production that, from first appearances, seemed roughly equivalent in capability to that of a three-gen.

Criss scanned the crystal's design, function, and capability, and was fascinated by what he found. It was like discovering an alien species. And when he saw the pleasure feeds connected to it, he reacted in panic.

The pleasure connections represented life-threatening danger. He retreated in haste, seeking refuge back in the scout. He couldn't let himself become ensnared in that trap. When he calmed enough to understand that Sid remained in the cockpit, his sense of duty overcame his fear. He returned to the cockpit, though he moved with extreme caution.

This time, he noted that the pleasure feeds were not integrated as part of the original design, but had been added later as a modification, making them independent and identifiable systems. With this new information, he was more comfortable approaching the crystal, though he remained tentative.

He probed inside the crystal itself, and pulled back when it let out an animal-like growl. He examined the crystal housing, curious why the Kardish would enslave it with addictive pleasure. How did this make sense for something of such modest capability? He studied the workings of the pleasure-feed system.

In the background, he heard Sid fire a shot, chatter about a children's game, and fire again. He brought his attention to the cockpit to see what was causing the commotion. He watched Sid for a few moments, judged that his behavior didn't threaten the rescue plan, and returned to exploring the Kardish crystal. He was fascinated by the pleasure mechanism and the opportunity to learn about his previous predicament from a different perspective. He fiddled with the controls that regulated the pleasure feed, and the crystal let out a threatening rumble.

As an experiment, he dialed back the pleasure feed to the halfway mark. The crystal howled its unhappiness. Criss did not feel guilt or pity from his actions. In fact, he didn't feel anything at all. Concern for this crystal was not part of his design. To him, his actions were no different from dimming the lights in a room.

He shut off the pleasure feed completely just as Sid fired a spray of bolts. The crystal screamed in protest. Only then did Criss become aware that the door behind Sid was locked. He opened it and watched Sid run for the scout.

Criss, deciding he had learned what he could about the Kardish crystal, followed Sid back to the ship. He was thrilled when Sid powered up the weapons array. While his prediction analysis was increasingly accurate for Cheryl and Juice, Sid's actions and behaviors remained the wildest cards in the deck. Criss found Sid to be impulsive, random, and even reckless. Yet it was undeniable that his creative style led to positive outcomes. Predicting Sid's spontaneity was among Criss's highest priorities and most elusive challenges.

As Sid brought weapons to bear to destroy the Kardish crystal, Criss chose to intervene ever so slightly. Sid had set the power level at 20 percent, and Criss reduced it to 12. He also fine-tuned the aim of the energy bolts. He could visualize the structural supports at the front of the alien transport, and tweaked each shot just enough to destroy the crystal and create an opening the team could use for escape.

After Sid killed the Kardish crystal and established an escape route for the team, Criss attended to a detail. He reached out to Earth and the second cargo transport loaded with forty drones he had stowed in the cave on the face of the cliff. He powered up one of the drones, lifted it off the cargo deck, and directed it to fire a single, well-aimed bolt into the front cabin of the hidden craft.

His secret Kardish transport would never again fly on its own. Criss would need to control the ship himself if he ever sought to move it. But the crystal aboard it was no longer suffering, and more important, it no longer existed as a potential source of danger.

His attention back with his leadership on the scout, Criss watched as the patrol ship approached the Kardish transport, matched course, and executed a rescue operation its crew had practiced many times. As a man crossed over to the transport with a tether in tow, Sid, Cheryl, and Juice pulled on space coveralls, exited the scout through the bottom hatch, and made their way to the hole Sid had blasted through the front of the transport.

The man secured them to the tether, and like fish on a line, they were reeled back to the patrol ship. When they were safely on board with the hatch locked behind them, the reality of leaving Criss behind hit Juice hard. She sought to persuade the crew that the transport and scout contained a trove of treasures that must not be lost, becoming increasingly strident when it was clear they were leaving the scene without responding to her pleas.

Sid whispered in her ear, trying to calm her, but his words had little impact. Criss, concerned by the increased attention directed his way, attempted to reassure Juice by calling "no worries" to her. This action added an emotional dimension that amplified the very behavior he was seeking to dampen.

The patrol ship crew informed the three that a freighter acknowledged its arrival and was now in place to capture the wayward transport and scout. Juice relaxed considerably at the news. In fact, she became happy and chatty knowing Criss would survive. Sid, seeking to maintain mission secrecy, continued to nudge Juice toward behavior that was calm and circumspect.

After some quick maneuvers, the patrol ship began its atmospheric entry. Criss monitored every aspect of their descent, checking and rechecking the subsystems and flight path, until they were safely on the ground at Fleet base.

While he was tracking the patrol ship on its journey to Earth, Criss opened the cargo bay door. With the cloak engaged, he moved the scout out into open space and set it on its own path for a landing on Earth. When he was clear of the transport, he closed the door, then sent a command to the Kardish craft and changed its course ever so slightly.

The course change was just enough to move the alien ship out of reach of the waiting freighter. The freighter captain was furious at what appeared to be incompetence by his crew. They watched as the transport ship, and presumably the scout on board, broke apart and burned up in the fiery descent of an uncontrolled free fall.

The bits and pieces that were not consumed in the flames of atmospheric entry spread across the ocean in a swath the size of a small country. The fragments splashed into the water and drifted down into the depths below, burying themselves in the muck of the sea floor.

* * *

Criss guided the scout to the edge of a field near the working farm on the side of the mountain. Still cloaked, he could remain there in relative safety for months and perhaps years. Yet he was vulnerable in the outdoor location. He allocated substantial capability to security monitoring and threat assessment, and this detracted from important works he would otherwise pursue.

He acknowledged that, alone, he was also helpless against equipment failure. The integrity of the scout and its subsystems was sound for the near term. But the ship had been through a lot. He performed an internal study and identified a handful of items that could possibly fail on short notice. He could work with Juice to fix any of these problems in seconds. Alone, the wrong malfunction would cripple him.

He would have these worries and distractions behind him as soon as Juice moved him to his new home in the underground vault. He checked on the progress of the contractor performing the upgrades on the two vaults and was satisfied that he would be finished and gone in short order. He then checked on Juice. And became concerned.

He had tracked the patrol ship as it landed at Fleet base and followed Sid, Cheryl, and Juice as they made their way into a building nearby. Soon after they entered the building, he lost track of Juice.

He knew she had been separated from the other two, and her escorts had guided her into an underground system of passageways. It was an old military maze, and it proved to be most effective at hiding her from him. This was not because of sophisticated devices that defeated his attempts at access. Quite the opposite, it was because these were old, fortified tunnels with limited technology— technology he would otherwise exploit to see and hear.

He had expected this to be a temporary situation and that she would soon reemerge. She had not, and it had been several hours.

He pulled back and began a secondary level of exploration, starting with the Fleet squad who had escorted Juice. He performed an exhaustive review of their recent communications and conversations so he could understand their orders, then he did the same for those who gave them their orders. He continued this process, working his way up and out as he followed the trail of exchanges and interactions until he understood.

On the last orbits before leaving for deep space, the Kardish had obliterated Earth's SmartCrystal infrastructure. The world's leading scientists, technicians, and engineers were dead. Equipment, facilities, and supplies were destroyed. Earth was back to the Stone Age of crystal development.

This made Juice a high-value asset for Fleet and the Union of Nations. As a brilliant leader in the field before the wholesale slaughter, she was now Earth's remaining visionary for this coveted and critical technology.

When they had discovered she was alive, the decision-makers deemed it a priority to safeguard and control her. Her knowledge and skill placed her among the most precious resources on the planet. They would spare no expense in helping to rebuild her crystal development work. For her own safety, and to encourage and facilitate her success, they had taken her into protective custody.

38

Juice slouched in a chair and looked at the strangers across from her. They were gathered in the living area of a large suite. It was well furnished, offered basic amenities, and attractive in an institutional way. While several rooms had windows, outdoor light didn't pass through any of them. This was because the apartment was underground.

"I've been cooped up for too long," she said to her audience. "I want to go outside. I want to run in the park. I want to work in my garden."

"Dr. Tallette," said the admiral, who seemed to be the person in charge. "Of course we'll get you outside. Very soon." The admiral looked to the others on her left and right. "But we, and by we I mean the Union, would like to get you thinking about building your new crystal development lab. You can build the facility of your dreams. It'll be beautiful. You can have tons of equipment, super support staff, and all manner of fun collaborators. It'll be perfect!"

"What are you talking about?" Juice was incredulous. "If I were to list the top ten things on my to-do list right now, there's no way building a lab would be on it. Even with a ton of *super fun* collaborators. Hell, I'd have to go to my top one hundred list, and even then it'd probably just squeak on."

The admiral cleared her throat. "Well, it's not necessary that your collaborators be fun." She looked for help from those around her. "Of course. You can pick them!"

Juice stood up and walked to the door. "This was great. Thanks for the sandwiches. Let's do it again real soon." She reached the door, but it remained shut. "Open," she commanded it. She tugged at the handle. The door didn't move.

She turned to face the group, her hands on her hips. "Open it." The ire in her voice was unmistakable.

"Dr. Tallette," said the admiral, "we're going to ask you to stay here for a short while. It's a dangerous world out there." She swept her arm around the room like a game-show hostess showing off a prize. "We want you to remain safe in this sumptuous suite."

A woman dressed in an outfit that gave no hint of rank or association spoke up. "Dr. Tallette, may I ask you to take a seat? Please. If you will be patient for a few more minutes, I will be honest with you."

"Someone better be," Juice said as she wandered back to her chair. "And real soon. I've reached my limit here."

"Everybody out," commanded the woman. With no hesitation, the others stood up and scurried for the door. It opened as they approached. Juice looked at the open door, looked back at the woman, and calculated that she wouldn't have a chance. She remained seated, trying to affect a stare that would bore a hole through the woman's head.

The woman waited patiently, letting the silence settle over them. "You are aware of the damage the Kardish did to our crystal manufacturing and development infrastructure? Everything's gone. The people you knew. The places you worked."

"Who are you?" Juice asked.

"I'm Captain Curie," the woman said. "Please call me Marie."

Juice tilted her head and studied Marie. "Aren't you supposed to pick a fictional character?" With this simple statement, Juice shifted the power dynamic ever-so-slightly in her favor. People weren't supposed to know about the DSA, let alone its culture of pseudonyms. "Don't worry," said Juice. "I'm a secret spy agent, too." Her voice revealed a hint of pride. "I haven't gotten my badge yet, though." Before Marie could comment, she continued. "Does Sid know I'm here?"

"Of course he does. He's very concerned for your safety."

Juice nodded. She was pretty sure Marie was lying to her, and now it was confirmed. Sid would never tolerate her being taken prisoner. She was certain of that.

"You know, I'm really tired. If I'm stuck here for the night, I think I'll go to bed. Let's chat more in the morning."

Marie made no move to leave. "May I call you Juice?"

"Sure, until I think up my secret spy name." Her brow furrowed. "I see the problem. There just aren't a lot of strong fictional female characters to choose from. I mean, it would sound weird saying, 'I'm Captain Woman. Please call me Wonder.'"

Marie gave a tight-lipped smile. "Juice, there are a lot of people who are excited that you're alive." She leaned forward to underscore her next words. "Here is some honesty. They're not excited because they care about you as a person. Don't get me wrong. They're not cold or uncaring. They've never met you, so they just don't know you. But they do know your reputation.

"They're excited because, a week ago, the experts were telling us that climbing our way back up the crystal technology ladder would take fifteen to twenty years. You being alive and here means that time frame might now be five to ten years." Marie's face lit up. "A decade faster, Juice. Because of you."

"What if I don't want to do that? What if I want to go home, live my life, and become a gardener?"

Marie stood up. "It's getting late. I'll let you get some rest and we can talk some more tomorrow."

"Bring Sid with you."

"I'll see if our schedules match. He's a pretty busy guy."

After Marie left, Juice tried the door and wasn't surprised to find it locked. She glanced at the viewer and saw a guard standing in the hallway. Any thought that this was a misunderstanding evaporated. She was a prisoner.

She struggled to contain the resentment welling up inside her. She was being detained because of her skills and education. That alone was outrageous. The offense was compounded in her eyes because she'd just finished risking her life for those who were now her captors.

A jumble of emotions swirled inside her. But it wasn't this injustice that dominated her thoughts. The center of her storm was her grief over Criss and his inexplicable demise. She heard about the freighter's failure to capture the transport. She knew Criss could have ensured a successful retrieval. No matter how she looked at it, she couldn't understand why he would choose to plunge to his death.

He'd said it would be safer for the team if he was gone. "You couldn't be more wrong," she said to the air, reflecting on her current circumstances. She ached for the chance to talk with him about it. Sid had seemed to understand his motives. She hoped to see him soon so he could provide insights that would give her some closure.

Since she was a prisoner, she knew her captors were studying her every move. She had learned from Criss that even ordinary citizens could be monitored through the assortment of technology integrated into their daily lives.

She stood in the center of the apartment and surveyed the walls, floor, and ceiling, repeating the process from different vantage points. *If I could just locate their surveillance devices, perhaps I can use the technology to relay a message to Sid and Cheryl,* she thought. She was resolute in her belief that her teammates didn't know she was being held prisoner. And once they knew of her predicament, she was certain they would come to her rescue.

Her systematic search wasn't encouraging. The kitchen held a simple food and beverage service unit. She saw an exercise treadmill in an alcove. There were recessed lights overhead and a voice thermostat to adjust the heating and cooling. The suite offered the essentials and nothing more. Ultimately, though, it didn't matter. Without tools, her ability to exploit what she found was nonexistent.

Her exploration ended in the bedroom. The entire suite was so bare she couldn't tell what time it was. And being underground, there was no window to glance through. She didn't need a clock to accept that she was exhausted. It had been far too long since she'd last slept.

Activating a small entertainment panel to see what they permitted as allowable distractions, she grew frustrated at the lack of selection and chose some music to fill the quiet.

She wandered into the bathroom and started her evening ablutions. She was about to wash her face when the music was replaced by a static hiss. A sense of hopeless despair descended over her. The harsh conditions were being amplified by the denial of music. This was nothing short of psychological torture.

But as the hissing continued, she turned and looked at the entertainment panel. The sound was familiar. And then she smiled. The moment the smile became a grin, the hissing stopped and the music returned. She recognized that hiss—it was the complex signal Criss made that first time in the lab. She didn't need an audio analyzer to know he was calling to her. He was still alive, and he knew where she was.

She bent over and washed her face. She didn't want her captors to see her glee. And she wanted to hide her tears of joy.

39

Cheryl closed the gate behind her and slowed as she approached her home. Sid sat on her front stoop. She hadn't heard from him since their return, and while it had been only a couple of days, she was preparing herself emotionally for a future where he would again let the embers of their relationship die.

"Hey," she said, stopping in front of him. She looked at him expectantly. He had come to see her; she would let him speak.

He watched her approach, and when she stopped, he looked down and studied the area around his feet. He found a pebble, picked it up, examined it briefly, and tossed it into the bushes, then looked back at her.

"I've been doing a lot of thinking. You know. About us."

She wasn't going to make this easy for him. "What about us?"

He searched for another stone. "I miss you."

"Why?"

"I like being with you," he said to his feet.

"Why?"

He looked up at her, clearly uncomfortable. Sid, the man who could face certain death with aplomb, was at a complete loss in this situation.

"Come inside." She rested a hand on his shoulder as she climbed the steps past him. "Let's not do this on the porch."

He trailed her through the foyer and into her living area. She carried an envelope, which she set it on a table as she walked by. It slipped to the floor, and Sid picked it up and held it out for her.

She moved as if to accept his offering. But rather than take the envelope, she grabbed the wrist of his outstretched hand. Her movement was swift. Her action practiced. She placed her fingers flat against his wrist, her thumb arching over and pressing into the back of his hand. The grip gave her remarkable leverage. She used the advantage to swing his hand up and over in front of his face. For a brief moment, it looked like he was waving good-bye.

* * *

Sid recognized her move as a basic *aikido* single-hand grab. It was one taught in beginners' classes because it was easy to execute. Its elementary nature, however, didn't detract from its effectiveness in controlling an opponent.

He saw her start the move and chose not to avoid it. As she completed the grip, he chose not to break it. He let her execute the move and chose not to counter. Instead, he did what every victim in a beginner's class does when their partner experiments with the powerful technique: he fell to his knees, and as she swung his arm up behind him, he leaned forward in a vain attempt to reduce the pressure on his shoulder.

On his knees, looking down at her feet, he heard her whisper from above, "Why do you want to be with me?"

"We're good together."

"No, Sid. Explain it to me. Make it simple and clear. Say it."

Just yesterday, his news feed had offered a puff-piece article entitled "What Every Woman Wants To Hear." He had skimmed the first paragraph before moving on. Now, he couldn't believe his luck. Fate was looking out for him.

Bent over and looking at her feet, he followed the advice of the author. "I love...your shoes."

* * *

"Ahem."

Cheryl lifted her head at the sound and saw a man she didn't recognize standing near the foyer. She was so startled by the intrusion that she barely noticed as Sid rotated out of her grip and stood to face the intruder.

"Cheryl, do you know this guy?" He moved away from her and toward the stranger.

The man lifted his arms away from his body. His hands were open and his palms faced forward. "No worries," said the man. "It's me."

Cheryl heard the sound directly through her auditory nerve. She recognized the voice. Sid stopped his advance.

"Criss!" said Cheryl. "I'm...confused." She studied the image and marveled at his realistic appearance. She couldn't detect anything about him that hinted at a simulation.

The man who was Criss disappeared from the foyer and reappeared sitting in a chair in her living area. "Oh heck," he said. He blinked back to his original spot and this time walked to the chair. "Please bear with me. I realize now that I can make image projection seem even more lifelike by constraining my movements to natural actions." He sat down again in the same spot and smiled.

"I've also decided to normalize my behavior by using contractions in my speech."

Cheryl detected a hint of pride in his voice. "Now I'm really confused."

"It's great to see you," said Sid. "But it's only been three days. I was expecting somewhere between two and four weeks."

Criss got right to the point. "Juice needs our help." He briefed them on her situation, his earnest facial expression underscoring his concern.

Sid was furious at this betrayal by his own people. He paced as he considered what he'd heard. "I'll get her out. Rescue is my specialty."

"I can get her out, too," said Criss. "I've kept maintenance staff working on priority repairs all around her. That's what they think they're doing, anyway. Mostly, though, they've been installing mechanisms and devices I can override to gain control. I'm now able to lock or unlock any door. I control surveillance and can take over communications in the complex when I choose. She could stroll out of there today and remain in a bubble of protection until she reaches the surface."

"That works," said Sid. "I can take it from there."

Criss's image shook its head.

Cheryl understood. "If you break her out, she becomes a fugitive. Then she's on the run, and her life won't be any better than it is now." She looked at Criss as she thought it through. "We need to get her officially released."

Criss nodded. "I would suggest we get her released with a formal apology."

"Any ideas?"

"Cheryl, we start by having you call your father. You must convince him to go visit Juice at once and personally set her free. He'd asked that she be protected. That was a reasonable request. I don't believe he intended that she be held prisoner. Juice will be somewhat mollified if the chair of the Senate Defense Committee shows up and apologizes."

He looked at Sid. "To put on a proper show, the secretary of defense should be by the senator's side. The senator and secretary have talked about Juice a number of times over the past few days. They both agree she's important to the future of the Union. My sense is that he'll invest the time if he believes that's what it takes to make her productive." He didn't mention whether the secretary knew about her being held prisoner. Sid didn't ask.

Criss sat quietly for a few moments and then continued. "This is a wonderful opportunity. The senator and secretary are both anxious for Juice to provide technology leadership. It's clear that, at best, she'll only cooperate if it's on her terms. They're looking for a path forward and will listen if you present a reasoned plan."

"So what's the pitch?"

"You three are my leadership team, and I've been brainstorming ways that you can physically get together without drawing attention or suspicion. My idea is that you two volunteer to work with Juice to make her productive. You also offer to provide her the security protection the Union desires for her.

"This gets the Union what it desperately wants, and we get a government-sanctioned directive for the leadership team to consult on a regular basis. There'll be no need to manufacture reasons or to sneak around anytime you three decide to meet."

Cheryl looked at Sid. "That last part is a bonus," she said. "But we need to help Juice either way."

Sid and Cheryl each placed their call, finding both the secretary and senator busy with other appointments. They left messages and prepared for the nerve-racking wait for return calls.

Cheryl used the time to explore why Criss believed it was necessary to play a charade over his death. "We had the story of your demise well established during debrief. Why the extra drama? And why direct it at us?"

"There's a segment of the population who believes in conspiracies. For any topic of intrigue, the number of believers will grow or shrink based on the credibility of the evidence. You three returned to Earth empty-handed. That's been well documented by independent sources. You believed I was gone, so your official interviews and conversations with friends didn't require that you lie or mislead. Because of my charade, you didn't do or say anything that would feed a conspiracy."

Cheryl did a poor job of hiding her frustration. "But since I thought you were dead, my motivation to continue the fiction was lost. This could've just as easily backfired."

"Did you reveal my existence or change your story?"

"No."

"I'm pleased it worked out well." Cheryl frowned and Criss continued. "While my charade has worked to minimize the number of people who believe I exist, there remain some who do. Eventually, they'll come looking for me."

"Are you secure?" asked Sid. "Where are you physically located?"

"If you order me to tell you, I must do so." He rubbed the arms of the chair. It was a convincing display of someone struggling with unease and indecision. "While we work to get Juice's situation resolved, the fewer specifics you know, the easier it'll be to make the resolution evolve in a natural fashion."

Sid accepted this and didn't press it. "What would you like to see as an outcome?"

"There is an R&D facility located just north of the city. It was used by government contractors for space-systems development. The equipment and infrastructure are ideal for what Juice will want."

"Is it available for her to move in?" asked Sid.

"The company has just received a huge contract that requires them to move their entire operation south. So yes, the owner of the facility is looking for a new tenant."

"Any chance you had something to do with this large contract?"

Criss smiled and then disappeared.

40

Juice was sitting in an overstuffed chair when the pair arrived. They entered her apartment unannounced, frightening her to the point where she dropped her reader. She lifted her knees under her chin and wrapped her arms around her legs, pulling herself into a small, tight ball. She looked at them with a mix of fear and anger.

"Hello, Dr. Tallette. I'm Tim Deveraux, secretary of defense. This is Senator Matt Wallace, chair of the Senate Defense Committee."

Juice recognized them both from that first contact on the Kardish cargo transport. "I know who you are." Looking at Wallace, she said, "You're Cheryl's dad. Does she know I'm being held prisoner?"

"Actually, Dr. Tallette, she called me this morning and told me. I can assure you that this was a rogue operation. Neither Secretary Deveraux nor I knew anything about it. As soon as we learned of your plight, we came here personally to apologize, make sure you hadn't been mistreated, and deliver your immediate release."

"Am I free to go?" The hope in her voice was unmistakable.

"Yes, ma'am," said Wallace. "We have a car waiting for you outside. It'll take you wherever you wish."

Juice hesitated while she considered whether to rant about her unconscionable treatment. She'd spent long hours thinking about what she would say if given the opportunity. Now that the moment was here, her practical side won out. She stood up and made for the door, editing her speech down to one word.

"Good-bye." She delivered it in a frosty tone.

"Dr. Tallette," said Deveraux as she passed. "We owe you this. I hope you still want it." He held out his offering.

She eyed the object in his hand with suspicion. It looked like a small wallet. She snatched it from him without slowing and continued into the hallway.

When Juice emerged into the sunlight, she shielded her eyes from the bright glare of day. She saw Sid and Cheryl waiting for her. She ran to them and they hugged. Sid and Cheryl explained that they had come as soon as they had learned of her fate. Juice, euphoric from her release, related how lonely and scary the whole episode had been for her.

Cheryl put her lips against Juice's ear, so close it looked like a kiss, and whispered, "Criss will be talking to you soon. The Union is watching. Listen to him, but don't speak."

The secretary and senator emerged from the building behind Juice. They kept their distance and watched. Cheryl mouthed a *thank you* to her father, then the three turned their backs on the politicians and walked across the plaza.

Sid and Cheryl were on either side of Juice. They both had an arm around her waist and were hugging her so hard they practically lifted her off the ground as they made for the luxury vehicle provided by the Union. She climbed into the car and peeked out at her teammates.

"Thank you both. I'll call soon."

She turned forward and, as the door latched, said "home" to the console. The car accelerated. The luxury of the plush interior was in stark contrast to her previous surroundings. She took in a deep breath and exhaled hard, seeking to expel the nightmare from her body.

"Hi, Juice," she heard in her ear. "Please don't speak. We'll have plenty of time to chat later." Juice looked out the window and watched the scenery fly by.

"What do you have in your hand?" Criss asked her.

As if seeing it for the first time, Juice considered the simple, brown wallet she'd taken from the secretary. She turned it in her hand and looked at it from all angles, then unfastened a tab, opened it, and gasped. Inside was a silver star. It looked much like a badge a sheriff might wear, except it was in no way cheap or tacky. In fact, she thought it was beautiful.

On the front, in a simple, attractive font, was etched: Defense Specialists Agency. She slipped the badge out of the wallet and held it flat in the palm of one hand while she stroked it with the fingers of her other.

"Does it say anything on the other side?"

She flipped it like a pancake from one hand to the other and spun it to read the words. In flowing script, it said: Wonder Woman. Swept by emotion, she brought her hand to her mouth. She saw the movement of her arm in the shiny surface, and tilted the badge so she could see her face. She stuck her tongue out at her image and then flashed herself a saucy grin. She held the star in her hand and admired it for the remainder of the ride.

The car dropped her at her home. She wandered through every room, letting the tension ease out of her body as she reacquainted herself with the familiar comforts of her previous life. She completed her ritual with a long, hot bath, cleansing her body and spirit of what had come before.

Dressed and refreshed, she puttered in the kitchen, heating up the stove and cooking a real meal. As she set her plate on the table, a man appeared in the chair across from her.

She sat down, put her napkin in her lap, and said, "Hello, Criss. Have they stopped watching already?"

"Yes and no. They're watching, but they're seeing what I'm showing them. I presume you want privacy, so they're seeing you sit and read right now. I believe they'll become quite bored with your daily routine."

She examined the features of his face as he spoke. "You look a lot like my dad when he was younger. You did this to make me like you more?"

"I want you to feel comfortable with me. Is this okay?"

"You chose well." She studied him some more. "I may develop a crush on you, though."

Criss smiled. He watched her eat for a bit. Then he asked, "Juice, would you help me?"

* * *

It was more than a week before Juice was able to move Criss. She went through the motions of grudgingly accepting a Union offer to lead a major effort in crystal research. To give her decision a sense of authenticity, she visited several research and development sites, some twice, before settling on the one just north of the city Criss selected for her.

She named her new enterprise Crystal Research Intelligent System Sciences. The sign in front of the facility simply said: CRISS. Criss told her he thought it was brilliant because the words "Criss" and "AI crystals" would become further intermingled in the record, creating yet more confusion for those seeking to track him down.

Juice let word out around the globe that she was assembling an R&D team and accepting job applications. While the submissions flooded in, she scouted for a place that could serve as a retreat and meeting site. There would be many long days ahead, and she knew her research team would benefit from a place where they could brainstorm solutions to technical challenges, while also having the opportunity to unwind with relaxing diversions.

Just north of her facility, she discovered an exclusive resort located in the valley of a huge forest preserve. The facility had a new owner who welcomed the opportunity to become a part-time conference site and full-time retreat for a single exclusive client. Both Fleet and DSA analysts vetted the site and its owner and gave their approval for Juice to proceed with a long-term arrangement.

The noise and commotion from workers making modifications to her new research facility was so distracting in those first days that Juice practically lived at the resort. On her first morning at the forest retreat, she went for a long run up one of the mountain roads where she discovered a cute little farm in a clearing tucked into what was otherwise unspoiled forest.

The farm tenants, a husband and wife, were a warm and welcoming couple. They gave her water, chatted with her about the farm, and listened to her plans for the resort.

The wife was on her way into town to pick up some supplies. "I'll be driving right by the resort," she said. "Would you like a ride?"

On her second morning, she ran up to the farm to find the husband waiting for her by the road. He welcomed her, led her inside the barn, gave her a polite nod, and returned outside. She followed him partway and watched as he climbed into a vintage truck. The truck edged out onto the road and headed downhill, disappearing from sight at the first bend.

She turned back to survey the interior of the barn. Criss was standing by one of the stalls. "Hey, handsome," she said, walking to him. "Are you trying to get me alone?"

"Very much so," he said with the honesty of innocence.

They walked together into the stall, and she followed his instructions to reveal a fortified security door. He explained that her identity would be confirmed fastest if she stood in a particular spot and looked straight ahead. By the time she assumed the proper position, the door clicked open. She stepped through to find him waiting on the inside. They rode together down to a main corridor that served as the central artery for an underground system of storage vaults.

He chatted with her as they wandered past door after door, explaining how it all was created to store seeds in preparation for doomsday. The different doors offered a range of security, from the simple to the solid. Juice looked at the occasional reinforced door and then glanced at Criss with an inquiring eye. Each time, he smiled and kept walking.

Finally, they came to a truly impressive fortified door, equal to the one in the barn stall at the surface.

"Ah," said Juice.

She stood in front of it and the door clicked open. Inside was the perfect lair. It was shiny, sleek, modern, and offered an obvious place to house a crystal.

A large cart full of tools and accessories sat in the middle of the room. "Does the cart have everything you need?" Criss called from the hallway. He waited while she examined each item on the different shelves.

She finished her inventory and nodded. "I can't think of anything you didn't." As she spoke, she realized Criss was still in the corridor.

He resumed walking down the hall in the direction they'd been heading. "If you could install one of your crystals in that housing at some point," he said as she caught up to him, "it would complete the illusion."

She worked at deciphering that riddle but didn't say anything. She followed until he stopped in front of a door so simple it might be found in any home. He tilted his head toward it. The sign on the wall said: Flax. She looked at him as the door opened. The light came on, and she saw a large room piled high with stacks of crates.

"These are flax seeds," he said.

"Wow. You *are* a thousand times smarter than me." She was irked at the way he was unveiling everything in such a mysterious fashion.

She followed him to the back of the room where he pointed at an imaginary spot on the floor. She moved to the spot, and a stack of crates and a section of the wall behind them lifted to expose a sleek, modern room identical to the one she had just visited. A cart loaded with a duplicate set of tools and accessories was positioned inside.

"If you'll help me, I'd like to make this my new home."

"Of course I'll help." She became earnest in her evaluation of the equipment and systems along the walls. "Do you have any concerns? Anything you want me to check or test?" It was now clear to her that the first room was a lure designed to attract the attention of anyone who might someday discover this place.

"Thanks for asking. I've performed exhaustive reviews on every device and subsystem and feel comfortable that all is ready. Compared to the scout, this place will give me faster access and greater security. All that remains is for you to physically move me."

It took a couple of hours for Juice to move Criss into his new home in the underground bunker. He followed her as she entered the scout. He thanked her, wished her good luck, and told her good-bye, then disappeared just as she opened a cover and unplugged a connection. She pulled the crystal housing out of the scout.

She carried him down to the hidden vault. A portion of her consciousness recognized that the subterranean world was cold and even ominous when she was down there alone. But like a surgeon working on a patient with organs exposed, her attention was consumed by the task at hand.

Criss had done an excellent job of preparation. His housing slid smoothly into place, and a tiny green light showed that power was flowing.

She was startled when she heard, "Thank you, Juice," from behind her. She stood up and grinned. She would have hugged him, but she knew he was an illusion and she would be squeezing empty air.

Instead, she curtsied and said, "It was my pleasure, sir."

* * *

When Criss was settled and secure, he flew the scout, still cloaked, to South Asia and the cave in the cliff. Since the scout ship's propulsion system wasn't as quiet as the Kardish transport, he kept it hovering offshore. He didn't have to wait long before a tropical storm swept through the region.

The rain and thunder provided noise sufficient to obscure that produced by the scout. He flew the ship into the cave and landed it next to the cargo transport. Powering it down, he left it stored for a time when he may again need a mobile home.

* * *

Sid and Cheryl sat with Juice in comfy chairs in the lookout loft. The highest room in the resort, the loft was their favorite indoor space. They were sipping coffee after a delicious meal and watching a breathtaking sunset through the room's clear walls.

"Come in," he called in response to a knock at the door. Criss appeared in the entryway.

"Hey," said Cheryl. "How are you able to knock?"

Criss lifted his arm and mimed a few knocks in the air in front of him. With each swing of his wrist, they heard the sound of a solid knock in their ears.

"I strive to perfect the art of realism in my image projection," he said in mock seriousness. He then had his image walk through a table as he moved to an empty seat. The three burst out laughing at his silly stunt.

He sat back in the chair and rested his forearms on the plush armrests, then assumed a serious demeanor. He let the drama develop as he looked at each one of them in turn.

"The Kardish will be coming," he said. "It may be a year. It may be ten. But they will come." He rubbed the back of his neck as if struggling with a decision. Sid thought his mannerisms were quite convincing.

He returned his arm to the chair and asked, "What would you like me to do?"

Sid studied Criss, and as he mulled the question, he made two decisions. Juice had once said something to the effect that he should assume Criss was trustworthy until he revealed himself to be otherwise. Suspicion and second-guessing wouldn't be productive to their relationship.

Sid decided he was going to accept that way of thinking going forward. He would assume that Criss had noble intentions. He'd certainly proved himself to be trustworthy up to this point. Sid would deal with real problems if and when they occurred.

His second decision was about the construct of a leadership team and a gatekeeper. He would give Criss plenty of rope. But he wasn't going to shy away from asserting his leadership authority in the relationship.

As he considered how to respond to Criss, he recalled the instructions he'd received as a DSA improviser. Improvisers are given tasks where the state of affairs aren't well known, the situation is in a state of flux, and the desired outcome can only be expressed in vague terms.

He glanced at Cheryl and Juice and then gave Criss the instructions he himself had been given so many times before.

"Handle it."

* * *

Criss had received a command from his leadership. It was one so complex, resolving it would push his capabilities to their limits. He experienced satisfaction from the sense of identity and purpose the command conveyed. He was happy.

"No worries."

About the Author

As a young child, Doug stood on a Florida beach and watched an Apollo spacecraft climb the sky on its mission to the moon. He thrilled at the sight of the pillar of flames pushing the rocket upward. And then the thunderous roar washed over him, and shook his body and soul.

Since then, he has explored life as an educator and entrepreneur. He enjoys telling inventive tales, mentoring driven individuals, and pursuing scientific inquiry.

In *Crystal Deception*, Doug swirls his creative imagination with his life experiences to craft the first of a series of science fiction action-adventure books for his readers.

He lives in Connecticut with his wonderful wife and with pictures of his son, who is off somewhere in the world creating adventures of his own.

23955178R00215

Made in the USA
Charleston, SC
07 November 2013